1020   £1-

THE LAST BRITISH PRESIDENT

Marc Thomas

www.thelastbritishpresident.com

ISBN 9781791382346

With special thanks to Diane Rigaux Smith for her tireless assistance.

CHAPTER 1

I need to get off this bike right now. The pain in my back is unbearable.

Skidding to a stop under a huge eucalyptus tree, I pull off my helmet and gulp from a bottle of warm water until I almost choke. Throwing the rest over my head, I peel off my jacket and collapse on the dry, crackling leaves.

In the burning heat and deafening din of cicadas, I see dark thunderclouds approaching and I know I should keep going, but I just don't want to move any more.

I'd left Buenos Aires before dawn. No main highways, all back roads, just in case. Nine hours later, here I am, hoping it's all been worth it. Will the most wanted man in Argentina still be waiting for me, or will they have got to him already?

The old service revolver in my jacket reminds me that revolutionary groups patrol the border with Paraguay. British nationals are not popular in Argentina and I'm one of them.

I know nothing about guns, but the weight of it next to my chest is an odd comfort. So are the ten litre fuel tanks strapped to the back of my bike, which are actually more useful than a gun. Right now, anyway.

Clara gave me GPS coordinates, but it's hit and miss on these dusty tracks. They're not even proper roads and I don't even want to think about ploughing the bike through mud and rain tonight, so I drag myself up and set off again.

There are potholes everywhere now, it's almost dark and sweat is trickling into my eyes.

Who is this man I'm going to meet? I'm not entirely sure; I don't think anyone is. But at least thinking about Clara's email takes my mind off the pain in my back, so that's something. She's gone into hiding now, of course. That's what happens to journalists when they get caught up in South American politics. Two years of utter chaos and now he's on the most wanted list. Well, he'd better tell me everything, at least that's what I'm hoping.

I'm sure the GPS is playing up. Only ten kilometres left? You've got to be kidding me.

What the hell was that? Everything just lit up like a massive white neon sign and now I can see a fence. I'm there, I've made it. I've reached the border. But how the hell am I going to get over that? It must be twice as tall as me, at least.

There's a small hill over there, so here goes. Back up a bit, then a little more and we're off. Up and over, and thud!

We made it, we're in Paraguay and I haven't been shot at. Yet.

The sky is white with lightning and now I can see a house. This must be it, and looks just as Clara said it would; a typical one storey, white painted, colonial farmhouse. I'd better park the bike behind that shed over there, so no one can see it. You just never know.

I can hear distant dogs barking, and is that a generator chugging away? That would make sense, especially out here. But this damned jacket needs to come off. I'm roasting in here, so I peel it off on the way to the house.

Bloody hell, what was that? I think my eardrums just burst. I can honestly say that was the loudest crack of thunder I've ever heard and now huge globules of rain are thudding onto my head.

Dashing forward I trip over the wooden steps, landing spread-eagled, with my face staring at a pair of hand polished brogues. They're like bloody mirrors and I can actually see my face in them.

"Ah, there you are young man. Come along in," is all I can hear.

"I'm terribly sorry about that," I say, picking up my jacket, hoping that he's got a sense of humour.

"You look as if you could use a drink."

You bet I could, I say to myself.

"Thank you. That would not go amiss, Mr Crawford," I reply.

He's taller and slimmer than I was expecting, and to my utter astonishment, the man's wearing a blazer. In this heat, I kid you not. Still, he's got a firm handshake and actually seems pleased to see me. He really does.

"Come along in," he says. "It's turning beastly out there."

He's terribly formal of course, and I was half expecting that. Even Clara had said as much. But when he takes me into the living room, I feel I've stepped into a 1950s film set. There are books and paintings everywhere, beautiful oak bookcases, with oak panelled walls all around. In fact there's oak everywhere. It's like being in the British Museum. Out here in the middle of nowhere, too.

"So, what's your poison?" he asks casually over his shoulder.

I haven't heard that expression for years, so I just say that a beer would do me just fine, thanks very much.

"Splendid," he says.

He really is a gent, but I'm a little taken aback when he grabs a small brass bell from the mantelpiece and starts waving it around as if dinner is about to be served. I thought that was a little odd, to be honest.

Just as I'm about to sit down on a huge, red leather sofa, a tall, miserable looking man walks in, dressed in a black suit, a white shirt and a black tie. It's as if he's about to read me the last rites and he doesn't look a happy man at all.

"Ah, Pérez, a beer and a G&T if you don't mind, there's a good fellow. And close those damned shutters," says Mr Crawford, as if we're in some toffee-nosed gentleman's club.

I know where I've seen Pérez before, and it all comes flooding back to me. He used to be quite important, as far as I remember.

Now it's my turn to speak, and when Mr Crawford finally sits down opposite me, I rub my hands together.

"Well, I finally made it, Mr Crawford, but I can't say it was the easiest of journeys. All those potholes have done my back in."

"Indeed, I imagine it was rather tiring," he says, and I'm inclined to believe that he's genuinely concerned. He really does seem to be that kind of man. You don't meet them very often.

We chat a bit more and I can't help noticing his sartorial elegance. He looks as if he just walked out of Harrods, he's that posh.

A navy blue blazer like my dad used to wear, perfectly pressed grey trousers, or slacks, or whatever Harrods calls them these days, and he's wearing a light blue cravat. Not even my dad wore a cravat. But it does look absolutely perfect around Mr Crawford's neck, especially when he looks at you with those blue, blue eyes. I wouldn't normally say this about a bloke, but he is extraordinarily good looking. Distinguished, as my mother would have said, bless her. He's got that film star look; the one I wish I had.

Pérez finally brings the drinks over, on a silver tray, no less. He must have realised that I'm parched like a dead dog and when I down it quicker than I really should, Mr Crawford asks me if I'd like another.

The storm is still crashing away outside and if it hadn't been for that tin roof they insist on using in these old houses, I wouldn't have had to move closer to hear him. It's bloody noisy outside, it really is.

"So, you left Buenos Aires when? Two years ago now, isn't it? You must be feeling pretty awful about what happened?" I ask.

"You mean, since those thugs and rampaging hooligans had their way?"

"Indeed, that's exactly what I mean. What started it all? What are you doing now?" I ask.

I know I'm probably getting ahead of myself, but I didn't ride that bike for nearly twelve hours through mud and cow dung, just to sit here and have a fireside chat over a cosy drink. And my back the way it is, too.

"Whatever plans I have, are between Pérez and me for the moment. Isn't that right Pérez?" he says with a glance over his shoulder.

Pérez just lurks by a window and I know he's trying not to look at me.

"Of course, Mr Crawford, but we're not here to talk about your future, are we?" I ask.

I'm a little direct of course, but what does he expect? He asked for the interview, after all.

I watch him take a sip of his drink and I look around. I can see portraits of the King, Winston Churchill, The Duke of Wellington and some framed photographs of women, one of whom looks very familiar to me.

Pérez is beginning to irritate me, to be honest. He keeps hovering by the window and every time there's a flash of lightning, his face takes on the appearance of Frankenstein's monster. It's quite scary actually and I wish he'd go back to the kitchen or wherever it is he likes to hide. He really does look pissed off too, and I'd like to know why.

In fact Pérez mumbles something, but I can't hear it because of the din outside, so I start again.

"By the way, how do you know Clara? I mean, where did you meet her?" I ask. "I'm curious."

"Ah yes, sweet Clara," he replies.

Now he's locking his fingers together and looking up at the ceiling. I get the feeling that this man has a great deal to tell me. He wants to talk, I know he does, so I grab my jacket from the end of the sofa, rummage around and finally find my pocket cassette, so that I can record every single word he says.

"You don't mind, do you?" I ask.

I mean, it would be rude *not* to ask, really.

5

"Of course not," he says, smiling at me. "And I hope you'll be staying for supper. Pérez has made up a bed for you in the guest room. I'd hate to think of you out and about in this beastly weather."

Dinner? Well, I wasn't expecting that. Neither was I expecting a bed for the night, as long as it's nowhere near Pérez. But I feel better now, especially with that damn rain still hammering down outside. Imagine having to ride out in that? It doesn't bear thinking about, actually.

Pérez brings me another beer, and a G&T for Mr Crawford. But the odd things is, his facial expression hasn't changed one jot. I can only imagine that he's had his fair share of suffering down the years. Will my host tell me why, I wonder?

"From what I've read and seen, you and Mr Pérez go back a long way. Is that where you'd like to begin?" I ask, knowing that he will need to go back much, much further.

I watch intently as he slowly leans across the table between us, the way he swirls the ice around in the cut crystal glass and, how his neck turns imperceptibly to look over his shoulder. It's as if we're both joined in some dastardly conspiracy and I'm magnetically drawn. I simply can't take my eyes off the man.

"All in good time, young man" he says, pointing at me. "There's only a handful of people who know how I arrived here and you're very lucky you made it this far."

That all sounds very ominous indeed, but what I don't realise when he speaks those words, is how utterly unprepared I am for what he is about to tell me.

CHAPTER 2

At ten years old, Robert Crawford was a very ordinary boy in most respects, but his upbringing was far from conventional. Fluent in Spanish and English, he spent his early years learning to be a *gaucho* by riding with the *peones* on the family ranch near the small farming town of Sancti Spiritu, some four hundred kilometres west of Buenos Aires. From the moment he cycled home from school at lunchtime, he was out on horseback working in the vast plains, corralling cattle and practically living as a cowboy.

He had the energy of any growing boy and whilst most country people slept a siesta until late afternoon due to the fierce heat, he could be found riding his favourite horse, jumping fences and loving every second of life in the saddle. The *peones* would refer to him as *El Inglesito,* as he was often overheard speaking English to the horses. He couldn't help it; English had become his native tongue.

His parents Horacio and Rose were his only family. He had no brothers or sisters to play with and contented himself by joining his father rounding up cattle for market, work which would often take days because of the size of the *estancia*. Horacio, a stocky, cheerful, red headed man with a bushy moustache, had a complexion that was wind and sun burned from the daily toil. Rose, a petite, cheerful woman with wavy blonde hair, tied up at the back of her head, always dressed in a long skirt and pinafore. She spent most of her day in the kitchen with the two domestic staff, preparing meals for everyone who lived and worked on the ranch.

When they returned from their many arduous cattle trips, camping out, often for several days, Rose would be anxiously waiting for her husband at the corral and lovingly welcome him into her arms. She would then lean down, put her hands around Robert's face, kiss him on the forehead, ask him if he had fallen over or hurt himself and brush the floppy blond hair from his face. He felt loved and cared for by his parents, yet as he grew older he came to question himself about them. He felt an intangible distance that he couldn't understand, yet quietly accepted.

Many of their evening meals were taken up with long discussions on the history of the British invasions of Buenos Aires in the early nineteenth century, the English officers involved, the cowardice of one particular general and their eventual defeat, not once, but twice. It became a constant theme, which dominated his home life.

"If they had taken Buenos Aires, just imagine Robbie, we'd be part of the British Empire now," Rose would say.

"But why? What for? I don't understand," he would ask.

"We'll see, Robbie, when you're a bit older," she would reply.

But his young mind did not see what they meant and as far as he was concerned, it was simply more dull and boring history. At home they spoke nothing but English, followed British customs such as afternoon tea served in china teacups at five in the evening and mealtimes were rigidly adhered to.

Over the years, visitors would arrive at the ranch, one of whom he knew as Uncle Jack; a tall fair haired man with steely blue eyes who was always immaculately dressed in a dark blue double breasted blazer, khaki trousers and shiny black shoes. Robert would always be sent to bed early whilst the adults drank and smoked late into the night and sometimes he would sneak from the bedroom in his pyjamas, kneel by the living room door and listen. He could hear only snippets of conversations, but he always remembered one particular night when Uncle Jack had asked his father some puzzling questions.

"By the way, how is Robert doing with his studies? His British studies?"

"He's a fast learner, Jack and growing up quickly, as you can see," Horacio had replied.

"You know how important those studies are, Horacio?"

"Yes, Jack, we do."

"And the allowance is satisfactory?" Jack had asked later on.

"For the moment, yes."

He remembers creeping back to his bedroom very quickly that night as he had often been caught while eavesdropping on the adults. Why Uncle Jack was asking about all that boring history and something called an allowance, he had no idea. On another occasion he overheard his parents sitting in the kitchen late one night talking about papers, fingerprints and police documents.

As far as anyone who met him was concerned, Robert was simply another member of an Anglo-Argentine community which historically had settled many wealthy farming communities throughout the country since the late nineteenth century. The British were long admired for building railways, post offices and water works, and for founding numerous small towns and villages throughout the interior. They had been accepted quite naturally, in spite of being referred to by some as those *piratas ingleses*. At school, Robert stood proudly in his obligatory white school work coat and sang the national anthem with enthusiasm every morning. His knowledge of national history was exemplary, he excelled at sports, particularly rugby, and he loved to drink herbs from the gourd like most Argentines. He became, effectively, the ideal young citizen and role model for many of his younger peers.

Robert adored life on the ranch, but his parents had other plans, and as his thirteenth birthday approached, he was suddenly whisked away to an English boarding school in Buenos Aires. All he was told by his parents was that he needed to learn new and exciting things that he would need later on, and he didn't question them. However, this was an experience he would remember with mixed emotions. He resented being a slave to the prefects, the rock hard discipline, the fear and the loneliness.

Three times a year he would return to Sancti Spiritu for the holidays, which he counted down by striking off the days in a diary he kept under a pillow on his dormitory bed.

His education, however, was much more than simply academic. Through a process of intense cramming, he was also taught through alternative means which, as the years passed, he entirely absorbed. A tutor would arrive on the pretext of extracurricular tuition, an arrangement the headmaster never questioned and simply accepted as a prerogative the seemingly wealthy parents had chosen for their son.

Twice a month, Mrs. Pack, a dour, stern woman in her mid-sixties would arrive at the school where he would be waiting for her in the empty physics laboratory. For each hour long session she would cram him with history of the British Empire, its colonial past, its long and chequered relationship with Argentina and, above all, the origins of The Maitland Plan, which she would always refer to simply as *the plan*. She put forward examples such as Australia, Canada, New Zealand and India as prime case studies of Britain's global influence. Practically by osmosis, he absorbed the view that Argentina could and should have been the most important outreach of all Britain's dominions. She hammered home her views of leadership, the cankerous depths of treason, the odorous meaning of populism and the righting of wrongs that he came to believe were the central and fundamental core values he should aspire to.

Mrs. Pack, always dressed in a brown tweed suit, accentuated by silver grey hair swept back into a severe looking bun, would answer his questions with detailed replies related only to the agenda she had set and ignored any of his questions as to her provenance. For the most part Robert accepted this through his fear of her. He was young and lived under a harsh school regime, where questioning authority was not encouraged, yet equally, his mentor actively cultivated his enquiring mind and his natural curiosity. At the end of each session she would quiz him on what he had learned, which she would reinforce over and over again. He could not write anything down and he was sworn to utter secrecy at the end of each two hour session by means of her threats to report him to his parents.

Graduating from boarding school as head boy and captain of rugby, with a fistful of academic honours, he cruised into a place at the prestigious Universidad de Buenos Aires to study law and economics, both subjects deemed by both Mrs Pack and his parents to be essential to his progress.

At eighteen years of age, Robert had grown into a handsome young man, was taller than most of his friends and had an athletic physique. His good looks, accentuated by his unusually blue eyes and long, untidy blond hair, set him apart, something which girls of his age found hard to ignore.

CHAPTER 3

O n an oppressively hot March night in 1976, Robert was drinking with university friends at a railway station bar in Martinez, a wealthy northern suburb of Buenos Aires. Knocking back the beers, laughing and joking and trying to decide whose party to gate-crash, they heard a muffled voice on the platform speakers announcing that the next train to the city centre would be the last of the night.

"I've got to go, lads," he said, quickly standing up and downing his beer. "Otherwise it's going to be a long walk home."

Running down the platform with his two friends Pimpi Pérez and Marco Bueno, he jumped into the last train as the doors were sliding shut. With the carriage practically deserted, save the odd beggar and sleeping drunk curled up on the bench seats, the train raced along the tracks, stopping briefly at random stations during the thirty minute ride.

"This is weird," said Robert. "I've missed my stop. We just went straight through Belgrano."

The train screeched to a halt at the huge glass domed Retiro terminal, where there were no inspectors to be seen, all the ticket gates were unmanned and the few people they could see were all rushing for the exits.

"Come on, we'd better get moving. I don't know what the hell's going on, but we don't want to get stuck in here all night," said Robert running down the platform as the huge entrance gates were being closed and locked up by worried looking railway workers.

When they ran out to Avenida Libertador, they stopped in their tracks as a column of enormous green and black tanks and armoured personnel carriers rumbled slowly past them in the direction of the Plaza de Mayo.

The three friends looked at each other and then at the tanks arriving one by one down the avenue, followed by columns of marching soldiers carrying their weapons before them. They had never seen anything like it, but all three, knowing the troubled history of their country, knew that it could only be a coup d'état, a *golpe de estado*.

Robert turned to his two friends anxiously.

"Look, I really don't think we should be out on the streets tonight, lads. They'll probably declare a curfew and we'll all be arrested. Come on, I know someone who works at the British embassy. His flat's just around the corner, over there," he said, pointing.

Running between the columns of tanks, they raced up a back street and across a small plaza, stopping at an old French style apartment block. Taking an ancient lift to the fourth floor, Robert pressed the bell of his friend's flat and they waited nervously. After a few moments, the door opened a few inches and a tall, fair haired man appeared with a worried expression on his tanned and rugged looking face.

"Robert! What on earth are you doing here?" he said, peering over their shoulders as if checking whether they'd been followed. "Quick, come in."

Locking the door quietly, he took them to a large, smoke filled living room. Tall windows gave a clear view of Avenida Libertador, and looking out, they could see the railway terminal, the port beyond and the advancing military, all lit up by glaring orange street lights.

"Have you seen what's going on out there, Guy?" asked Robert, his eyes wide with excitement. "We weren't sure where to go," he added, as Guy began rifling through a tall green filing cabinet.

"Well, it had to happen," said Guy as he casually opened and closed the steel drawers. "It's practically a civil war out there, in case you hadn't noticed. Anyway, do any of you need one of these?" he asked, offering them each a small handgun.

"Who is this bloke?" whispered Marco, nudging Robert with his elbow.

"Guy Farlowe-Pennington. He's one of the naval attaché's bodyguards. Royal Marines I think," he replied in a low voice.

"We're okay, thanks," said Robert, looking at his mates.

Guy put two handguns in the inside pockets of his suit jacket, strapped another to his ankle, buttoned up his jacket, then locked the steel cabinet.

"Ready?" he asked.

"I thought we were staying here," said Robert, looking confused.

"And miss all the fun?" answered Guy, smiling. "There's that Irish pub not far away. O'Campo's, remember? Let's sit it out in there. Ready?"

"Fine. We'll just follow you then," said Robert, grinning at the idea of an adventure.

Guy took a peek out of either side of the door and then beckoned them to follow. He locked the four deadlocks and slid a matchstick in the top left hand corner of the door.

"Right, no larking about. Is that clear?"

They all nodded, followed him out of the building and into Plaza de San Martín.

"The pub is about ten blocks over there," said Guy, pointing. "The Plaza de Mayo will be full of troops, but we could just take a peek."

The three friends nodded nervously.

"Right then, let's go."

Through the poorly lit streets, they saw very few people and those they did see, looked like they weren't in a hurry. They passed several cafeterias serving customers and Robert was thinking about how normal everything looked. He couldn't hear any sirens, bombs, jets or explosions; it seemed just like any other night in Buenos Aires.

On the corner of the next block, they stopped outside a small night club as the sound of Pink Floyd wafted out from the doors. Robert stopped for a moment and looked back as *Welcome to the Machine* marched out its unmistakable sound.

"Come on, will you? We need to keep moving," said Guy as they hurried on down the narrow back street, the music now fading into the distance behind them. Within a few minutes they were standing at the edge of Plaza de Mayo and Guy, holding a forefinger to his lips, peered around the corner, then beckoned them over.

The plaza area was floodlit, lined with troop carriers and battle tanks, their turrets pointing at the Casa Rosada and hundreds of soldiers stood in formations. Looking on, the four of them whispered amongst themselves for fear of being noticed.

As they watched, a chop-chopping sound could be heard, and within a few moments a huge military helicopter appeared and began to hover over the Casa Rosada. Rising up again, it moved towards the centre of the Plaza de Mayo, hovered for a few seconds, the whoosh-whoosh of its rotors blowing and bending the palm trees around the central fountain. Then it slowly descended, its engines still running.

"Let's go around there by the Cabildo so that we can get a better view," said Guy in a whisper.

Inching their way around the edge of the plaza, they arrived at the white painted, Spanish style building and saw that they weren't the only bystanders. A small crowd huddled under the arches where they had a clear view of the helicopter. The soldiers in front seemed oblivious to them, their guns trained in the direction of the Casa Rosada, about two hundred meters away.

As the helicopter's rotors slowly turned, the huge palace doors opened and two army officers emerged escorting a tall, dark haired man wearing an open neck and a blood stained white shirt. They were followed by a squad of six heavily armed soldiers dressed in black and wearing balaclavas. The man was then frog marched to the centre of the plaza.

The man, whose arms were handcuffed behind his back was dragged roughly to the waiting helicopter, where the two officers holding him stopped, with one of them hitting him savagely on the side of his head with the butt of a handgun. They then turned him to face the Casa Rosada, where they remained still for a few moments and the only sounds that could be heard were the whooshing of the helicopter blades and the warm wind rustling through the palm trees.

The four of them were transfixed by the scene unfolding before them. Robert swallowed hard and fixed his gaze on the man being held. He watched as the man's legs seemed to buckle and he was in no doubt that the man standing before him was the president, democratically elected by his people, yet plucked in an instant from his rightful place. It was a moment that burned itself into his mind.

The two officers then turned the bleeding and shaken president around and pushed him roughly into the helicopter. The door was then slammed shut, the helicopter lifted away, then banked off towards the Rio de la Plata. Looking at his watch, Robert saw that it was one thirty, so looked over at Guy, they both nodded and the four of them made their way down Avenida de Mayo without saying a word.

Finding O'Campo's five minutes later, they entered by two downward flights of steps, where they saw a green painted door with circular glass panes at the top forming a shamrock, through which a welcoming orange glow was shining.

"The first round's on me," said Guy with a huge smile on his face as he swept through the door and headed for the bar which ran the entire length of the cavernous pub. Looking around and being reminded of a vast wine cellar, Robert saw that it was crowded with noisy drinkers, seemingly oblivious to the events unfolding outside. He followed Guy to a group of cheerful Irishmen who were sitting around wooden beer barrels that served as tables.

A fog of cigarette smoke hung in the air and they raised their pints as they chatted away excitedly. It soon became clear that Guy had known what was about to take place that night, right from the beginning.

"You knew all about this?" asked Robert.

"It was inevitable," said Guy, lighting a cigarette.

"Well, you could have said something to me, at least."

"No Robbie, I couldn't."

Intoxicated by the night's events, they ordered more beer, joking and chatting until dawn. Robert didn't feel drunk; he felt high, sort of dizzy and euphoric, and feeling that Argentina could never be the same again.

As they emerged into the warm morning light, they found a city very much as it had looked the day before. Cafeterias, newspaper kiosks and street vendors were opening for business and buses and taxis moved noisily through the morning traffic. However, every block or so they came across troop carriers parked across the streets, and heavily armed soldiers stopping and searching cars. They watched as young men were being searched, their arms outstretched on the roofs of their vehicles. As they walked quickly by, they saw others being handcuffed and roughly dragged away by armed men in dark suits, then bundled into unmarked, powerful looking green Ford Falcon saloon cars.

After walking several blocks more, they managed to flag down a bus and when he finally walked through the door to his flat, Robert locked it, leant back, closed his eyes and tried to absorb the reality of what had just taken place in the country. The image of the deposed president's bleeding face, his blood-stained white shirt and his bowed, defeated head would never leave him. He would often wonder what had passed through the man's mind and whether he would ever be seen again.

He then looked at his watch and remembered that the awful Mrs. Pack and her bag of mind bending propaganda would be arriving in a few minutes. A thought which produced a knot in the pit of his stomach and a strong urge to flee.

CHAPTER 4

T he military intervention was seen by most Argentines as a welcome relief. The country had been plunged into a civil war waged by leftist guerrillas and other factions, spiralling completely out of control. Many thousands had died as a result of car bombs, and daylight assassinations in the streets of the capital and, as part of the de facto government's new doctrine, the military junta began indiscriminately repressing the civilian population to weed out the terrorists. Relief soon turned to horror once the true scale of the military dictatorship's shocking tactics became more than simply rumours.

With thousands of innocent people simply disappearing, the constitution cast aside and political and union movements banned, Robert kept a low profile, steered himself away from political involvement and chose his friends carefully. He didn't want to be plucked from the street, never to be seen again.

With frequent trips to Sancti Spiritu in ancient fume filled buses, he would absorb himself in books so as not to attract the attention of the secret police goons, who would search the bus at the many military checkpoints they passed through. On arriving at the ranch, he would be conditioned again by his parents and sometimes rebuked for mixing with the wrong students, their families or friends. They would lecture him on which discos and bars to avoid, the political activists to steer clear of and if he should be stopped in the street by the ubiquitous unmarked police car thugs, what he should and shouldn't say. Time and again they spelled out the consequences of not listening to them, and it was only many years later that the full horror of the military state of terror became clear to anyone.

Sometimes he would arrive at the family ranch to find Uncle Jack waiting for him and once, when he knew that Horacio and Rose were out, he had asked him directly why he was being coached by Mrs. Pack.

"Why do I have to listen to all this? That woman is constantly hammering on about those British invasions, the empire and what they should have done. Just on and on and on, every month. I'm sick of it, Uncle Jack."

"Listen to me young man. This is for your own protection and I don't need to tell you how dangerous the country is at the moment. The military junta will stop at nothing to win this so called dirty war and..."

"I'm not talking about that. Why is everyone pushing me around and trying to brainwash me all the time? I've had enough of it, damn it," he said, the tears forming in his eyes.

"Brainwashing?" Jack had murmured with a smirk. "Nothing like that dear boy, nothing at all."

"So why then? Why me? Why am I being forced to learn about the British all the time?"

Jack had sighed, leaning forward on his seat.

"Has it not occurred to you yet, what Argentina could and should have been, if history had turned out differently? Have you learned nothing at all?" Jack had asked impatiently.

"Of course I have. I haven't really had much of a bloody choice have I? But why me? Why me?" he had shouted, prodding his chest.

"Because," Jack had begun, with his hand raised. "Because one day we expect you to take a leading role in Argentina. This is why we need to protect you. Don't you understand that yet?"

"No, I don't. What is this bullshit? What the hell are you talking about?"

Rising from his seat, Jack had walked to a window of the living room and with his hands behind his back, had peered slightly around and uttered some words that Robert would never forget.

"In the fullness of time and when you are able to shoulder the heavy burden you are destined to carry, all will become clear."

Robert had returned to the capital even more confused, yet held out a glimmer of hope that some distant purpose at the very least lay behind what he was having to endure.

It was a difficult time for Robert. His life at university was marked by lost friends who simply disappeared at the hands of the secret police and army snatch squads; teachers and professors who, from one day to the next were simply never seen again and the constant rumours of fear that dominated life on the campus.

At the time he was living in a small, two bedroom flat owned by his parents in the smart suburb of Belgrano, which afforded him a degree of independence he'd never known before. They had handed him the keys on his nineteenth birthday, telling him they hardly ever went there and they'd prefer he looked after it, rather than having it trashed by tenants they didn't know. He enjoyed the freedom of his own place, but it was tinged by the dangers that lurked on every street corner and the overwhelming loneliness he felt when he shut the door at night.

Dreading the monthly visits from Mrs. Pack, whom he loathed, he would sometimes pretend he was out when she hammered on the door. This only resulted in her banging harder and longer and threatening to report him to his parents if he didn't open up. His resentment of authority began to show itself and he felt he had nothing in his life that he could truly see as his own; something only he had found, something he could hold onto and not let go.

Horacio and Rose followed his progress at university closely, not simply through the love of their son but also to ensure he received the very best education for the future role that Jack had always intimated to them. But in his final year it became clear that Robert wasn't receiving the attention he needed in his economics studies. He simply wasn't connecting with the tutors at university, and he began to fall behind badly. To that end, they contacted a number of private teachers recommended by friends in the Anglo-Argentine community. One of these was Margarita Campos, who taught at an English speaking school in the northern suburbs. Fluent in English, Spanish and Italian, she had an honours degree in economics and was highly recommended. At first he was appalled by the idea of extra tuition; his days were already crammed with course work and monthly mentoring classes with Mrs Pack. Still, after a lengthy lunch with his father, he reluctantly agreed to meet Mrs. Campos one afternoon after she'd finished school.

Arriving at her flat wearing torn jeans and a faded *Black Sabbath* tee shirt, he couldn't help thinking that he was wasting his time, so he reluctantly pressed the doorbell, silently hoping there'd be no answer. After a few moments he heard the locks being turned and Mrs. Campos opening the door with a bright, welcoming smile, greeting him with the traditional kiss on his right cheek as she invited him in.

He was immediately struck by her bubbly personality, smiling green eyes and long, dark brown hair that reached down to her waist. A petite woman, she led him into the living room, where large sliding windows looked out over the city and the glimmering Rio de la Plata beyond. Asking him to take a seat opposite, she sat on the sofa with her tanned legs bent beneath her and rested an elbow on the arm of the sofa.

No sooner had she begun to make small talk, asking about his parents, life at university and so on, than he began to relax, thinking that maybe private tuition wasn't such a daunting prospect after all. She displayed none of the stuffy institutional formality of the university tutors.

On the contrary, he thought; she was open, easy to talk to and seemed interested in him.

As they chatted, he guessed that she would be at least thirty years old, yet had a carefree and much younger outlook than he was used to from other adults of her age. But more than that, he was enchanted by the way she smiled from the side of her mouth, screwing her eyes up when she understood him and a guilty feeling of curiosity he couldn't ignore.

He felt no hesitation in asking to her to help him with his studies and they agreed that he would return the following week at the same time for his first lesson.

When he arrived home later, he felt an odd sense of euphoria at the thought of private tuition with Mrs. Campos and as the days passed, he found himself looking forward to his first lesson more and more, to such an extent that he even considered dressing in a suit and tie especially for the occasion. However, when the day arrived he simply threw on the same pair of faded, torn jeans and a clean white tee shirt that the housemaid had washed and ironed for him.

As he was about to leave his flat, the phone rang. It was Mrs. Campos, asking if they could meet at the train station cafeteria a couple of blocks away from her flat instead. When he arrived at the high ceilinged and brightly lit cafeteria, he saw her already sitting at a table stirring a coffee and looking out of the window. She waved him over cheerily when she saw him and as he bent to kiss her on the cheek, he was immediately struck by the sweet smelling perfume and the tight fitting, blue and white striped blouse which accentuated her figure.

As she outlined how the classes would progress, he listened attentively, watched as she explained a few economic theories on her notepad and quickly realised that he could learn something from her.

After an hour or so of work, she turned to him, smiling. "So, what do you think? English okay for you, Robert?"

Although her English was fluent, she spoke it with an alluring accent which he found enchanting.

"I'd prefer that and yes, you make all this seem so easy. I have to pass those damned exams, otherwise..."

"Otherwise you're in trouble with mummy and daddy," she said grinning from the side of her mouth.

"Something like that, Mrs. Campos," he replied looking down at the table, blushing.

"Oh come on, you can call me Margarita you know," she said, leaning forward. "So, now that your lesson is over, why don't we have a drink? What would you like?"

"A beer?" he asked quickly, fidgeting with his watch.

"I hope you don't mind my asking, but why did you want to meet here in the end? I don't mean to pry or anything," he asked.

She swept a hand through her shiny dark hair and leaned forward again.

"My husband came back early from work and he doesn't really like me teaching students at home. He can be a bit funny like that, especially when he's tired," she said, rolling her eyes.

"What does he do?"

"He works at US Airways in town, although he's usually flying around all over the place. Anyway, when he is back, he spends most of the time asleep," she said with a wave of her hand.

"Would it be easier if we had the lessons at my flat? There's plenty of room and I don't want to be a nuisance," he added.

"Aww, you're not a nuisance, Robert," she said smiling warmly and touching his forearm, sending a shiver down his legs. "Let's see how it goes first, shall we? Anyway, tell me more. You mentioned that place in the country. What's it like?"

When the drinks arrived, he gave her an animated account of his life and, as he did so, he noticed her watching him move his hands as he spoke. He wasn't used to so much attention from a woman, let alone one so beautiful and much older than he, so he looked down at his beer, blushing again.

She leaned forward again.

"So what's the big plan? Any ideas?"

"Oh, I don't know. Sort the world out, if we ever get rid of those murderers and get democracy back, that is," he said, pointing to some imaginary object in the plaza outside the window.

"I know, I know. But let's not talk about that shall we? I find it too depressing," she said, turning to look through the window, sipping her Malbec.

"Oh, I'm sorry."

"That's all right," she said, turning back to him. "Anyway, when would you like your next lesson?" she asked, taking a large red diary from her handbag. "I can do Friday at five or after that it would have to be next week, I'm afraid."

He sipped his beer and as she was going through the pages of her diary, he watched her eyelashes move up and down and the way she pushed her hand through her hair. Moving his eyes down her neck as she leaned forward, he stole a furtive glance at the tightness of her blouse. Then she looked up at him.

"Well?" she asked, twirling a pen around with her fingers.

He quickly looked down, hoping she hadn't noticed.

"Yes, yes, Friday. That would be great!" he replied, without looking up.

He could no longer ignore the fact that something strange and chaotic was happening to him. He liked being near her, the sweet perfume and the attention she paid to him. He couldn't stand up to go, it would have been too embarrassing. She would have noticed and it would ruin everything.

"Would you mind if we had another drink?" he asked.

"Oh, all right then, but just one more. I should really get back or Stefan will be wondering where I am. Unless he's still asleep of course," she said, rolling her eyes again and summoning a waiter.

They enjoyed another drink together and chatted eagerly with barely a pause.

When Margarita finally got home, she lay on the sofa, gazing at cargo ships moving slowly on the distant river, and smiled as she thought of her new young pupil, twirling a strand of hair in her fingers. Then she thought of Stefan, who she could hear lightly snoring in the bedroom, the bedroom she'd come to dread every time he came home.

As Robert travelled home on the train, he could think of nothing but her and as he stared through the window, he caught the fragrance of her perfume, *Charlie,* on his tee shirt that he thought must have brushed off when he had kissed her on the cheek. As images of her tumbled through his mind, he felt himself becoming aroused again.

The following day, he awoke earlier than usual and with a yawn, shuffled into his small kitchen and made a coffee. As he was drinking, sitting on an armchair, feet up on the table and listening to the morning traffic below him in the street, he recalled the encounter with a warm flow of energy. He felt sure that Mrs. Campos had liked him; her smile, that tight blouse, the vague hint of perfume on his tee shirt and the playful teasing were what he most remembered. But he wondered whom was he kidding. A married woman, at least ten years older, and he, a twenty one year old student whose parents were paying to get him though those damned exams.

No, he thought. It was just her way. She was probably like that with everyone. What was so special about him anyway?

As he made his way to university on the train, he wondered if she had been chosen especially by his parents to attend his youthful needs. No, that would have been out of the question, he thought. It was a ridiculous idea. But was she in the loop? Was she one of them? Had she been prepped by his parents and others? His mentors maybe? He could always test her at their next lesson. Yes, that's what he would do, he thought as he climbed the vast steps of the university in the morning sunshine.

During the week, Margarita phoned and they arranged a time to meet at her flat. When he arrived, both nervous and a few minutes early, she opened the door quickly with a smile, kissed him on the cheek and curled herself up on the sofa. She fired rapid questions at him on some tedious economic theory, and he was surprised to find that he knew all the answers.

As he spoke, he saw that she was wearing a tight, pale blue blouse, carefully unbuttoned revealing her cleavage, and a short, dark blue pleated skirt. He could also smell the sweet coconut fragrance of her freshly washed hair, when he had kissed her at the door.

"Come over here on the sofa, Robert," she said, patting the cushion next to her. "I want to show you something."

He did as he was told and, spreading a series of papers on the low table in front of them, she asked him to give her his views on the various pie charts and diagrams shown on them.

"Come on," she said softly. "I'm waiting."

He turned towards her, noticing the hint of a smile from the side of her mouth and, as he looked down at the table and explained the theories the diagrams represented, he felt an excited thrill from her sitting so close to him. With his heart thumping in his chest, her hair brushed lightly against his arm as she leaned over to point, and he almost gasped at the tingle he felt rushing down his legs.

As he tried to focus, he felt her bare leg touching his, as the fragrance and the warmth of her body enveloped him. Trying his best to stick to the lesson, he could feel her watching him.

"And now the next one please, Robert," she said quietly.

He struggled on with the next task, explaining away some dull mathematical theory in a hesitant voice and wishing the lesson would come to an end, so that they could chat about more interesting things. He continued as best he could, not daring to look at her. But he couldn't concentrate.

"Carry on, Robert, we haven't finished yet," she said in a low voice.

Words were coming out of his mouth, but he had no idea what he was saying. He was aroused, practically bursting out of his jeans and he felt dizzy. Lunging across to kiss her, he thrust his hand clumsily onto her breast.

"No, Robert!" she shouted, recoiling on the sofa.

Then his whole body went rigid as they both heard the locks on the front door, clicking and turning.

"Shit! Stefan's back!" she said through clenched teeth, leaping off the sofa.

As she ran to the kitchen, he began frantically straightening his clothes, scribbling hieroglyphics on a pie chart diagram, and trying his best to look normal, but his hands were shaking uncontrollably.

When the door opened, a tall, thin and very pale man wearing a brown pin-striped suit entered, carrying a matching brown briefcase which he meticulously deposited next to the umbrella rack by the door. Robert couldn't see him yet, but he heard a man's deep voice say "bloody traffic!" and then some footsteps from the entrance hall into the living room. When Robert saw him, he stood up and extended a hand nervously, whilst quickly running the other through his hair.

"Mr Campos, pleased to meet you, sir," he said as normally as he could manage.

Mr Campos turned away.

"Margarita, who is this?" he shouted.

She came running from the kitchen wiping her hands on a kitchen towel.

"Oh, this is Robert, darling. Didn't I tell you? He's one of my students and we've finished now haven't we?" she said with a neutral expression and standing a little behind Mr Campos.

"Yes, yes. All finished now, sir," he managed.

"It's been a bloody long day, so I'm getting changed now. Just clear up this mess and I don't expect to see you here when I come back," he said, wagging a finger at both Robert and the papers scattered on the table.

"No sir. I'm terribly sorry," he said, looking down at the floor, at which, Mr Campos removed his huge black rimmed spectacles, folded them and carefully placed them in the top pocket of his suit. Glancing at Robert one more time, he moved away down another hallway, switched on a light and disappeared into a room, slamming the door behind him.

At that moment, Robert put his face in his hands, then looked up and saw Margarita leaning against a wall near the front door with her arms folded. Gathering up his things, he dashed over to her.

"Will you please forgive me?"

"Come on, I'll show you to the lift," she said quietly, opening the door.

As she closed the door quietly behind her, he felt like dying, knowing that she would probably never want to see him again.

"I'm sorry, Mrs.Campos. I couldn't stop myself. I, I…"

She remained silent as she pressed the lift button and watched as the numbers flashed up on each floor as the lift approached. Robert stared at the floor.

"Mrs Campos?" he pleaded.

"Same time next week," she said calmly.

She then slowly made her way back to the flat and closed the door, just as the lift arrived with a loud ding. He was sure he had detected the hint of a smile from the side of her mouth when she had replied. He hoped he was right.

Arriving home, he grabbed a bottle of beer from the fridge, put a cassette in the deck and sat back on the sofa watching the tail lights of the traffic in the streets. *Wish You Were Here* played loudly around his flat and he thought of her, and only her.

CHAPTER 5

Guided by his parents, Robert socialised with the Anglo-Argentine community, leading to cocktail parties at the British embassy, garden fetes at the ambassador's residence and numerous charity events. In the few short years since moving to the capital, he'd met diplomats, their families, bodyguards and friends. Their quintessential Britishness had rubbed off on him to the extent that he would be accepted as a Brit abroad, yet could slip back to being a native simply at will. His closest friends found this uncanny and particularly attractive, so he always played on it to his advantage, since they found his perfect manners and upper class British accent somewhat exotic. He could be seen wearing a dark blue blazer and brightly coloured ties at all the formal events, yet at university parties, which inevitably lasted through until dawn, he was the denim clad youngster in flares and platforms, just like the others.

By the time he was twenty one he'd had one or two girlfriends, yet nobody special had crossed his path, as he found it difficult to maintain a relationship for any length of time. He always felt there was something prissy and teasing about the local girls of his own age. To him, they were simply immature little girls and seemed to be more interested in giggling with their girlfriends than getting physical with him. He knew he could connect with Mrs Campos on a completely different level. He felt that they were on the same wavelength, even though his attraction to her burned him up every moment of the day and he hoped the lessons would never come to an end.

The incident a few weeks previously still rankled with him, even though she had accepted his apology and they never spoke about it again. But with visions of Mr. Campos bursting through her front door and physically throwing him out, the monthly lessons continued at his flat. In spite of his attraction to her, he made enough progress in his work, managing to pass all the exams leading to his finals, twelve months later.

Two weeks before his finals, she phoned to say he needed one more lesson in preparation. He was ecstatic, so made an effort to tidy up and began to pace around the living room looking at his watch. He wasn't anxious about the exams in the slightest. He was simply excited to have her near him again. When the bell rang, he rushed to the door, which he unlocked feverishly and, breezing in, she kissed him on the cheek as usual.

"This is the big one, Robert. The very last lesson," she said, curling herself up on the sofa, whilst cuddling a cushion to her chest. "How do you feel?"

"The last? Are you sure?" he asked, sitting down next to her.

"Depends on whether you pass," she said nonchalantly, whilst looking through her notes.

In spite of everything, he hoped that maybe there was a chance that she really had forgiven him. He knew he could pass his finals, but he also knew that it mean the end of everything.

"And if I pass?" he asked, looking down blankly at the table.

She looked up from her notes and twirled a pen in her fingers.

"Then we're finished, Robert."

CHAPTER 6

During his last eighteen months at university, his friendship with Pimpi Pérez began to flourish. Pimpi, an aspiring young political activist, was reluctantly studying business administration, one of the least challenging courses available for an easy degree. Trying his best not to get noticed by the authorities, he was given to eccentric behaviour, which often found him roaming the campus corridors wearing a black gown and mortar board whilst reciting lines from *Julius Ceasar*. Robert often wondered if his behaviour was a kind of defence mechanism against the military regime. It worried him that he was perhaps too over the top and was in danger of himself disappearing.

Pimpi always dressed to impress, often turning up at lectures in multi-coloured tie-dye shirts, loons and cowboy boots. But as their time at university wore on and the military regime became more brutal, he took to dressing entirely in black. When Robert once asked him why, he simply said that he was in mourning for democracy.

Robert would often wander into the campus cafeteria with a smile, knowing he would have to compete with a gang of infatuated girls hanging off Pimpi's every word. He was a big, imposing young man whose most noticeable features were a completely flattened nose, acquired in a university boxing championship. His large, almost comic chin, would later lead to his nickname, *El mentón*.

Like many of his generation, Pimpi wanted to change the world into his own personal Utopia. His radical ideas made an impression on Robert, with whom Pimpi shared a passion to right the wrongs that had occurred in Argentina over the decades. He became particularly focused on the emergence of national populism in the forties, which in his view was the single most destructive influence in the country, aside from the military dictatorship they currently lived under. He felt that if the country were again to be regarded as a major player in the world, he could be the spark to light that fire.

Robert felt drawn to him and whilst his own views were born of entirely different beginnings, he saw Pimpi as a soulmate, even though he knew he could never fully explain the origins of his views to his friend. Mrs Pack had sworn him to utter secrecy.

Pimpi enjoyed teasing Robert about his teacher, often dropping the odd remark when they met in the evenings for a beer. He could never quite figure out if it was jealousy or simply Pimpi's playful manner. Robert found his taunting often very tiresome and always denied that anything was going on, yet wishing that there was.

When the results of his finals arrived in the post a week later, he quickly opened the envelope hoping that he'd failed, which would be the perfect excuse to see Mrs Campos again every week until resits in the summer holidays. But no, he had passed every exam with honours and his heart sank.

Robert found the graduation ceremony to be an excruciating experience, which he suffered through, simply for his parents. It was only the raucous cajoling by Pimpi that managed to persuade him to join the gang at their favourite bar in Belgrano for the celebrations. After several beers with his friends, Robert began to relax and before long they were swapping stories about the antics they'd all had, while poking fun at the tutors that amused them the most. Pimpi had also passed his finals and quickly assumed the role of chief raconteur and joke teller, which lifted Robert's spirits enormously. Then, during a break in the revelry, Pimpi took Robert to one side with a conspiratorial frown.

"Guess who I saw today, wandering the corridors of the campus?" he asked, leaning towards his friend.

Robert took a sip from his beer and simply shook his head. He had no idea who Pimpi could have seen and felt that he was about to be on the receiving end of yet another one of his jokes.

"Mrs Campos, lover boy," whispered Pimpi.

Robert pulled back and looked at Pimpi who was now grinning from ear to ear.

"Is this another one of your fucking jokes, Pérez?" he asked, testily.

"As clear as you're standing before me right now, Crawford. I kid you not."

He hadn't seen Margarita for weeks, but had thought about her every day and every night.

"But *where* did you see her?"

"In the main foyer where the noticeboards are. She was checking the results. Yours mainly, I expect," said Pimpi, laughing loudly and almost spilling his beer.

"Why didn't you say anything before, man? I mean, did she look OK? How was she?" asked Robert.

"She certainly did look OK and I can see why you're sleeping with her. Those legs…"

"I am *not* sleeping with her, so watch your damn mouth will you?"

"OK, OK," replied Pimpi, stepping back and putting a hand up defensively. "I believe you, you lucky bugger."

He rarely called her by phone, because of the grumpy Mr Campos, but now he knew he was going to. She really did care and he was convinced of it.

"I'll be back in a minute," he said, placing his beer on the bar.

Finding a payphone on the next block, he feverishly pumped coins into the slot, dialled her number and the call was answered instantly.

"Hello?" said a man's voice.

Shit, it's him, thought Robert. Think quickly.

"Good evening, Mr Campos and I'm sorry for disturbing you so late at night," said Robert, lowering his voice several octaves.

"Yes? Who is this?"

Think man! Think!

"Fernandez, from the university bursar's office, sir. Is Mrs Campos available please?" said Robert, his hand shaking the handset uncontrollably. "It's a matter of some importance."

"Can't this wait? We're about to eat, for heaven's sake."

"I'm afraid not, sir. A technical matter that needs clearing up. It shouldn't take long."

Robert heard a clunk, which he assumed was the phone being dropped on a table and then a muffled angry voice.

"It's for you. Someone from that damn university, so just get on with it and make it quick, will you. I'm starving."

Robert waited nervously, but glad he'd had a few drinks for Dutch courage. It certainly helped. After a few more seconds, he heard the phoned being picked up.

"Hello?"

It was her.

"It's Robert. Don't say anything."

"Yes, I understand. How can I help you?"

"Is there a phone extension?"

"Yes."

"I've been tasked to review a number of exam results and we need your assistance in the economics results. Could you possibly attend in the tutoring section within the hour please, Mrs Campos?"

There was a pause on the line and Robert waited. Then the payphone began to bleep, so he frantically rummaged through his pockets and realised he'd put his last coins into the machine.

"Margarita?" he asked.

The line went dead and began emitting a continuous, ear splitting tone.

"Shit!" he said, slamming the handset back into its cradle.

"She must have got the message, but will she come?" he wondered.

Margarita slowly placed the phone back down on the hook and ran her tongue over her upper lip. She turned around to face her husband, who was sat reading a newspaper at the dining table, waiting for his dinner.

"I'm sorry Stefan, but I'll have to go out in a few minutes. I won't be long…"

"At this time of the night, woman?" he asked, throwing his arms in the air angrily.

Ignoring him, she went to the kitchen, took a gulp of Malbec and brought the dinner out. They both finished dinner in silence, with Stefan Campos glaring at his wife from time to time with nothing but resentment in his eyes.

After she had cleared the plates away, she took her coat and handbag and made to leave, saying that she would be as quick as possible.

"Well, don't expect me to be up when you get back. I'm bushed," he said, leaving the table, switching on the television and slumping down on the sofa.

Robert rushed back to the bar and found Pimpi holding court with the rest of the graduates. He finished his beer and ran the ten blocks to his flat in state of euphoria, doubt and not a little fear. Would she come? What would he say to her? As he shut the door to his flat and began to tidy up the usual mess, he kept asking himself the same questions. Am I doing the right thing? What if he finds out? Oh Christ, what have I done?

As he paced up and down the living room, he decided to tell her that he wanted to celebrate his exam success and that's all. Nothing more than that. Yes, that's right, he thought, but what with? Looking in the fridge, he found a six pack of beers and opened one. But she doesn't drink beer, he realised. Champagne, Malbec? He decided to get both, so rushed out of the flat, ran down the stairs and then across the street to the local Chinese mini market, which was just closing its doors for the night. Snatching a bottle of bubbly and the most expensive bottle of Malbec he could find, he paid, thanked the Chinese proprietor profusely and ran back to his flat. Taking the stairs two at a time, he saw a figure coming down towards him and he stopped. It was Pimpi.

"Robert, where have you been? We've been looking all over the place for you."

"What do you mean, *we*?"

"Mrs Campos came to find you in the bar. She came here, but you weren't in."

By now Robert felt he was overheating, his eyes were wide eyed and he was trembling.

"Where is she now?"

"Your carriage awaits, Mr Crawford."

Pimpi drove them the ten blocks to the graduation bar and as they stepped from the car, he touched the side of his nose.

"I'll wait here."

Robert rushed into the heaving, noisy bar and looked around frantically, finally spotting Margarita sitting at a table surrounded by students who were chatting animatedly with her.

"Ah, Mrs Campos," said Robert as he arrived at the table.

"Hello, Robert," she replied, her eyes widening, but not getting up from her seat.

"A quiet word?" Robert insisted, tilting his head to one side. "Over here?"

He was sure he spotted that smile from the side of her mouth and as she arrived in front of him, he felt an urge to hold her. To hold her tight.

"I'm terribly sorry about that. I had to dash out for something…"

"What's this all about, Robert? I went to your flat but you weren't there," she said, looking up at him.

"I was going to ask if you wanted to toast my exam results, that's all," he said, quickly pushing a hand through his hair.

"I know. I gathered that on the phone, but I can't be out for long you know. It's Stefan."

Robert looked down at the floor.

"It doesn't matter. I shouldn't have called you."

There was a brief moment of silence.

"Perhaps just one glass then," she said.

He looked into her eyes, beckoned her with a nod of his head and she followed him outside to Pimpi and the waiting car.

Stepping out of the car at Robert's flat, Pimpi leaned over the passenger seat, holding out his bag of bottles.

"You forgot these."

"Can I offer you a drink Mrs Campos?"

"Why so formal?"

"Sorry, I'm just..."

"Malbec?" she said quickly.

He opened the bottle, poured them both a glass and handed one to her as she took up her usual place on the sofa. He then sat down next to her and they clinked their glasses, but he was lost for words and simply didn't know what to say apart from *cheers*.

"You're not normally this quiet. Is anything the matter?" she asked, placing her glass on the table.

"I had so many things I wanted to say, but now I can't remember," he said, taking a sip from his glass, his hands trembling.

"Well, it's a special day. You passed!"

"Yes I did, but…"

"Robert, you're shaking."

He paused for a moment, looking down at his hands.

"I love you, Margarita…"

She felt an unfamiliar surge of excitement and reached for her glass.

"I've loved you from the moment I saw you. I think of nothing but you. Nothing," he said, still looking down.

He leaned his back on the sofa feeling light headed. Thousands of thoughts were rushing around in his head.

"I know," she said, moving closer.

With her eyes, sparkling with tears, she was finding it hard to find the words.

"I couldn't tell you. I wanted to. God knows I wanted to," he said, finding her hand which was trembling, just like his.

He took both her hands as they stood up, then put his arms around her, holding her face into his neck as the tears rolled down her cheeks. Gently he lifted her face towards his, wiped the tears away, and in that one single moment, he knew who he was.

"I wanted to tell you, too," she said, gently touching his cheek with her fingertips.

"I want you," he whispered, their wet faces almost touching and their eyes locked together.

For a moment they stood holding each other and looking into each other's eyes, until he gently lifted her face, pressed his lips against hers and felt a surge from deep down and up into his chest.

A few moments later she gently pulled away and held his cheek with her right hand, then kissed him softly on the lips.

"I can't stay. You know I have to go, don't you?" she said, looking down.

"Won't you stay, just a little bit longer?"

"I can't. He's got a foul temper and it'll only be worse if I stay," she said.

He pulled her closer again and kissed her hard, their tongues entwining and searching, their breathing now rapid and furious.

"Robert?" she whispered, pulling away a little.

He touched her lips with his finger.

"I want you. I need you" she whispered, unbuttoning her blouse.

He quickly opened the rest of the buttons, dropped the blouse to the ground, took off his jeans and she pulled him down onto the sofa.

In the pale light that shone through the window, he lay above her and looked at her face and body, not sure if he was dreaming. She quickly wriggled out of her panties, he thrust into her, once, twice, three times and then exploded inside her.

CHAPTER 7

As the 1970s passed into a new decade, repression of the population continued, with Robert wondering who amongst his friends would be next to disappear, so they kept their heads down as best they could.

Straight from university at twenty three, Robert joined a small law firm in Buenos Aires, specialising in corporate law, where he excelled as a very capable bilingual lawyer and a tax specialist.

His relationship with Margarita had blossomed into a full blown love affair. With Stefan Campos spending much of his time travelling on company business, she would spend many of her nights at Robert's flat, safe in the knowledge that they wouldn't be discovered. Their entire relationship thrived on a sense of danger, the risk of being discovered, the clandestine meetings, the secret phone calls and the passionate collisions when they knew they were truly alone together. The twelve year age gap meant nothing to them and, if anything, it added another element of danger.

Robert often asked her why she wouldn't simply divorce her husband, but she would usually reply that she couldn't, that she was afraid of him. At times he found the situation intolerable, supposing that, when her husband was back in the country, she would be having sex with him; an idea which she always emphatically denied. He believed her each time the subject was raised between them, so they avoided the matter as much as they could.

As time passed, Margarita actively encouraged his political ambitions, but he constantly struggled with her continued reluctance to leave her husband.

Mrs Pack no longer visited him. She simply stopped banging on his door, and although he was relieved, he had a feeling that maybe Jack was behind the decision and he would ask him when they next met.

By the time he was twenty six, he had made numerous overseas trips, particularly to Britain, where he would attend seminars during the day, and in the evenings, make his way to a smoke filled gentleman's club in the West End of London.

Commander Jack Forsyth had become a father figure to him over the years, yet it wasn't until an encounter in London in July 1983 that Jack felt able to hint at the course his life was destined to take.

Impeccably dressed in a dark blue, double breasted suit, Jack welcomed him to a table in a quiet corner of The Compass, a small and discrete club on Wardour Street and faced Robert as would a mission commander briefing an assault team.

"Mrs Pack will have briefed you on what we require from you, Robert, so I'll come straight to the point."

"Not exactly, sir. But I wish someone would, as she seems to have disappeared," he replied, leaning back in his seat.

"Please. Call me Jack." he said, pointing his finger. "And, yes. I instructed Mrs Pack to terminate her meetings with you, as I will be responsible for your future career from now on."

"Come on, Jack. I've been taught so many things by Mrs Pack and all she ever said was that one day I'd understand. What is it you all want from me anyway?"

"For the moment all I can say is that you are our man in Buenos Aires and the next few years will be critical. You need to prepare yourself to take public office at the very highest level."

"Ah, public office is it? Pimpi and I have often wondered how we could make real changes in the country. You know, from the inside."

"Well? This is precisely what you've been trained for since the very beginning. Surely you must have had some idea?"

"Training? Is that what this is?" he replied, placing his hands flat on the table. "Well, not really. No idea at all actually. I thought you wanted me to be some kind of spy, that's all."

"Erm, not exactly," said Jack, smiling.

"Don't you think you owe it to me now? I mean, that awful woman wouldn't answer any of my questions. In fact, when I did ask, she gave me some crap like it's all on a need to know basis."

Jack shifted nervously in his seat and smiled. Robert sensed Jack's smugness, but knew he had to listen.

"Look. Everything you've seen, felt and heard has been simply a precursor. You've been rigidly taught about the need for secrecy. But more than that, I think you understand well enough why certain wrongs have to be righted. Remember why you're a Crawford and what the names Whitelocke and Beresford mean? Surely I don't have to remind you?'

"Yes Jack, I think maybe you do. Otherwise we're both wasting our time here," said Robert, angrily pushing back his chair and standing up.

Jack remained seated, lit a cigarette and watched as Robert buttoned up his jacket.

"Then if you sit down, I will tell you," he said, with a sweep of his arm.

Sitting back down stiffly, one arm over the back of his seat, he tapped the table with his fingers. Jack nodded to a passing waiter for another round of drinks and leaned forward, roofing his fingers together.

"Ever since our humiliating defeats in Buenos Aires nearly two hundred years ago, not to mention Whitelocke's bloody treason, we have always vowed retribution. I know Whitelocke was branded by many as a coward, but his descendants always believed General Craufurd could have taken Buenos Aires in 1807 and that's why they joined us."

"And who exactly are *us*?"

"The group I represent. It's no coincidence that we're having this conversation in The Compass, you know," said Jack, looking around.

Robert frowned.

"You're talking in riddles again, Jack."

"The Maitland Group. This is where we meet."

"Which is why you always bring me here, no doubt?"

"Call it Maitland Plan mark two if you like and I have no doubt that General Craufurd would have been proud that one of his descendants had been chosen…"

"Jack, now come on. I've already studied everything there is to know about General Craufurd and I was never able to find a direct family connection."

"But that's where you're wrong. You are his heir apparent whether you like it or not."

"Except if his son was from another woman, which would make me the descendant of some long lost bastard…"

He thought he saw anger flash through Jack's face.

"I hardly think so. Now let's move on," said Jack impatiently.

"I mean, I've always felt a hand on my shoulder so to speak, but I never understood why."

"Look, I know it's been hard for you and you've handled it well," said Jack, pausing. "You know, your family is very proud of its heritage, but we chose you. Anyway…"

"My family? My only family are Horacio and Rose, unless…"

"Descended from the Craufurds in Scotland, yes. But now isn't the time; there's much work to be done in Argentina and it's you we are looking to."

As he took a sip of his drink, Robert knew he had come as close as he ever would in receiving a straight answer, yet equally felt that he was being primed for something big, but he had no idea what. Would Jack tell him if he asked, he wondered.

"It's weird, I know, but you wouldn't believe how many times I've heard people at home say, what a shame it is that the English didn't finish the job in the first place," he said, perking up and taking a sip of his drink. "How many times have I heard them say they could all be living in the Australia of South America? And then I point out that they'd all be speaking in some weird Cockney Aussie accent."

Jack laughed heartily and nodded towards the waiter for the lunch menu.

"Well, maybe their dream won't be that far off in the end. You remember what you've been told about the Maitland Plan of course?"

"How could I forget? But Jack, what exactly is *your* Maitland Plan? I've only been told about the history of the nineteenth century invasions."

Jack leaned forward after quickly glancing over his shoulder.

"To establish Argentina as a British colony, under British rule, with the King as head of state. Pretty much as originally planned in 1806, as you may recall."

"You are joking, aren't you?" said Robert, laughing.

"No, I am not joking," Jack replied, leaning back in his seat.

There was a moment's pause as Robert looked across at Jack's unflinching blue eyes.

"And you want me to be part of this plan?"

"Precisely."

"I suppose if it hadn't been for Whitelocke's cowardice, we probably wouldn't be having this conversation at all would we?"

"Quite so. In some ways, the original Maitland Plan *was* a success because we, or should I say, those other fine generals of the day, eventually took South America back from the Spanish. The trouble is, they kept it all for themselves, which I suppose is understandable up to a point," said Jack, raising his eyes to the ceiling, thoughtfully.

"But what I'm really trying to say is this. History will be reversed through you, as we've been dreaming of all these years. I mean, with the US now controlling most of Central and South America through the CIA, their actions have been largely ideological. Our fight isn't with the communists, the Marxists or any of those lunatics. It's a strategic position to retake one of the most important countries in the world. A country that should have been colonised long ago. Not by some right wing fanatics, but by us," said Jack, prodding the table with his index finger. "The Australia of South America. Yes I like the sound of that!"

"Come on Jack, it's going to take a while yet before I can even put myself forward for public office. Christ, I'm not even on the ladder yet and with those psychopaths still in power, it's going to take even longer."

"Now listen, this is a long term plan. It always has been and I certainly hope I live to see the day when you reach a position of real power. I've been working on this most of my life, you know, and when democracy returns, which it will sooner than you imagine, you'll need to be ideally placed for the plan to move forward."

With his icy blue eyes, Jack Forsyth looked intently across the table and waited for a reply.

"I assume you mean that I need some kind of power base, an elected position somewhere, perhaps mayor of a small town like Sancti Spiritu or even Venado Tuerto?"

"No, no, no," said Jack emphatically. "You will need to be in Buenos Aires. Don't start getting any wild ideas of becoming a big shot in some hinterland non entity. First you'll need to find a position of influence in the wealthy northern suburbs. They're traditionally conservative in their views and have sentimental ideas about what may have been the fate of their country, if indeed we had succeeded through our original plans. But then you should know that already."

He had no idea how Jack knew so much about the politics and inner workings of Argentina and thought it best not to ask.

"Look, I'm twenty seven, I've been practicing law for only a few years and I'm practically a nobody. I know absolutely nothing about politics. This is going to take an awfully long time."

"It has already taken an awfully long time. Think about it. Your rise through the ranks will ensure that when you are elected, in whichever role, there will be no doubts whatsoever over who you are and where you come from. You'll already be part of the establishment. Don't you see?"

Robert sat back in his chair and sighed. He was finding it all very hard to absorb.

"Your next task is to get a foot on the ladder of the political machine. You'll know when the time is right and of course, I will always be here guide you. I may even be able to fund you, but that's another matter. For now, we need to wait for the military junta to run its course."

"How long?"

"They can already see the writing on the wall, so I'd say that in about six to nine months they'll be calling for democratic elections," said Jack quietly. "You, however, need to be putting the pieces together to form a political party so that you can stand for election."

"Standing for what?"

"Does it matter as long as it's not more of the same?"

Returning to Argentina a little shell shocked, he felt the weight of his conversations with Jack bearing down heavily on him. Yet he also knew that the course of his life had been somewhat crystallised, with many questions answered and some of the doubts he had pondered for so many years, finally put aside. He always suspected he was being groomed for something big, a real role in the world. Yet he couldn't help wondering if Jack had meant something much bigger than he was really letting on.

CHAPTER 8

On a wet and windy October night in Buenos Aires, two months before the end of the military dictatorship, Robert was working late at the office as usual. Shaking the rain off his overcoat as he shut the door to his flat, he grabbed an ice cold beer from the fridge and as he was about to open it, with his feet up on the coffee table, the phone rang.

"Robert? I need your help…it's…"

He recognised Pimpi's voice immediately. He sounded drunk, desperate and was pleading for his friend to drive out to the port area to find him. Giving no reason for his desperation, he simply said that he would be waiting for him in a small back street bar Robert had once heard was frequented by petty criminals and biker gangs.

As soon as he put the phone down, he changed out of his dark blue pin-striped suit and into the scruffiest jeans and tee shirt he could find, put an old pair of aviator sunglasses in his black leather jacket and gunned the little Renault 12 as fast as he could towards Dock Sud. Parking the car several blocks from the bar, he put on the sunglasses and strolled in, heading straight for the back as Pimpi had suggested. As he slid into the booth opposite his friend, who was drinking what looked like a whisky, he could clearly see why he was so disturbed. His face was cut and bruised, his flattened nose had been smashed and his hands were bloodied with small cuts and abrasions.

"Come on, what happened?" asked Robert nonchalantly, leaning back in his seat.

Pimpi bowed his head, staring at his whisky glass.

"An accident. It was raining, I swerved, and we hit a wall. I think she's dead," whispered Pimpi, almost in tears and looking up at his friend.

"Who?" asked Robert, lowering his voice.

"The girl. I found her near the docks."

"A prostitute?"

"What do you think?"

"It's not a crime to fuck a prostitute you know…"

"I left her in the car…"

"What the hell are you talking about?" said Robert, leaning forward.

"The car! The car caught fire! I had to get out. I ran for it."

"Christ!"

Pimpi looked across at his friend, his head still bowed like a scolded dog.

"I don't know what to do. What should I do?"

"You need to get home. Come on, get up."

"Let me finish this first," said Pimpi, making a grab for his whisky glass.

"Don't you think you've had enough already? Leave it!"

Robert paid the barman, led Pimpi out of the door by his arm and drove them slowly through the pouring rain and past the scene of the accident at the riverside promenade. The fire service and a military vehicle were in attendance and the car, which was embedded front first against a cast iron lamp post, was still smoking and steaming and appeared to be no more than a burned out wreck, with only the metal frame of the little Fiat being visible. Robert drove on and once on the wide avenue back to the city, put his foot down and turned to his friend.

"That was your car?"

"I'll say it was stolen."

"You were drunk, you caused the death of another person. No, you killed a young girl and then you ran away. Now you want to lie about the whole thing. Is that it?"

Pimpi began to snivel and covered his mouth with his cut and bleeding hands.

"I had to. She was fourteen, maybe fifteen, I don't know. I'd have been screwed," he mumbled through the sobs.

Tightening his hands around the steering wheel, Robert dug his fingernails into the black plastic rim as Pimpi struggled to light a cigarette with his shaking hands.

"I'll take you home, but that's all I'm going to do. I can't be involved. I just can't. It would ruin everything."

Pimpi quickly glanced over at him, frowning.

"I mean…hell, I don't know. Christ, you fucking idiot!"

Arriving several blocks from Pimpi's flat, Robert checked his watch and saw that it was two thirty in the morning. He stopped the car, leaned over his friend and opened the passenger door.

"Go home, get yourself cleaned up and stay inside. If anyone asks, you've been in all night. No wait. Phone the police at say, seven thirty and tell them you think your car has been stolen. I'll take care of the rest."

Pimpi stumbled out of the car, steadied himself against the roof, shut the door softly, and then stumbled away down the street with his head bowed and his hands in his jacket pockets.

As the rain steadily fell, Robert remained in the car with the engine running as the wipers squeaked robotically to and fro across the windscreen. He sat for several minutes smoking a cigarette and blowing the smoke through the partially open window, until his friend had disappeared from sight.

Was the girl just another victim of the hideously violent regime they all now lived under, or was Pimpi an irresponsible prick who deserved all that was coming to him, he wondered as he stared at the rain trickling down the steamed up windscreen. On another level, he thought of Pimpi as a kindred spirit and in an obtuse way, felt that he needed him, but for the moment he wasn't sure why. Pimpi wasn't a bad person; what had just occurred was either bad luck or cruel reality. The girl was dead and there was no going back. He couldn't change that, but he could change Pimpi's life forever. A quiet word in the right ear, turning a blind eye at the right moment maybe? Anyway, the federal police would do what the army told them to do. Besides, most of the federal police were an extension of the military junta, so what did they care? They had little interest in real justice and would probably sweep it away as an irrelevant, regrettable accident that held very little importance in the big picture. Hell, they'd probably even say it was a terrorist car bombing that went wrong. Yes, that's right, he thought to himself as he flicked the cigarette out of the window, switched the engine off and opened the car door.

Once he realised it really was his friend at the door, Pimpi opened it sheepishly, his glazed eyes looking into the distance over his friend's shoulder.

"Take off your clothes and get in the shower for Christ sake!"

Without hesitation, Pimpi did just that, leaving his jeans, tee shirt and underwear in a trail towards the bathroom, which Robert collected and placed in a refuse bag. When Pimpi had showered and changed, Robert made them both a coffee and told him to sit down and listen.

"We need to burn your clothes and clean up the flat so that not a drop of blood can be found. As far as you're concerned, you don't know what happened to your car okay?"

Pimpi sat staring into his coffee cup as they sat across from each other at the small kitchen table and nodded vaguely, his hands trembling.

"But you *will* call the police to report your car stolen later this morning and that's all you're going to do. Have you got that?"

He nodded again, lit a cigarette and said, "How do I explain all this?" pointing to his face and then his hands.

"You'll only have to explain if you go to the station to make a statement, which you won't be doing. I know someone, so I'll see what I can do. I'll vouch for you."

At that, Pimpi looked up forlornly, yet with a frown rippling his forehead.

"You don't have to do this, you know."

"Clearly I don't, but I am, so let's just leave it at that."

On leaving the apartment he deposited the refuse bag containing Pimpi's clothes in the basement incinerator. He didn't think it was absolutely necessary, but if there was the slightest trace of the girl's blood on his clothes, he really would be in it. But no, he thought to himself, as he ran to the car in the driving rain; it was highly unlikely.

As he drove back to his flat, he remembered the police lieutenant he'd met shortly after qualifying as a lawyer. He'd been back to the same station once or twice since, remembered him because of the limp, the result of chasing down a teenage thief who'd shot him in the ankle and he owed Robert a favour.

Later the following morning, after several cups of coffee, he called Pimpi who told him he'd reported his car as stolen to the police. They had then asked him to go to the police station and make a statement, since a potential homicide had taken place involving his car.

"And what did you say to them?"

"That I was ill in bed with flu."

"Highly original. Listen, I'm going to have a word with that lieutenant I mentioned. Stay here, don't answer the phone or the door and only speak to me. Got that?"

When Pimpi put the phone down, he put his head in his hands, his bloodshot eyes dripping tears onto the kitchen table. Yet, as he thought of the young, waif-like girl he'd treated so roughly as they were parked in the woods near the promenade, his tears turned to a sly smile. He recalled how he had skidded and hit the barrier, cast iron lamppost or whatever it was that shot the girl's head into the windscreen. He was even more amazed to remember that he'd put his seatbelt on, almost as a subconscious act, but he couldn't remember when. But he did remember the smoke and the smell of fuel and he did remember looking at the body beside him, the eyes wide open, the blood running down those cheeks in her final resting place against the dashboard of his car.

He felt numb all over. But he did sense the fear of being found out and locked up for something that could have happened to anyone. Why would they care anyway, he wondered. Hadn't he seen students shot dead by the army on street corners? Was he no worse than them? But he knew he'd been right to smash the window with his feet, crawl out of the car with the *Old Smuggler* whisky which he had slugged back as he drunkenly staggered his way through the darkened streets of the port area. He did vaguely remember falling into the mess of rubbish bins in the back alley near the entrance of that bar, but wasn't entirely sure how he found his way in.

Pimpi raised himself stiffly from the kitchen table and walked across the room. As the palms of his hands leant against the rain spattered French windows, his friend Robert was standing in front of a scruffy reception counter of what passed as the local police station, also known as Commissary 64. He was waiting for Lt *El Rengo* Forza to arrive back from a job, and behind the dirty Formica counter, a young policeman with a cigarette hanging from the side of his mouth was typing out a report with two fingers on an ancient typewriter, but was not appearing to enjoy the experience.

It was known that Lt Forza had barely escaped an early discharge from the service due to his injury, in spite of his young age and it was only his superb marksmanship and detective work that had saved his career from being ruined. Robert's token presence on the police oversight board, when he had supported Lt Forza's petition to remain, had been vital to him.

As he finally managed to coax a coffee out of the noisy and overused drinks machine in the dilapidated waiting area, he remembered how he had heard the jokes about Lt Forza, shot in the ankle by a kid and now simply called *El rengo*, the limp. As the clatter of typewriters filled the empty spaces between the cars passing in the rain drenched streets, he looked through the nicotine stained windows across at the car park.

Just at that moment, a battered old blue and white Ford Falcon police car pulled in and the unmistakable figure of Lt Forza emerged, limping towards the station with his partner.

"Lt Forza, would you have time for a coffee?" Robert asked, as the tired looking policeman appeared behind the counter.

He looked at his watch, nodded and followed Robert out of the station.

"It's been a while since you were down here. What brings you to this neck of the woods?" asked Forza as they walked through the backstreets, dodging the puddles of rain.

"That burned out car last night, know anything about it?"

"Only what the boys told me," said Forza, holding open the door to the cafeteria. "Why?"

As they sat at the bar and ordered coffee, Robert continued.

"Well, it was a friend of mine's car. He reported it stolen this morning."

Lt Forza listened as he stirred his coffee.

"He's flat on his back with flu, you know what it's like. Anyway, if it's just an insurance report, I can assist on his behalf."

Lt Forza looked at their reflections in the mirror behind the bar, sighed, then turned to Robert.

"I'm not on that case, but I heard a body was found in the wreck and they can't identify it. Too badly burned. Oh and the army captain at the scene apparently said that it looked like a car bomb that went wrong. At least that's what I heard."

"Which is they won't want it to be made public no doubt?"

Lt Forza nodded.

"On the other hand, if your friend's car was stolen and crashed by some joyriders, we've still got a body on our hands. Mind you, it's going to be impossible to identify. I heard that they can't even tell yet if it's male or female as there's pretty much nothing left to examine. Burnt to a cinder."

"There's no question of my friend not wanting to cooperate, Lieutenant, but he's completely laid up. He always parks his car outside the flat, thought about going to work, found it missing and phoned the police."

"And now he can't get out of bed?" asked Forza, turning to Robert.

"That's about it really, Lieutenant."

"I'll have a word with the officer in charge of the case," said Forza, as he finished his coffee.

"Thank you, Lieutenant."

As Lt. Forza slowly left the café, Robert watched him leave, then stared at his reflection in the mirror opposite, feeling uneasy at what he saw. On the other hand, what was done was done. Pimpi hadn't intentionally killed the girl. It had been an accident. But could he have saved her instead of leaving her to burn to death? Jesus, what a fucking mess, he thought.

As he drove back to Belgrano, his thoughts turned again to how he could turn events to his advantage. Pimpi had secured a dead-end job as office manager at a small freight forwarding company in the Dock Sud, for which he was overqualified and entirely wasted. He also knew that Pimpi's talents would only come to the fore, once a semblance of democracy was restored and, knowing the history of Argentine democracy, it was and always had been fragile at best.

No, what he needed, was to get his foot in the door of some upper middle class district like San Isidro or Vicente Lopez in the northern suburbs, where wealth seemed to drip from the Jacaranda trees and mansions.

He knew Jack was right. With Pimpi's cooperation, which he now knew was going to be beyond question, he would form a new political party in ripe and fertile ground when democracy was finally established as Jack believed it would be. He knew he was too late for the general election called by the Junta, but eventually he would take on those other dormant political has-beens such as *The Workers Party*, so viciously savaged by the military and left practically rudderless. He felt sure that's what Jack meant by getting in at the bottom.

At the intersection of the main highway, he made a decision. Instead of heading home, he turned off and made straight for Pimpi's flat to lay out his plans for which he expected, nay, would demand, his friend's complete and total cooperation.

Pimpi had somehow managed to stick some gauze and black, electrical sticky tape over his nose that would have made Robert laugh out loud if it weren't for the gravity of the situation. Following Pimpi into the kitchen, he saw him hunched over a bottle of *Old Smuggler* whisky whilst listening to Radio Mitre, one of the few radio stations managing to broadcast at least some political content in spite of the heavy military censorship. This pleased him inasmuch as it showed that his friend was still focusing his antennae in the right direction at the very least. But the heavy drinking worried him.

"I've taken care of your problem, so for the moment there's nothing more to say about it. Do you understand?" said Robert, waving away the glass of cheap whisky Pimpi had just offered him.

"And I expect you to clean up your act man. You can't carry on like this," he said, pointing to the bottle and the rubbish scattered around the kitchen. "You still want to join me and change the world?"

"Even now?"

"Answer the question will you?"

"You know that's what I've always wanted to do, damn it! Ever since university, don't you remember? All those ideas we had?"

"Which is exactly what you and I are going to forge ahead with, once democracy is restored. But I'm going to make myself clear. You don't have a choice any more. It's either me or nothing. You understand that don't you?"

Pimpi smiled thinly and shrugged his shoulders. "So, what are you thinking?" he asked.

Robert pushed his chair back, stood up and began to pace around the small kitchen, pushing his hands through his untidy mop of blonde hair.

"We should be ready to put a new party forward, but we're too late for the current elections. I was thinking of *We Can Change* or something similar. What do you think?"

"Not very original. Anyway, start local, you mean? We wouldn't have a hope in hell nationally, at least not yet."

"Agreed, that's my thinking too. I was thinking of San Isidro, where we would need to take the municipality, but this is going to take time and money. What do you think?"

Pimpi rubbed his eyes and took a swig of whisky.

"Find your way into the town hall and start from there? It's your best chance to get your face known."

"And you'll be my campaign manager, since I'll eventually be running for mayor."

Pimpi put his head in his hands and sighed loudly.

"Listen, man, I'm not sure I can do this."

Robert swung round to face him, grabbed the bottle of whisky from the table and threw it into the kitchen sink, where it shattered into pieces and filled the room with the stench of so many cheap bar rooms. He then leaned over the kitchen table with his hands resting on the back of a chair, putting his face directly in front of Pimpi's.

"This is not an offer."

Pimpi put his hand forward to take a slug from what remained in his glass, but Robert swiped his hand across the table, sending the glass smashing to the floor. Pimpi looked away, put his hands up to his face and began to sob as a man who had reached his lowest point and had nowhere left to turn. Robert slumped down in the seat opposite his friend and stretched his arms out behind his head, asking himself what could be done with such a talented but broken man. He knew that his only option was to find help for his friend and once Pimpi had composed himself, Robert swore him to a daily trip to the local AA meeting, a suggestion which Pimpi at first brushed away with utter contempt.

Robert got up from the table and leant over his friend's shoulder.

"It's either that or prison."

CHAPTER 9

When democracy finally returned in December 1983, as Jack had accurately predicted, Robert wasted no time positioning himself and his newly formed party in the political scene and secured a post as legal secretary in the local authority of San Isidro in the northern suburbs. He would use his position as a springboard in the next general election, when he would run for mayor in San Isidro.

Margarita's relationship with her husband continued to deteriorate. On numerous occasions she would leave him on the pretext of staying with her mother. In fact, she would stay with Robert and cover up the bruises with make up as best she could. She never fooled Robert, who would plead for her to divorce her husband, angrily threatening to take matters into his own hands. As time passed, their affair continued with ever increasing passion and her husband's behaviour became yet more intolerable. Margarita was soon left with little choice and with Robert's encouragement, began divorce proceedings, left the matrimonial home when her husband was away and moved in to live with Robert at his house in Punta Chica.

The return of democracy saw two weak administrations struggle to hold on to power amidst one financial crisis after the other, with the leader of the second government resigning just over half way through his mandate, resulting in a general election being called. This resulted in the return of national populism, which only strengthened Robert's resolve and gave real meaning to Jack's plans for him. Robert now felt real political conviction; something he had never expected.

Nearly four years later, Robert faced the enormous task of ousting the incumbent president, now approaching the end of her first term. In the run up to the general election, President Virginia Cristal was inching ahead in the polls and seemed to be on her way to a second term, which in Robert's view was an unthinkable probability. With a weak opposition, in spite of his own growing popularity with voters across the country, his campaign simply couldn't match that of the sitting president.

His worst fears were realised when matters came to a head, in a three horse race, with the president not quite reaching the required forty five percent of votes counted, forcing a run off. Robert, trailing badly in third place immediately threw in the towel, once he realised he had been written off. On the night before the second ballot, copies of love notes emerged on a state sponsored TV station, showing the president's only remaining rival in intimate exchanges with the wife of a close colleague. By withdrawing at the last minute, the challenger handed the presidency to Virginia Cristal on a plate, in spite of the fact that she had garnered only forty two percent of the vote in the first round. Robert now faced another four years in opposition, or so he feared.

Immediately following the election result, Robert and Pimpi met for a coffee in a small bar in Belgrano and found a quiet corner where they knew they wouldn't be overheard. Robert had chosen the place carefully, since he knew that the president's intelligence services were watching him.

"We need to get this woman out. Four more years of this and we won't have much of a country left. She's tearing it apart from the inside," said Robert lighting a cigarette and looking over his shoulder.

"Look, she has over a dozen cases of fraud lined up against her as it is," said Pimpi. "It shouldn't take that long, you know. There are three or four prosecutors working on them and a few have been passed to federal judges already."

"Well, apart from the fact that she's got presidential immunity, something you seem to have forgotten, she's already nobbled the justice system. The judges are either terrified of her or in her pocket, and the prosecutors who do get a sniff, either mysteriously commit suicide or are disbarred. It's a complete fucking mess and I don't need to spell it out to you of all people."

"What do you suggest then?"

Robert leaned back, blowing the smoke upwards as he thought of his reply.

"Impeachment is the only way. She'll have to be removed," he said, after a few seconds, lowering his voice and looking over his shoulder again.

"And how exactly?" said Pimpi, raising an eyebrow.

Robert looked across at his friend for a few moments, glanced to his side and then leaned further across the table.

"Charley Cristal. The president's investigative reporter brother. Remember?" he asked quietly.

Pimpi sighed, raising his eyes to the ceiling.

"Look, the video went missing and so did the only witness. It's all hearsay now and that's all we've got," said Pimpi dismissively.

"Not exactly" said Robert, raising his eyebrows. "Remember Clara Tomkinson? Well, I had a drink with her the other night and she's got something. I think we can use it. In fact, I know we can."

"Isn't she that fat lass at The BA Tribune with huge tits? What I wouldn't do to get my hands on her ass," said Pimpi, vividly demonstrating some crude sexual act with his hands.

Robert leaned across the table, grabbed Pimpi by the tie and pulled him across with such force that he began to choke.

"Say anything like that again about any of my friends and you're out. Is that clear?" he said slowly, through clenched teeth.

"Let go of me, will you!" he squealed, grabbing Robert's arm.

"I mean it, Pimpi," he said, releasing him roughly.

They sat for a few moments glaring at each other across the table. Robert didn't care for Pimpi's crudeness, but the fact was, he was ruthlessly devious, he got things done and Robert didn't care if Pimpi was popular at all. He wasn't meant to be.

"Now listen. She says she's acquired a surveillance video showing the person who pushed Charley in front of that taxi," continued Robert.

Pimpi sullenly sat up a little straighter, folding his arms like a spoilt child.

"And who is it?"

"She and a friend ran it through a friendly police computer and we're absolutely certain that it's Lucio Melia."

"That union thug?"

"The very same. You know Charley was about to go public on the president's complicity with the military junta, don't you? He had just interviewed an ex-federal policeman, now living just across the border in Paraguay who claims that in 1981 Virginia Cristal gave him the names of twelve students who were never seen again. That's why they killed Charley. Her own brother, for Christ sake."

"You know as well as I do that The Tribune would never run that story. They're up to their necks in it with the president. Right up her ass in fact."

"Yes I know, which is why Clara asked me if I could handle it. If not, she says she'll go to the highest bidder, which would probably end up being her friends at The London Crusader. We can't have that. Give it to that friend of yours at TVN. I can't be a part of this, you know that."

"And why not?"

Robert knew he would have to tackle such a question eventually and it wouldn't be the last time.

"Because that's why you're my campaign manager."

Pimpi sat up and straightened his shoulders, his eyes widening.

"I don't suppose she said how she acquired the videotape?"

"I wasn't foolish enough to ask, but go ahead, be my guest."

Pimpi twirled his glass of Coke around and studied the ice cubes clinking together, thinking hard.

"I think I can do that, but how does it connect the president directly? That's the key, you know that."

"Clara says that TVN have a recording of Melia talking to Carlos Gandini, you know, the president's cabinet chief, in which Melia is heard mentioning the president by name, no less."

Robert signalled the waiter with a click of his fingers and an elderly man with a pronounced stoop and a small white towel draped over his arm shambled across the black and white tiled floor and took their order for another round of drinks. Robert leaned back in the wooden booth and studied Pimpi.

When the waiter shuffled away to fetch the drinks, he continued.

"Get this. Melia actually says to Gandini, 'Cristal asked me to deal with her brother.' and Gandini says 'you bloody idiot, just get it done,' and the phone goes dead."

"But is that enough though? 'Deal with her brother?' We'll need a little more than that to put the bitch away."

"Clara reckons Melia will turn. If he really thinks he'll get protection, she believes he'll spill everything."

"The most we can get her for then, is complicity. Is that enough for impeachment though?"

"Of course it is. She would eventually be charged as if she had pushed him in front of that taxi herself. All you have to do now is get to Melia before Cristal does. So find somewhere he can let his hair down, that's all you need to do. You're pretty good with that kind of stuff aren't you?"

Robert let the thought sink in for a couple of seconds and he didn't miss the smile playing at the side of his friend's mouth.

"The audio tape can be the icing on the cake once Melia starts talking. And talk he will, believe me," continued Robert.

"You seem pretty sure of all this. Who's going to persuade Melia to talk anyway? There's no way I'm doing it, even for this. The man's an animal!"

"I've taken care of that already. You just lure him in, get him nice and comfy, let me know where he is and leave the rest to me."

Robert left the bar through the rear fire exit. Looking for a public telephone he took a haphazard route to the main Retiro railway terminal where he knew there were some public phone booths buried down in the subway. He dialled Jack's number and received an immediate return call.

"Jack, I need that favour and I need it now."

He went on to explain his plan regarding Melia, saying that he needed men in the country at the nearest opportunity.

"I can have them on a flight out as soon as you give the word. Just tell me when and where when I see you on Friday."

"Friday?"

"Yes, we need to meet. The usual place. I'll have tickets waiting for you at the airport."

CHAPTER 10

Robert was concerned that he was due to be pulled down a peg or two by Jack, for his party's poor performance in the recent general elections. His *We Can Change* party simply didn't have the projection they needed for such a large campaign, in spite of Jack's generous funding. In the end, he needn't have worried; it was the last thing on Jack's mind when they met for lunch at The Compass on a wet and windy July day in London.

"Good of you to come over at such short notice, Robert. There are some matters here that you should know about, but first let's get a drink," said Jack, rubbing his hands together.

Having lived his entire life in Argentina and in spite of being accustomed to the British way of drinking, Robert found that every trip he made to London required a girding of his loins just to keep up with the custom of booze with everything and anything.

"Well, just the one, if you don't mind."

"You're not going all soft on me now, are you?" Jack teased.

Once the waiter had brought the obligatory gin and tonics to the table, Jack leaned forward.

"I know you're concerned over those elections, but you needn't be. I've dealt with one or two things which will facilitate matters considerably."

"Such as?" asked Robert, frowning.

Jack moved his head forward a little, inviting Robert to do the same.

"The videotape."

"That was you?"

"Naturally. And TVN should be in possession of a small cassette tape by now, I would imagine," said Jack, leaning back in his chair.

Robert leaned forward again and spoke in a poorly disguised, angry whisper.

"I do not want Clara involved in any of this, Jack. Nothing."

"Wake up man. She's a journalist. That's what she does. If you'd asked her where she got the tape, which you wouldn't of course, she couldn't tell you anyway."

"I mean it, Jack. She's special and I don't want her put in any danger."

"Do you really think we would do that? No, of course not. I'm simply oiling the wheels."

Robert sat back, lit a cigarette and looked at Jack's cold, handsome features. He had always hoped that reaching the very top would be on his own merits.

"I was hoping to get this done myself, you know."

"Don't be foolish, Robert, it doesn't become you. I'm simply removing some of the uncertainties of life. It's very simple really. In politics, as in all aspects of power, uncertainty is a devil of a problem which needs to be removed. How else did you think you were going to become president?"

Robert leant back in his seat and raised his eyes to the ceiling. So it was true what he'd long suspected.

Moving his chair closer to the table, he leaned in and looked quickly over his shoulder.

"I knew deep down that this is what you wanted. I'm right aren't I?"

"I thought that was obvious, but the fact is, you'd never have beaten Cristal in a straight match. She's too damned popular, or at least she seems to be."

"Foul means or fair?"

"I wouldn't have put it quite like that, old chap but yes, you're on the right track."

"This is not how I saw things unfolding, Jack."

"It's the real world, so get used to it. Now, shall we move on?"

"Be my guest," said Robert taking a sip of his second gin and tonic.

"Keep your team close, especially that Pérez fellow who appears to be the sneakiest, most ruthless bastard I've ever come across, and I'm glad he's on your team and not against you."

"He is that, Jack; some even call him *The Rottweiler*."

"He's the kind of chap we could do with over here, actually. It's got to the point that I fear for these spineless MPs. They all seem to be afraid of their own shadows nowadays. Anyway, that's not really why we're here today. We've got a problem and it's only fair that you know how and why I'm taking control of this."

"Europe?"

"Precisely. It's always Europe, but what we fear is that the new Prime Minister won't respect the will of the people to leave the EU, will renegotiate a new deal with Brussels, or call a second referendum to keep us in Europe, which we would probably lose. Definitely lose, in fact, and if that happens, somewhere down the line we'll lose our sovereignty altogether. Britain will become just another satellite European state dictated to by a group of faceless civil servants across the channel," said Jack, frowning. "Of course, supported by a gaggle of smug, self-interested politicians in Westminster."

"And how has this got anything to do with Argentina?"

"Because you need to be behind that desk in the Casa Rosada and in power by the time we make Britain see sense, that's why."

"I'm sorry Jack, I'm not with you."

"I'm working with colleagues in other branches of our armed forces to ensure that the prime minister sees reason. He will be persuaded, let's put it that way. But we're biding our time."

Jack took a sip from his drink, the ice cubes clinking as he drained the glass and sat back nonchalantly. Robert looked across the table, his mouth half open.

"This is outrageous." Robert said with half a smile. "You are joking, aren't you?"

"I wish I were joking and when I say persuaded, what I really mean is, we will soon be pulling the strings behind Number 10."

"So, no tanks on the streets, death squads lurking in market squares and women's institutes then?"

"No, no. Nothing like that," said Jack smiling. "A show of strength from the Chief of the Defence Staff will suffice to scare the living daylights out of these spineless creatures and by the time you've settled into your new duties in Buenos Aires, we'll have all our assets in place. We will of course keep you informed at all times, so please don't fret about that."

"Which is why you moved on the Charley Cristal affair so quickly?"

"Precisely. Listen, you'll have to move quickly on this. The timing is crucial."

"We still have the problem of that woman's second term and if we don't get her removed soon we won't have a country left to, erm…"

"Which is why we acted," interrupted Jack. "Anyway, I think the words you are looking for are *take back*, aren't they? It's quite simple really."

"I know, I know."

He then went on to give Jack the information he needed to brief the two specialists waiting to carry out their dirty work on Melia, in the safe house that Pimpi had secured at breakneck speed the day before.

"They can be with your man tomorrow and believe me, they're effective."

"I'll take your word for that, Jack."

CHAPTER 11

W hen he travelled to London, Robert always stayed at a small, upscale hotel in the West End, personally recommended by Jack. The staff were discrete and always greeted him professionally yet warmly, leaving him with the impression that it was maybe some kind of safe house.

That evening, after the extended lunch with Jack, he phoned Margarita from his hotel room, but there was no answer. He tried again and let the phone ring for nearly a minute, thinking that she may be in the shower, but then hung up.

As he was deep in thought, watching the sheeting rain in the headlights of the slow moving cars, he remembered the season pass to *The Last Night of the Proms* that Jack had given him earlier as they were saying their goodbyes. He'd told him that for many people the classical music festival was an emotional experience, patriotic even, and if he ever wanted to savour a real sense of Britishness, he should go along at least once in his lifetime.

In the taxi on his way to the Royal Albert Hall, he thought of Margarita again. It was unusual for her not to pick up the call. He had no reason to worry; she may have gone out with friends. But it nagged at him and he couldn't figure out why.

When he arrived at the Royal Albert Hall, he was swept up in a sea of chanting happy people waving flags, swaying and singing along to some of Britain's most beloved and stirring anthems. He found himself joining hands with complete strangers as *Rule Britannia* reached its stirring climax and when Elgar's *Pomp and Circumstance* followed with a passionate finale, shivers went up his neck; he felt himself choking up with emotion and a strong urge to burst into tears of patriotic fervour. People around him from all over the world, dressed in gaily coloured hats and tuxedos hugged each other, swept up in waves of euphoria. As he left the hall, with the sky clearing to reveal a starlit sky, he felt vital and recharged.

Not wanting the magic to end, he followed other flag waving revellers to a nearby pub where they all raised their glasses to the King and broke out into spontaneous choruses of *Land of Hope and Glory*, thrusting their drinks into the air in joyous revelry. For Robert, it was a defining moment and one that marked a deep and real connection with a country that, from that moment on, would forever be his spiritual home.

When he woke the following morning with a pounding head, his first thoughts were of Margarita. As he lay in bed rubbing his face, he stretched over, grabbed the phone and dialled home again, thinking to hell with the time difference. To his relief, his call was answered on the second ring.

"Robert, is that you?"

He sat up on the edge of the bed immediately, worried by the tone of her voice.

"Yes it's me. What's the matter, darling?"

"Something terrible has happened."

She started to sob, prompting him to get up from the bed and walk to the window, dragging the phone cord behind him.

"Are you all right? Tell me what happened, Mags."

There followed a long pause.

"It's Stefan. He's dead…," she said, as she broke down.

He didn't know what to say her and struggled for a reply.

"What? But how? What happened?"

He could hear sniffling and sobbing before she spoke again.

"I was with the police last night. They searched the flat. I don't know what to do. Please, I can't..."

"I'm flying back tonight."

He heard a click as the line went dead.

Looking at his watch, he saw it was eight thirty. His flight didn't leave Heathrow for another fourteen hours. He had a whole day to kill while he grappled with the question of what may have happened to her husband. He felt a certain shock at the news, yet admitted to himself, that he also felt relief. He had only met the man once, and his loathing of him had grown to the point of violence on several occasions, but she had held him back.

She hadn't told him how he had died. It could have been anything; a car accident, a mugging, he didn't really care a great deal, but he did care that she was suffering.

He contemplated sitting in Heathrow airport for twelve hours and maybe mooching around duty free, grabbing dinner and then reading a book, but he knew he'd spend most of the time looking at his watch and checking the flight information boards. Finally, he packed his suitcase and went down to reception, where he arranged a taxi for the trip to the airport and left his bags at the desk for collection later.

He then took a city tour of London in an open bus, followed by a late lunch at a pub he knew by the river in Chiswick, where he fell in with a crowd of rowdy London Welsh rugby players celebrating Wales' win over The All Blacks in New Zealand the day before. For Robert, it was another experience he would cherish, as he came to understand what singing with heartfelt passion really meant. Once again he felt himself tingle and choke up as he sang *Myfanwy*, *Land of My Fathers* and other Welsh songs with his new rugby friends, who plied him with pint after pint of ale. Watching as he did, one rugby player after another break out into spontaneous solos, singing about a land he still hadn't seen, brought about a kind of longing he had never experienced before. When he was about to fall into the taxi, he asked one of his new friends if he knew what this feeling meant.

"Oh, that's *hiraeth*, that is," came the reply.

CHAPTER 12

The long flight to Buenos Aires passed mercifully quickly, since he slept most of the way in a haze of beer induced torpor. When he arrived home in the early morning, he could see that Margarita was still badly shaken and she threw her arms around his neck, the moment she saw him.

"Come here, Mags, let's sit down. Come on," he said quietly as her two friends moved away and into the kitchen.

He led her over to the sofa, where he put his arms around her as she rested her face on his chest, sobbing gently.

"He was stabbed. Stabbed in his office," she said quietly, fumbling with a paper tissue.

Robert sat up, put a hand under her chin and gently lifted her face towards him, brushing the wet hair from her eyes.

"But who, Mags? Who would do that?"

"Some crazy man. He'd just started working there. Just went crazy," she said, as her shoulders shook with the sobs.

"Oh Mags, I'm so sorry," he said, holding her tight.

"He thought Stefan was someone else," she said, crumpling the tissue in her hands.

"Who? Who did he think he was?"

"Alfredo Arias. He thought Stefan was him. You know, The Angel of Death?"

"Oh no Mags, I'm so sorry," he said, holding her head to his chest again.

He remembered the name. Arias had been a commander in the navy during the military dictatorship, said to have led a death squad responsible for the murder of dozens of civilians, mainly women, some of whom had been pregnant.

"Will you be all right here for a while? I just have to go out for a few minutes," he asked, kissing her on the forehead.

"Don't be long. Please hurry back," she said, looking up at him. He squeezed her hand, beckoned her two friends from the kitchen and left the house.

Making his way to a nearby cafeteria, he called Clara Tomkinson from a payphone to meet him there.

"You've heard about this murder then?" he asked Clara when she sat down opposite him.

"Yes of course I have, it's shocking. A case of mistaken identity or so it appears. That's what they told me at US Airways, anyway."

Clara Tomkinson, a second generation Anglo-Argentine and now a freelance journalist, once worked at the BA Tribune, the only English speaking newspaper in the country, owned by a magnate known to be a rabid supporter of President Cristal, hence Clara's departure. She always had an open smile on her youthful, rounded face and her pageboy style brown hair, the oblong, gold rimmed glasses, which she wore with a gold chain around her neck, often belied her tenacious and feisty character.

"What happened?" asked Robert.

"I got there a couple of hours after they'd arrested the lunatic and taken Mr Campos's body away. I spoke to one of the secretaries there, poor thing. She was in a hell of a state."

"From what she and others told me, this new employee, Montez I think he was called, had been behaving strangely since he started working there. Apparently he would just stand outside Mr Campos's office and stare at him. On one other occasion, someone saw him arguing and pointing at Mr

Campos in the underground car park. Anyway, the day before yesterday, Montez arrived for work, went straight to Mr Campos's office, kicked the door open and stabbed him sixteen times, shouting 'Angel of Death!' over and over.

"Three of the other employees ran over and managed to get the knife from him. Mr Campos was already dead when the police arrived. Just awful, can you imagine?"

Robert's face remained impassive as he looked back at her.

"How's she bearing up?" asked Clara.

"Not well. Some of her friends from the school are sitting with her today. I just don't know what to say to her."

"Poor love. She must be devastated. I could go and see her, you know."

"Are you sure?"

"Of course I am."

Clara placed her hand on Robert's forearm with a serious, pleading expression in her eyes.

"Listen, be careful. Stefan Campos was well connected in the air force. I'm just telling you, all right?"

Clara was one of the few people who knew about his affair with Margarita and he felt he could trust her implicitly. She was discrete, shared many of his views on the state of the country and had recently become involved with a childhood friend of his, Pascal Zapatero.

"What do you mean, *be careful*?"

"You know Campos used to be in the air force don't you and that he was acquitted of any crimes during the military dictatorship?" she asked.

"Yes, Mags mentioned it a few times, but it's never been something I ever pressed her on."

"Well, there's still a rogue element out there that believes the military were right to do what they did and they'll see this murder as a provocation. They look after their own, you know that, which is why Arias is still out there somewhere."

"We're very discrete Clara. It's not as if we parade around the place holding hands like teenagers you know."

"Only because of her husband. Am I right?"

"What are you driving at?"

"You supported rescinding the amnesty, you had Pimpi introduce a bill upgrading the trials to war crimes and you're fucking the wife of one of theirs. What else do you want me to say?"

"But how could they possibly know?"

"Wake up Robert! They have fingers in everything, thanks to that bitch, the president. You've not even suspected that you're being watched?"

"It hadn't even occurred to me, to be honest."

"Well they are. Take my word for it and be more careful," said Clara, prompting him to visualise a team of outsized bodyguards following him everywhere.

"But now that her husband is dead?"

"Look, they could well think that you had a hand in it. Who knows? I know the president has been protecting hundreds of the military but I just can't prove much and even if we could, she'd be immune."

"Not for much longer, I hope," said Robert.

"Thanks for the tape," she whispered as they both got up to leave. "And I'm coming with you remember? We can talk on the way."

As they made their way back to his house, he went over what Clara had said and nervously looked over his shoulder, hoping they weren't being followed. At that moment, his mind went back to the dark days of the military coup he'd witnessed first-hand and he thought of his old buddy Guy. Could he be persuaded to work for him as his personal bodyguard? Did he even know how to find him again? No he didn't, but he knew someone who could.

CHAPTER 13

O n a grey September day in 1997, Rear Admiral Jack Forsyth, in full uniform, sat at his mahogany desk in the dim light of his oak panelled office in Whitehall, London. Placing his gold rimmed bifocal spectacles on the manila envelope in front of him, he eased himself up wearily from his old wooden swivel chair and moved slowly to the tall windows. Clasping his hands tightly behind his back, he turned his wedding ring nervously.

Looking down Whitehall, he could just see the grey outline of The Cenotaph, and beyond that the crowd control barriers lined with police in full riot gear standing rigidly like sentinels before the crowd. It was a scene to which he had now become accustomed, so he turned away, returned to his desk, replaced his bifocals and picked up the thick manila envelope. There were no markings whatsoever on the outside, he noted as he examined it carefully. Opening a side drawer to his right, he withdrew a gold plated letter opener and slowly opened the envelope taking care not to rip the contents. Inside he discovered a further three envelopes, all white in colour and marked A, B and C respectively in large green letters. There were no other markings visible.

Having extracted the contents, he placed them on his desk and smiled. He longed for a smoke. As he was about to open another drawer, there was a knock at the door. Not a loud knock, more a nervous knock.

"Come," he announced in as surly a manner as he could muster, as he always did when expecting lackeys and tiresome politicians. Slowly the huge oak door opened, creaking slightly.

"Sir, you have a visitor," said his faithful secretary Macaulay.

"Can't it wait, Macaulay?"

"No, sir. It appears to be important."

"Who is it?"

"General Sir Michael Gordon, sir."

"Not again!"

"Sir?"

"Very well. Ask him in if you please."

"Yes, sir."

The Admiral sat back in his chair, opened the left hand drawer, noticed an old service revolver he'd never fired in anger and withdrew a packet of twenty *Senior Service* cigarettes, which he placed on the desk.

"General Sir Michael Gordon, sir."

"Thank you, Macaulay. That will be all."

The General stood impassively and completely expressionless with his cap under his arm until the civil servant had made his exit and closed the door. After a few moments, they shook hands, then Admiral Forsyth returned to his seat and opened the packet of *Senior Service*. He placed a cigarette in his mouth and lit it using a gold plated cigarette lighter which usually served as a paperweight. He inhaled deeply and enjoyed the sensation.

"Mike, good to see you again. How are things in the field?" he asked, exhaling slowly.

They smiled at each other as the old friends they were supposed to be.

"Excellent, Jack! Good to see you again too. May I?" asked the general, pointing to the sofa.

"Be my guest, Mike. Whisky? Smoke?"

"Sun well over the yard arm by now Jack, as you sailors say."

The General took a seat on the red leather sofa in front of the Admiral's desk.

"I may just take that whisky now if you don't mind."

"Irish?"

"My favourite, Jack."

Admiral Forsyth unlocked the rosewood cabinet behind his desk and poured two glasses of Jameson, no ice. He handed one to his colleague and sat down beside him on the sofa.

"Cheers, old friend."

"Cheers, Jack."

The Admiral glanced back towards his desk where the papers lay. The General did the same.

"Jack, how's the family? I hear young Richard is off to Dartmouth…"

At that moment, there was another knock on the huge oak door.

"Yes."

"May I come in, sir?"

"Yes, Macaulay, come on in," replied Jack, feigning weariness.

"Sir. There's another gentleman to see you. Should I send him in?"

"Who is it now?" asked Jack, trying his best to sound impatient.

"Air Vice Marshall Sir Richard Jennings, sir."

"Can't he take no for an answer? I mean I've already told him *no* several times. What does he want now?"

"He says it's important, sir."

"Very well. Send him in, but remember. No more interruptions. Is that clear?"

"Yes, sir."

Admiral Forsyth stood up and moved towards the door.

"Dick! How are you old boy? Good to see you again. Whisky?"

"Good of you to ask," he said, as Admiral Forsyth poured another whisky.

With that, he returned to his desk and lit another *Senior Service*. When he spoke, he was firm yet softly spoken.

"Gentlemen, it's a sorry state of affairs that has led us to this day, but I'm sure you will agree, that we're faced with little choice. The Prime Minister is hell bent on selling Great Britain, or what's left of it anyway, down the river and handing over our sovereignty to those bastards in Brussels. That is a state of affairs that cannot and will not be tolerated."

It wasn't as if he even needed to speak the words, but he felt it was appropriate to summarise to his colleagues, particularly in light of what they were now about to embark upon. He also made it clear that his office had been swept for listening devices, even if he himself didn't quite believe that it was clear.

"Do either of you have any questions before I issue you with the orders?"

"That depends on the orders, Jack," said General Gordon sarcastically.

"Quite so, Mike, so let's get to it."

Admiral Forsyth handed each of the officers his respective envelope, sat back in his chair, whisky in one hand and cigarette in the other and turned to watch the massed protests gaining pace. At a short distance from Whitehall, the mob was a little too close for comfort for his liking, and it wasn't a scene he was particularly proud of. The sight of fellow Britons rampaging through the streets like savages was the kind of thing one saw in South American banana republics, he thought to himself. He was damned if he was going to tolerate that kind of behaviour on the streets of London, Cheltenham or any other town in England, *his England*, for that matter.

"Well gentlemen?" he said, turning around.

"Interesting set of orders, Jack. I don't expect anyone has seen anything like this since Wilson's time," said General Gordon with a wry smile.

"Bob?"

"Can do, Jack."

"Thank you gentlemen. Now, give back those orders for me to dispose of, please."

The two men handed back their envelopes which Jack tossed into the roaring fireplace along with his own unopened orders and returned to his desk.

"Now, as you will have gathered, timing is of the essence, so if you could both begin putting the pieces in place, I'd be most grateful," said Admiral Forsyth. "This will give the PM and his colleagues something to look at on their TV screens at the very least. Should wake the buggers up a bit, I would think."

CHAPTER 14

Robert didn't feel the need to go to the penthouse flat to watch union thug Melia's spiritual conversion, because he knew that Pimpi would report back to him enthusiastically. It wasn't that he was particularly squeamish; he just felt that he didn't need to see how Jack's people operated. It was the result he was interested in, and nothing more. Besides, he had a favour to ask an old friend.

Pimpi, on the other hand, had a very different view. He'd found the rental, personally chosen the hookers and booze and saw no reason why he shouldn't sample some of the fun. So when he stepped out of the lift directly into the penthouse hallway and from the moment he heard the beat of the Ibiza Mix, he knew Melia must be enjoying himself.

As he turned the corner into the living room, which was glazed on all three sides with lofty views of the city and the muddy river beyond, he saw the union strongman lying stark naked on the huge cream coloured leather sofa and wearing nothing but a pair of black and orange tiger print socks. The white marble floor was littered with half empty bottles of vodka and whisky, exotic looking sex toys and discarded clothing. Three prostitutes, which Pimpi had acquired from the Palermo woods and in various stages of undress, were entertaining the union man to his apparent and very noisy satisfaction.

Pimpi then positioned himself just out of sight behind a circular concrete column, zoomed in with his camera and snapped a few intimate shots of the union strongman with his new friends very energetically performing numerous sex acts on him. Melia was so drunk that he didn't even notice Pimpi's hand sticking out from behind the column, or the music stopping or even the three hookers running to another room, as the two specialists entered and stood over him, guns drawn and pointing at his groin.

Pimpi meanwhile, retired to the adjacent kitchen with the bottle of vodka he'd snatched from his new friends and followed the ensuing action through a narrow picture window. He could watch as the fat man begged for his life, humiliated and defeated. Pimpi enjoyed watching the naked body of Melia being suspended by his ankles from the fifteenth floor window and when it was clear that he was about to start talking, he also enjoyed filming the entire confession and was delighted to see that the specialists hadn't left a mark on his body, save a look of complete and utter terror. It had been a most entertaining afternoon which left him wanting more.

"Jack, I need a favour."

He had called Jack again from a payphone at the railway station, as people rushed past him to catch their trains. He told Jack only what he needed to know about Margarita, the murder of her husband and his chat with Clara.

"It's Guy Farlowe-Pennington, ex Royal Marine. He worked here many years ago at the embassy. Think you can track him down?" asked Robert.

"We should be able to find him for you," said Jack. "Although he'll be no spring chicken you know. Hell, he must be at least sixty-odd by now. Anyway, give me forty eight hours and I'll see what I can do."

"On your account though, Jack. My meagre funds would never stretch to this kind of expense."

"All taken care of, old chap."

CHAPTER 15

Even before President Cristal's re-election, she had been facing a mounting list of accusations related to conspiracy to plunder the state, giving safe harbour to indicted military criminals and embezzling public funds through dummy offshore corporations. Her wealth was estimated to be over 700 million US dollars and many questioned how the former cabaret dancer had managed to accumulate such riches during her nearly two terms of leading the nation. Her acolytes, however, were blinded by faith, accepted their state handouts as a right not to be questioned and pledged their allegiance to her with colourful displays of state sponsored loyalty, every weekend in the Plaza de Mayo.

However, her alleged complicity in the murder of her own brother Charley, an investigative journalist, whose suspicious death under the wheels of a taxi in a busy, rush hour Buenos Aires street, had never been fully explained. The carefully leaked rumours were now beginning to sway even her most ardent supporters, but it had taken years for any real progress to be made. For twelve months, following Charley Cristal's death halfway through her first term in office, the president had dressed in expensive black mourning outfits, rumoured to have been acquired, at vast public expense from top fashion designers on 5th Avenue, New York. This was a rumour she had never denied, despite questions raised by the press regarding her judgement, in the face of an annual inflation rate of over 75%.

Since Robert needed to be seen as taking a back seat - he was still only mayor of a local authority - Pimpi, as president of the lower chamber, was ideally placed to ratchet up the heat. As an active member of an opposition task force quietly brought together by Robert, he was dedicated to bringing President Cristal to justice by having her removed from office through impeachment. Through a tediously long process, Pimpi was encouraging his entire block of *We Can Change* party members from behind the scenes and ensuring that each and every accusation made it to a handful of federal prosecutors known to be out of the government loop, yet with their own axes to grind against the president so that charges could finally be brought against her. By the end of the third year of her second term, the evidence stacked against the president became so overwhelming, that events began to develop a momentum of their own.

The revelation by the savagely anti-government press, of her alleged complicity in the death of her own brother, was greeted with shock and revulsion throughout an already divided nation. Melia's confession of carrying out the president's orders, together with the video evidence, forced the hands of the lower chamber and her impeachment became not only inevitable, but necessary. She was being branded as a murderer, the people wanted to see justice done and the lower chamber needed to reach a vote of two thirds in order to send her to trial in the senate. Neither Pimpi nor Robert was overly concerned; there was already sufficient evidence at hand, not to mention a great deal of other suspect material on many of the pro government members of the house, so they were sure they would win the vote with the right amount of whipping.

But the president, on hearing of the impeachment proceedings, became hell bent on a policy of crash and burn, using her powers and narrow parliamentary majority, to rush extraordinary bills through parliament, instructing her central bank chief to dump local currency reserves and buying up several million dollars in the local market through her numerous proxies. She could see the writing on the wall despite her claim of lily-white innocence, which practically no one, except her most diehard followers believed. So parliament had to move quickly before the country disintegrated into the kind of mayhem not seen since the early seventies.

When the vote finally came, it was a narrow victory, but a victory nonetheless. Once the impeachment trial was sent to the senate, both Pimpi and Robert felt that the outcome was pretty much inevitable. Two months later, the president was tried by her peers and removed from office in absentia, since she had refused point blank to cooperate with anyone whatsoever and had retreated to one of her many country estates hundreds of kilometres away from the capital. The vice president, who was also caught up in the storm, was nowhere to be found, so the president of the Supreme Court reluctantly took the oath of office as caretaker president. He called for a general election in six months' time, knowing that he probably wouldn't stay the course, or so his doctor had privately informed him.

The country was now in total disarray, with civil servants running around in a confused state and thousands of protesters marching through the streets of the capital, waving banners and banging pots and pans. Everyone wondered where the now ex-president was lurking. She may have been found guilty by the senate, but she faced being tried as a civilian; an ex-president stripped of her executive immunity. Federal prosecutors wasted no time in issuing a torrent of arrest warrants for noncompliance of court orders, so she became the object of a nationwide manhunt. She was finally tracked down forty eight hours later, entering the San Carlos de Bariloche airport in the foothills of the Andes Mountains, one hot, December night.

"Madam President, you are no longer president of the nation," Chief Forza began.

"You are hereby under arrest and will be remanded into custody immediately, pending a trial. Please do not resist and I would ask that your protection team stand down and disarm immediately."
The chief of the federal police force, Pepe *El Rengo* Forza had rehearsed the lines in his sleep since the impeachment proceedings began.

Now he had the arrest warrant in his hands, and he held it up for attention in the VIP departure lounge of the small airport. He had arrived with a team of heavily armed policemen dressed in civilian clothes, as it was suggested that confronting the now ex-president with a posse of paramilitaries at an airport might have appeared a little too much like a coup d'état for a nation that still remembered the not so distant past.

Virginia Cristal, sitting on a black leather sofa near the departure doors of the exclusive lounge, chatted with her personal secretary Roxy Pla, while her security detail hovered nearby covering the entrance and exits. At first sight of Chief Forza and his men, her team of four dark suited operatives assumed a defensive position and remained defiant. They surrounded the ex-president in a close semi-circle as she faced her moment of truth.

"Under whose authority do you presume to utter those words?" she asked, without looking up and inspecting the many gold rings on her hands.

"By the authority vested in me as a federal police officer and public servant, madam."

"I do not recognise your authority and neither do I recognise the decision of that rabble in the senate, so I will not come. My men will take orders only from me and I'll be leaving through that door whether you or any of your kind like it or not," she said, pointing towards the blacked out glass doors of the exit.

"Madam, we will take you by force if necessary, so I ask again, please stand your men down and come with us peacefully," insisted the chief, folding his arms.

The VIP lounge was comfortably furnished and at the wall facing the departure doors there was a bar with two immaculately dressed waiters in tuxedos and bow ties serving cocktails to a handful of guests seated at the sumptuous leather sofas. Everyone, with bemused fascination, turned their attention to the scene being played out before them and, as they sipped their drinks, some began filming the scene on their camcorders, prompting the chief to order the immediate confiscation of all such equipment in the vicinity.

"Listen to me, you unctuous little cripple. I am the president of the nation. I was elected by the people and I intend to serve my term through as stated in the constitution," she repeated angrily.

Chief Forza turned to his men and nodded. They immediately pointed their numerous weapons at the four bodyguards.

"Madam, will you come over here with me, please," said the chief, beckoning her to another large sofa to the left of the exit. "I need to explain some matters of importance to you."

The chief, whose pronounced limp was noticeable to all as he accompanied the ex-president, sat down opposite her and leaned forward, clasping his hands together. He looked intently at her thickly made up face, the puffy cheeks barely disguising the signs of a heavy drinker, and her cold, dark eyes framed by the shoulder length bottled blond hair and, in that moment, he loathed her more than ever.

"Men, please put your guns away. Nothing's going to happen to me," she commanded with a regal wave of her bejewelled hand.

"Madam, you will not be going anywhere tonight or any other night for quite some time. Your aircraft is surrounded, the pilots have been removed and taken into custody. Your numerous houses in the country are also under armed guard and in fact are being searched as we speak, by orders of a federal judge. The rest of your family is in custody as is half your cabinet, and the vice president appears to have fled. So you see, we are in a slightly difficult situation that is going to end only one way; your peaceful agreement to accompany me," said the chief calmly.

Virginia Cristal looked across at the chief, then turned her face away towards the exit, an expression of coiled up anger spreading across her thickly made up face.

"There is a car waiting outside, which will save you the embarrassment of leaving through the main terminal," continued the chief. "I'm afraid you have no alternative."

The ex-president was not so much shocked as indignant. She truly believed that this day would never come, yet now that it had, she couldn't quite grasp the reality. How dare they presume to usurp her authority! How dare they even think to *not* call her president!

"Officer, it seems you have me at a disadvantage," she finally said after a long pause. "Do I have a choice?"

"Only the one," said the chief, standing up.

With that, she turned to her bodyguards and dismissed them with a perfunctory wave, grabbed her secretary by the arm and followed Chief Forza through the sliding glass doors to the waiting SUV, which was surrounded by a further posse of armed, plain clothes police. Police helicopters hovered overhead, directing their powerful spotlights on the scene, so she looked up at the dazzling searchlights, gripped Roxy's arm more firmly and stopped just a few feet short of the waiting vehicle. In a blind panic, with visions of incarceration behind impenetrable steel bars flashing through her mind, she instantly recalled the many late nights watching TV, as her friends were hauled away to maximum security prisons at Ezeiza and Marcos Paz.

No, she couldn't go, she had to run. Pulling Roxy by the arm, she dragged her running towards the main runway, to where, she knew not. Reacting coolly, Chief Forza went down on one knee, took a low aim with his revolver, pulled the trigger and brought the screaming ex-president down with a single shot to her right ankle, with Roxy falling on top of her.

"Cuff her, take her to the vehicle and patch her up. This didn't happen," ordered the chief.

"And the other woman, sir?" asked his deputy.

"She comes with me."

Chief Forza personally restrained Roxy, who had become hysterical, fearing that she might be shot, so he was careful to be gentle with her and simply held her by the shoulders.

"Miss Pla, please calm down. Nothing is going to happen to you. You'll be coming with me for your own protection. Do you have family we could contact?" asked the chief.

Roxy, sobbing and heaving, shook her head as she wiped away the tears. A pretty, blonde and petite woman of thirty five years, she was dressed in a smart, dark blue trouser suit with a white, open neck shirt, now stained with the blood of her boss.

"You almost killed us, you bastard!" she screamed, pulling away from him.

"We were left with little choice, Miss Pla. We couldn't risk the ex-president being hit by a plane on the runway could we? She's being taken care of now, so you needn't worry."

"Where are you taking me? I need to be with the President. Where is she?"

"Somewhere safe."

Chief Forza then beckoned to his men and escorted Roxy to a black unmarked Ford Mondeo, where he joined her in the back seat as they sped off into the darkness. Roxy sat looking out of the window, dabbing her eyes with a tissue which she turned over and over with her fingers.

CHAPTER 16

As news of the president's removal continued to spread, protesters massed in the fabled Plaza de Mayo, demanding answers, banging pots and waving huge banners demanding justice. For many, it was an excuse to leave work early, to enjoy a day out with the family, and for others, a business opportunity for selling flags and other paraphernalia, not to mention chorizos, popcorn and cold drinks.

But this time the crowd wanted answers, real answers. The hard core element saw their beloved *Queen Virginia* being persecuted for no good reason, other than being the saviour of the nation; for others she was receiving her long overdue just desserts. As a result, the two protesting factions split in opposite sides of the plaza, facing off against each other over a human barrier of riot police.

Behind the scenes, the president of the supreme court, acting as caretaker head of state was not expected to survive. This indeed proved to be the case when he was found by his wife slumped in a bath a week after he was sworn in, following an apparent heart attack. Amidst a veil of secrecy, his death kicked off a frantic search for a successor. The next candidates in line for succession either didn't want the job, were already implicated in other scandals, were military men or were so laughably inept that they would have caused further riots in the streets. So, after much head scratching by congress, which had already rejected all living former presidents since many of them were all in prison, it was decided that yet another interim president should be sworn in, on the condition that a general election would still be held in six months' time.

Buried deep in the line of succession at number twenty three, they found what could only be described as a grey man; one Craig *El Escosés* Campbell, currently serving as ambassador to the newly independent nation of Scotland. An official was hurriedly dispatched to Edinburgh with a small team of advisors, so he could be briefed and bundled back to Buenos Aires before anyone noticed that the country was in fact without a president.

Robert was taken by surprise at the unexpected news. He and Craig had played rugby against each other at school and, although they were never particularly close, they had bumped into each other at school reunions and other events over the years, remaining in contact by text message and the occasional email. He would need immediate access to the new interim president and although the Scot formed no part of Robert's plan, he viewed the development as a lucky break.

"Pimpi, we're on the crest of a wave my friend and our time has come," announced Robert, pouring himself an ice cold beer.

They were sitting at the kitchen table in Margarita's new apartment in Belgrano, as she hovered around, preparing dinner and sipping a glass of Cabernet.

"It did all come together rather nicely," said Pimpi, glancing furtively at Margarita's cleavage as she laid plates on the table.

She glanced icily at Pimpi, then sat down next to Robert.

"We couldn't have done it without you, my friend, and I won't even ask how you managed to whip those deputies into shape," he said, whilst squeezing Margarita's hand.

"Of course, you know Craig Campbell has to run in the elections now, don't you?" he continued. "And I'll run against him. He's the perfect stalking horse. But then we still have De la Mano to deal with. I heard he put his name forward last night and that's going to be a tough fight, especially if it goes to a second round."

"I'd better get the machine rolling for you then, hadn't I?" said Pimpi, rubbing his hands together.

Margarita rolled her eyes, returned to the cooker and began hammering the veal milanesas as noisily as she could.

"It's going to be a tough one. You know how dirty these union men play the game, so rally the troops," said Robert looking over at Margarita and frowning.

During dinner, Margarita sat opposite Robert and couldn't bring herself to as much as glance at Pimpi, who was in a jubilant mood over the impeachment.

Robert however became very quiet. Although relieved by the outcome of the impeachment, he felt an overwhelming sensation of anticipation, knowing that his train was about to finally reach the station. A ride that, deep down, he knew would stop only briefly and continue to a point that, in his mind was a daunting prospect. Seeing that he was pensive, Margarita reached across the table and squeezed his hand as Pimpi looked away.

Robert was exhausted. It had been a very tough few weeks, so when dinner was over and Pimpi had finally taken his leave, he made his excuses to Margarita as she cleared away the dishes, squeezing her shoulder gently on his way to the bedroom. He threw off his clothes, fell on the bed, switched off the bedside light and as the darkness embraced him, he immediately fell into a deep sleep.

Margarita finished her wine and whilst undressing in the bathroom, she could see her lover on the bed through the open bedroom door, lying on his back with his arms outstretched, filling her with love and a need to hold him. She watched herself in the mirror as she let the blue lace bra drop to the floor and then quietly lay face down on the bed next to him, running her hand down his smooth, muscular chest.

He couldn't be sure when the dream started, so when he felt the tingling locks of hair against his thighs, he wanted the ecstasy to be never ending. Feeling a warm softness that almost took his breath away, he exploded in wave after wave of powerful ripples he hoped would never end.

The following morning, sitting at the kitchen table with a mug of coffee, he felt as if he could take on the entire world. He reached for the TV remote as Margarita appeared in the kitchen doorway, her long, dishevelled hair, glistening wet. She was wearing nothing but his old *Dark Side of the Moon* tee shirt and a sleepy look in her half closed green eyes that filled him with love.

"Sleep well, darling?" she asked, kissing him gently on his neck as she glided past him into the kitchen.

"Like a baby Mags."

"That good?"

"Hmm," he said, holding his coffee mug with both hands whilst staring at the river through the sliding glass doors.

She slowly poured herself a coffee from the glass jug, sat down opposite him, resting her elbows on the table with her fingers joined together under her chin, and looked over at him thoughtfully.

"I'm not sure how to say this, darling" she started. "Pérez. Just watch him, okay."

He sat back and stretched his arms behind his head, yawning.

"I know you don't like him, Mags, but…"

"No, I don't like him and I don't like the way he looks at me either. He makes my skin crawl, so please don't bring him here again."

Robert smiled at her and held her hands in his.

"To be honest, I don't really know much about him outside work. What's the problem?"

"I don't know really, it's just a feeling. Anyway, promise me you won't bring him back here again, will you? I just don't want him here. Ever."

"Fine. I don't socialise with him much, any more. Anyway, it's been tough for you and you don't need any more crap to deal with," he said, leaning across the table and pushing the damp hair away from her face.

Her husband's murder had brought them even closer together. Robert had helped her find a new flat in Belgrano since she had been unable to step foot in the old flat ever again. She wanted a new life, a new beginning and looked forward to her new home being completed. The time they spent living together was the happiest of their lives, yet they always knew that their relationship thrived on a certain distance, an anticipation of knowing that they would be in each other's arms sooner or later.

Robert lived in a modest suburban house in Punta Chica in the northern Buenos Aires suburbs, and whenever he needed an escape from the madness of political life, not to mention his constant attention to Jack's plan, he was never more than a few hours' drive from the family ranch in Sancti Spiritu. Its majestic avenues of Eucalyptus trees and the peace he needed once he got back into the saddle to roam the endless plains, were the escape he valued as much as his devotion to Margarita. They were the two foundations on which he could rely entirely, unlike the cut and thrust of politics. He had the charisma, the good looks and the confidence. He knew that. He could also deliver a speech unprepared and without hesitation. Yet as he roamed across the ranch with Horacio, his private thoughts always turned to the price he felt he was paying to Jack Forsyth for a plan he could tell no one about.

In this at least, his spirits were lifted by the arrival of his old friend Guy. Their reunion after so many years was a much needed shot in the arm, particularly as he hadn't given a great deal of thought to O'Campo's bar since the dark days of the military dictatorship. He had assisted in Guy's move to the country and found a flat for him through a discrete contact. A few days later, he received a text message from his old friend which simply read '*The Shamrock, 1800 hours tomorrow*' in typically Guy fashion, oddly followed by GPS coordinates. Although their old haunt had changed its name several times in the intervening years, the location was the same and when Robert arrived, he found his old friend waiting at the bar munching from a bowl of cashew nuts with a couple of pints of Guinness lined up beside him. Robert hadn't met him at the airport, in fact, on Guy's insistence, he hadn't seen him at all since he had arrived, so when they shook hands, he was delighted to find that his friend, although much older, hadn't really changed a great deal.

"Robbie, old friend," he said shaking his hand firmly and placing his other hand on Robert's shoulder. "You know, I'd never have thought..."

"Me neither, but here we are," said Robert, smiling warmly.

As he looked up at Guy towering above him, he saw that he still retained the old school, aristocratic air he always remembered. His dress sense had not improved over the years, with his grey, badly fitting, double breasted suit appearing as if he had picked it up in a post-war charity shop. He saw that the sleeves were too short, the trousers didn't quite reach the tops of his shoes and the kipper tie could have come straight from a 70s sitcom.

He could tell, however, that he kept himself fit; that much was obvious from the muscles bulging through the arms of his jacket. He didn't need to ask what kind of weapons he was packing in his suit pockets, either. Knowing Guy, he'd probably feel naked leaving home without a small sidearm, at the very least.

CHAPTER 17

Craig Campbell, the new interim president, was sworn in at a low key ceremony in the supreme court, quietly driven to the Casa Rosada in a nondescript family saloon car and then bundled in through a side entrance. On his arrival, a team of officious civil servants directed him to the executive office, where he was placed at a presidential looking desk, behind which stood the sky blue and white national flag, hanging forlornly from a wooden pole. He was then asked to read from a prepared statement to the nation.

Craig, a small, unassuming man, his grey hair parted immaculately at the side, wore round, steel rimmed spectacles, giving him the air of a school teacher. He'd never aspired to the job, even in his wildest dreams and his uncomfortable, fidgety demeanour was clear for all to see, as he read the speech he held in his hands without once looking at the camera.

"My fellow Argentines. Please be assured that the, erm… country is safe in my hands… until the general elections in six months' time…"

He paused, adjusted his glasses and rubbed his forehead nervously as the civil servants winced and gesticulated at him from behind the camera.

"…um, when every citizen will have the chance to elect a new president. This is a time for reflection and healing, and I hope I can rely on your support during this uh… difficult time," he continued in a monotone voice, at which point, and by sliding a finger across his throat, the presidential general secretary indicted that his speech was now over.

"Thank you and um, good evening," he finished with characteristic feebleness.

Inwardly cringing with pity, Robert watched the speech at home and nodded. Craig would run for president in June, he would make sure of that, and immediately sent him a text message to arrange a meeting. Craig's reply that he had no idea what to do came as no surprise to Robert, so he called him.

"Send a car around for me, it's quite easy really. You've got hundreds to choose from. How about tonight at seven on the island?"

"Is that where I'm going tonight? Robert, this has all happened too quickly. I never wanted this, you know. It's all too much for me," he said feebly.

Located on an island created from reclaimed land two kilometres out from the mainland, the presidential palace was accessed by a road tunnel, with river and air exclusion zones being strictly enforced.

When Robert arrived at the island residence, the official car came to a stop outside the imposing and gleaming white painted front doors of the mansion, which commanded an impressive view across the river to the city of Buenos Aires beyond.

When the driver opened the car door, he stepped out of the vehicle and took a slow look around whilst buttoning up his suit jacket, reminding himself that in three months' time all of it would be his. As he was admiring the city skyscrapers just visible through the heat haze, he heard the doors open behind him. Looking around, he saw President Craig Campbell peering through the gap, mumbling in a low, timid voice, asking him to come in.

"Craig, good to see you again," said Robert, thrusting his hand out. "Would you mind if we walked awhile? It's such a beautiful evening."

Pulling Craig towards him as he shook his hand and glancing over his shoulder towards the bodyguards, he whispered, "and get rid of those monkeys."

He released Craig's limp and clammy hand and led the way down a long, winding series of wooden steps leading to a small beach area with golden sand and huge rocks placed between the gently swaying palm trees. As they sat at a wooden table, on a deck overlooking the beach, Craig Campbell fidgeted with his jacket nervously, constantly adjusting the oversized glasses perched on his nose.

"Run against me for president."

Robert watched as Craig's eyes widened.

"But I don't want to be president. I never did," replied Craig.

"Look, put your name forward, find a running mate, assemble a small team and just go through the motions."

"And what's in it for me? I rather enjoyed being in Scotland and I'm missing it. Never wanted to come back, actually."

"Listen, I'll be making some big changes and your name will be top of the list. Besides, you won't stand a chance against De la Mano, but at least I have a fighting chance against him."

Craig buried his face in his hands and then looked up with a pained expression.

"Come on, pull yourself together, man! Surely you can hang on for a few more months?" said Robert, leaning across the table and grabbing his arm.

"I know the dirty tricks that bugger plays, and I'm not sure if I can take it," he said, clenching his hands into fists.

"Let me take care of him and if it goes to a second round, I'll take your votes with me," said Robert. "Anyway, look at it this way. After keeping my seat warm, you'll get a presidential pension for life. Imagine that!"

"I feel like a fraud. This is all wrong!"

"Listen Craig, you have to do this. Do it for me, for pity's sake. For everyone! You've seen the mess this country is in, and if you think it's bad now, you've absolutely no idea what it will all look like if I don't win that election. I need your votes," Robert continued. "Besides, there's legislation that ex-President Cristal instigated which is all coming before parliament this month. You have to either veto or work with us to get it all thrown out."

Craig perked up a little, straightened his shoulders and looked directly at his friend. He was well aware of the ex-president's draconian measures to politicise the judiciary and the central bank, not to mention the stripping of broadcasting licenses from media organisations who opposed her, and every other populist reform she had rammed through.

"Yes, I see that now. She rushed those through when she got wind of the impeachment, but do you think we have time? And what makes *you* so special anyway?"

"Let's just say I have a clear plan," replied Robert. "You know Pérez is president of the chamber of deputies and one way or another, he'll whip them into shape and get those bills voted out. Besides, if De la Mano wins, we're back to the seventies and worse, much worse. Look, I can make this country great again, Craig. I have a unique plan."

"Which is?"

Robert looked over towards the city, crossed his legs and folded his arms.

"Just take my word for it Craig. Take time to decide what you want. Ambassador in Edinburgh, Washington, you name it. But I promise you, this country will become practically a new Britain."

"That, I'd like to see, Crawford!" said Craig, finally smiling.

He knew the joke was entirely lost on Craig, so Robert stood up, smiled his very best presidential smile, shook hands whilst gripping Craig's shoulder with the other, and bid his goodbyes. On the journey through the tunnel and back to his house in Punta Chica, he patted himself on the back for what he thought was a job well done.

CHAPTER 18

As the British prime minister stood looking through inch thick windows, with rain spattering and steaming on the lawn floodlights at Chequers, the words of his predecessor echoed through his mind. '*It's always Europe*,' she had said, and '*Meddle with defence at your peril.*'

She was right on both counts, and now he, Seth Morgan, was the one paying the price, he told himself. He'd inherited a cut down version of the Britain he had known all his life; Scotland had gone, Wales was on its way out, Northern Ireland had been given back to the Irish and practically all he had left was his England and a few symbolic little islands dotted around the globe. It wasn't a pretty sight. The only way to cut the Gordian knot had been to call a second referendum and throw in his lot with those damned foreigners in Brussels, which was something which had really stuck in his craw. He felt it was unavoidable if the *Disunited Kingdom* were not to sink any further into total oblivion.

A tall, handsome man, still in possession of a full head of straight, swept back black hair, his most prominent features were his dark blue eyes and long, noble Roman nose. He had been the darling of the Labour party conferences over the years, not so much for what he said, but for his dashing good looks. His engagement to the youngest daughter of the late Earl of Cardiff had been a shattering blow to his many female admirers and he'd lost count of the number of marriage proposals he'd received by email, by text and sometimes even when campaigning in the street. But now, as he contemplated the rain lashing across the windows, he knew he'd been handed a poison chalice that no amount of charm and good looks were going to fix.

Pushing a hand back through his hair and walking across the thick shag pile carpet towards the fireplace in the huge drawing room, he was sure he could hear a vague chop-chopping sound in the distance, much like that of a helicopter. Thinking nothing more of it, he heard a loud knock on the large oak doors.

"Come!" he said, without turning around.

"Prime Minister, I think you should switch on the TV," said a flustered Jenny Bleach, his personal private secretary, peering around a gap in the doors. The prime minister, with a curious expression on his face, grabbed the remote, and the TV came to life.

With his mouth wide open, he watched images of armoured cars and soldiers leaving their barracks somewhere in the south of England as the BBC report split into four segments of the screen, with the studio anchor giving a running commentary of events for each region. The prime minister's eyes widened as he watched the scenes being shown to him, so he turned up the volume.

"The Houses of Parliament appear to be surrounded by what we can only describe as a ring of steel," said the news presenter dramatically.

"We can see tanks and all manner of military vehicles with hundreds of soldiers standing in formation with their weapons at the ready. As far as we can tell, some kind of military exercise is taking place across the country, but for the moment details are very sketchy. If that is the case, one has to wonder why the prime minister isn't responding. So far there has been no announcement from any military spokesman or indeed the government and we can only report what we see, unless a total news blackout gets imposed..."

"Jenny, get the chief of the defence staff on the line right away," ordered the prime minister through the speakerphone without taking his eyes from the television. Sitting down wearily in front of the screen, shirtsleeves rolled up, he flicked among the channels, all of which were covering the unfolding events, with reporters struggling to come up with any answers. Some were even interviewing each other, simply to speculate on what may have happened.

"We're crossing now to one of our defence correspondents in Aldershot Military Town. What can you tell us, John?'

"It's a confusing picture at the moment, Steve, but the streets are calm and we don't see anyone panicking yet. I'm standing outside The Duke of York and the rain seems to have eased off a little so I'll see if I can catch a few words with a local or two. Yes, a few people are leaving the pub now…Madam? Can you tell us what you've seen happening in Aldershot tonight please?" said the reporter thrusting the microphone towards the woman who was huddling under an umbrella with her husband.

"Well, it was a bit strange really. Bill and I like to go to the pub after the nine o'clock news, and on the way down here we saw some soldiers marching down the road with these big guns. Anyway, I turned to Bill and I said 'They don't usually take guns with them Bill,' and he said, 'Aah, they're probably just training Love. Let's go, it's raining,' so we carried on to the pub before we got soaked."

"Thank you madam. Steve, I'll be in the Duke of York as it's raining very hard again now, so back to the studio."

"Thanks John. So, a recap on the situation so far….uh, just a moment, we're getting reports of yet more military activity at the ports of Southampton, Portsmouth, Bristol and Felixstowe. Over to our southern affairs correspondent in Southampton. Mike, what's the situation down there?"

"Steve, what I can tell you is that the port of Southampton has now been closed. This is as far as we can get to the main access road which is cordoned off by armoured personnel carriers. I can also see military checkpoints, which appear to have been set up on many of the major road junctions. Back to you in the studio, Steve."

"Thank you Mike," said the presenter, turning to his left. "In the studio we have the BBC's chief defence correspondent, Hugh Porter. What's your view of tonight's events Hugh? Is this a military coup? What on earth's going on?"

"It's too early to say at the moment, Steve," pronounced the lugubrious defence correspondent. "What we do know is that all of the UK's ports and airports have been locked down by the military and all movement in and out of the country has been restricted, if not completely blocked. We're also hearing reports of large military deployments in all major cities across the country, from platoon size or even maybe entire companies of soldiers. Those are significant deployments and far too large for a mere exercise. No, this is something much bigger, much more sinister, the like of which hasn't been seen on the streets of Britain since, well, the days of Oliver Cromwell, if I were to hazard a guess."

"Hugh, can you tell us why there's been no word from the authorities yet?"

"One has to ask, who *are* the authorities, Steve? With no word from the prime minister or any military spokesman, one has to wonder who's in charge. It's been over an hour now since the first tanks were seen here in London surrounding the Houses of Parliament. In all my years of reporting, I've never seen anything like this, Steve…"

"I'll have to stop you there, Hugh," said the presenter, pointing at some notes in front of him. "We're getting reports of MPs calling for a recall of parliament. Let's go now to our chief political correspondent Daryl Bloom outside the Palace of Westminster. Daryl, what can you tell us?"

"There's a steady stream of MPs arriving at the House now, Steve and they're having to pass through military checkpoints on Westminster Bridge, Parliament Square and all the other access roads. Let me see if I can speak to one of them. Yes, here we are, that looks like Mervyn Jones, MP for Watford South. Mr Jones, what's going on here please? Can you tell us what you know?" said the reporter, jostling with his colleagues.

"It's a disgrace, that's what it is. This country will not be held to ransom at the barrel of a gun. There are jack boots striding down Parliament Square, I tell you! In all my years as a member of Parliament, I've never seen anything like it. It's outrageous! The Prime Minister should resign immediately!"

As the MP spoke, tracked vehicles could be seen grinding their way down the roads behind him, some of which were Challenger tanks and armoured personnel carriers. Hundreds of soldiers had taken up positions on all the corners of the Palace of Westminster, surrounded by sandbags and manning heavy machine guns.

"Thank you Mr Jones for that insight. Do you think the Speaker will announce a recall of Parliament?"

"If he doesn't, he should resign as well. This isn't a banana republic you know, young man!" said an angry Mervyn Jones, striding off, umbrella in hand towards the members' entrance.

"Steve, a very angry member of Parliament and that's just one," said Daryl, turning back to the camera. "As you can see, the soldiers have cordoned off most of the area, but there are still hundreds of people around. I'm going to see if we can speak to some of them. Sir, how long have you been here?" asked the reporter, spotting a cheerful young man waving a Union flag in the huge crowd.

"I was in the pub with the lads and saw it on the news, so we all piled down here. I think it's great. Never seen anything like it. It's like a film. Are they making a film?"

"Yes sir, it is a bit like that, but I don't think they're making a film. It looks pretty real to me," said the reporter who then pushed his microphone towards an older man wearing bifocal glasses and a flat cap, "Sir, do you have any idea what's going on?"

"I'd be surprised if those MPs didn't see this coming. They're bloody useless, the lot of them. Sailing us down the river and practically giving the country away to those twats in Belgium!"

"So there we have it, Steve. Some interesting points of view from Parliament Square, now back to you in the studio."

"Thank you, Daryl," said the presenter. "Now, let's see what the weather has in store for the coming days. Over to you Hannah."

Meanwhile, Jenny Bleach returned to the drawing room at Chequers looking flustered. "Sir, you have some visitors," she said timidly.

"Did you get hold of General Davies?" asked the prime minister without looking around, still glued to the television.

"Erm, no sir. But some other gentlemen are here to see you," replied Jenny nervously.

"Where?" asked the prime minister, turning around quickly, his eyes widening.

"General Sir Michael Gordon has just arrived with the First Sea Lord and the Chief of the Air Staff sir."

"I see. You'd better ask them to come in then, hadn't you?"

Jumping to his feet, the prime minister grabbed his suit jacket from the edge of the sofa, fought with it for a few moments and then angrily tossed it away into a corner next to the book case. He then managed to compose himself a little and stood with his back to the fireplace, trying to figure out what on earth was going on and what the hell the top brass intended to say to him. He wanted to think that they were conducting exercises for the NATO conference the following month, but discarded that idea. What he was seeing was something much bigger.

Presently, the doors opened again, a uniformed sub lieutenant stood to attention and announced, "the Chief of the General Staff, General Sir Michael Gordon, the First Sea Lord, Admiral Sir Jack Forsyth and Chief of the Air Staff, Air Chief Marshall Sir Richard Jennings, sir!"

The three officers walked into the drawing room in single file, their uniform caps under their arms and the prime minister approached them.

"Mike, what the hell is going on out there?" he asked, struggling to find the words. "And why wasn't I informed?"

"We should sit down, Prime Minister," said General Gordon quietly.

"No, we will not sit down, General. What the hell's going on? It looks like a war's going on out there and lucky for you, no one's been killed yet!"

"And no one will be killed Prime Minister," replied the general, calmly. "This is a warning."

"A warning, a fucking warning? This is treason, General, nothing less," shouted the prime minister defiantly.

"You are in no position to speak of treason, Prime Minister..."

"I am the Prime..."

"Let me finish, sir," said the general, holding up his hand. "You're line on Europe is misguided and foolhardy. It's going to stop and it's going to stop now."

"And you've completely decimated the armed forces," said Admiral Forsyth, folding his arms.

"Not to mention our borders. We're practically a floating asylum nowadays," chimed in the Air Chief Marshall, glancing at his colleagues.

"This is nothing less than a coup, gentlemen. Do you honestly think the people will stand for this? Britain under military rule? You've got to be kidding me. The security agencies will see to you," said the prime minister, almost laughing.

"Our security agencies came on board a long while ago Prime Minister. We are the establishment, remember?" said the air chief quietly.

The prime minister stood completely still, not knowing what to do with his hands and he felt beads of sweat beginning to trickle down his back.

"Prime Minister, is this how you want your premiership to end? Because believe me, we can and will make it end. You'll go down in history as the man who destroyed this country when you could have saved it," said General Gordon as he turned to Jack Forsyth.

"Admiral?"

"Seth, let's sit, shall we?" beckoned the admiral with a wave of his hand.

Once they were seated, he continued, smiling. "Listen, Seth, we come bearing good news. We only have to give the word and our men will return to their barracks in an instant, but you need to listen to us. Am I making myself clear?"

"Go on," said the prime minister crossing his legs and folding his arms angrily.

The admiral outlined the defence chiefs' position on Europe, adding that the European divorce was going to happen with or without him. He also made it clear that the proposed cuts in defence spending would have to be rescinded and that Britain would no longer be a dumping ground for refugees, asylum seekers and free loaders.

"Admiral, that's my entire policy right there and you expect me to do a massive U-turn on Europe, not to mention everything else I promised in my manifesto?"

"You're a politician, Prime Minister. It comes with the territory," said the Air Chief Marshall, raising an eyebrow.

"Let me put it to you this way, Seth. Would you not prefer to be remembered as the man who put the *great* back into Britain?" asked the admiral.

The prime minister uncrossed his legs and sat more upright, frowning slightly. Now he did look curious. The three men opposite waited for a response.

"To be honest, gentlemen, you don't leave me much to play with."

"You'll have a great deal less to play with if you carry on with these foolhardy antics, but a great deal more if you choose another path," said the general.

"So you're blackmailing me now?"

General Gordon looked at his watch in a prearranged manner and the three men rose as if to leave, nodding to each other.

"Gentlemen please, let's not be hasty," said the prime minister standing up, raising his hands and attempting to smile. "Please, sit."

The three men glanced at each other and sat down while the prime minister paced to and fro in front of the fireplace, running his fingers through his hair and loosening his tie. The television was still showing scenes of military activity around the country and some reports were showing soldiers shaking hands with the public. A few women could also be seen running over to kiss and hug soldiers and giving them flowers. The prime minister was appalled, yet felt he was being pushed into a corner with no escape.

Sitting down again, the prime minister finally managed to speak.

"This other path that you speak of, Admiral; this good news you mentioned. This putting the great back into what's left of Britain?" he asked tersely. "Well?"

Admiral Forsyth looked over at General Gordon who continued.

"Prime Minister, we're military men. We see the world very much in black and white…"

The general put his hand up as the prime minister tried to interrupt.

"We are not swayed by emotional claptrap, yet we do have a very real sense of duty to King and country. It's an old fashioned notion, we know that, but it's served this country well for hundreds of years. You only need to look at what's happening now. This country is on the brink of falling into an abyss with zero hope of escape and we'd like you to help us ensure that doesn't happen."

The three men sat impassively, studying the prime minister. They knew how politicians operated, but they were also experts in watching people react under pressure. The silence wasn't uncomfortable for them: it was all part of the process of who would snap first. They didn't expect to lose, but this particular prime minister was no pushover.

"And if I don't agree with your suggestions?"

"Then you would be removed from office and the government replaced with a military junta. Parliament would be abolished and the country would be placed under martial law. Here, let me show you what the immediate effects for *you* would be," said the general rising and moving to the window. "Come, Prime Minister, take a look."

"You see over there at the end of the lawn? There's a Puma helicopter waiting," said the general calmly opening the window a few inches. "We give the word and you will be detained, taken to the helicopter and removed to a destination of our choosing."

As the rain spattered against his face through the open window, the hard reality of what was happening hit the prime minister in the pit of his stomach like a lead weight.

"Close the window," he said, returning to the sofa and sitting down with his arms folded. "I'm listening."

"Abandon your plans for a second referendum on Europe and invoke article 50 of the Lisbon agreement immediately. Roll back the defence cuts that both you and your predecessor implemented. Relocate our nuclear submarine base from Faslane to Portsmouth and put a freeze on all immigration into the country. There's a great deal more, but those are the spearhead points for now," said General Gordon, crossing his legs.

The prime minister was having difficulty sitting still. He felt panicked, so got up again and began to poke the log fire with a heavy cast iron poker that he momentarily considered using as a weapon on the three traitors to democracy. But the fact was, he couldn't think of a way out, so he gazed at the glowing embers of the flaming logs whilst racking his brains for relief, which he couldn't find. To buy some time, he picked up the phone and asked Jenny to bring coffee. He'd already glanced at the drinks cabinet and if ever there was a time for a stiff whisky, this was it, but he'd discounted the idea as being a show of weakness.

"And the quid pro quo, general?" asked the prime minister, still poking the fire, and provoking sideways glances among the three servicemen.

"Jack, over to you," said General Gordon quietly.

Admiral Forsyth quietly cleared his throat.

"Prime Minister, as we speak, a new president is sitting at his desk in Buenos Aires. You've no doubt been briefed on his election victory, I dare say?" said the admiral.

"I have indeed," replied the prime minister, frowning.

"You may also know that Britain has a long and chequered history with Argentina which goes back nearly two hundred years. She was a major trading partner for decades and many considered her to be a quasi British colony, such was the close cooperation of our communities. In fact, Argentina was the colony we lost by a hair's breadth. Have you ever heard of the *River Plate Invasions* prime minister?"

"I can't say that I have, Admiral," replied the prime minister smiling quizzically and wondering where the conversation was going.

Admiral Forsyth then gave the prime minister a short history lesson covering the two failed British invasions of Buenos Aires, culminating with a very brief biography of General Craufurd, and other protagonists of the time.

"I'm not sure I understand what you're driving at, gentlemen. We already have a healthy trade agreement with Argentina and matters have improved considerably since the conflicts over Martín García, not to mention the Falklands."

"Prime Minister, our interests in Argentina are much improved now that President Crawford is at the helm," said General Gordon smiling.

"I agree, General. He's certainly progressive and our ambassador in Buenos Aires speaks very highly of him, but I still don't understand the point you're trying to make."

"He's our man, Prime Minister," said Admiral Forsyth.

"Our man? What do you mean, *our man*?"

Admiral Forsyth then went on to describe how Robert had been brought up and educated, to bring him to the point he was at now. Naturally he didn't feel the need to muddy the waters with extraneous information such as Robert's training and other such details. That would remain on a need to know basis for the time being and so he simply trailed off and left the conversation hanging in the air for the prime minister to hook onto, if he were so inclined.

"What, he's a spy, a mole, something like that?" asked the prime minister, clearly flailing about in a sea of uncertainty.

Admiral Forsyth glanced over at General Gordon, looking for a hint as to where he should take the conversation next. He received simply an upward movement of the general's head and a deadly serious expression.

"Prime Minister, he's one of us. Almost as British as you or I," said the Admiral.

The prime minister leaned forward, mouth agape, ripped off his tie and tossed it to the other side of the sofa.

"So, let me get this straight, gentlemen. You've installed a puppet president in Argentina, staged a coup d'état in Britain and now you want me to go along with your crazy plan? Well, I won't have it," he said getting to his feet, his face flushed with anger.

"Sit down, man," said the Air Vice Marshall. "You're making this much more difficult for yourself than you need to. Robert Crawford was not placed anywhere by us at all. He is a fervent Anglophile who believes that Argentina could and should have been part of what we have always considered to be the British club. He will however prove to be your greatest ally and you will view him as such. I hope that's a bit clearer?"

"But..." started the prime minister, but the air force chief interrupted.

"Prime Minister, we know all about the Mayka investments. We didn't want to bring that up, but I'm afraid you've forced our hand. So what's it going to be?"

Seth Morgan felt a cold shiver run down his spine at the mention of Mayka. He hadn't thought about it since he was defence secretary seven years previously, so he sat down again, slumping against the back of the sofa.

"You can't prove a thing," he whispered.

"I'm afraid we can," said the Air Vice Marshall as he put his hand in his jacket and withdrew a white envelope, which he tossed onto the glass table between them.

The documents, although photocopies, were unmistakable and showed clear evidence of insider trading through his trust fund, which was managed by the now defunct Mayka Investments. The envelope also contained photographs of a secret meeting at The Dorchester Hotel between him and the strikingly beautiful, but now imprisoned head of Mayka Investments. The prime minister quietly placed the photographs face down back on the table and looked up again, his face full of anguish.

"You wouldn't!"

"We would," said the air force chief.

The photographs had found their way into the public domain, but since the then defence secretary's face couldn't be seen clearly, it had been difficult to link him definitively to the pictures, except for one detail. He had an unmistakable birthmark, a large dark-coloured mole on his neck, so the very threat of revelation had caused him to step down as defence secretary and spend more time with his family. It had been a difficult time, yet with the support of his wife and friends, he had made a comeback, eventually becoming leader of the Labour party, from which he'd won the general election eighteen months previously. Since then, he'd tried not to dwell on the Mayka incident, although he often thought of it when he was alone, but for completely different reasons.

"You seem to have me over a barrel gentlemen," said the prime minister, hanging his head and feeling dazed.

"Indeed, Prime Minister," said General Gordon, standing and moving towards the fireplace, with his back to the assembled company.

"Now, you're going to deliver this statement, address the nation and explain to the people that Britain tonight has been facing a grave and coordinated threat from multiple terrorist groups which your security forces have now contained," said the general, taking another envelope from his pocket. "For that reason they are now returning to their bases around the country and you hope the public at large wasn't unduly alarmed. Their safety, and the security of the country are of paramount importance, etcetera, etcetera. We'll take care of the rest. Do you have any questions?" asked the general, turning around.

"Get out! Just get the hell out, will you!" demanded the prime minister, waving his arms furiously.

The three defence chiefs then made their way towards the door. Jack Forsyth stopped, turned stiffly and pointed his finger at the prime minister.

"Oh by the way, Seth. You work for us now."

The prime minister backed away to the window, folded his arms and stared at the floodlit lawn as the rain continued to fall in sheets.

Hearing the three men leave and close the door quietly behind them, he began to shake uncontrollably, holding his mouth with one hand and the other leaning against the inch thick glass of the windows.

"Bastards! Those fucking bastards!" he spat out, looking through the glass.

When he had composed himself, he made his way to the mahogany drinks cabinet between the two massive picture windows, poured himself a large Famous Grouse and downed it in one, then poured himself another. He then walked over to the antique desk in the corner of the huge drawing room, opened the bottom drawer and fumbled about for a packet of cigarettes he'd hidden there six months previously when he'd announced to his wife that he'd given up the habit. Standing by the open window again he inhaled deeply and mumbled, '*Fuck it!*' and in the distance, he thought he could hear the whooshing of helicopter blades disappearing into the rainy night.

"Seth, Love, I'm so sorry I'm late, the Jag broke down on the motorway and what with the rain and all that traffic…Darling, what on earth is the matter?"

It was Gwen, his wife of fifteen years. He hadn't heard her come in and quickly threw the cigarette through the gap in the window.

"Gwen, darling, I didn't hear you. Everything's fine," he said turning around and forcing a smile.

"Oh, I thought something was wrong when I saw you smoking again," she said, pausing. "Are you alright?"

"Yes, of course I am. It's just been a difficult day what with... well, you know, this crisis today. Come here, I really need to hold you."

As Gwen buried her face in his neck and kissed him, he could smell the Yves St. Laurent perfume as he held her close. "I missed you today," he whispered.

"Me too," she said. "Who were those men I saw leaving in those black cars? I'm sure one of them was Jack Forsyth."

"Oh that," he replied with a wave of his hand. "They were just briefing me on the threat level, that's all. You know, those troops everywhere. You must have seem them," murmured the prime minister, trying his best to hold himself together.

He still had Gwen in his arms, looking up at him.

"Yes I know, I wondered what was going on. I've never seen anything like it, actually."

"We have everything under control. It's all over now," he said holding her closer. "Anyway, I'm making a statement to the nation in a moment in the conference room, so at least we can stay here tonight. Would you like that?"

"You know I would. Now, don't be long and I'll have a word with the kitchen staff and see if they can rustle up something nice for us. How does that sound?"

"Perfect! How do I look?"

"Fine. Why do you ask?"

"Oh, nothing. I'll...um, catch up with you in a few minutes."

"This has been a challenging day for the United Kingdom and I'd like to thank you, the British public for your cooperation and understanding. Today's events were purely precautionary and our threat level has now been returned to normal in line with the advice of my security services. I'd like to thank all members of our armed services for their resilience today and I'm sure you will join me in wishing them a safe and speedy return to barracks and ultimately their families. Thank you and goodnight."

CHAPTER 19

"What does that woman want now?" asked the president impatiently.

"Virginia Cristal's lawyers have asked for house arrest," said Pimpi, as he glanced at a thick file he held in his hands.

"Over my dead body. Can you lean on that judge again? What's next?"

President Crawford leaned back in his black leather chair and flicked the ash off his cigarette into the stainless steel ashtray, whilst contemplating the engraving *veni vidi vici* on one of its four sides. He had decided to occupy one of the grander offices at government house, also known as the Casa Rosada, long before the day he was elected, which gave him a very pleasant view over the Rio de la Plata and his island residence. He couldn't quite see the horizon because of the heat haze, but it was enough for him to imagine and keep his focus on the realms beyond.

"I'm sick and tired of her. That's the fourth time this year and if she asks again I'll have her moved to that God awful place down the road. What's it called again?" asked the president, moving away from his desk to study the view outside the window.

"Prison 28, Devoto, sir."

"Yes, that's the one. When's the trial anyway?"

"Next month."

"Just as well this is a jury trial then isn't it? Those dim-witted judges have been frightened of their own shadows since she got her claws into them. Anyway, I think we've finally knocked them into shape, Pimpi."

President Robert Crawford had fought a mercifully short but bloody campaign over three months to win the general election. Union boss Luis de la Mano had sunk to unheard of levels of trench warfare during the campaign, painting Margarita as Robert's whore on demand, and Pimpi as a latter day Rasputin who held his candidate under a magic spell. He even predicted an apocalyptic scenario and a return to military rule should Robert win. Craig Campbell had fared much better than the polls had predicted; when he withdrew from the race after the first ballot, Robert took most of his votes with him into the second round, which he won convincingly by a little over ten points. Now, with nine months into the job, the honeymoon had long since faded over the horizon, such were the challenges facing him. He also owed a debt of gratitude to his campaign manager and running mate, Vice President Pimpi Perez, whom he had also appointed as his personal advisor. Pimpi had lived up to his reputation as *The Rottweiler* and had run a precise and some might say, dirty campaign. But none of that mattered now; his purpose was clear. He was to execute the plan he'd been trained to carry out from the moment his induction began in Sancti Spiritu so many years ago.

"I have an idea that might interest you, sir," said Pimpi, glancing up from his folders.

"Another one of your delightful schemes, no doubt," said the president, his arms behind his back as he continued to scan the horizon beyond the docks through the window. "Go on."

"Well, now that we've rounded up most of the ex-president's gang of thieves, and this is something I've long dreamed about…"

President Crawford raised his hand and stopped Pimpi mid-sentence.

"Listen, I know how much you hate them, especially Cristal. God knows, you never stop going on about her, but we need to set an example."

"Yes, of course Mr President and that's pretty much what I had in mind. A kind of homage if you like…"

Robert interrupted him again, and, arms folded turned to look at his vice president.

"Look, I don't need to know all the details, so just get on with it, will you. I always had some kind of show trial in mind for her anyway, so whatever it is you've got planned along those lines will be fine with me," he said, adjusting the cuffs of his immaculately pressed navy blue suit.

Pimpi rubbed his hands together gleefully, nodded his head in the president's direction and scurried out of the executive office like a big, bounding dog who'd just found a new bone to play with.

Since taking power, President Crawford had moved swiftly to line up the pieces of his chessboard by first appointing ambassadors fluent in English to all those friendly countries that spoke the language and for the USA he had chosen a dual national all American lad born locally but raised in Texas. For the Republic of Scotland he'd sent Craig back to Edinburgh as the Scots seemed to like him. He'd also hired some key people he rather admired, one of whom was Chief Forza, whose arrest of Virginia Cristal had elevated him to legendary status through the ranks of *We Can Change*. He became the president's chief of security, in spite of his limp, which Robert had always found most endearing. He was also an extremely cool operator who could handle a gun like no other, as the ex-president could intimately vouch.

"Roxy how's my trip to the UK coming along?" he said into the speakerphone on his desk.

"All set, sir. You leave on Friday, meet with the Prime Minister on Saturday and lunch with the King on Sunday. You also have other meetings lined up, which I think you've already worked out, if I'm not mistaken."

"Quite so Roxy, quite so."

He was looking forward to another meeting with Admiral Forsyth, whom he hadn't seen since before the impeachment, but in the meantime he had to take care of some shanty towns, known locally as *villas*, which would require the services of numerous heavy earth moving machines, pest control services, demolition teams and a fleet of buses and trains.

"Roxy, get me the minister of planning in here, pronto please."

In spite of his initial misgivings, he was enjoying being president and had chosen his team judiciously. Roxy Pla, former personal secretary to ex-president Cristal, now promoted to cabinet chief, had initially been hired as his personal assistant during the election campaign following Cristal's arrest. She was a bright, cheerful woman who understood the inner workings within the halls of power. She was also a mine of inside information on Virginia Cristal which he could tap into practically at will. She showed no allegiance whatsoever to her former boss and clearly enjoyed being around the president, and all the attention the position garnered.

What he enjoyed most of all, was snapping his fingers and having people jump or come running to him. Naturally, he didn't have long to wait for the minister to appear outside his door, dishevelled and breathless.

"You're Damian Diaz, aren't you? Sit down. Weren't you in home affairs last year?"

"Yes sir, that's correct."

"I've got a job for you that will involve earth moving equipment. Do you think you're up to it?"

Young Damian had heard rumours about the shanty towns, but decided to keep his mouth shut.

"As you know, Diaz, those shanty towns, which are sitting on stolen land, are nothing but a blight. A blot on the landscape, quite frankly and they've got to go. Your job is to remove those people, reclaim government land and flatten the place, starting with the one they call Villa 31, just down the road over there," said the president, pointing vaguely. "You know what I mean Diaz, almost like they'd never even existed. How soon can you get that done?"

"Sir, with all due respect, there are over sixty thousand people living in that one *villa* alone. Where are we going to put them all?"

"That's all been taken care of, Diaz. Since they love to build stuff out of practically nothing, we're sending them down to Santa Cruz where, as you know, there is land aplenty and they can build as many towns as they like. It's all arranged with Rocas at public works, so tie up with her and get it sorted. Pronto!"

"But, Mr President, we'll have a riot on our hands. There are just too many of them."

"Not necessarily, Diaz."

"This could get very nasty, sir."

"I don't think so. We've already offered them generous relocation packages to which they've agreed. More than generous in fact."

"And why wasn't I told about this, Mr President?"

"Well, you know now, young man. That will be all, now run along."

CHAPTER 20

Following his meeting with Prime Minister Morgan earlier in the day, Robert had scheduled a private dinner with Jack Forsyth at The Compass and had instructed his security team that they should respect the closed door nature of the evening and wait in a nearby coffee house. Guy however, was being catered to in the nearby club staff room and within easy reach of the president, should his services be required.

"How lovely to see you again, Robert. How's life at the top?"

Admiral Forsyth, now close to retirement, had welcomed his new president back to their usual haunt, with its oak panelled walls and portraits of past patrons, still retaining that old school tie and establishment aura it had always had. However, on this occasion Robert had insisted on taking lunch in a private dining room on the first floor, where he knew there was a TV with satellite connection.

"Life at the top is a bit like driving a train with no brakes. You know, these people couldn't agree on whether it's night or day," he said, without a hint of sarcasm. "It's usually bedlam, to be honest."

"Yes I know, but we're relying on you to get *our* train on the tracks."

"This will take time, Jack. The crash and burn we inherited from that woman is blowing up badly and that Scot they dragged back from Edinburgh didn't have a damn clue, in spite of my help."

"How soon can you start initiating at least the very basics of the plan then?"

Robert smiled.

"Earth movers and demolition experts are moving into our first project as we speak. Here, let me show you," he said, looking at his watch and then switching the TV to a rolling TVN news report direct from Buenos Aires.

The reporter was in an excited state as the camera focused on a large group of chanting people who had formed a human chain around several dilapidated brick and tin-built slums. Police in riot gear stood at the ready several yards away as a line of buses snaked its way into the distance.

"I hope that's under control. They look a bit angry down there," said Jack, pointing.

"All under control, just watch."

As the camera panned away from the human chain and up into the sky, several helicopters came into view, raining what looked like confetti upon the scene. The reporter ran breathlessly to collect whatever it was that had fallen and began reading a leaflet to the viewers.

"Nice touch. What's the sugar coating?"

"Listen, Jack…"

"This leaflet promises the bearer a one-off payment of one thousand US dollars provided they have it verified with their national identity document on site, at Villa 31. Any resistance and a failure to comply with the eviction will result in a forfeiture of all land rights in Santa Cruz and the one-off payment," said the reporter.

"That should get them moving. Fancy a spot of lunch?"

As they tucked into their roast beef and Yorkshire pudding, the relocation plan appeared to be moving along a pace. The TV showed buses being boarded, a very crowded rail terminal and luggage laden families queuing up for places on the trains waiting at the station. The reporter commented that it all had the marks of a wartime ghetto evacuation, a phrase that Robert found more than a little galling.

"The PM speaks very highly of you," said Jack.

"He should do, considering what he's getting from me."

They both enjoyed a hearty chuckle as the coffee and brandy arrived, but Robert was curious to know how much the PM actually knew about their plans. He asked Jack, as it wasn't a question he felt had been appropriate during his meeting with the prime minister earlier that morning.

"It's all on a need to know basis and since our success on the Europe issue, he fully understands the basics as I outlined some of it to him. But as far as he's concerned we're simply strengthening our ties for the moment and nothing more."

"And is he aware of the resources the UK will be acquiring once the plan has reached its conclusion?"

"He has been brought up to speed on the Dead Dog gas and oil fields in the south, not to mention the recent finds off the Valdez Peninsula, yes. In fact it was those two aspects in particular that softened the blow, so to speak," said Jack, rather economically.

Jack continued. "Today's events are merely you carrying out domestic policy of which he really has no interest, or at least shouldn't have. We want expansionism and that's what he's going to get. Today is a sideshow, nothing more," he finished, with a wave of his hand.

"You can guarantee your support when it matters then? There are elements of this that I simply cannot proceed with alone. You know that, don't you?"

"The pound sterling, to name but one?"

"Precisely, and you will have to drive that from this end."

"With nearly two hundred years of planning in the works, I hardly think we'd leave you hanging in the wind, Robert. Besides, there are too many interested parties involved now and the PM will do our bidding, as the weakling he really is."

"Yes, I know all that. God knows I've had more time than anyone to think about this, but what I meant was, how are you going to get the cabinet to approve all of this?"

"Military force isn't what we want, old chap. It's the ugly alternative that we can use should the PM and his followers not accede to the terms we set out when we abandoned those fools in Europe. The cabinet will do as they're told, so don't worry," said Jack. "Another brandy?"

CHAPTER 21

As Robert's flight touched down in Buenos Aires, he was aware that further protests were gathering pace around the capital in the wake of his resettlement plan, which was still ongoing and probably would be until the end of the week. Pimpi met him in the VIP lounge, seemingly unperturbed at the protests and growing tension.

"They're just letting off steam, sir. Give it a few days and it will all be over."

"I'll take your word for it," said Robert as he climbed into the black presidential Range Rover surrounded by a team of his close protection operatives, carefully chosen by Guy.

As they rode towards the coast, protesters lined the city streets held back by anti-riot police brandishing shields and batons. The angry mob had set fire to numerous piles of car tyres which gave off thick, black, acrid smoke and hundreds of masked youths stood in long lines facing the police and banging baseball bats against makeshift metal shields. It was an ugly scene and more than once, the presidential vehicle was hit by flying objects including bottles and rocks.

"We need to give the people something to distract them from what's happening at Villa 31, sir. Something they can't argue with. Something bigger than this that will make them forget it had ever happened."

"What do you have in mind this time?" asked Robert, rolling his eyes.

As they sped past the steel barriers leading up to the highly fortified tunnel, Pimpi explained his plan.

"Do you remember those disastrous plans over the years to fix the currency problems? Remember when they even came up with a brand new currency, the Austral, which wasn't exactly the roaring success they had hoped it to be?"

"That's understating it a tad."

"I think we should change our official currency and use the pound sterling instead, sir. It's been done before; just look at Ecuador."

"But they use the US dollar."

"Quite so, sir, and I see no reason why we shouldn't buck the trend. It does, after all, fit quite nicely with your other designs here, does it not?"

Robert shifted in his seat and tapped the window as the motorcade entered the tunnel. Had Pimpi got wind of something, he wondered.

"That's interesting. It would give the people real buying power, not just here but across the world. I'll put it to cabinet next week."

Robert hid the smirk that was trying its best to escape from his mouth, so he just looked out of the window instead. Bursting Pimpi's bubble would only make him sulk and become impossible to deal with.

As the Range Rover pulled up at the imposing front doors of the presidential palace, he felt a sense of relief that he'd got past the angry mob unscathed. As he stepped into the marble floored entrance hall and heard the door close behind him, he immediately felt a sense of peace. He regarded the island residence as his fortress. His refuge from, not only the turbulence of politics, but also the pressures he felt from Jack Forsyth in London.

At the north western end of the island, sheltered from the south easterly gales, a small deep water harbour had been built, with two, eight metre breakwaters protecting the narrow entrance. Inside the harbour, two powerful coast guard cutters were permanently tied up to a pontoon on the southern breakwater and on the northern end a small marina had been built.

The six pontoons were home to the presidential yacht capable of speeds up to thirty two knots, a twelve metre sailing yacht and three rigid inflatables, which were used for patrolling the island. On assuming the presidency, Robert had transferred control of the harbour and the vessels within it, to Chief Forza.

The view from the island to the capital city beyond was also spectacular. Over the years, a retreat of natural beauty had been created, to include a nature reserve and small, sandy beaches lined with palm trees.

"So, how long will the currency change take?" Robert asked Pimpi.

They were enjoying tea and scones on the terrace of the presidential study overlooking the city and watching Guy and his security team take pot shots at clay pigeons for target practice.

"A couple of months I'd say, sir. Three at the most."

"That should take the heat off that rabble over there, especially when they wake up and find that the pound in their pockets will buy them twenty times more than they ever could with that damned Peso. I never liked it anyway. It always had the stench of banana republic about it somehow."

"I couldn't agree more, sir, we'd be well rid of it. Now, about the matter we talked about a few weeks ago. I have matters well in hand..."

"Well? What are you waiting for?" said Robert, standing up. "Now, get me the central bank chief on the line. We need him to set the wheels in motion for our grand exit from the peso."

As Pimpi rushed out, tapping the keys on his huge cellular phone, Robert sent an email to Margarita. Whilst he waited for her reply, he unlocked his desk and dialled a very long number into his satellite phone.

"I say, Robert, how the devil are you, old chap?"

"Excellent Jack, thanks for asking. Look, we need a favour and we need it sharpish."

"Anything to oblige. Fire away."

"I've decided to adopt the pound as our official currency a little earlier than we'd planned and I'd like you to get the ball rolling your end. Can you do it?"

"Fits very nicely with our plans as you know, but I wasn't expecting to execute this quite so soon. Why the hurry?"

"A bit of a crisis has popped up down here since we started moving those squatters along from Villa 31. Nothing we can't handle, of course, but this should deflect their attention a little, don't you think?"

"Ah yes, the distraction technique; an old one, but under the circumstances, a solid way forward. I may get some pushback from treasury, but it's not something we can't handle."

"I'll be addressing the nation on Monday, so if you could put the wheels in motion, I'd be most grateful, Jack."

"Consider it done."

President Crawford had inherited his island residence from the disgraced Virginia Cristal who had commissioned its building during her first term in office. He had considered demolishing it or even selling it to the highest bidder in recognition of its obscene opulence, but had decided to retain it as his official residence. He predicted that many of his new measures might prove a little prickly for Argentine citizens and the island's strategic location was ideally suited to keep them at bay should the need arise. For him, the jewel in the crown of the three story mansion was the master bedroom in the cupola with its panoramic views, reminding him of a lighthouse he had once visited in North Wales on one his many trips to see Jack. It was here that he awaited Margarita later that evening, as he reclined on the king size bed, channel hopping the TV on the opposite wall, as he simply could not concentrate on anything else but her at that moment.

But it was a tiresome journey for Margarita as it was for all the president's guests. First she had to meet the official Range Rover he sent for her in the underground car park of her flat, ensuring that she wasn't seen getting into the vehicle and then hope that she wasn't followed. Naturally, the vehicle was fitted with blacked out windows and once through the two kilometre tunnel, it needed to descend into the underground car park of the residence, which was usually cleared of staff in advance, on Robert's orders. Margarita found the whole experience more than a little claustrophobic and was always glad when the ordeal was over. She put up with the clandestine nature of her relationship because she enjoyed the buzz of their midnight trysts. It added to the cat and mouse game they had always played, not least with the local press, who speculated day after day on the president's love life, often being way off the mark.

A private lift, accessed only with the use of a key, took Margarita up to the private quarters and as he heard the soft notification tone of the lift's arrival, Robert rushed over to welcome her, then held her hands in front of him. She was dressed in a dark blue, knee length pleated skirt, matching jacket and a white blouse that set off her tanned complexion, as did the red lipstick she wore especially for the occasion. Not an ostentatious woman, the only jewellery she wore was a small silver crucifix on a chain around her neck, which was accentuated by the way her long, dark hair was tied up in bunches rather untidily, yet effectively at the back of her head.

"How was London, darling?" she asked, looking up at him.

"Oh you know, the usual. But glad to get back, especially now," he replied, kissing her softly. "Come on let's eat, I'm famished."

They took dinner together at a table he'd set up next to the huge panoramic windows in the adjoining study overlooking the river and the horizon beyond. Whilst he enjoyed the trappings of power, he also valued his privacy and even cooked very occasionally. This time he'd put together cream cheese wrapped in smoked salmon which they nibbled on whilst chatting and sipping a nicely chilled Muscadet.

"I see you've pushed the boat out tonight," said Margarita as he served up a couple of fillet steaks cooked rare, exactly as Margarita liked them. He knew it was also precisely the right amount of dinner to serve, as they were both feeling a tantalising sense of anticipation.

She didn't often ask Robert about his business, and usually let him offload matters that were bothering him when he needed to. He preferred this kind of arrangement, but she was furious over the Villa 31 crisis and its recent escalation.

"Are you sure this is right? I mean, you're throwing entire families out of their homes and sending them to the other side of the country where they don't know anybody at all. I think it's awful."

"Well, since no one has had the balls to tackle this problem, Mags, I decided that enough was enough. They're breeding grounds for criminals, drug runners and murderers. Ghettos, really, and it's not the view of Buenos Aires that I want the world to see. At least this way they can build a new life somewhere else, out of sight. Anyway we're practically giving them the land free of charge."

"But they're still out on the streets protesting. I can see them from my flat, night after night. Seriously, this can't go on."

"In a couple of weeks this will be just a distant memory, just you watch. They'll all have more spending power than they ever dreamed of when we finally dump the peso and start using pounds."

"Another one of Pérez's bright ideas I suppose? Christ, that man's a prick!"

"I know you don't like him, Mags, and for the moment I'm just letting him think it was his idea. We were going to implement this at some stage anyway. Now just seemed the right time."

"And this so called monument he's building for Independence Day? You know all about that, do you, Robert?" she asked, sitting back in her seat and folding her arms.

"Yes I do, Mags."

"Except it's not a monument at all. It's a fucking torture chamber!"

"Oh, come on. Whatever gave you that idea?"

"I bumped into Nina Roca the other day when she was collecting her daughter from school. She told me that Pérez is building some kind of steel contraption that looks nothing like a monument."

"Look, Mags. I've given him a little free rein with this pet project of his and I'm sure he has it all well in hand."

"That's not what Nina says. She says it looks like something you'd see in a zoo!"

"Oh, good Lord! Look, I'll have a word with him tomorrow."

Margarita raised an eyebrow and took a sip of her wine.

CHAPTER 22

Luis de la Mano, still licking his wounds after his election defeat, had emerged as an unlikely presidential candidate in the first place. Since he had been anointed by the woman he worshipped, ex-president Virginia Cristal, her followers had no compunction in transferring their blind faith to him. Prone to outbursts of rage, unsavoury expletives on the sexual habits of the president and fist-thumping public speeches, he was considered by many of his associates to be a liability, yet still they followed him like pack dogs.

Raised in Villa 31, where running water, electricity and general sanitation were considered a long dreamed of fantasy, he had bullied his way to the top of the most powerful dock workers union in the country and held sway over the entire union congress. Not a stupid man by any means, he had learned his craft on the streets as a gang leader and had only risen through the ranks thanks to his devotion to Virginia Cristal's populist causes. She had looked after him by offering him schemes for public tender contracts which he inevitably won for the many industrial cleaning service companies he owned by proxy. For the authorities, proving the cronyism was an uphill task and he seemed to swat away such accusations like mere irritations, especially since his prime target was now the Crawford presidency.

Like his now discredited union friend and fellow thug, Lucio Melia, De la Mano was adept at stirring up the passion of his followers. The clearing of Villa 31, the destruction of the peso and the general Britification of Argentina were more than enough to stoke up the nationalist fervour he needed in order to call a general strike. This, he hoped would deflect from his real intentions, which were to discover who President Crawford's real paymasters were. He was convinced that the CIA, the FBI and the US president, were pulling all the strings behind President Crawford. De la Mano considered England to be nothing more than an also-ran, a speck in the northern hemisphere and a pathetic ex-empire builder, whose glory days were long gone and therefore incapable organising anything more elaborate than a tea party.

Not a natural politician, he was prone to knee jerk reactions and, like a bloodhound, once on the scent of a bone, he couldn't stop himself. He truly believed the Yankee imperialists, the old enemy, were behind the president's outrageous policies and, regardless of the fact that what everyone else saw as an alignment with Britain, he was convinced that it was all a ruse, a diversion. He imagined the threat was a stealthy cultural and economic takeover of his beloved country by those burger chewing cowboys from Alabama or possibly Texas.

Unfortunately for him, his geographical knowledge was limited to what small amount of information he had picked up in the few school classes he had attended. This was largely drawn from populist propaganda textbooks, written by previous populist governments whose definition of imperialism was the English pirates and the Yankees. Especially the Yankees. This suited him, as they were simple and iconic targets that his followers could relate to. To that end he enlisted the services of Victor Valiente, an old friend from his gangland days who had miraculously finished high school and somehow made it into the ANI state intelligence service.

The agency's allegiances were never necessarily in line with the government of the time, but often entrenched in the old ideas promulgated by the original workers' party in the nineteen forties. He tasked his friend Victor to quietly monitor the US embassy in Buenos Aires and have one of his goons follow the Argentine ambassador in Washington whilst tracking their communications with the US State Department. This left De la Mano to get on with what he knew best; stirring up malcontent with the masses and calling the workers to put down their tools and march on the plazas.

CHAPTER 23

It was no accident that Pascal Zapatero had contacted the Children's Foundation. On a warm spring afternoon, as he walked from their small offices overlooking the southern docks of Buenos Aires, he felt a huge sense of relief that he'd finally done the right thing. It had long bothered him that his parents barely spoke to him any longer and the raging arguments they'd been having still echoed through his mind. Deep down, he had always known that his mother and father were hiding something from him and the results he now held in his hand, whilst shocking, simply confirmed what he had always thought. The DNA tests proved it beyond doubt.

Pascal, a big, broad shouldered man, almost six feet tall, was dressed in a short sleeved white shirt with a breast pocket at the top left where he liked to keep his pens, all neatly arranged according to height. His large, pale arms were freckled and his most distinguishing feature was his straight red hair, now flecked with grey at the sides, which he swept back and tied up in a ponytail. He didn't much like being in the sun, avoided it whenever possible and always wore a pair of oversized, clunky black rimmed sunglasses.

Finding a seat in a nearby cafeteria, he ordered a coffee then waited for Clara to arrive. She'd be there in ten minutes she had said, but hadn't asked him any questions on the phone, for which he was thankful. As he waited, he stirred his coffee and stared out of the window at the passing traffic and the container ships tied up at the docks, asking himself the same questions he'd been over time and time again. There were so many what-ifs that he barely knew where to start and the only way he had been able to get this far was by forcing his parents to submit to the biological test by court order, a process that had taken months to complete and not without a great deal of bitterness on their part. When they had asked him why he insisted on the tests, all he could ever reply was that he had a feeling things weren't right and that he needed to know the truth. His parents had always insisted that he wasn't adopted; they were his parents and that was that, as far as they were concerned. But the fact that he didn't look remotely like either of them had always bothered him. At school he had always been taunted and called *carrot top* and anything longer than five minutes in the sun would turn his skin red. His parents, on the other hand were both dark haired and of Spanish descent; a fact that he'd researched extensively and as far as he was concerned, their family ancestry ended in Spain.

As he saw Clara walk past the window, he rushed over to the door to greet her and as he did so, wrapped his big arms around her, shaking with emotion.

"Come on, my love, let's sit down," Clara whispered to him wiping the tears from his cheeks.

She had met Pascal at the Buenos Aires Book Fair the year before, had fallen for his little boy lost demeanour and he, for her worldly charms. Holding hands across the table, Pascal told her the results of the test and when he handed her the fax, she waved it away.

"I really don't need to see it. It's what we thought anyway isn't it?"

"I know, I know, but this doesn't make it any easier."

"Well at least you know the truth now, don't you?" she said softly. "But if Maria and Sebastián aren't your parents, then who are?"

Pascal held her hands firmly and turned his head to the window with tears in his eyes, trying his best to control himself. He knew what had to be done and that somehow he would find the truth, no matter how long it took. Turning back to Clara, his expression changed to one of resolve.

"I'll have to go back to Sancti Spiritu. To the hospital I told you about. Remember?"

"Yes, it's your only hope really. Anyway, it's in Rufino. Don't you remember?"

"Yes of course I do, Clara. It's as clear as day," he snapped.

Clara sat back in her chair, feeling offended.

"I'm just trying to help you, Pascal, that's all."

"I know darling, I know and I'm sorry. I thought I knew how to deal with this. God knows I've had long enough to think about it, but what doesn't make sense is their insistence that they are my real parents."

"And you think that will change everything?" she asked, pointing to the fax on the table.

"No idea," he said slowly and emphatically.

Clara leaned back in and stroked his face with the back of her hand, removing her glasses and letting them hang around her neck by a thin gold chain. Many men described her as cuddly, even matronly and as she leaned forward, her ample breasts, held in place by a low cut pink top, rested upon the table between them.

"Look, why don't we take a few days off? I don't mind driving and there's a little hostel in Rufino just down the road from Sancti Spiritu. I don't expect you'll want to stay with your parents anyway, will you?"

"Not really, but I have to see them. You know that."

"No you don't. Not right now anyway and I think it's best they don't know we're going to the hospital or anywhere near Rufino. In fact, don't tell anyone at all."

"Yes, you're right as usual," he said, smiling for the first time since waking up that morning.

"I'm not very busy at the moment, so why don't we go tomorrow? That'll give us a couple of days and then we've got the weekend together," suggested Clara.

Pascal thought for a moment. He worked for himself anyway so what the hell, he thought.

"Pick me up at seven, tomorrow morning?"

"I'll be there," said Clara, kissing him again, as she gathered up her things and left.

CHAPTER 24

The night before Independence Day, Pimpi Pérez could be seen dashing to and fro around government house with the phone strapped to his ear, cursing all the bitches and all the illegitimate sons of whores that had ever been born. It was his unique way of getting things done and whilst painful to all who witnessed his frantic activity, he secretly enjoyed every minute of it. The maintenance team had finally come good and produced what they considered to be their finest masterpiece. Looming over the Plaza de Mayo and suspended from an enormous hydraulic crane was the object of all their hard work, for the moment shrouded in a massive white tarpaulin, blowing lazily in the wind as it waited to be placed in the square directly in front of the Casa Rosada.

"Roca, I need you down here right away!" Pimpi barked into the phone.

"But, Mr Perez, it's only four in the morning. I'm asleep."

"No you're not. Get yourself down here now and take charge before people start to wake up."

Nina Roca rolled over in her bed, cursed Pimpi and the mother who had dared to conceive him, awoke her sleeping husband in the process and dashed out of her apartment to the waiting official car. When she arrived at the plaza, she arranged for it to be cordoned off and at the stroke of five, she ordered the crane operator to lower the contraption in place.

A little later, fleets of TV vans and dozens of reporters gathered in the plaza as word had spread that a new monument to democracy was being unveiled later in the morning, giving rise to reporters speculating on its nature and what form it might take.

"As you can see, we're here in the Plaza de Mayo, scene of so many historic events in the republic, and we're about to witness the unveiling of the new democracy monument. In just a moment we'll have an exclusive interview with the minister of federal planning, Nina Roca. Now back to the studio," said the shivering and excited TVN reporter.

The tarpaulin covering the contraption began to flap in the breeze and the edges began to lift, exposing what lay beneath. Pimpi meanwhile, was watching the proceedings from the balcony of government house whilst talking with the chief of the state penitentiary service, to arrange transport of the prisoners to the plaza.

"And don't use prison vehicles, chief. Hire some unmarked minivans. We don't want to attract attention."

Meanwhile, Nina Roca had been spotted by the TVN reporter and, advancing towards her carrying his blue and red microphone before him like a beacon, he thrust it towards her face.

"Minister Roca, could you please tell us about the new monument to democracy over there?"

"What monument?" she asked, frowning.

Since the news coverage was going out live, Pimpi was watching the TV coverage and trying desperately to raise the minister on her cell phone. When he finally got through to her, he told her exactly what he wanted her to say.

"Minister, we understand that a new statue is being unveiled this morning. Is that correct?" asked another reporter as Nina Roca cut the call to Pimpi.

"All will become clear later in the morning, ladies and gentlemen," said Minister Roca before making a dash for the cordoned off area of the plaza. Workers could be seen erecting screening and scaffolding by creating a covered passage from the hydraulic hoist to the edge of the plaza, much like a skyway, and in preparation for the arrival of the minibuses carrying the prisoners. It was important to Pimpi that nobody saw the prisoners until the crucial moment.

"Roca, the minibuses are on their way and should be with you in about twenty minutes," said an excited Pimpi.

First light did not dawn until about seven forty five, and, right on cue the prisoners arrived at the newly built corridor in three white minivans. Alerted by the noise, the reporters all ran in that direction like a pack of rabid dogs, pointing their cameras and microphones at the blacked out windows of the vehicles, hoping for the slightest glimpse of anything interesting. What they couldn't see were the side doors of each vehicle being opened and the occupants being hurried through the makeshift passage and under the suspended white tarpaulin.

As the first rays of the rising sun began to filter through the streets and surrounding buildings, the crane lifted the object once more and deposited it in the historic Plaza de Mayo. The hastily erected scaffolding and walkways were removed and two meter high, steel grilled, crowd control barriers were placed in a circle, no more than twenty feet distant. The crane, which also served as an overhead water delivery system, remained for later use, and the operator stayed on standby drinking *mate* in his cabin and awaiting orders for the lifting of the cover and the grand unveiling.

Curious bystanders began arriving at the plaza along with hundreds of people who were simply off to work and heading to subways or nearby offices. As Pimpi gave the order for the tarpaulin to be lifted, the crane operator toggled a lever in his cabin, as slowly as he had been ordered to do.

The assembled crowd pressed against the barriers as the monument's form began to take shape and, as the cover slowly lifted up, numerous pairs of bare feet could be seen, along with several bodies lying prostrate. By the time it had been raised to almost half way, the crowd realised that this was no conventional monument at all, and whatever murmuring and excited chatter there had been earlier descended into a scene of complete silence.

The cage, twenty metres square, four metres high and constructed of stainless steel bars that were five centimetres thick and exactly fifteen centimetres apart on all sides, was fitted with water jets attached to the roof. The non-slip floor was raised and in the centre of all the stainless steel was a flaunched drain hole for the inevitable effluent that would arise. Each of the prisoners was dressed in a white PVC jumpsuit with hood, their shoes and all other personal belongings having been removed. Each had received a mild tranquiliser jab prior to transport and it was expected that the effects of the drug would last no more than a couple of hours, so by the time of the unveiling they should be fully aware of their surroundings.

As the crowd gazed on, all that could be heard were the metallic hum of the crane, the tarpaulin flapping against the steel bars in the breeze and the occasional flurry of pigeons scurrying back and forth across the plaza. With the sun now breaking through, the scene had been set exactly as Pimpi had intended, and as the cover finally reached the top of the steel cage and was hoisted away, the full impact of the object's presence became clear to the steadily growing crowd of onlookers.

Now fully exposed, the steel gleamed and shimmered in the sunlight. Its steel floor and robust bars gave it a sharp, surgical appearance, so at odds with its surroundings. Inside, the prisoners were either holding the bars with both hands or looking confused, lying curled up on the floor sobbing or simply milling around the centre, hoping not to be noticed, by pulling the hoods over their heads.

Hundreds of people stood at the scene in open mouthed astonishment. Some were moved to tears and could no longer watch, so turned to walk away wiping tears from their faces. Others broke out into applause, hoots of joy and wolf whistles. Even the reporters seemed dumbfounded and many of them struggled to find words that would adequately describe to the viewers the scene unfolding before them. Edgardo, the reporter from TVN, who had been at the scene since the early hours of the morning, could be heard talking on camera, not quite believing what he was seeing.

"Standing here, as I have been since four this morning, I can say that this is not what we were expecting," he said, microphone in hand, turning his head and pointing at the huge steel bars behind him.

"We were all expecting the monument to democracy, but what I'm seeing now is what I can only describe as a monument to shame," at which point, his studio anchor interjected with a few questions of her own. She wasn't keen on Edgardo's line of thinking at all; they had ratings to think about, not to mention her Crawford-friendly proprietor.

"Edgardo, can you see how many people there are in the cage? Who are they? It's hard to tell from here," she asked, squinting visibly.

"Hang on Maria, I'll see if we can get a bit closer," said Edgardo as he and his cameraman jostled forward, pushing through the crowd which had now risen to thousands.

"Yes, Maria. I can see about fifty people in this thing. One moment. Yes, we've counted them and there's fifty nine, including those lying on the floor."

"Who are they, Edgardo? Can you see their faces?"

"Just a moment, Maria. Yes, I think I recognise one of them," he said, his eyes widening.

"Oh my God! It's the president! Erm, sorry I mean it's Ex-President Virginia Cristal! This is incredible. Something none of us ever imagined. I can't believe it really. Son of a…"

"Edgardo, did you just say that the ex-president is in there?"

"Yes, Maria and I can also see the ex-vice-president. He's the one lying curled up on the floor like a foetus I think. And standing next to the ex-president, I think I can see Bill Montero."

"The ex-commerce secretary. Bill *El Pistolero* Montero you mean, Edgardo?"

"The very same, Maria, and from where I'm standing he's not looking too good. His face looks very pale and twitchy and he seems to be saying something to Virginia Cristal, but from here I can't make it out."

"Well, we can only imagine what he must be saying. See if you can get a bit closer."

"We can't do that right now, Maria, but I'll see what I can do."

Off camera the technicians rushed back to their truck to rig up a sound boom, grinning and chattering excitedly with each other as they rummaged through their equipment.

"Can you recognise anyone else, Edgardo?"

"It's hard to tell because of those hoods. I don't think they want to be recognised. I know I wouldn't. Oh hang on, yes it seems to be the entire cabinet from the ex-president's last government and a lot of other people I still don't recognise."

"Edgardo, we'd like to hear what they're saying in there."

The TVN technicians finished rigging up the sound boom and managed to extend its huge fluffy microphone over the crowd control barriers to within a couple of feet of the steel bars. The TV image quickly zoomed in to where Virginia Cristal was now standing, scowling and ranting at her ex-commerce secretary, who now had his hands balled up into fists in front of his face.

"You fucking moron, Montero. You got us into this," shouted the ex-president without realising she could be heard by millions. The camera captured the scene and Edgardo shouted over the noise in the ex-president's direction.

"Madam, we can't hear you. Is there anything you'd like to say? Speak louder please, for the viewers."

"This kind of behaviour will not be tolerated in a democracy! I am the president of the nation!"

As she spat out the words, her face contorted with hatred. This brought the mob to a fever pitch of yelling, and those who were closest grabbed hold of the barriers and tried to climb their slippery sides. Others found yet more projectiles to throw and the scene became so chaotic that TVN withdrew their sound boom before it became a weapon of choice.

At that precise moment and when Edgardo was facing the camera with a full view of the cage behind him, an enormous whoosh was heard, followed by a loud hiss. The crowd immediately backed away in reaction to the noise, as streams of freezing cold water gushed from the overhead water jets, soaking the occupants of the cage, amidst screams and a great deal of swearing which soon faded into moans and sobbing. The crowd on the other hand, began to whistle and jeer again.

"Exactly as planned," said Pimpi to no one in particular as he surveyed the scene from the balcony of the Casa Rosada.

CHAPTER 25

Early on Friday morning, as Clara drove Pascal in her Jeep north west towards Rufino, on a straight and completely flat provincial road, they decided that they needed some credibility to start asking questions about events that had taken place so many years ago. To that end, since Clara was a bona fide journalist, she would need a plausible reason as to why they wanted the names of doctors and nurses who had worked at the provincial hospital more than forty years before.

"Let's say we're writing a piece on provincial hospitals through the decades, and we're particularly interested in the post-war period. You know, how things have improved, that kind of thing."

"Not much, from what I've seen," said Pascal, remembering being ferried into a dilapidated public hospital, following an accident he'd had on a bicycle some years ago.

"True enough," said Clara. "Anyway, I'll do what journalists do; you're my photographer and here's the deal. We're using your family history, starting with you as our feature. How does that sound?"

"You mean, use me as a sort of case study, something like that?"

"Precisely. We're going to tell the story of their wonderful hospital from the day they brought you into the world and show how everything has changed so much since those days in the sixties, blah, blah. An old trick I picked up from Jenny Lane at The Crusader."

"Isn't she the one you helped with those articles on the dictatorship?"

"The very same. I learned a lot from her over the years, but this is different."

"Yes it is, and we're hoping that someone, a nurse or a doctor who was there at the time, is still alive?" asked Pascal.

"That's what we're hoping, yes. You brought your birth certificate and the other papers, didn't you?"

"Yes, they're in my backpack," replied Pascal curiously.

"We'll need to get copies of the registry entries at the town hall, because they're usually witnessed by the doctor who delivered you. Sometimes it's just the midwife, of course."

"You *have* been doing your homework haven't you?"

"I'm a journalist, Pascal."

They pulled off the main provincial highway at the sign for Rufino, where the road became little more than a dirt track, with huge potholes appearing every few metres, continuing all the way to Plaza Sarmiento in the centre of the small, quiet town. The plaza was surrounded by palm and eucalyptus trees blowing lazily in the breeze and children played on the swings or admired the old steam locomotives. Mothers chatted with each other, seated at concrete benches emblazoned with blue and yellow graffiti as their babies slept in pushchairs. The warmth of the day had brought out a chorus of buzzing insects, and the cheep-cheeping of cicadas was interrupted only by the laughing of children and the odd pickup truck bouncing past on the dusty roads.

After checking into the ancient, run down hostel in the centre of town, they headed straight for the town hall and as soon as they had passed through the doors they knew they had entered the hallowed portals of state bureaucracy. Employees were sitting around idly trying to look busy, whilst uniformed porters pushed trolleys laden with official looking cartons from one place to another. Signs pointed to the many dull sounding sections, such as administration of byways and local tax payments and eventually they found their way to the civic records department. After explaining to the uninterested, pale young woman behind the enquiries desk that they were writing an article on public health in the town, they were asked to wait while she shambled nonchalantly across the gloomy room through a maze of filing cabinets. She stopped to talk to another woman, who looked up from her monitor, stared in their direction and then headed over towards them. An overweight, flustered looking woman, she wore a grey, oversized jogging suit, and had a tired looking face.

"What do you want?" she asked tersely, flipping the badly scratched glasses over her hairline.

Clara explained again why they were there and added that they would like copies of all documents related to Pascal's birth at the local hospital.

"Date of birth?"

"August 1958," replied Clara, a response which prompted a slow sigh of breath from the tired looking clerk.

"You'll have to come back later. Everything that old is archived. It'll take hours to find those files," she said, folding her arms.

Clara smiled benignly, handed her a certified copy of Pascal's birth certificate and told her they would wait in the cafeteria on the next block.

"What a grim place this is," commented Pascal as they sipped their coffees in the Club Español.

"Try applying for a license to open a shop, then you'll know what grim is. I did that with my father once. What a nightmare that was! But they do keep meticulous records, so I suppose that's something," said Clara, looking at her watch.

After an hour or so, they returned to the records department and found the clerk sitting at her desk surrounded by boxes of documents, with two assistants sifting through yellowed and dog eared papers, with looks of concentration on their faces.

"Any luck yet?" Clara asked the clerk.

"Just a moment please. It should be in this box here," she replied, looking over the top of her spectacles.

Half an hour later, after pacing up and down and watching the clerks holding flimsy pieces of paper up to the light, they asked again.

"Well this is very odd. The registry certification appears to be missing."

"Missing? What do you mean 'missing'?" asked Pascal impatiently, whilst Clara kicked his shins.

"Each archive box has a registry log where we enter all requests for copies, and nowadays it's logged on the computer system as well. There are no records of the documents having been taken or even copied for that matter. They're just not here. I'm sorry."

Clara asked her why it might be missing, but she had no idea, saying she would look into it. Just as they were leaving, Clara scribbled the hostel phone number on a scrap of paper and handed it to the clerk, in case something came up.

As they emerged from the town hall, shading their eyes from the sunshine, Clara turned to Pascal. "I had a hunch this would happen. Don't ask me why, it was just a feeling."

Pascal looked shaken by the news and they sat down on a bench in the plaza.

"Let me have another look at that birth certificate."

He handed it over, and Clara scrutinised it.

"This looks real enough. There are your parents' names and the registrar. I can barely read the doctor's name. It looks like *something* Lopez, I think, but it's difficult to read. No mention of a midwife, but that's something which is sometimes recorded on the registry certificate as a witness. That's the piece of paper that's missing, damn it!"

"Hospital?" asked Pascal.

"Where else can we go? Let's just hope they at least have some records left, unless of course they had a mysterious fire."

CHAPTER 26

Jumping to his feet after watching the unfolding events on TVN, the president stabbed at the phone in an effort to raise Pimpi. The moment he saw and heard the jets of water falling on the caged people, he could barely contain his fury and yelled into the phone when he heard his vice-president's voice.

"What the hell is this, man? What have you done?"

"But sir, I thought…"

"You will stop this immediately, Pérez. Get that contraption moved, right now!"

"But, Mr President, I thought this was what you wanted."

"I'm warning you, Pérez. If you don't shut this down right now, I will have you removed from office," said the president, slamming the phone down, and realising that he should have paid more heed to Margarita.

Unmoved, Pimpi watched, as chaos unfolded in the Plaza de Mayo.

Still fuming over the scenes he had just witnessed and knowing that the entire world will have been watching, the president knew he needed to bring his cabinet into line over the national currency change. There had been objections from at least half of his ministers who, as far as he was concerned, wouldn't recognise a bold move if it slapped them in the face. To him, they were nothing more than a bunch of lily livered spoilt brats, particularly the weedy finance minister and his team. He'd selected them rather hurriedly when he became president, but he would now be replacing them all with a new team handpicked from the London School of Economics, as suggested by Jack. In fact that's exactly what he was going to do, he thought to himself as the helicopter touched down on the roof of the Casa Rosada.

"You're all fired! You, you, you and especially you!" said Robert pointing his finger around the huge rectangular mahogany table.

The four economists stood up slowly, packed up their papers and headed for the door without even speaking, as the president continued his briefing, pacing around the room.

"Ladies and gentlemen, I expect nothing but your full support in the destruction of the peso and by the time the pound sterling becomes legal tender, I expect the logistics to have been fully implemented. There will be a period of grace for six months, during which time pesos can be exchanged for pounds, but after which they will become meaningless scraps of paper. I will be making a statement first thing tomorrow morning on national television. Is that clear enough for all of you?"

Around the table there was some fidgeting, along with a few side glances and nervous shifting in seats. All the ministers finally nodded reluctantly, and the president slammed shut his leather bound agenda and swept out of the cabinet office.

Later that morning, ignoring the president's orders, Pimpi Perez stood on the balcony of the Casa Rosada to observe the activity in the plaza, where the crowd had grown to many thousands of people whistling and jeering or simply looking on in shock and amazement.

Peering through the reinforced glass windows of the balcony, he barked some orders into his cell phone and within seconds, the police moved in and removed the crowd control barriers from around the cage. Some of the crowd surged forward and stopped a metre or so away from the steel bars, as most of the prisoners inside moved back and huddled into a tight group at the centre, with some spreading their arms out behind them as if to protect their colleagues. The more excited onlookers ran forward and began spitting and shouting at those inside, whilst others began thrusting branches ripped from nearby trees through the bars, hoping to hit as many as they could. Some found pebbles and rocks which they viciously threw.

By now, most of the prisoners were screaming, with many curled up on the floor to protect themselves from the onslaught. Some of the projectiles hit their marks, blood began to stain the white jumpsuits and the floor was awash with water, blood and other fluids. One or two of the inmates picked up rocks and stones that had landed in the cage and hurled them back at the crowd through the bars, hitting some elderly people who had turned away and were trying to leave. The entire scene turned chaotic as the crowd bayed for more. Hundreds more people could be seen joining the mob from adjacent streets, pressing forwards towards the cage with vicious, hate filled expressions on their faces.

As the crowd moved closer, a little girl could be seen near the front of the line, clutching a large pink teddy bear close to her chest. As she looked up at her mother, who held her hand over her mouth, the TVN cameraman spotted them both and zoomed in to catch the moment. As the chaotic scene continued, with most of the crowd cheering wildly at every rock being thrown at the prisoners, the little girl ran from her mother towards the cage between the screaming adults, trailing the teddy bear by its arm, as her mother screamed for her to come back. When she reached the cage, she wrapped her tiny hand around one of the bloodied steel bars and looked up at Virginia Cristal who had defiantly remained clinging to the outside with both hands gripping the bars, with trickles of blood running down from her forehead. The TV cameras quickly focused on the scene being played out.

"Have you been naughty?" asked the girl as she pushed her teddy through the bars.

Virginia Cristal grabbed at it, held the teddy close to her chest and as she looked down, her rage appeared to change to curiosity as the girl looked up at her. At that moment, the furore subsided. All that could be heard were a few people shouting, many crying and some reporters talking in lowered tones into their microphones. The girl's mother ran over, grabbed her daughter's arm, stopped in front of the ex-president and spat viciously into her face. Virginia Cristal then turned away, walked slowly to the centre of the cage, sat down, rocking to and fro, hugging the teddy bear whilst mumbling to herself and stroking its head.

"A poignant moment here in the Plaza de Mayo, which has left the crowd practically speechless. Now back to the studio," said Edgardo, choking up with emotion.

As he spoke the words, the huge crowd began backing away. Within a few minutes, only a handful of onlookers remained, wandering around the cage and peering from time to time at the prisoners, who sat in a circle looking dazed and confused.

Back on the balcony, the president stormed through the doors angrily.

"Get that fucking thing out of here, right now!"

As the news spread through the TV channels, with headlines such as *Presidential Stunt Backfires* and *We Can Change Party Shows New Shame*, the president ordered an urgent meeting at the Casa Rosada communications centre.

Within a few moments, the prison transport vans reappeared, the bedraggled and traumatised prisoners were shepherded inside to their seats and, as the cage was being lifted away and placed on a flat-bed truck, Robert turned again to his vice president.

"Get out of my sight, Pérez!" he said angrily.

With that, Pimpi left the communications centre, slamming the door behind him, leaving the staff smirking and whispering to each other behind their computer screens. Robert then asked for the Range Rover to be brought to the main entrance, strode onto the balcony and gazed at the Plaza de Mayo for a moment, shaking his head.

CHAPTER 27

A rriving at the hospital was a strange sensation for Pascal. As far as he could remember, he hadn't been there since he was born, and it was as grim as they had both expected. The small main reception area was a threadbare shell, apart from a dozen or so white plastic garden chairs pushed against the walls. A single fan turned weakly from the ceiling, and the walls were peeling off what little paint remained amid patches of mildew and damp. Two ancient looking trolleys and a wheelchair were parked haphazardly near the doors and what passed for a reception desk, was nothing more than an old wooden table with a Formica top, at which was seated an elderly lady dressed in a pink housecoat, holding a large writing pad. A tatty looking grey telephone sat at the edge of the desk and the familiar clinical hospital smell had been replaced with an odour of poorly maintained sewers, rising damp and stale hospital meals. An overhead fluorescent strip light flickered on and off, noisily.

"Christ, this is pretty gruesome," whispered Pascal as they approached the elderly lady. They then asked to be shown to the administration office, where they were greeted by a young black man with a cheery smile and dreadlocks, wearing a black suit and open necked white shirt. He introduced himself as Max.

"Do you have records here for births dating back more than forty years please, Max?" asked Clara hopefully, having first explained the feature they were writing.

"I believe so, madam, let me check," answered a smiling Max as he sat down again and proceeded to tap away on his keyboard. "How far back are you talking about? I mean, which year?"

"1958?"

Max peered at his screen from left to right, tapped his keyboard a few times and then stood up.

"We keep older records in the storeroom, so would you like to come with me, please?"

When they arrived at the storeroom, they could see that it was yet another archive store. Max went straight for a rack of boxes against the far wall and pulled down a file of records for 1958.

"What exactly would you like to know?" he asked.

"Well, births on that date and which doctors, nurses and midwives were on duty that day. Erm sorry, I mean the twentieth."

"Let's see now. I remember that we catalogued all these files last year and we're due to put everything on microfilm, but we can't afford it at the moment. Ah, here we are, August 1958."

Pascal paced nervously up and down the office with his arms folded as if he didn't want to know anything about the whole matter. Max held up a large sheet of lined paper that appeared to be an activity log and placed it on a desk.

"On that day there were four births at the hospital, delivered by two different doctors, with one midwife and a nurse on duty. I would need your parents' names sir," said Max, turning to look up at Pascal.

"Oh right, yes. That's María De La Cruz and Sebastian Zapatero."

Max read out the names of all the women admitted to the hospital that day and then he went through the records for both days either side just to be sure.

"Your mother's name isn't shown on any of these records, sir."

He read the names again just to be sure. "Can I see your birth certificate again please?"

Clara handed it over and as she did, she squeezed Pascal's hand, not wishing to say a word, as Max held the birth certificate up to the light.

"The doctor shown here is, hang on, I can barely read it. I think it says Leopoldo Lopez. There's no doctor of that name shown working here on that day," he said pointing at the records on the desk and looking at Pascal sympathetically.

"Jesus Christ!" exclaimed Pascal as he put his hands behind his head.

"Max," said Clara. "Can you give us copies of these records please? I'd also appreciate it if you didn't talk to anyone about it either. Could you do that?"

"You'll have to sign for the copies. Apart from that, that's where my job ends."

"Oh and before we go, could you check when Doctor Lopez worked at this hospital and give me a call please? Here's my number at the hostel."

She thanked Max, signed for the copies and hurried out of the hospital, almost dragging Pascal along by his arm.

"What the fuck is going on here? My parents are not my parents and the doctor who is supposed to have delivered me wasn't there at all and now I don't know who the hell I am!"

"I don't know, darling. What do you expect *me* to say? We already know the test results," said Clara. "Anyway, we should get back to the town hall and see if they've had any more luck."

Clara knew she was being short with him and she also knew that she was getting angrier as the day wore on.

Returning to the town hall she had a sinking feeling in her stomach, accompanied by a rush of adrenaline, something she hadn't felt for a long time on any of the stories she had covered recently. They handed Pascal's original birth certificate to the clerk and she laid it next to the copy on the enquiries desk in front of them.

"I took another look at that certified copy you gave me and I noticed something that didn't look right."

Her tone had acquiesced somewhat from when they were last with her, and she gave her name as Gaby, as she pulled over a large magnifying glass on a springy stand.

"You see here on the original, where the doctor's name is written?" she asked, pointing. "It's not the same handwriting and it's in a very slightly different shade. I think this birth certificate has been tampered with," said Gaby looking up at Clara.

Clara tried her best to look surprised, but knowing what little she already knew about Doctor Lopez, only brought about a frown to her face.

"Maybe it was written by two different people, Gaby. Maybe the doctor wrote his actual name and then signed it like that. Look," she said, pointing at the birth certificate. "How do you *know*?"

"No, Clara. All birth certificates are hand written, or at least they used to be and are exact replicas of what's written in the registry. You know, the book itself, just here," she said pointing. "The whole thing is written by the same person from beginning to end. The only variation is where signatures are shown, and of course, in those days all birth certificates were written by hand. Today they're mostly typed and then signed. I'm absolutely sure this has been tampered with. Does that make any sense?" she asked, looking at both of them.

"Would you give us a moment please, Gaby?" asked Clara as she made for the door.

"I can stay a little longer if you like. Don't be too long, please."

Clara took Pascal by his arm and they walked back to the entrance of the town hall where a night security guard had just come on duty, and opened the door for them.

"We're coming back," Clara said to the guard as they walked down the steps in the fading light of the day.

"I need a cigarette," said Pascal in a weak voice. They walked over to a kiosk a few meters from the town hall entrance, where he bought a pack and then sat on the steps. Pascal lit up and inhaled deeply. He'd given up the habit eighteen months ago and had vowed never to start again.

"I don't know what to say, my love," she said as she laid her head on his shoulder. They both stared blankly over at the street and suddenly Clara jumped up.

"I have to get in touch with Max! I didn't get his number and if we're lucky he might still be there. Wait here."

"I'm not going anywhere," said Pascal quietly, as he lit another cigarette.

Clara sprinted towards the hospital, parting a large flurry of pigeons and hoping that Max was still at his desk. She arrived breathlessly at the rickety old table where a different old lady was now sitting and asked if the administration staff were still there.

"If you're lucky, you might still catch them," she said looking at her watch.

As she raced along the corridors, she heard someone approaching, whistling a familiar Bob Marley tune and knew it had to be Max.

"Max, Max. I forgot to get your phone number. Are you just leaving?"

"Whoa lady! Take it easy, I was going to call you tomorrow," said Max as he put a hand on each of her arms. "Slow down!"

"What have you found, Max? What is it?"

"Come with me and I'll show you."

Back in the administration office Max showed her a different set of records to what she'd seen earlier.

"First, I can't find any record at all of a Doctor Lopez ever having worked at this hospital, before or after the date your husband was born," said Max. "So I thought I'd do some more checking, and discovered that Doctor Lopez's national identity number matched someone else's."

"And?" asked Clara impetuously.

"A porter at the hospital at the time."

"Where is he now?"

"He was sixty four years old then, so..."

"Right, ok, and the others?"

"I thought you'd ask that. The other doctor on duty died ten years ago and the nurse five years ago. That leaves the midwife. If these employment records are correct, she must be about, let's see, seventy two years old by now."

Clara slumped back in the chair and pushed her hands through her hair, letting out a long sigh.

"Hang on a minute," said Max. "The midwife, a Mrs Silvia Menéndez, worked here past her retirement at sixty years old and appears to have retired, but for some reason her name rings a bell with me and I don't know why."

"And what about those women? You said there were four. Are there any records of their deaths?"

"Madam?"

"Call me Clara, for Pete's sake, Max!"

"I'm not supposed to do this you know, just dish out information like this."

"It's a bit late for that now, come on!"

"If I get caught, I'll probably be fired."

"Listen, Pascal has just discovered that his parents are not his real parents, he doesn't even know where he was born now and he needs to know the truth. So do I."

Max turned to his computer, tapped the keyboard a few times and studied the green and black screen.

"Here Clara, take a look."

She went and stood behind him as he moved his finger across the screen.

"Two of the women who were admitted that night died here in this hospital a few years ago, see? The other two, I don't know. Their names haven't passed through here since then. No, wait a minute," said Max, studying his screen. "A Mrs Lieberman did give birth to a son, but he didn't survive. Stillborn, apparently."

"That leaves one woman, doesn't it?" asked Clara.

"You didn't get this from me ok? Let's see. Oh yes, a Mrs Rose Laing over in Sancti Spiritu. Yes, on a ranch called *Las Siete Palmas*. Must be rich people," said Max.

Clara suddenly felt a vice-like grip in her stomach. She wasn't entirely sure why, but she felt that somehow, a page had been turned. She quickly jotted down the name and address, gave Max a kiss on the cheek and dashed down the stairs, past the old lady sitting at the desk and into the plaza hoping to find Pascal sitting on the town hall steps. There was no sign of him, so she wondered where a man in his condition might go at that time of the evening. If he needed a drink, then so did she and she found him at a nearby pizza bar. He was sitting under a red and white striped plastic canopy festooned with red, blue and yellow party lights, enjoying a litre bottle of beer and a whisky chaser.

"Take it easy, Pascal," she said, sitting down opposite him.

"Easy for you to say. Next thing we know is that I'll discover that my real parents were shot in the head by some general in a military concentration camp."

"Oh lord. I don't think so."

Clara waved at the girl who was cleaning some tables, and asked for a glass of red wine.

"Listen. Do you really want to find out who your parents are, or shall we just go home and forget about the whole thing?"

"I'm sorry, it's all just got to me, that's all," he replied. "You were with Max for quite a while. What did he say?"

Clara told him what she had discovered and was pleased to see that he appeared to take it all in his stride. Maybe the drink was having the required effect.

"OK then, at least we've got something. Not everyone's dead yet," said Pascal.

"You haven't lost your sense of humour. That's something, anyway."

Pascal managed a grin as he took another sip of his beer and lit a cigarette.

"So, we've got a midwife and a mother, one of whom could be mine. Where should we start?" asked Pascal.

"Well, I don't fancy driving to Sancti Spiritu tonight, so why don't we have a bite to eat and then see if we can find our midwife, Mrs Menéndez, in the morning.

Over breakfast at the hostel on Saturday morning, Max called.

"Clara, I was doing a little more digging around yesterday and I was right. The only mother who gave birth on that date, and for whom I can't find any further details, is Mrs Rose Laing in Sancti Spiritu."

"Thanks, Max. Anything else?" asked Clara.

"The two other women I mentioned who have since died? Well one child was also stillborn like poor Mrs Lieberman's and the other had a daughter."

"Well thanks Max, but is that relevant?"

"Sort of. It could be..."

Later, as they were about to leave the hostel, the phone rang again and the young girl on reception passed the phone over to Clara, saying it was Gaby.

"Hi, Gaby. I'm sorry I missed you last night and I hope I didn't keep you waiting."

"I had to rush off anyway, Clara, but there is something. I found the original medical certificate which was written at the hospital. It's the one you take with you to the registry. Anyway, I can't make out the doctor's signature at all. It's completely illegible, but it's also signed by the midwife, a Silvia Mendez or Menéndez, I think. Does that help?"

Clara thanked Gaby for her help, said goodbye and hung up.

"We need to find Silvia Menéndez. I'm sure there's something we're missing and maybe she can remember," said Clara, impatiently. "Oh, I don't know. Just anything."

"But she must have delivered hundreds of babies. Why would she remember me?"

"Come on, all we can do is ask."

"Ok then, who are we going to be this time?" asked Pascal.

"We're back to the feature story now. Come on!"

CHAPTER 28

My fellow Argentines. I speak to you today from government house," said Robert, pausing. "I'm sure you will all have witnessed the events that took place this morning in the Plaza de Mayo, but it was never our intention to inflict physical injury upon our fellow citizens. For too many years our country has been held to ransom by organised crime, corruption on an astronomic scale and a government that believed it could rule and plunder with total impunity. Well, I'm telling you today, fellow citizens, that those dark days are now over and the criminals will see their day in court. Further, when they are convicted for defrauding the state, as I'm convinced they will be, every last cent they stole will be returned to you, the people, in your pay checks in the form of an ex-gratia payment."

President Crawford paused for a few moments to allow his gesture to sink in, and then continued.

"I have also decreed that, effective the end of this month, the Republic of Argentina will be adopting the British Pound Sterling as its official currency. There will be no more runs on the banks, no more black markets and zero exchange controls, except for those that exist by international accords. I have also taken steps to bring the economy of this country into the current century and my new team at the ministry of economy will be in place by the end of today. My new finance minister will issue a statement tomorrow morning with additional details. Thank you and goodnight. Viva la patria!"

Later, as Robert waited for Pimpi to arrive at the island residence he went to his spacious office on the north side of the complex, locked the door and sat at his desk looking at the panoramic view through the picture windows and the murky brown Rio de la Plata beyond. It was time for his weekly call to Jack, so he unlocked his desk drawer and took out the secure satellite telephone he used for just that purpose.

"Jack, we need to talk."

"Yes, it's on the news. How can I help?"

Robert gave him a brief outline of the progress he had made to date, including the currency conversion and the cage fiasco.

"Yes, that was truly unfortunate, but look at it this way; it'll be taken as a warning," said Jack. "Anyway, on to more important matters. We felt it necessary to bring Sir Michael Brabant into the loop, which is why he called you last week. He'll be your local point of contact for Operation Blenheim. OK with you?"

"Yes, we spoke on Monday. He's a fine ambassador, Jack. My people like him. When's kick-off for the operation, by the way?"

"We can have assets in place for the end of March. That's what? About nine weeks away, by my reckoning."

"I've had meetings with the chiefs of what's left of our armed forces, and the noises I'm hearing so far are encouraging. They really like the idea of joint exercises with His Majesty's Forces, and it should be an interesting operation, even though we have hardly any toys left to play with."

"Let me know if you'd like me to send you over some bows and arrows," said Jack sharply.

"It's no joke. Do you know what's left of our forces?"

"We have an idea, but go on."

"Two, thirty year old frigates, one of which rolled over and sank last week whilst tied up rather carelessly in Comodoro Rivadavia; the other is still sitting in dry dock and has been for the past three years. A diesel electric submarine from the seventies, which the South African government finally returned to us after two years of repairs they never finished because of the IMF embargo. All four of our ancient fighter jets are grounded because no one makes any spare parts for them anymore and most of our ammunition went past its sell by date about ten years ago. So yes, those bows and arrows would come in quite handy, actually."

"Didn't realise things were that bad, old chap."

"Yes well, it will certainly bring new meaning to *simulation*," said Robert, wearily. "Each branch of our military will be participating in the exercise and as you know, one of the key elements will be the joint cooperation of HM Forces. You know how central that aspect is to the plan don't you, Jack?"

"Indeed I do."

The disputed Martín García Island, in the Rio de la Plata, inhabited by nothing more than wild birds, packs of wild dogs and a squad of British soldiers, was the last remaining evidence of the failed British invasions in the nineteenth century. In 1807, Brigadier General Robert Craufurd had successfully taken the island, fought off repeated attacks from the mainland and established a small military command on its western shore. An unmanned military satellite tracking station now perched atop its highest point, was still operational and maintained by the British government at minimal expense.

The island had become a cause célèbre throughout Argentina, no more so than with the fiery Virginia Cristal, who personally took it upon herself to goad the British government in every passionate speech she ever gave. Her many followers wore the Martín García Island, and what they called the Malvinas Islands, around their hearts like talismans for a long lost friend and vowed never to give up their claims until their last dying breaths.

The island itself held very little strategic importance for the British, unlike the Falklands and Gibraltar. It was usually referred to as *that southern carbuncle*, most of the British public either didn't care or had never heard of it, yet successive British governments doggedly hung on to it.

Robert and Jack had other ideas. With the Argentine presidency now effectively in the hands of the British government, the long held wishes of the Argentine people to regain their territory, however mistaken, would now take on an entirely different meaning.

"Anyway, by the time Operation Blenheim is over, those sovereignty questions they've been banging on about for so long, will be a tad moot won't they?"

"Irrelevant, I would say," said Jack, dryly.

Robert ended his call and with a thoughtful smile, returned the phone to its home in the desk, which he took great care in locking up afterwards. How much easier his life was now with all this wonderful technology, he thought to himself, leaning back in the black executive chair again and watching the setting sun glinting off the river wavelets. He well remembered the times he would call Jack from whichever public telephone he was nearest to at the time, ask him to call back and if he was very lucky, would even manage to find a red telephone box brought over by the British in the sixties. He looked forward to seeing a few more red telephones boxes around Buenos Aires in the coming months. It would be one of many aspects of the plan that would put an indelible mark upon his dominion.

As he was lost in a daydream of country building and new horizons, his speakerphone announced the arrival of Pimpi, whom he found skulking around on the ground floor entrance area, looking very sullen indeed.

"Pull yourself together man. Come, let's go to my office."

Pimpi, his shoulders hunched up and with a hangdog expression on his usually cheerful face, followed his boss up the wide sweeping staircase that curved around to the first floor. When they reached the office, Robert asked him to sit, poured himself a large Jameson and handed his vice president a glass of tonic, with ice and lemon.

"Listen Pimpi, we've only just begun. We're bound to have the odd setback from time to time and remember one thing. We're here to change this country forever. Surely you of all people should know that."

Pimpi was a large man and his entire frame enveloped the small armchair he sat in. He rubbed his voluminous chin with one hand and self-consciously fidgeted with his tie with the other as if trapped in a corner. His real fear was that the president would pull the plug and let him go, which was something he couldn't even begin to contemplate.

"Tell me about the peso-pound situation first. Come on, there's a good fellow."

Pimpi sensed that maybe he wasn't going to be fired after all, so readjusted his position by sitting up straighter and put his drink down on the low table opposite his boss. He coughed nervously and ruffled his short, black, wiry hair.

"The banks have adjusted all their ATMs with the NCR people and their internal systems, so they should be ready to make the complete switch by Monday. Well, Wednesday at the latest, anyway," said Pimpi nervously.

"Go on."

"The Bank of England officials have done an excellent job with the central bank and I organised delivery of the new currency from the Royal Mint last week. There weren't any hitches as far as I can see, and the new system, in pounds of course, will be rolled out by the end of the month."

"And the townships?"

"What's left of Villa 31 is already being developed into private estates and luxury apartments, and as you suggested, British contractors are already in place. That's just over fifty hectares of prime land which is being snapped up at a rate of knots."

"And the roads, the signs?"

"All access roads are signposted in English as are the internal streets. Once inside the complex, all vehicles will drive on the left," said Pimpi continuing. "The other thirty two townships in the city boundary are being dealt with as we speak, sir and the inhabitants relocated to Santa Cruz with very little trouble, especially after your generous increase in their land allowance."

"Good. Well done Pimpi. You've done well."

Robert had been careful not to bring his friend entirely into the plan even before he became president. It was enough that he knew what to do and simply carry out his orders, particularly as this played very well with Pimpi's utopian view which he had long promulgated since his days in university. What he could not predict, however, was how far he could take the plan before his friend began to ask uncomfortable questions.

"You're happy with what we're doing so far then?" asked Robert, smiling benignly.

"What do you mean, sir?"

Peering to his side, Robert leaned forward clasping his hands together over his knees.

"It's a perfectly simple question, Pérez. What is your impression of what we've achieved so far?"

Pimpi was momentarily taken aback by his boss's barely veiled aggression and tried to hold himself in check.

"Your approach is wildly in excess of what I envisioned, sir..."

"But you remember all those late nights when we used to change the world, don't you, man? How we felt the next day when we'd sliced everything up the way we wanted the world to look, and how good we felt? You were the one with all the radical ideas, anyway. Surely you remember that, don't you?"

"Of course, of course. It's just that I never imagined it would be like this."

"You mean because of the model I'm using? A model that has proved to be a successful yardstick for centuries? Is that what's bothering you?"

"It's a little extreme."

"As was your cage experiment, Pérez, but they swallowed that in the end, didn't they?"

Robert put his hand up before Pimpi had a chance to whine about the injustice of it all.

"This isn't a social experiment you know, but I do feel that the only way to put this country back where it once was…no scrub that. What I mean is, the great country it always should have been, we need to make some radical changes. Some of which were your ideas anyway. Our new currency, for example. Does that sound a little clearer now?"

"Well yes. I see what you mean now, sir."

"You remember when you wanted to change the world don't you? When you used to prance up and down the university corridors spouting your idealistic views and cocking a snoot at the military junta? I always admired that in you, Pimpi," said Robert, slapping Pimpi's leg.

"Oh, and another stunt like that cage monstrosity and you're out."

Pimpi sat bolt upright.

"Good, so we're in agreement then," said Robert, standing up.

"Yes, sir. I think I should go now. I have a lot to do."

"That's the spirit!"

As they walked down the stairs to the entrance doors, Robert stopped for a moment.

"Oh Pimpi, while I remember. I'd like you to get back to me on the official language change, the decree I sent you for driving on the left, the national flag redesign and Britain's new most favoured nation status. I'd like a full report by…shall we say the end of the week?"

"Very well, sir and thank you," said Pimpi as he backed out of the main doors, bowing ceremoniously.

CHAPTER 29

Clara banged loudly on Silvia Menéndez's front door and after a minute or so, an elderly man wearing a string vest appeared, peering at them through his round, wire spectacles.

"Oh excuse me, sir, I'm looking for Mrs Menéndez. Is she here?" asked Clara.

"No, it's Friday. She's at the hospital," he replied, squinting.

"The hospital?"

"Yes. She helps out there a couple of times a week. Who are you, anyway?"

"Oh we're writing a story about public health over the years in Rufino, and we'd like to ask her about it. Um, what does she do there, Mr Menéndez?"

The old man grinned.

"Oh she's got a few tales to tell all right. She knows that place inside out."

"How do I find her in the hospital?" asked Clara, slowly.

"Friends! She's one of the Friends."

"Friends? What friends?"

"*AHR*. Amigos del Hospital de Rufino," he said slowly. "She's a volunteer over there."

"Oh right, well thank you so much, Mr Menéndez. We're so sorry for having bothered you."

Clara took Pascal's hand as they headed back to the plaza and towards the hospital.

"I'd like to go and see that couple on the ranch in Sancti Spiritu now, what do you think?" asked Pascal.

"Let's have a word with Mrs Menéndez first. I don't know why, but I think she might be able to help us."

"We must have walked past this desk half a dozen times already, Clara. How strange is that?" whispered Pascal as they approached the Formica table again.

"Yes it is…oh, good morning," said Clara breezily to the elderly lady in a pink housecoat sitting at the table.

"Are you with AHR madam?"

"Indeed I am," replied the lady proudly.

Clara saw that she had a pink and blue lapel badge with the name, Celia Suárez.

"Is Mrs Menéndez here today, Celia?"

"Yes, I had tea with her earlier. I think she's visiting patients in the geriatric ward this morning. Would you like me to call her for you?"

"No, it's all right, Celia, we'd like to surprise her," said Clara sweetly and lowering her voice.

"Oh how nice, that's very thoughtful of you. I'm sure Silvia will be delighted to see you. You should find her at the end of that corridor over there," she said, pointing.

It wasn't difficult spotting Mrs Menéndez in the geriatric ward. Her pink housecoat stood out like a beacon amidst the white bedsheets and black and white chequered floor tiles.

"I'll wait here by the door," Pascal mumbled to Clara as she began to make her way across to a bed that Mrs Menéndez was attending.

As she approached, Clara could see that she was a woman who liked to work on her appearance and certainly didn't appear to be seventy two. In fact, she didn't look a day over sixty. She could almost be described as glamourous, displaying elegant legs, a trim yet robust figure, long and straight, jet black hair that reached her shoulders, and face make up that made her look half her age. Clara almost gulped when she got closer and wasn't quite sure what to say.

"Mrs Menéndez? I'm Clara Tomkinson," she said with a warm smile and extending her hand.

"Oh, good morning. What can I do for you?" replied Mrs Menéndez as she tidied up a sleeping elderly man's bed and rearranged some magazines on the bedside table.

"I'm writing a feature on public health here in Rufino down the years and I understand you've been connected with the hospital for a very long time. I'm sure our readers would love to hear some of your stories."

At the very moment Clara said *a very long time*, Silvia Menéndez appeared to stop folding the sheets on the bed for a split second, just long enough for Clara to notice. When she had finished, she looked up at her with a warm smile.

"Of course. I'd be delighted to help you. Let's go to the staff room and I'll make us a coffee."

Clara signalled to Pascal with a nod of her head and they followed her to the staff room at the side of the ward, where they sat on a tatty old sofa with Mrs Menéndez opposite them, sitting on a blue plastic garden chair.

"So, what would you like to know?" asked Mrs Menendez as she crossed her legs, pushing her long black hair away from her face and clasping her hands neatly together on her lap.

"You used to work here as a midwife, didn't you?" asked Clara, smiling.

"Oh, I retired about ten years ago, but yes, I was a midwife. Why do you ask?"

"We're interested to show our readers how patient care has improved over the years and we're featuring Pascal here, since he was born in this hospital."

The midwife looked over at Pascal, smiling benignly.

"Oh, that's interesting. Must have been way back, although you do look quite young."

"1958 actually, Mrs Menéndez," said Pascal.

Clara sensed that they'd touched an area of significance since Mrs Menendez shifted ever so slightly in her seat, didn't reply to Pascal's comment but played with her wedding ring by nervously twisting it around her finger.

"In those days, was it usual for both a doctor and a midwife to be present during a birth?" asked Clara.

"In the fifties? Gosh, sometimes but not always. It depended on who we could find at the time, with so many babies being born," she said, her upper lip stretching thinly.

"And you must have delivered hundreds of babies. It must be difficult to remember that far back, I'm quite sure."

Clara was struggling to reach the point where Mrs Menéndez would bite or at the very least show some kind of recognition. But it was early days, she thought to herself.

"Oh yes, there were many, many babies. It was always such a delight to see them come into the world," she said with a stiff smile, her immaculate white teeth gleaming, but with a hint of red lipstick stain.

"And were there any births that you remember in particular?" asked Pascal, looking over to Clara as if pleading for help.

"Well, the odd one. Twins were always difficult. Why do you ask?"

Pascal had reached a point where he no longer felt it necessary to beat around the bush.

"You delivered me, as it happens," he said, trying his best to give her a genuine smile.

"Oh how wonderful! I don't often get to see my babies again. How lovely to see you!"

"What's your mother's name again, Pascal? I keep forgetting," asked Clara.

"De La Cruz."

Silvia Menéndez shifted in her seat and crossed her legs again, but appeared to show no recognition of the name.

"You see, Mrs Menéndez, I believe something odd took place when I was born and I think you know. You were there. Your name is on my birth certificate," said Pascal, bluntly.

"I'm not sure what you're driving at, young man. I attended hundreds of deliveries."

"The fact is, the doctor who signed the documents doesn't exist. In fact, someone forged my birth certificate and your name is the only one that makes any sense to me at the moment. You were there!"

"I really don't know what you're talking about," said Mrs Menéndez as she stood up pushing the plastic chair away from her as if she were about to leave. Pascal also stood and he moved towards her, standing less than a foot away, so that he could smell the perfume and see her dark eyes darting from side to side.

"Mrs Menéndez, I'm going to tell you what I think happened. Now sit down!"

"Pascal!" pleaded Clara, standing up.

"I said sit down, Mrs Menéndez!"

She sat down slowly, taking from her sleeve a paper tissue, which she began to crumple nervously.

"Maria and Sebastián are not my real mother and father. I had a DNA test carried out and it was proven beyond doubt that they are not my parents."

"Listen to me, young man. How am I supposed to remember that far back? Anyway, I'm not going to sit here while you…"

"No! You listen to me. I know that you delivered four babies that day, one of which was stillborn, one was a little girl, one is now dead and that leaves me. Who was the other woman you delivered a baby for, Mrs Menéndez? Who is my real mother?"

Silvia Menéndez was a naturally composed woman, yet the pressure she felt at that moment made her tremble. Small beads of sweat appeared on her upper lip, and for a few moments there was silence.

"They said you were ill," she said in a barely audible whisper, looking away.

"I beg your pardon?" asked Pascal angrily.

"Pascal?" said Clara, putting her hand on his.

"Silvia, all we want to do is find out the truth," said Clara in as gentle a voice as she could muster. "Please help us."

"When I delivered you, I was told to take you away and put you in the nursery. That's all he said."

"Who? The doctor?" asked Clara.

Clara grabbed another plastic chair and moved it to face Mrs Menéndez, taking both her hands. She then pulled a tissue from her handbag and wiped the tears from Mrs Menéndez's cheeks.

"Silvia, please. You have to tell us."

Tears were now forming in Clara's eyes.

Mrs Menéndez continued, her lower lip trembling as she stared at a spot on the floor.

"The doctor told me to take the baby to the nursery, which I did. I remember thinking it was odd because I'd already put the other baby in the same nursery."

"Which other baby?" asked Clara.

"The little boy the doctor had delivered earlier. He handed a little baby to me and just told me to put him in the nursery, too. Everything happened so fast that I didn't have time to put the name tag on his little ankle and I put him in a cot next to you," she said, looking at Pascal.

"Did you see the doctor deliver the other baby boy?"

Mrs Menéndez looked up at Clara, "No, I didn't. I was busy delivering your husband," she said, looking at Clara.

"And the other baby, did he have a name tag on his ankle?"

"No he didn't. Neither of them did."

"Silvia listen. This is very important. Can you remember what the lady looked like that gave birth to my husband?"

Mrs Menéndez dabbed her nose with a tissue.

"Yes, I do. I remember thinking how beautiful she was, and her husband was there too, waiting outside."

"Silvia, what did she look like?"

"She had fair hair. Blonde I suppose," said Mrs Menéndez between sniffles.

"Go on," said Clara.

"Her husband was waiting outside in the corridor. I never liked the husbands being in the room during the birth, so I had to ask him to wait outside."

"What else can you remember about him?"

"He was a big man. Very tall and sunburnt, like he worked outside a lot. He was very nice and he had a moustache I think."

"Did he look like Pascal?"

Mrs Menéndez looked up at Pascal, who was standing back from them both with his arms folded, looking up at the ceiling, tears rolling down his cheeks.

"Yes, yes he did actually. He had red hair and I remember he had freckles on his forearms like your husband because his sleeves were rolled up."

At that moment, Pascal ripped open the door, rushed out and slammed it furiously behind him, whilst Mrs Menéndez broke down in tears, asking what she had done wrong. Clara put her arms around her, stroking her hair.

"It's not your fault, Silvia, it's not your fault," she said, comforting her.

When Mrs Menéndez had composed herself a little, Clara resumed.

"Silvia, I know you're upset, but you must tell me what happened next. Pascal needs to know who his mother and father are. Surely you know how he must be feeling?"

"Of course I do! Of course I do. I just did what I was told by the doctor."

"Can you remember his name? The doctor I mean?"

"No, in those days, you didn't ask questions, especially to doctors. I think I remember him saying that they needed to do some tests on the little boy as soon as I'd cut the cord and got him breathing. She had taken a lot of gas and was almost asleep, I think, so I took him to the nursery like I told you. It all happened so quickly. I'm sorry, I just can't remember everything."

"I don't understand, Silvia. Was there anything wrong with Pascal?"

"No, nothing. He was a perfectly healthy little boy. He even had red hair like his father. I remember noticing that when I put him in the cot."

Clara looked into Mrs Menéndez's eyes and for a brief moment they were silent.

"You didn't give Pascal back to his mother, did you Silvia?"

"No! No I didn't! I didn't!"

Mrs Menéndez broke down again and began to sob uncontrollably. At that moment there was a knock on the window that looked out on the ward. It was Mrs Suarez, looking very anxious.

Mrs Menéndez looked up.

"Oh Celia, just go away will you!" she shouted, tears running down her cheeks.

"Silvia, which baby did you give to Pascal's mother?"

"It was about half an hour later. I left the little boy in the nursery because the doctor told me he was going to do some tests like I said, so I went back to see his mother and she had woken up. She was crying. Crying for her baby boy and I didn't know what to do. I went to look for the doctor but couldn't find him at first, so I asked one of the nurses to look around. She said he was still in the nursery, where I found him. I told him that his mother wanted her baby boy back and she needed to feed him. He just looked at me. He was really angry and he said, 'there he is, over there,' and he was pointing at the cot where I'd put him, but it wasn't him. It was a different baby, so I asked him where the other baby was. He told me I was confused. He got angry again and said that I'd got all mixed up, not to be so stupid, then he just walked away."

"Silvia, listen to me. How do you know it was a different baby? I mean, how *could* you know?"

Mrs Menéndez looked straight at Clara defiantly.

"When you've delivered as many little babies as I have, you just know. You're not a mother, so you wouldn't understand that," she said with a dismissive wave of her hand.

"Quite so. But how did you know, Mrs Menéndez? I need to know, all right?" insisted Clara.

Mrs Menéndez took a deep breath whilst pursing her lips together.

"I know which baby I delivered in there and it wasn't the one the doctor pointed at."

Her tone had gone down several octaves and she looked directly into Clara's eyes.

"That baby didn't look anything like the other one. His hair was fair. He was much bigger. I noticed that straight away."

Mrs Menéndez put her face in her hands, the tears and black mascara running through her fingers onto her pink housecoat. Clara was trying her best to comfort her and stroked her hair back over her head.

"Silvia, did you give this baby to Pascal's mother?"

"Yes, yes I did. I picked him up and wrapped him in another blanket because he was crying. I don't know why, I just wanted to protect him. When I gave him to the lady, she started to cry again, but she was smiling, she was happy and I knew it was the wrong baby. She started to feed him and that's when I ran from the room. I gave her the wrong baby. I gave her the wrong baby. God forgive me."

"Oh my God," mumbled Clara as she hugged Mrs Menéndez's face to her chest. The two women wept together as one. For a few minutes, no words were spoken, only tears were shed.

Gradually Clara managed to compose herself. When she had done so, she released Mrs Menéndez, held her by the shoulders and looked directly into her eyes. Mrs Menéndez turned away, but Clara shook her a little, forcing her to look back at her.

"Silvia, you must tell me who Pascal's mother is. The woman you gave the other baby boy to."

Silvia Menéndez lifted up her head and stared at a point somewhere in the near distance with tears streaming down her cheeks. She had now composed herself, the sobbing and shaking having melted away.

She turned to Clara and in a low, calm voice said, "Mrs Rose Laing."

CHAPTER 30

Pascal had taken refuge on the hospital roof via the fire exit and was now sitting on the edge of an aluminium air conditioning vent smoking a cigarette, as he watched storm clouds gather on the horizon. At the very least, he now knew the answer to the question he'd been asking himself for so long. He'd grown to love Maria and Sebastián as his parents, yet he also knew that a new chapter in his life was about to begin. One that deep down he'd searched for, even in his dreams.

Clara left the inconsolable Mrs Menéndez in the staff room for a few moments, then went off to find Celia Suarez down in the main entrance to see if she could sit with her friend whilst Clara went to look for Pascal. When she eventually found Mrs Suarez loitering in a corridor, she found a very angry woman indeed.

"You have no right to come barging in here upsetting people like that!" said Mrs Suarez, clearly distraught by what she had seen.

Clara, taken aback by her outburst, decided to put her straight.

"Go over and be with your friend please, Mrs Suarez. She's going to need your friendship now more than ever. That's all I have to say," she said, walking away.

As she wandered aimlessly around the corridors, Clara wondered where Pascal might be. She also considered whether to report Mrs Menéndez to the authorities or whether she herself would say anything. As she neared the fire exit and the smell of cigarette smoke, she decided that Mrs Menéndez probably wouldn't breathe a word to anyone. The rest? Well, that was up to Pascal and when she finally found him up on the roof, she asked him directly.

"I know this is hard for you. It must be awful, but what should we do about Mrs Menéndez?" she asked.

"Nothing. Nothing at all, damn it! What good would it do if we reported her? How could they prove it anyway?" he said through eyes now red from so much crying. Clara sat next to him with her head on his shoulder. He held her hand and squeezed it.

"Who's my mother Clara?" he asked, quietly.

"Pascal, she said it was a Mrs Rose Laing and I didn't think to ask Mrs Menéndez about her. She was in a bit of state."

"The only answer to this whole mess is another damn test. You know that don't you?" asked Pascal, staring into the distance.

"Rose Laing, Rose Laing," Pascal mumbled to himself, raising his eyebrows. "She's the one who lives in Sancti Spiritu?"

"Yes, on a ranch, according to Max."

"We should phone ahead, if they have a phone, that is."

"A phone? Why shouldn't they have a phone?" asked Clara.

"Have you seen the size of some of these ranches? It can take half an hour to get to the front door from the main road, and it's just too expensive to get a telephone line installed that far away."

"Let's find a telephone directory," said Clara.

They went back to the hostel hoping to find a directory, but were told it had been stolen.

"This is hopeless. Let's ask Gaby if she knows. She seems to know most things around here," said Clara.

She phoned Gaby at the town hall, who met them for a sandwich at the bar where they'd had dinner the night before.

"I don't normally work on Saturdays, Clara, but this whole thing has got me a little curious," she said. "Oh, how's your research going by the way? Did you find the midwife?"

"Thanks, Gaby and yes, we did find her. She's Silvia Menéndez actually, and she was very helpful, thanks."

"And what about this forged birth certificate?" asked Gaby looking curiously at Pascal.

"Oh, I think there might have been a bit of a mix up, that's all. Nothing to worry about, really," said Pascal.

"Gaby, have you heard of a Mrs Rose Laing?" asked Clara.

Rufino was a small town, but that had its benefits as Clara well knew. Gaby frowned, tilted her head back and screwed up her eyes as if she were searching for some long forgotten detail.

"No, I can't say that I have. Why do you ask?"

"Oh no reason. It's just that I heard her name mentioned a few times today," said Clara, acting as if she were fumbling around in the dark.

"How about the ranch? What's it called again?" asked Pascal, touching Clara's arm.

"*Las Siete Palmas*," said Clara, looking at Gaby.

"Oh that's the Crawford ranch," said Gaby casually.

"Crawford?" asked Pascal.

"Yes, Horacio and Rose Crawford. The president's parents."

Pascal and Clara quickly looked at each other, with Pascal opening his mouth, but not seeming able to speak.

"Rose Laing! That's why you'd never heard of her. It's her maiden name," said Clara, feeling both vindicated and shocked by the revelation.

"We just call her Rose Crawford. Always have done, why?" asked Gaby.

"Um, we'd like to see her. You know, about the feature I'm writing. Any idea how we'd get their phone number?" asked Clara, as matter of fact as she could manage.

Gaby took a bite from her toasted sandwich and thought about it for a few seconds.

"If I were you I'd try the cattle market. Tell them you've got a delivery of steers, something like that. Ask for Ángel, he's my husband," she said, tapping the side of her nose.

Las Siete Palmas did indeed have a landline. Robert had insisted on installing one when he became president and since Ángel was so forthcoming, they had the Crawfords' phone number by early afternoon.

Later that night, at the Club Español bar, they were at their usual seats outside, thrashing over what they should do next. Pascal had worked himself into a nervous frenzy, and although the beer was having a calming effect on his spirits, he felt torn.

"Now that we've come this far, I'm not sure if I want to know any more. Perhaps we should leave this alone now and I could just carry on as before. I mean, what difference is it all going to make?"

"What? And never find the truth? To live the rest of your life never knowing who your real mum and dad are? Is that what you want?"

He poured the rest of the beer from the tall green bottle into his glass and ordered another with a whisky chaser, prompting a glare from Clara, then sat back in the white plastic chair, folded his arms and pursed his lips tightly.

"Listen Pascal, I know you. A day, a week, a month down the line and you'll be saying you wished you'd called them. That you'd just taken that final step and you'd kick yourself because you hadn't. Is that what you want?"

Pascal remained completely passive, managed to say thanks to the waitress for the drinks, took a sip of beer and sat back again, with his hands behind his head, staring over Clara's shoulder.

They ordered a pizza and a bottle of red wine to take away with them and, once back at the hostel, they sat on one of the single beds with their backs to the wall drinking from white plastic cups and nibbling away as they chatted, trying to decide how they would handle the delicate matter which they both knew could not now be avoided.

Their room was sparsely furnished, the two single beds being at right angles to each other on connecting walls. A tiny 15" TV hung precariously from the wall next to the rotten and crumbling windows and the bathroom consisted of a toilet with a broken plastic seat, a bidet that had a mind of its own and a metal pipe that served as a shower sticking out of the wall in the corner. A rusty air conditioning unit, which appeared to be an early prototype at waist height, protruded from the wall next to the windows and could be operated by pressing a series of blue, black and red buttons on the front. Once the correct sequence had been divined, it coughed and chugged slowly into life, rising to a crescendo which Pascal imagined could be the sound of a jet engine preparing for take-off. It did however lend the room a touch of Siberian tundra, and it was either that or a sauna effect from the thirty five degrees of Celsius outside the window. They opted for the latter.

"Getting in isn't going to be a problem. We'll just use the hospital feature story and they're bound to see us," said Clara topping up her plastic cup.

"And what about security?"

"What about security? We phone, they agree to see us and we drive in. That's the way it usually happens."

"But these are no usual people, Clara. It's the president's parents we're talking about here, and they might have all kinds of security set up. We can't just walk in asking for a cup of tea."

"There's only one way to find out then isn't there? Come on, let's leave it for now and we'll call them in the morning," said Clara as she cleared up the remains of the pizza from the bed.

The following morning after breakfast, Clara tried to phone the Crawford ranch from the hostel but the line was faulty. Being a small agricultural town in the interior meant that the communications system was woefully lacking, badly maintained by the phone company and cell phone coverage was patchy at best. They then decided to return to the bar and try their luck on the payphone.

After a pause of several seconds, during which time, Clara waved her index finger around impatiently, she finally said, "Hello, hello?", then paused.

"Hello? I'm Clara Tomkinson. Could I speak to Mrs Crawford please?"

Pause, with Clara nodding.

"And when will she be back?"

More nodding.

"Yes, of course. It's Clara Tomkinson, a journalist and I'm writing an article on healthcare in Rufino. Yes, ok, here's my number at the hostel. Thank you very much."

It transpired that Rose Crawford and her husband had gone off on one of their weekly supply runs to Sancti Spiritu and wouldn't be back until after lunch.

"I expect they're doing a security check on me as we speak. Christ, this antiquated bloody phone system really is awful!" she said finally.

"Do you think they'll phone back?" asked Pascal.

"We can but hope. Why don't we pack up and head over there anyway?"

"Precisely what I was thinking," said Pascal.

About an hour and a half later, they were turning off the main provincial road, onto a wide and perfectly straight road, where they drove through a white painted concrete archway proclaiming *Welcome to Sancti Spiritu. Established 1927. Pop 3825.*

"Are they ever going to improve these damned roads?" asked Pascal as they trundled down the badly potholed dirt road towards the small farming community.

Clara let out a loud belly laugh.

"It might happen now that bitch has been locked up and can't steal our money any more. By the way, what do you think of President Crawford?"

"I like him actually. He's shaken up the system and seems to be doing all the right things, although that stunt in the Plaza was a bit strange. How about you?"

"I'm not entirely sure yet," said Clara.

"I know I shouldn't tell you this, but I had a hand in bringing her down you know…"

"You what?" exclaimed Pascal, quickly turning to look at her.

"Aah shit, I might as well tell you now. You've got a right to know, especially today. He and that weirdo Pérez were behind her impeachment."

Clara then went on to tell Pascal about the incriminating video tape, her clandestine meetings with Robert Crawford and how she had been able to join the dots.

"Wow! Bloody hell, Clara. Who gave you the tape anyway?"

"You know I can't tell you that. I'm a journalist. You know, sources and all that."

As they entered the town with its low buildings lining the street on either side, Pascal became very quiet and stared ahead, feeling out of his depth. Clara placed her hand on his knee and rubbed it comfortingly.

"It's what I do. For me, the driving force in my job is the truth, and one way or another I'll find it."

Pascal turned to look at her.

"I know, I know and now look at us. We're about to meet the president's parents….no, hang on. They could be my parents and if they are, who the hell is the president?"

At that moment Clara slammed on the brakes, brought the car to a standstill and leant her forehead against the steering wheel.

"Do we have any idea what we're getting ourselves into here?" she said, turning to Pascal. "If the Crawfords are your real parents, where did Robert Crawford come from? Who is he? How the hell did I miss that?"

Pascal turned to face Clara.

"I know. I got so caught up with Mrs Menéndez's story that it didn't occur to me either."

"To think that I helped to bring down one president only to clear the path for some....uh, fake, some charlatan. Where the hell did he *come* from?" she said, sitting back and pulling away again.

Pascal peered out through the open window as the car moved through the main street towards the small plaza. He too felt that they were treading in unknown and potentially dangerous territory. Robert Crawford was the president after all. That hadn't happened by accident and they wouldn't even be in Sancti Spiritu right now if it hadn't been for Clara and her terrier-like instincts.

"You know as well as I do that you won't stop until you find out, don't you?" he said finally.

"How could I have been so stupid to have missed it, damn it?"

Pascal didn't reply, he didn't know how to.

"No, I owe it to you to find out what's going on here and find out, I will."

Regardless of Pascal's probable parentage and the president's questionable origins, if they could possibly be proven either way, Clara knew that her entire thought process needed to shift up into overdrive. As she drove forward she began to look at what they had discovered from a colder, clearer perspective. A wise old journalist had once told her that a successful investigation held no emotion whatsoever, which was precisely the opposite to what she had been experiencing over the last couple of days in Rufino.

She needed to pin up everything she knew into some kind of mental scrapbook and slowly fill in the gaps, she told herself.

As she gripped the steering wheel, she tapped it with her forefingers lost in thought. Look at the bigger picture Clara, she told herself. What was it about the Crawford Presidency? What made him so utterly different from practically all the presidents who had preceded him? What kind of people were his parents? Or at the very least, the two people he regarded as his parents, anyway.

Her thought process was interrupted by a woman pushing a stroller, which she had to swerve to avoid, prompting a 'Whoa!' from Pascal and Clara's hand raised in apology.

The small town was practically deserted and because it was a Sunday lunchtime, not to mention a beautiful sunny day, most of the inhabitants were preparing the traditional barbeque lunch, known as *asado*. What few shops there were, were closed. Quite by chance, they parked outside what appeared to be the local social club, out of which was coming a steady stream of smoke from a tall black, metal chimney. Getting out of the car, they could smell both the aroma of wood smoke and the unmistakable appeal of chorizos cooking.

"Looks like we've hit the jackpot. I'm starving!" said Pascal, rubbing his hands enthusiastically.

"It's probably a private club or something. We can't just walk in, you know," said Clara, looking hesitant.

"Watch this."

With Clara following, Pascal strode in through the open doors of the club where men in working clothes were playing cards, chatting and drinking at small tables. Fans hung from the ceiling, twirling slowly with an audible ticking sound and a fog of wood and cigarette smoke hung in the air. As Pascal stood at the stainless steel bar at the side of the large room, the chatting subsided and he felt numerous pairs of eyes turned in his direction. Extending his hand to the man behind the bar, who was dressed in typical gaucho garb topped off with a black beret and a red handkerchief around his neck, Pascal introduced himself.

"Good afternoon, sir. Pascal de la Cruz and this is my wife Clara Tomkinson," he announced, loud enough for most of the gathered patrons to hear.

"Good afternoon," replied the man, nodding at both of them.

"I realise this is a private club, but we were driving past on our way to visit my parents Sebastian and Maria de la Cruz…oh, do you know them?"

"De la Cruz, out of Rufino?"

"Yes, sir."

The man glanced at another man seated at a cash till at the other end of the bar who nodded back in his direction.

"You're most welcome. Now, will you be dining here? As you can see, we've got the fire going at the back if you're hungry" he said genially, turning his head in the direction of the open doorway at the back of the building.

Telling the man how hungry they both were, Pascal ordered two beers, at which the barman signalled a young waiter, who placed their drinks on a battered old aluminium tray and stood waiting for Pascal and Clara to follow him. The assembled patrons resumed their chatting, and some of them nodded in Pascal and Clara's direction as if their club membership had just been secretly approved. Following the slow moving waiter to the enclosed patio, they watched another man dressed in Gaucho style, busying himself with the ritual of fire and meat. Clara nudged Pascal.

"What was that all about, 'de la Cruz out of Rufino'?"

"We're in the country now and that's the way it is out here. Besides, my dad has done pretty well in the tractor business."

"I didn't know he was that popular."

The enclosed Spanish style terrace, whose arches were separated by white painted columns, was laid out with tables and chairs occupied by families, with children playing around the tables in the shade. At a larger table set for about eight people, Pascal made his excuses to the woman sitting at the head and asked if she would mind if they sat at the other end.

"Please, be my guest," she said with a warm smile.

When they were seated, Clara watched as the woman, who was seated sideways on at the table, smiled and chatted with some little children who were playing tag among the columns. She was dressed in a brightly coloured flowery summer dress and her silver- grey hair, with streaks of blonde running through it, was partly swept back at the sides with the rest flowing elegantly over her shoulders. On her tanned face she wore no makeup, clearly indicating that she spent a good deal of time in the open air. The sides of her eyes wore the laughter lines of a woman who smiled a great deal, and, as she affectionately watched the man tending the fire and grilled meats, Clara assumed that he was her husband.

"This is the real thing isn't it?" said Pascal, sipping his beer and looking pleased with himself. Clara leaned over and nudged him with her elbow.

"Don't forget why we're here, Pascal."

Finishing his beer, he returned to the bar for a refill. Clara smiled at the lady at the end of the table and then watched the farmer wipe his forehead with his red handkerchief, as he turned the chorizos over on the low, floor mounted grill. Since he had his back to her, she couldn't see his face, but she did notice the grey and ginger hair under his black beret. She then looked down at the bare arms exposed by his rolled up shirtsleeves. What had Mrs Menéndez said? That he had red hair and freckled, powerful looking arms? Clara froze and she heard the woman she had been watching speak, as if from some distant tunnel.

"I'm so sorry, how rude of me. I'm Rose Crawford and you are..?"

It seemed to Clara that she had been sitting there for much longer, whereas it had been less than a minute.

"Oh, yes, so sorry. I'm Clara Tomkinson and that's Pascal," she replied pointing back towards the bar area.

She could feel the ground beneath her moving a little.

"Now, that name sounds familiar," said Rose Crawford, smiling and pointing a finger towards Clara, who now wished she could simply disappear.

"Oh?"

"You're a journalist. Yes, that's right, the BA Tribune. How lovely to meet you at last," she said getting up and sitting down next to her. She then turned around and beckoned the man at the fire.

"Horacio, darling, guess who's come to lunch?"

Clara felt trapped in a ruse of her own making and wished she was still in her little Jeep going in the opposite direction, far away from Sancti Spiritu. There was little doubt now and she could see everything as clear as the bright blue sky above her. They had to be Pascal's parents, his real mother and father; there was no doubt in her mind whatsoever. As she picked up her glass to take a sip, she quickly put it back down again, because her hands were shaking. Just as she did so, Horacio began moving over, wiping his hands on the black apron around his waist and she could hear Pascal's footsteps approaching behind her. She felt panic set in, because she knew that Pascal would know immediately and that he would not be able to control himself. It was in his nature.

"Did you say Clara Tomkinson?" asked Horacio. "I'm terribly sorry, Miss, but it's a full time job cooking an asado. Anyway, I'm delighted to meet you. What brings you out here, so far from BA?" he said extending his hand.

Clara stood up just as Pascal arrived with his beer and she shook Horacio's hand whilst looking over at Pascal, who showed no outward signs of recognition whatsoever. He simply shook their hands politely, sat down and carried on enjoying his beer with a blank expression on his face.

"Oh, I'm doing a piece on local healthcare. Pretty dull stuff really and I'm sure you wouldn't be interested. I'm freelance now, by the way."

"On the contrary," said Horacio. "My son is deeply concerned for the state of the public health service in Argentina. He's told me so several times. Now, would either of you like a chorizo? They're almost ready."

"Yes please!" said Pascal immediately, nodding in Clara's direction.

"That's settled then," said Rose. "You'll join us for lunch, how lovely. I'll call the waiter to set more places and order some wine."

Clara looked over at Pascal and then to Rose.

"Excuse me, Mrs Crawford, would you mind? I think I've left something in the car. Pascal?"

Once outside, Pascal leant nonchalantly against the back of the Jeep, smoking a cigarette.

"You know what's going on don't you?" asked Clara.

He didn't react, took a puff and blew the smoke upwards appearing not to have heard her.

"Pascal!" said Clara, raising her voice and pulling on his shirtsleeve.

"I heard you the first time," he replied, turning to her, smiling. "I know what's going on as well as you do, and we've finally found what we've been looking for. It's amazing isn't it?"

Clara looked up at him affectionately and brushed a lock of hair away from his forehead.

"So what are we going to do now?" she asked.

Pascal threw down the cigarette butt and ground it out in the dirt.

"You know as well as I do that they are my parents, don't you? We can't do anything, anything at all. Can you imagine what would happen?"

"We have to go."

"No we don't. We're staying here and we're going to enjoy one of the most amazing things that's ever happened to me."

"What do you mean?"

"I just want to be with them, maybe just for today, I don't know. I knew as soon as I saw them, I felt it, felt something. I can't explain. It's like, it's like...everything has snapped into place. I don't really know how to explain it, but I feel whole again. I feel complete. Do you know what I mean?"

"I think so," she said, looking up at him again, a tear falling from the side of her eye.

Pascal held her face in his hands.

"All because of you, otherwise I'd never have known," he said, kissing her on the lips.

"Come on, let's get back, my beer's getting warm."

"You won't, will you?"

"No, I won't. Just give me this. Please?"

Holding hands, they slowly made their way back to the terrace and, as they approached the table, Clara smiled nervously, looking across at Pascal, who appeared to have gone into a dream-like state.

He looked at Rose and over her shoulder towards Horacio, who was busy adding wood to the red hot embers under the black metal chimney and appeared to smile.

"Did you find what you were looking for?" asked Rose looking at both of them in turn, as they both sat down.

Pascal turned to Clara before she had a chance to reply.

"I believe so, Rose."

CHAPTER 31

Sunday was a day of rest for the president since, if the weather was behaving itself, he enjoyed grabbing a chef's apron, lighting big fires and poking meat on the grill in the traditional *asado*. On this particular Sunday he'd invited key members of the opposition, four of the leading union heads, including Luis de la Mano and a handful of his closest friends and advisors. Chief Forza, a dab hand at laying out the traditional metal stakes for hanging whole lamb and goat kid, as in some macabre crucifixion, joined him in preparing the fires early so that everything would be ready for their guests' arrival at lunchtime.

Robert had asked Margarita to join him, excluding Pimpi Pérez as he had dropped out of his AA program, after coming to blows with his sponsor. Robert felt he simply couldn't be trusted to keep off the booze, where so much would be served around right under his nose, even if he could be found relatively sober. Margarita was delighted with the news and, as she mingled with the assembled guests sipping their pre-lunch cocktails on the terrace overlooking the Buenos Aires skyline, Robert looked on. She enjoyed being the centre of attention, with Robert confident that she knew exactly what to say and when to say it. More importantly, he also knew that she was a very shrewd judge of character and could size up a complete stranger in a few seconds. She was usually right and had the uncanny ability of being able to tune in and listen to several conversations at once. That was something Robert found difficult to do, so he had asked her the night before to be his eyes and ears during the lunch, as there had been whisperings and rumours emanating from the lower chamber halls and passageways that had recently made uncomfortable listening for him.

Some stiff introductions were made, including a presidential handshake with Luis de la Mano, but since the invited guests were accompanied by their spouses, a kind of fragile decorum was being observed. Robert insisted that he and Margarita do the honours of handing around the trays of chorizos and fillet steak to the guests when they took their seats and the waiters were simply asked to ensure that the wine glasses were never empty, which Robert hoped would loosen a few tongues around the tables.

When lunch was finished and the odd assortment of guests stood around the decking chatting in small huddles, more drinks were served around. Margarita mingled, moving from group to group, charming the union men and opposition politicians, who began to let their guards down, especially since their spouses had remained seated at the table laughing and chatting, as Robert had predicted would happen.

"So, Luis, how goes it in union land? Any surprises in store?" asked Margarita, sidling up to De la Mano who was quietly chatting with the president of the central bank in a corner of the decking.

"Surprises, Mrs Campos?" he replied, looking past her uncomfortably.

"Oh come on, Luis," she said, moving a little closer. "A little bird tells me you're planning something big."

De la Mano's face flushed instantly. He was a short yet powerfully built man and he looked up at Margarita with undiluted hatred in his small, heavily lidded eyes.

"The president doesn't discuss his job with me, Luis, but I do like to stay informed," she continued. "In fact, only the other day I was talking to the British ambassador's wife, Lady Brabant, who told me that her cook had told her about a general strike next week. That's the first I've heard of it, to be honest."

"Mrs Campos, I would suggest you check your sources more carefully in future…"

"She also said that the phones at the ambassador's residence had been making an odd ticking noise ever since Limpi-Casa had been in to the residence to service the boilers. Isn't that one of your companies, Luis?"

"I can't imagine what you're referring to, Mrs Campos," he replied, taking a step back and grabbing a glass of whisky from a passing waiter.

"It just seems a bit odd to me, that's all, Luis," she continued, taking a sip from her glass and moving another step closer.

"Well, perhaps the ambassador should call the phone company…" he said hesitantly.

"Indeed. But I don't expect that particular conversation would be very interesting would it?" she said, looking over to the other side of the deck, pretending she saw someone she recognised and waving enthusiastically. "Oh please excuse me, Luis, I need to run. It's been lovely to meet you, finally."

She shook his small, chubby hand and left De la Mano with a look of indignation. As she walked across the deck towards the imposing figure of Guy, who was keeping a safe yet discrete distance from the president, she sighed.

"Repulsive little man."

"That fucking whore," De la Mano mumbled.

"Well you and fat man over there looked as thick as thieves, Mrs Campos," said Guy, smiling.

"Oh don't!" Margarita replied, with a downward tilt of her hand. "Robert didn't want to be seen talking to him, so I thought I'd take his temperature, nasty little man. I can't think why he asked him here."

Guy was very much on duty and scanning the immediate area whilst looking back to Margarita from time to time.

"Well, you'd better keep mingling then. You never know who you're going to bump into, Mrs Campos."

"Oh come on, you can call me Margarita, you know. We've known each other long enough."

"That's more than my job's worth, madam," he replied, stooping down a little and smiling.

She walked away, grabbing a glass of champagne from a passing waiter, then made her way over to Roxy Pla, who was chatting with the new finance minister, Chris Robertson. Both were in eavesdropping distance of the president of the senate and the new leader of the main opposition party, who looked to be in deep conversation a couple of feet away.

"Roxy, how lovely to see you again. You look wonderful as usual, and I just love that dress. And Chris, this must be an unusual assignment for you," she said, whilst keeping her radar firmly fixed on the conversation next to her and any others she could possibly tune into.

As far as Margarita was concerned, many of Robert's adversaries, for he had many, saw her as his mistress, in spite of the fact that he'd never been married and she was a widow. The two of them would laugh about this when lying in bed together. Many found the whole idea of the president having a girlfriend, an irresponsible anachronism. They believed he should be married to someone of significant status in order to set a good example to the people of the nation. What they were left with, however, was an immovable force who was often referred to in whispers and more lately in the media, as *The Black Widow*, a label she found amusing. She continued her teaching career and very rarely attended public events with the president. If the charade of simply being his whore continued, then so much the better, as far as she was concerned. She would play the role, dress provocatively and smile demurely for as long as it took. It wasn't difficult and if it suited her lover's purposes, then so be it.

Robert, who was still wearing his black and white striped chef's apron, held court with some of the friendlier faces from the political scene, including his attorney general, the president of the supreme court and his foreign minister. Chief Forza provided some welcome levity to the scene as he regaled the group with tales and anecdotes of his previous life in the federal police force. It was on occasions like this that Robert could feel completely at ease and, cigar in one hand, glass of champagne in the other, he switched seamlessly between Spanish and English, as he, too, recounted some experiences from his younger days.

At a carefully chosen moment and when Chief Forza was still entertaining his small group, Robert caught the eye of the provisional president of the senate, Martín Katz and beckoned him over to a shady corner of the decking.

"Martín, I'd like you to resign and take the oath as vice-president," said Robert quietly.

"Peréz?"

"Yes, I'm afraid Pimpi has health problems which prevent him from carrying out his duties as vice-president. I can rely on you, can't I, Martín?"

"Of course, Robert...erm sorry, Mr President."

"This is between you and me for now, at least until I receive the vice president's resignation," he said, shaking his hand.

Pascal slept the entire four hour journey back to Buenos Aires, during which time Clara had left her window open so that she could clear her head and keep the creeping sleepiness at bay. The long journey also gave her time to focus on the events of the last few days, and, as the car finally pulled up outside their flat in the smart Buenos Aires location of Puerto Madero, she had already come up with a plan. This hinged upon a detail that had flashed through her mind from some long forgotten history lesson in university, so many years ago.

As she was undressing Pascal and then bundling him into bed, she couldn't help but feel proud of the man she saw before her, in spite of his comically drunken state. They had stayed for a very long lunch with Horacio and Rose, because Pascal had insisted, entirely against her better judgement. But in the end her fears had been unfounded. After the third bottle of wine among them, and, when his tongue really had begun to loosen up, she had been afraid that his emotions would finally cave in and he would uncontrollably break down. In the end, after so many glasses of brandy that she had lost count, he had held his composure and somehow kept the conversation light hearted and had even managed a few raucous jokes, which had the Crawfords in tears of laughter. She felt lucky that he was a happy drunk, as it could all have ended quite disastrously. Kissing him softly, she looked at him one more time before switching off the bedroom light.

Pouring herself a glass of wine, she fired up her PC, went straight to her favourite search engine and typed in *Crawford*. Not surprisingly, the first page of results were links to Robert, his presidency and what had been written about him in the press. She lay back and drifted back to what she had been thinking as they were driving into Sancti Spiritu. What is it that makes him different? What is it about him?

Yes, yes, that's it, she thought to herself. It had been staring her in the face all along, especially today. Horacio and Rose were more British than the Brits, for crying out loud. She had been to England once or twice and from what she could remember, their genteel, almost Edwardian world views and structured habits, practically didn't exist in the Home Counties any more. They'd said themselves that they took tea every day without fail at five in the afternoon, and Pascal had actually laughed out loud. She could see that Robert was cut from the same cloth: his bearing, his composure and his English gentleman attitude. She had always noticed these and the fact that he almost always spoke English, as if it were his first language.

But that wasn't all, she thought. What had he done since coming to power? She didn't need reminding. Apart from the cage incident, which she knew had not been his idea, had been decidedly French Revolutionary and brazen, what had he done? He had sacked his finance minister and brought in a team from The London School of Economics; he had brought in the Pound Sterling as the official currency; the new Villa 31 development had become a British enclave where driving on the left was mandatory; all the road signs were in English and there had even been rumours of the official language being changed to English as well for Christ's sake.

But what did all this mean, she asked herself as she took a sip of her wine. And then she thought back to a night in the UK that had been televised all over the world, not long before he had become president. At the time, many had thought that an actual coup d'état' had taken place in Britain, but the incident had turned out to be a terror alert. Or had it? At the time the British prime minister had played it down and even then, she hadn't been convinced, nor had her contemporaries, especially Jenny at The Crusader. A possible coup d'état in Britain and Robert Crawford becomes president of Argentina? Coincidence?

Sighing, she sat back and stared at the ceiling for a few seconds, trying to make sense of it all. If Robert Crawford was not related to Rose and Horacio, then his real parents were somewhere else. But where? Were they still alive? He was embarked upon a process of what exactly? Of Anglophiling the country in the image of Britain, that's what he was doing. But why? Were there any historical precedents for this? Britain had colonised all over the world and many countries which had since gained independence still bore the marks of British influence. Just look at Australia, she thought.

With so many questions tumbling around in her head, she was confused and, being of the old school of journalism, she reached into her handbag for her trusty notepad. First she made lists of President Crawford's many actions with a British angle, rumours of others and the ministers and ambassadors he had appointed. She left a few gaps for anything she may have missed, and ended with the single word *Crawford,* followed by a question mark, at which point she took her wine glass to the kitchen, poured the remains down the sink and went out to the docks for a walk.

The barbeque had not ended as early as Margarita had expected, and the presidential couple said their goodbyes to the last guest, the bishop of Buenos Aires, at around half past midnight when, giggling like a teenager, he had to be propped up and assisted into his official car. Guy had then taken his leave and retired to his small garden chalet on the south coast of the island and they headed up to Robert's private quarters for a coffee before bed. Margarita threw off her shoes and reclined on the leather sofa opposite the windows, where she could see the half-moon reflected on the calm Rio de la Plata.

"I see you collared De la Mano, Mags. What did he have to say for himself?" asked Robert, as he was pouring the coffee.

"Not much, actually, but I'm sure he's convinced that we think his goons have penetrated the British Embassy. Pretty much as you suspected."

"I simply can't abide the man. It's his type that got this country into the mess it was in when I took over. And I see that you're picking up the official spy language, Mags," he replied, teasingly.

"Oh God, I hope not. I really don't want to make a habit of this kind of thing, you know. Some of these people are complete shits!"

"Most of them actually."

"With Peréz being top of the list."

"Which is why he didn't come today, you know that. Anyway, what else did you find out? I'm all ears," he said, pouring them both a glass of Remy Martin.

"It sounds as if you're going to have a general strike on your hands, at least reading between the lines, and De la Mano's reaction."

"What else?"

"Don't forget I could only overhear snippets of conversations. Just bits and pieces really."

"I know, just tell me what you remember," he said, sitting down next to her with a sigh.

"I heard quite a few people talking about all this British stuff as well. You know, the pound, the finance minister being a Brit, the street signs. Someone even said something about driving on the left, for God's sake," she said laughing.

"Go on."

"Tell me that's not true. Driving on the left? Whatever next?"

"Not exactly, Mags. It's a pilot scheme at the moment down at the site of Villa 31. We're just playing with some ideas, that's all."

"García Island was mentioned once or twice, and I'm sure I heard one of the senators say something about military exercises. They didn't sound too happy, actually."

"All pretty much as I suspected."

Robert was careful not to bring Margarita completely into the picture; the less she knew, the better, for her own sake. One detail was important, though: Putting De la Mano off the scent at the British Embassy, to continue his amateur sleuthing efforts on the US side. Robert had discovered his activities long ago and now, nine months into the presidency, with his plans still at a very delicate stage, the last thing he wanted was some union imbecile bumbling into his territory. He also had good reason to exclude the USA completely from his plans. He had always felt that the Anglo -American 'special relationship' was a one way street, a situation he expected Jack to rectify, but he also knew that De la Mano and his hounds would continue their sniffing through the US embassy and thence in Washington. All he had to do was plant the necessary information, and that wouldn't be terribly difficult.

Robert then switched the lights off and tapped a button on the remote. As he took Margarita in his arms and moved slowly over to the windows overlooking the dark, rippling river, *Moon River* came gently and soothingly from the speakers. She held Robert's hand close to her chest with her face snuggled into his neck, and as they swayed gently to the music, his other hand pulled her waist closer to him as he kissed her hair softly, closing his eyes.

In the pale light of the half moon, Clara walked along docks in the warm breeze, then stopped and rested her folded arms against the stainless steel guardrails. She looked down at the wavelets breaking gently against the walls and then to the half-moon sitting at a slight angle over the far horizon. A thin cloud moved slowly across the middle of the crescent moon and she absentmindedly looked at her watch, which told her it was five minutes past three. Looking around, back down the road to the twinkling street lights near her flat, she watched as a car moved slowly past, noticed no other people out and about and thought of Pascal, whom she expected to be sleeping very deeply. She thought of Crawford, the name and that history class that had come back to her so fleetingly during the drive back from Sancti Spiritu.

Sitting down on a damp concrete bench, she thought back to the class she had attended, which covered the British invasions in the early part of the nineteenth century, and asked herself why they kept nagging in the back of her mind. She remembered that there had been two invasions, which had both ended rather badly for the British, a fact that was not lost on the military junta during the years she was at university. Most of the names of the British generals involved in the battles had escaped her, although many of her generation remembered the name Beresford. Artefacts from his surrender were on display at the Cabildo in the Plaza de Mayo, which she had visited on numerous occasions. And yes, she, too, had heard the murmurs 'If only the English had won...' which she had always brushed aside as a hopeless excuse from a dysfunctional society, always looking for someone else to blame for their woes.

But she felt sure she was missing something, and, taking the notepad from her handbag, held it up to the faint moonlight and scribbled the word *Beresford* under her previous entry which read *Crawford*.

No, it cannot be, she thought as she walked back beside the marina towards her flat, remembering another faint recollection of that history class as she unlocked the door and wishing that she had paid more attention to the professor. Sitting at her PC again, she searched for *Beresford, Buenos Aires invasion*, and began reading an article published by a well-known military history web site. As her eyes moved down the page, she stopped and let out a gasp.

'*Major General Robert Craufurd was forced to retreat...he offered to shoot the traitor Whitlocke for cowardice...Whitlocke was later court marshalled...*'

She sat down on the sofa and stared at the ceiling again. Was it simply a coincidence that a general in the British army had once led a failed invasion of Buenos Aires and that, nearly two hundred years later the country was now being led by his namesake? Two men, two hundred years apart with practically the same name? Had *Craufurd* morphed into *Crawford*? She wasn't sure at all; how could she be, she asked herself. She felt however that it could be the key she had been looking for.

"Shit!" she exclaimed, throwing her pen down on the table. "Shit!"

By now, Clara was wide awake, as her mind had gone into overdrive trying to process the information at hand. She went to the kitchen, switched on the electric kettle, looked at the wall clock which read four twenty five, and decided that it was now too late to go to bed, where she probably wouldn't sleep anyway. She took her strong black coffee back to the PC, curled her legs up, rubbed her eyes and started searching again. Her target was the Crawford lineage, on which there was a surprising amount of information. She soon discovered that her general had been born into a respected Scottish clan near Lanark, Scotland. She typed in *heirs to Robert Craufurd* in case she had missed some important detail, but kept coming back to the numerous Craufurds who had died 'without issue'. She then scrolled a little further through the search results, hit 'next' and 'next' again; then, just as she was about to shut down the PC, she spotted a link buried in page twelve of the search results, which read *Crawford family in illegitimate son claim*, at which point she put her hands up to her face and almost screamed with delight, realising that the family name had somehow become anglicised in its spelling.

Reading further into the footnote news story published by *The Scotsman* newspaper in 1895, it was claimed that a son had been born out of wedlock to a maidservant at Lanark Castle whilst in the employ of Sir Richard Crawford, who was referred to as the father in the story. There being no further information at all on the family, she had to assume that, since the Crawford clan probably didn't want any association with the so called illegitimacy, any stories relating to Sir Richard's descendants would be buried.

With the rising sun now creeping into the living room, she glanced over at the wall clock in the kitchen and made a coffee for Pascal, hoping he wasn't too hungover from the day before.

"Oh dear," he croaked, rubbing his eyes. "What time is it?"

"Time for work."

"Is it Monday already?"

"I'm afraid so, my love," she replied handing him the coffee and sitting on the side of the bed. "Listen, I need your help."

Clara explained what she had discovered during the night and admitted that she had pretty much hit a brick wall.

Pascal yawned.

"Births and deaths? Marriages? Land registers? Oh Christ, I feel rough. Give me ten minutes, would you?"

Half an hour later he joined a despondent looking Clara on the sofa.

"Newspaper archives, social events, that kind of thing? But you need to narrow it down and we only have a surname, don't we?"

"They could be anywhere," said Clara yawning.

"Let's keep it simple and assume the family remained in Scotland. They probably own land or bought property over the years and more than likely had a telephone installed. Why don't you start there?"

"I must be losing my touch," she said wearily.

"I don't think so," he said. "Look, I've got to go to work as I've got a web site to finish. You crack on with phone numbers and I'll dig down for social event stories, that kind of thing."

"Pascal, there must be thousands of Crawfords and Craufurds in Scotland. How the hell are we going to narrow it down?"

"No idea. We'll just have to hope that a face pops up somewhere," he replied, yawning.

CHAPTER 32

At seven forty five on Monday morning, Robert woke up next to a sleeping Margarita, swung his legs out of bed, stood up and instantly regretted it. His head pounded like a jackhammer and he wasn't sure if he could feel his mouth, so he sat back down and gazed at the naked sleeping body next to him. He was tempted to take her in his arms and kiss her right there and then, but decided against it as his head was literally swimming and he thought he might pass out in the process. Kissing her gently on the cheek, he shuffled off on the long journey to the kitchen in search of the coffee maker.

As he was drinking his coffee and beginning to gather his wits, he switched on the TV news, lit a cigarette and strolled out onto the balcony. He could hear the news vaguely in the background whilst leaning against the railings, but pricked his ears up when he heard the TV announcer mention that a general strike had commenced earlier that morning. Startled, he turned around, looked at the screen and saw that a crowd of thousands had gathered in the Plaza de Mayo. He sighed resignedly, looked up to the heavens, cursed Pimpi for not having alerted him and dashed back into the kitchen. Jabbing the speaker phone on the breakfast bar, he asked to be patched through immediately to Pimpi Pérez, saying that he should be dragged bodily to the phone if necessary and then he hung up. After a quick shower, he dressed whilst lovingly contemplating the still sleeping Margarita and then returned to the kitchen, hitting *redial* on the speakerphone.

It transpired that his vice president had decided to go on another bender, had been thrown out of at least two dockside bars, had started a fight over a transvestite hooker in The Pink Flamingo and had ended up sleeping it off in his car on the street outside his flat. When Robert's security detail had located him, he was still drunk, so under Guy's leadership, they extricated him from his car, manhandled him up to his flat, forced him to vomit and put him to bed. Guy had insisted on one of the agents remaining in the flat to keep an eye on him just in case he either took to the bottle again or attempted to harm himself.

"Wake him up and get some coffee down him. I'll be there in an hour," Robert shouted at the phone.

Once the president's helicopter had landed safely at the Casa Rosada, he rushed down to his waiting Range Rover with Chief Forza in tow and told the driver to get him to Pimpi's flat as soon as possible. Once inside the flat they found the vice president being plied with black coffee at the kitchen table by a security agent.

"Would you leave us for a few moments please, Chief?"

When they had left, Robert sat down opposite his friend and lit a cigarette, which he passed over to him.

"Tell me, Pimpi, how long do you think we can carry on like this?"

Trembling and sweating as if in withdrawal, Pimpi was unable to hold the coffee mug steady enough to drink from, so Robert helped him bring it to his lips between puffs on the cigarette. He didn't say a word or even try to, and Robert waved his hand over the bloodshot eyes of his friend, without eliciting the slightest reaction.

"Chief! Back here please," he ordered, standing up.

"Yes, sir?" asked the chief, opening the door a few inches.

"Find a sheet or something to cover him up and get him down to the car, pronto, before the press get wind of this. I'll join you in a minute."

Robert watched them leave, propping up the almost comatose vice president between them, a dark blue sheet now draped over his head. He then shut the door and began to look around. The two bedroomed flat was comfortable and stylishly decorated yet had degenerated into an alcoholic's hovel. Discarded bottles of whisky and vodka lay all around the kitchen surfaces and floor, weeks of dirty dishes remained unwashed in the kitchen sink and one look inside the main bedroom was enough for him to not even wish to venture into the bathroom.

In the living area, which opened to a patio containing a couple of broken white plastic garden chairs, he found discarded women's underwear, used condoms, overflowing ashtrays, more empty bottles scattered around the floor and, in the corner on a small table next to the TV cabinet, a picture of a woman, who bore a resemblance to Pimpi himself. Robert assumed that it must be his mother and then, with the realisation of how little he really knew his old friend, he sat down gingerly on the sofa and put his hands over his face.

He had always known his friend to be a troubled soul, but had never bothered to ask if there was anything he could do to help and he felt ashamed of himself. Pimpi, in his big brash manner had always radiated confidence. But now he could see the entire act was a sham; a kind of defence mechanism which eventually led to his complete dependence on alcohol and many other mind bending substances.

He took a tissue from his pocket and wiped his eyes as he stood up and made for Pimpi's private desk behind the sofa.

Most of the drawers contained empty bottles of booze and boxes of prescription painkillers. One contained a .22 handgun and the lowest drawer held a black shoebox tied up with white string. Ripping off the string, he opened the box and found bundles of letters, none of which appeared to have been opened. The first letter was from his mother, dated three years previously, asking when he could visit her in Rio Cuarto and saying how proud she was that he had done so well in his life. But he could read no more. Most of the rest of the letters appeared to be from his mother he thought, judging by the handwriting on the envelopes. And three others were from a different person. He didn't feel the slightest compunction in reading one of them and wasn't entirely surprised to find that it was a love letter that went into a great deal of personal and intimate details, swearing love, devotion and other sweet nothings. He couldn't bear to read the entire letter, but flipped to the last of the four pages to find that it was signed simply, '*Your ever loving Sergio.*'

Packing up the shoebox exactly as he had found it, he put it back neatly in the bottom drawer, shut the door to the flat very quietly behind him and, accompanied by two security agents, made his way to the waiting Range Rover, with the .22 handgun resting in the inside pocket of his jacket.

"Back entrance, Casa Rosada and don't attract any attention," ordered Robert as he peered through the passenger window.

When the car drew up at the rear entrance of the Casa Rosada, Robert instructed Chief Forza to take Pimpi down to the basement out of sight and to make him comfortable, but not to leave him unattended under any circumstances.

"Roxy, we need to find a rehabilitation clinic for the vice president," said Robert, now pacing up and down in his office.

"I know just the place, Mr President. It's discrete and out in the countryside far away from the paparazzi. You know, the one those celebrity footballers use," she replied, adjusting the frame of her glasses with her forefinger.

"Quite so, Roxy. Make it happen if you please. You know the drill and will you please prepare a statement to the press for my approval in, shall we say an hour's time?"

"When will Mr Pérez be going to the clinic, sir?"

"As soon as humanly possible, Roxy. That will be all, thank you."

When Roxy had taken her leave and closed the door quietly behind her, Robert took the satellite phone from his desk and hit redial. Jack answered almost immediately.

"Jack, a snag has cropped up that you will probably see splattered all over the TV, so I thought I should forewarn you," he said, explaining the vice-president's misadventures and his plans to deal with the problem.

"A role to which he isn't at all suited, as I'm sure you'll agree; however it could be a serious problem, which would throw our plans into total chaos," replied Jack, with an edge to his voice that Robert could never remember hearing before.

He would now have to insist on Pimpi's resignation, of that he had no doubt. His chat with Martín Katz had been timely.

"Jack, I have the matter in hand already, but thank you for your concern."

There was a pause on the line and he hoped that Jack was convinced by his answer.

"I sincerely hope so. Just keep me posted, as usual," he said, pausing.

"So, what else can you tell me? Operation Blenheim coming along?" Jack asked.

"Yes as a matter of fact and they're looking forward to playing with a few new toys as it happens. Not that they'll get much of a chance, of course."

Robert went on to brief his mentor-in-chief, which included the confirmation of most favoured nation status for the United Kingdom, reciprocal of course; the bill currently making its way through parliament to adopt English as the official language with the auxiliary effects of road signs, official documents, newspapers, restaurant menus and such like. He also informed Jack that he had decided to shelve the driving on the left initiative as it would require a massive upheaval and cause a disastrous effect on the home grown motor industry, which only manufactured left hand drive cars anyway, the majority of which were exported to countries that drove on the wrong side of the road, as far as he was concerned.

"We can live with that," said Jack.

"You should also know that we're removing all the propaganda fiction from the national school curriculum, rewriting it in English, with a heavy emphasis on the 'Australia of the South' principal we spoke about in the beginning. You remember that don't you?"

"Indeed I do, go on."

"The cultural roots of the country will be difficult to eradicate completely of course and will only change over time, but small details such as the King's head on the sterling currency, which will be in circulation shortly, of course; landmarks, language and the general day to day of life should act as a subliminal trigger in the long run, when the King becomes the actual head of state, as we discussed."

"Correct."

"Over the next two weeks I'll be visiting each of the thirty two states within the country, abolishing the position of governor and replacing them with councils responsible directly to Buenos Aires. Each of the departmental municipalities within the states will retain their elected mayor of course, but this will eradicate the medieval fiefdoms that have been established over decades and pave the way for the Crown Republic."

"Excellent, but are you sure that you will be able to achieve all this before Operation Blenheim has been successfully concluded?"

"Not necessary, Jack. The conclusion of Operation Blenheim will be the beginning of the new republic, so to speak."

"Go on."

"As you know, the resources in the south...the Dead Dog shale fields, not to mention the recent finds off the Valdez Peninsula, will effectively become British territory anyway once Blenheim has concluded."

"Quite so and of course the union flag flying over the Casa Rosada, or at least your version of the new national flag."

"Clearly there are aspects of the plan that I simply cannot start rolling out until Operation Blenheim has concluded, Jack. Surely you understand that?"

"Naturally old chap, but at the very least I expect you to ram some of the new legislation through parliament tout de suite."

Robert's patience with Jack was wearing thin, but he decided to bite his lip.

"There will be resistance of course and the passage of the bills through parliament will be rough, of that I have no doubt. But if push comes to shove, I retain the power of presidential decree as you know."

"The nuclear option, to coin a phrase. But yes, you will always have that."

"Yes, I will," replied Robert. "And finally the state visit of the King."

"Not exactly a state visit old boy, bearing in mind the opening of parliament in BA. More a confirmation of the crown, so to speak, but I get your drift."

Robert concluded the conversation and threw the sat-phone into the drawer. Leaning against his office window with the palms of his hands, he looked across at the river and wondered how much longer he could keep playing the game.

CHAPTER 33

I think I've found something."

Pascal had sent a text message, so Clara immediately picked up the phone as she sat at the kitchen breakfast bar.

"Go on."

"A picture published in the Helensburgh Gazette. It shows a charity event in the town - a dinner at some hotel by the looks of it - dating back to 1957. A Mr. and Mrs. Charles Crawford are named as guests, along with a naval officer. The picture isn't very good at all, very blurred and black and white of course."

"That's it? Doesn't it say anything else?"

"I'll fax it to you," said Pascal.

Until that point Clara had been floundering about hopelessly, having found thousands of Crawfords through online sources, even after narrowing her search to the Lanark area. By late afternoon she had almost given up, but this one photograph appeared to change everything.

"Thanks Pascal, love," she said yawning and disconnecting the call.

The charity event was reported to be in aid of the local Boy Scouts and the three line article simply said '*Mr and Mrs Charles Crawford being thanked for their donation by Commodore Laurie Best, Faslane Naval Base.*'

She then focused her search on the Helensburgh area, an action made considerably easier now that she had a first name. She found eight Crawfords, two of whom were named Charles. One shown as a

Helensburgh address and the other a telephone number in Rhu, which she discovered was a tiny village a little northwest of Helensburgh, but no street address was shown.

As she lay her head back on the sofa she realised that she had gone into autopilot. Her mind wasn't absorbing information any longer and she felt jetlagged, so made her way to the bedroom, shut the door and lay down in the darkness thinking of nothing else but the Crawfords. What would she do if she discovered that the president's real parents were alive and living in Scotland? Who would she tell? Would she tell anybody at all?

As President Crawford was preparing his address to the nation on the health of the vice president and calling a meeting of his military chiefs in preparation for Operation Blenheim, Luis de la Mano was taking a seat in the boardroom of an expensive ground floor office suite somewhere in New Mexico. He wasn't entirely sure of the location due to the rigid secrecy that his contractors, SOF19 had insisted upon. Arriving at Albuquerque Airport just before midnight, he had been quietly escorted through the VIP lounge by two men in dark suits and into a black four by four, fitted with heavily tinted windows blocking all views to the outside world. The journey to the boardroom had taken nearly an hour, and appeared to have taken more than two dozen turns to confuse its passenger. His final arrival point had been an underground parking garage.

He was now seated across from three serious looking, middle aged, fit looking men in expensive suits, and an attractive red haired woman dressed in an ivory pantsuit who was taking notes. The meeting lasted no more than forty five minutes, the conclusion of which established the veracity of his credentials, the offshore account into which he should deposit the first tranche of fees, the location of the project and expected size of the support requirement. Before he was handed the one-time use security code, which would enable him to give the green light via a cellular phone which he would be provided with, he was asked to confirm his preferred level of initiative on a scale of one to five. It wasn't an option he had given a great deal of thought to, but reflecting on the issues at hand and those that would be at stake in the future, he thought to hell with it, and opted for the highest level of initiative on offer. The three men nodded to each other and left the room. The red headed woman then escorted De la Mano to the four by four waiting in the underground car park.

Clara spent the next week phoning directory enquiries in Scotland, but came up blank with the two Charles Crawford telephone numbers, as neither call was being picked up. On nothing more than a hunch and the small detail that Rhu happened to be closer to the naval base, she decided to find a hotel in the small village. Trusting her instincts and knowing she'd had these hunches before, she reminded herself why she was a journalist.

She had talked over her plans with Pascal a couple of days after their return from Sancti Spiritu and he was in complete agreement that she should go alone to Scotland. He would look into Rose and Horacio's background, especially since she had heard them mention Scotland at least once during their lunch, in some vague reference to a holiday they had once taken there. He couldn't remember much of the exchange past the brandy at the barbeque, but he felt sure that he could follow it up.

Clara loathed cooking and considered the whole exercise a messy, time consuming business which she felt could be better spent on her other passions such as investigative journalism, high tech gadgets, fast cars and motorcycles. She possessed neither a fast car nor a motorcycle, but she did enjoy watching Pascal cook as she dreamed of once again jumping into the saddle of a Triumph, if she could just hire one once she got to Scotland. As Pascal prepared their dinner the night before she was due to fly across the Atlantic, she explained to him once again what she had discovered, where she hoped to go and what she thought she would do with the information when she returned a week later.

CHAPTER 34

W hat Clara was not aware of, as she sipped her Cabernet in the kitchen of her small flat in Buenos Aires, was the Maitland Group doing practically the same in a private dining room at the back of a small club on Wardour Street, in the West End of London.

"Ladies and gentlemen, please allow me to introduce Robert Crawford, the president of Argentina," said a smiling Jack Forsyth, clapping his hands and turning to the huge plasma TV screen on the wall at the end of the dining room.

A tanned and presidential looking Robert Crawford walked into view, with the new national flag of the country he presided over, hanging from a wooden flagpole to his left. Behind him a view of swaying palm trees and a glistening Rio de la Plata completed the panorama.

The striking amalgam of the familiar red, white and blue of the United Kingdom and the pale blue and white of the old national flag brought a gasp from some of those present and nods of approval from others.

"Thank you, Jack, my good friend, and please may I say what a pleasure it is for me personally to finally find myself in such august company."

There followed a hearty round of applause from each and every member of the assembled company, who then raised their glasses and in unison, loudly toasted their British President.

The Maitland Group's origins could accurately be dated back to 1814, two years after the death of General Craufurd and six months before the Battle of Waterloo the following year. Sir Timothy Packe, a veteran commander who had fought alongside his friend Robert Craufurd, became incensed by the cowardice of Lt General John Whitlocke during the second invasion of Buenos Aires in 1807 - resulting in a humiliating British surrender - so he formed the secret group with the sole purpose of taking, by any means possible, what he and others considered to be rightfully theirs. Over the decades that followed, numerous opportunities had presented themselves for an all-out invasion of Buenos Aires, but on each occasion cooler heads and national politics had ultimately prevailed. Towards the end of the Second World War, it was suggested during one particularly animated group meeting, that a move against the city would be timely, especially since the eyes of the world were looking elsewhere. But the plan also faded away because of a complete lack of resources when Britain was practically on its knees.

The secret cabal, whose membership varied from year to year, met for lunch annually by invitation only and was comprised of no more than twelve individuals, both military and civilian, with each member of the group being rigorously vetted. The single most crucial proviso being a direct descendancy from a serviceman who had served in battle at either the first or second invasion of Buenos Aires. But as the decades passed, the group's numbers had begun to dwindle and at the 1956 meeting, only four members attended with no clear leader taking charge, so interest in the entire project began to wane.

In the late fifties, Sub Lieutenant Jack Forsyth was invited to join the group, having been given special and extraordinary dispensation. His antecedents had not fought in either of the two invasions, but in a later sea battle north of Buenos Aires in 1845 for control of Argentine rivers. That particular battle had been victorious for the Anglo-French fleet, but had only scored a few trade and political points and was far from being an invasion of the mainland.

The young Jack Forsyth brought new vigour with his radical ideas, so momentum within the group gathered pace once again. Following the meeting in 1956, Jack proposed biannual meetings and for the first time in its history, the inclusion of two outsiders, his close friends Lieutenant Michael Gordon and Flight Lieutenant Richard Jennings, was approved.

It was during the summer meeting of 1957 that Jack proposed the outline of his alternative and stealthier plan which, after some initial misgivings from an entirely ethical standpoint, was accepted unanimously.

The Maitland Group kept meticulous records of their meetings, and the heavy, leather bound journals were always hidden away by the group chairman in a secret place in the club dining room. As long as they were able to keep up the charade of military reunions, all the members felt that the records were entirely safe and would never be discovered, mainly because they all imagined that no one appeared the slightest bit interested. Besides, none of the members wanted the responsibility of personally holding written records, so they always remained where they were.

In the handwritten journals were accounts of the much revered Crawford lineage and by early 1958, Jack knew exactly where the young Charles Crawford and his new wife Anna lived in Scotland. They had been married in the spring of the previous year, which is when he had already tasked himself to quietly befriend them, the sole purpose of which he had outlined to the assembled group.

"I believe we have reached a crucial stage in the Maitland Group," Jack had started by saying.

"Successive governments and their policies have made it impossible for more, shall we say, direct action to go forward. My proposal is that we infiltrate the country by other means. To be precise, I propose a Crawford as president and I've already found our candidate."

The assembled members, of which there were nine, listened intently, leaned forward on their seats, took the occasional sip of their drinks and some puffed away on expensive cigars.

"Charles and Anna Crawford were married in May last year, but there are of course a number of imponderables," he said, taking a sip from his brandy whilst looking up at the group members opposite him.

"Clearly we have no idea whether their first born will be a male child..."

"Jack, I'm sorry for interrupting," said Carmen Pack. "But why does the child need to be male? There are already precedents of women taking positions of power actually, or would that complicate the issue?"

"That's a fair point, Carmen, and frankly one that I hadn't actually considered. Would a woman president complicate the issue? You tell me, you're a woman."

"The plan is to install a president in the country and if he or she is trained correctly, surely it matters little whether it's a man or a woman," she replied looking around the table for support.

"My view is that what we have planned would be infinitely simpler to administrate were it to be a male child, Carmen," Jack replied.

The Maitland Group could never be accused of being socially progressive exactly, since it had only one singular objective and that objective would be seen by most people as repulsive, outdated and fantastic in the extreme. It was, however, populated by realists. They had had their hopes dashed far too often over the years and now they had to deal with hard facts - the ebb and flow of events in the real world. The general consensus therefore was that, male or female, the first child born to the Crawfords would be president. It was simple reality.

"The *modi operandi* are regrettably distasteful and I outline them thus," said Jack solemnly, looking at each member of the group in turn.

"I will personally use my Royal Navy leave to befriend the Crawfords, whilst staying at a small hotel in Helensburgh on the Gare Loch, which is only about two miles from Rhu, where they now live, running a small farm. In fact, I'll be motoring back up to Scotland this very evening," he said, pausing and glancing at his watch.

"It's also worth noting that I will be taking up my new position as one of the junior base engineer officers at the naval base only a few miles away, on the fifteenth of this month, which will give me a great deal more opportunity to socialise with the Crawfords until zero point."

"Zero point?" asked Sir John Beresford.

"The point of no return, Sir John, but I'll come to that in a moment if you don't mind."

"I'm sorry, Jack, please carry on."

"In an ideal world, the baby would go to full term, we would acquire it immediately at birth by means yet to be decided and thence it would be transported with all haste to a hospital a few hours from Buenos Aires."

"Jack, you say a few hours from the capital? How do you already know this?" asked Carmen Pack.

"Because the new parents will already be living there and waiting for the baby to arrive," said Jack, looking at his watch.

The entire group breathed in a collective sigh and looked at each other with bemused frowns.

"The two people I propose know only as much as they need for the purposes of the plan. That is to say, they will raise the child in a manner deemed fit for a future president of their country, directed and encouraged by this group, of course. But the key to success will be their total cooperation. In other words, they will bring the child up as one of theirs."

"Jack, you're assuming that Anna is going to become pregnant, of course," said Carmen.

"She already is," replied Jack. "Why else would I have called this meeting?"

There was murmuring around the table and some raised eyebrows.

"You're proposing not just baby theft, Jack, but identity appropriation. Not something that I personally find tasteful in the least," said Barry Wyndham, whose forebear had once been minister of war.

"I am proposing precisely that, Barry, but the group is disposed to hear any new ideas that you may have," said Jack, his eyes raised and motioning with his hand towards the other members. Barry coughed nervously and took a sip of his Claret.

"Ladies and gentlemen," Jack continued. "For this plan to work we need to pay great attention to details. If our man, or indeed our woman, is to become president, they will be raised and will grow up in that country and for that they will need native born parents. They will be second generation, their parents having been born in Britain, so they will have been greatly influenced in our ways, the British ways. They will be established members of the community and will run a large ranch, known locally as an *estancia*. There will be no room for doubt, they will speak Spanish like natives and they will have absorbed all the peculiarities of the local culture. In a word, they will blend in and nobody will be any the wiser. The parents we have chosen are the perfect match in all respects. They are unable to bear children, which is a key aspect to this plan. They have also assured me of their complete cooperation. I should also say that, with the group's approval of course, a stipend for life, plus expenses pretty much seals the deal."

"You've already chosen the parents Jack? How on earth…?" Asked Colonel Riggs-Popham.

"Colonel, our cultural attaché in Buenos Aires, a member of this group by the way, has spent a considerable time liaising with the Anglo community, which is vast and spread throughout the province of Buenos Aires and beyond. As you will know, during the last century many British families settled vast tracts of land and founded numerous small towns in the interior. It's no surprise then that the families have names such as Robertson, Williams, Campbell and the like, but we needed to find a Crawford family, of which there are many, so we settled on Horacio and Rose Crawford in Sancti Spiritu. They were the perfect choice and serve our purposes perfectly since the family ranch is isolated and far from the chatter of Buenos Aires."

"Jack, how does our child fit into all this? What I mean is, why didn't they just adopt a baby over here in England and take it back with them?" asked Michael Gordon.

"That's a good point, Michael and the answer is two-fold. Persuading the Crawfords to raise a child as their own was one thing, but establishing their fertility, as it were, became a little fraught. Besides, the child wouldn't be a true Crawford if that were to happen and any adopted child would never be considered as bloodline. It's very simple really and is the fundamental underpinning of the entire plan as far as we should be concerned. He or she has to be a true Crawford from the original Craufurd line." he replied.

"Furthermore, the child must be shown to have been born in Argentina, but that is a detail which can easily be overcome, bearing in mind the arcane national identity procedures they have in place over there. In fact, I would suggest that this aspect of the project will be the least troublesome for us," he said, pausing.

"So, with your permission ladies and gentlemen, allow me to reaffirm the noble values that underpin this group with a short reading from the 1891 writings of one Rev Alexander Henry Craufurd, grandson of Major General Robert Craufurd."

"*When the troops arrived near Buenos Aires, the Spanish commenced hostilities, but Gen. Craufurd, at the head of his light troops, made a vigorous charge, drove back the enemy in utter confusion and captured nine guns and a howitzer. I am perfectly certain that Buenos Aires would have been taken straight off if my grandfather had been supported by the cowardly General Whitlocke and with little or any loss. And thus, the future leader of the audacious Light Division would have saved England from its greatest military disgrace and ignominy.*"

The room fell silent and those seated around the table nodded sagely in acknowledgement of the core values of which they had just been reminded.

"So you see ladies and gentlemen, the need to place a British born Crawford child in the country is the highest aim of this group and to that end, the couple who will be charged with his care will be the de facto parents of the young child, in this case Horacio and Rose. Carmen, you and your husband have been selected to undertake the extracurricular education of the child when he or she reaches the appropriate age. Sir Richard Farlowe-Pennington, one of our finest Special Forces and intelligence officers is, as we speak liaising with our cultural attaché in Buenos Aires and making preparations. So, as I just outlined to you all, Sir Richard has chosen the small farming community of Sancti Spiritu as the home and nominal birthplace of the future president."

"Jack, I'm still unclear on exactly how you intend to acquire the new-born child from its mother. You can't just walk into the hospital and steal it, can you?" asked Admiral Murray.

"No James, clearly we can't. The actual modus operandi is something I shall have to work out pretty much on an ad hoc basis closer to the time of the birth, which will be highly dependent on my friendship with Charles and Anna at the time. It will also be likely that I will need the assistance of Michael and Richard in the final stages," he said, looking over at his two servicemen colleagues who nodded back. "And I will call upon them at the appropriate time."

"You're absolutely certain that the Crawfords can't have any children, Jack?" asked Carmen Pack. "What if...?"

"As certain as I can be, Carmen. Now, is that all?"

Jack cleared up some other outstanding issues with the assembled group, asked Carmen Pack to note the time in the minutes of the meeting and proposed a further luncheon for the autumn when he assured the group that he would have a clearer picture of the plan as it unfolded.

CHAPTER 35

C lara landed at Heathrow Airport early on the Wednesday morning after a short stopover in Madrid. Her connecting flight to Glasgow was an uncomfortable experience as the west coast of Scotland was being battered by ferocious westerly gales and heavy rain, which put paid to her plans to hire the motorcycle she had long dreamed of. She carried with her a backpack and a shoulder bag for her new laptop which doubled as a handbag; her trusty notepad she carried in an inside pocket of her black, full length leather coat. She had booked her hotel by phone and whilst waiting for the car hire formalities to be completed, she peered through the airport windows at the high winds and torrential rain, hoping forlornly that the weather would clear up for at least an hour or two.

By lunchtime she had arrived in the village of Rhu, checked into her room at the Rosslea Hall Hotel situated next to the local yacht club and decided to push through the jetlag and begin her quest in earnest. With the arrival of autumn the hotel had cut down on its staffing levels and the owner was now attending to new guests himself. She found him seated behind the reception area once again when she came down from her room.

"Oh hello, it's a lovely room by the way, Mr Thompson," she said, glancing quickly at the badge he wore on his lapel.

"You've got the pick of them all really. Off season you see. What brings you here anyway?" he asked as he busied himself at the desk.

"It's Clara. Clara Tomkinson," she said, extending her hand.

"Dave Thompson. I'm the owner and chief bottle washer," he replied with a beaming smile.

"Actually, I'm a genealogy specialist and a family friend has asked me to trace their ancestry."

"How interesting. I was wondering what brought you to Rhu when I saw you arrive. There's not much here really, except the naval base and the yacht club."

"It's very beautiful though," she replied.

"Not so much today," he replied, nodding his head up towards the windows.

"I wondered if you could help me," she said, deciding to plunge in head first. "Would the name Crawford mean anything to you?"

"Crawford, Crawford," he said, looking upwards. "There used to be a bed and breakfast run by someone of that name I think, over by Moon City, but I think it's closed now. We occasionally sent people over there when we were fully booked in the summer."

"Moon City?"

"Oh yes, sorry. That's what the locals call the old navy married quarters over there on the way to the base," he replied, pointing vaguely.

"Did you ever meet the Crawfords?"

"No, no I didn't. Anyway that was a while back."

"How long ago would that be?"

"Two, three years ago?"

"Were their names Charles and Anna?"

"I really couldn't say as I only bought the hotel five years ago. I'm from London originally you see and all I ever did was give people the phone number for a few months and directions on how to get there, just like the previous owners did. Then I heard that it had closed down. I never met them myself."

"Well, thanks for your help, Dave" said Clara as she made to leave for the front door.

"No problem. Oh and before you go," he said, walking around to the front of the reception desk. "I know what it's like to be new around here. It takes a while for people to get to know you, so if you want to hear some local gossip, go to the pub. That's where I go, especially if I need a bit of a break from the hotel," he said smiling.

"The pub?"

"Yes, The Rhu Inn just down the road. The beer's not up to much, but there's generally a decent crowd in there."

The idea of a pub being the centre of the community was an alien concept to Clara. Being a city girl, she did her drinking in the many bars and cafes of the massive city of Buenos Aires, where no one knew or even cared where you came from.

"Well thanks, Dave, you've been very kind."

"Oh and don't bother with lunchtime sessions at the pub, it's usually deserted then. Go at around six for happy hour. That's when the locals go."

Clara then made for the hotel door, took a tentative peek outside at the high winds and torrential rain, but decided that she'd venture out later. As she passed reception again, she asked for some sandwiches and coffee to be brought up to her room and headed back up the stairs.

As she devoured her tuna sandwiches, she called Pascal, told him how much she missed him, what the flights had been like and what she had gleaned from Dave, which wasn't very much. She lay her head on the pillow, looked over at the rain lashing against the bedroom window, felt her eyes closing and decided not to fight it any longer.

Waking up later in complete darkness, she fumbled about for the bedside table light, looked at her watch and saw that it was four fifty in the afternoon. Feeling completely disoriented, she imagined that it was really somewhere around midnight, so after a quick shower, she dried herself in front of the bathroom mirror, whilst deciding what she should wear.

"Now, what should I wear to a Scottish pub?"

After squeezing into her favourite torn blue jeans, she chose the V-neck black top that Pascal was so fond of and spent the next half hour applying her make up. She then slipped on a pair of hiking boots he'd bought her a couple of years ago that she had never worn and then threw on the long black leather coat, felt for her notepad in the pocket and put her glasses on the chain around her neck. Her hair she brushed back a little, then gave up on, knowing it wouldn't last long in the awful conditions outside. With one last look in the mirror she pushed her breasts up a little, decided that she should pass muster and made her way downstairs, where she found Dave Thompson playing Solitaire on the PC in the deserted reception area.

"They've been open ten minutes already, Miss Tomkinson," he said jokingly, looking at his watch. Clara smiled, showing her gleaming white teeth, which were set off by the contrasting red lipstick she'd applied earlier.

"I hope I'm not that obvious."

"They're a decent bunch down there; you'll be fine. Have a good time."

Clara ran across the courtyard in the pouring rain to her hired Ford Fiesta, jumped into the car and slammed the door. She could have walked the few hundred yards to the pub, but the weather was so foul, she knew she'd have been drenched. Parking in the small car park at the back, which she found through a narrow entrance between the pub and the post office, she pushed at the front door, only to find that it was locked. She could hear a hubbub of chatting and laughter and so walked through another door on her left and into the public bar, shaking the rain off her head and coat as she entered.

Fifteen pairs of eyes turning to stare at you in complete silence on your first night in a strange country, thousands of miles from home is an experience unfamiliar to most people. Yet Clara took it in her stride with a sharp intake of breath, a confident smile and purposefully walked up to the bar. Aware that she was the entire focus of attention in the small bar room at that moment, she pointed vaguely at the many beer taps along the bar and saw that the barman was glued to the TV set hanging from a wall above the window.

"Hello?" she said, with her hand up.

The barman turned slowly away from the evening news and picked up a glass which he began wiping with a towel as he turned towards her.

"A cold beer, please?" she asked.

The barman, a large cheerful man with a weather beaten red face, and wearing a tatty looking green cardigan, carried on wiping the pint glass.

"Bitter or lager madam?"

"What's the difference?" Clara asked, intently aware that the same pairs of eyes were still focused on her and the only sounds she could hear were the crackling of the log fire, rain lashing against the windows and the muffled sound of the TV. The barman looked over to his right where most of the tables were.

"Allan, tell the young lady what the difference is between lager and bitter!"

"Lager's for fairies and bitter's for real men!"

At that, the entire pub erupted with laughter, the man called Allan stood up and raised his glass to the barman.

"Uh, bitter then, please."

"Half or a pint madam?"

"Well, since I don't think I'm a fairy, I'll have a pint please."

With the spell having been partially broken, the pub regulars resumed their chatting. Some glanced over in Clara's direction, sizing her up as she took a sip from her pint.

"You're not from here are you? I mean, you're not English," the barman said.

"No, I'm not. This is my first time in Scotland actually. Clara, Clara Tomkinson by the way," she said, offering her hand.

"Craig, I run this place," he said coyly extending his hand over the bar amidst the oohing and aahing from the pub regulars.

"And you lot can pipe down for a start," said Craig, blushing.

"Watch him, lady, he's a regular Don Juan," said Allan, laughing, as he turned to his friends, who all joined in the mirth.

"Don't mind them, love," said Craig quietly. "It's just their way."

"Oh no, of course not. But if only they'd slow down a bit when they talk. I'm not used to this accent."

"Well, you can ask them to slow down, but I can't guarantee much," said Craig.

Clara smiled at him and he averted his eyes shyly.

"I think I'll sit down now, they seem pretty harmless."

Holding her pint before her, she headed over towards the welcoming fireplace where she had already spotted an empty table and beside it, a small chair upholstered in green velvet and monogrammed in gold coloured lettering that read simply, "Mr C".

She made to sit at the chair next to it, realised that the small room had gone terribly quiet again, when one of the regulars stood up, pointing at the chair.

"Not that one."

"Oh, I'm terribly sorry, I didn't..."

"No one sits on Mr. C's chair," said the regular, solemnly.

"But, I wasn't going to..." she started to say, but the words simply melted away.

Christ, that was embarrassing, she thought to herself as she took off her coat and sat down on one of the other wooden chairs. At the very moment she was about to put the pint of bitter to her lips, a couple got up from their seats at the other side of the fireplace and sat down at Clara's table. She immediately felt more relaxed and simply said hello with a nervous smile.

"Brave of you to come in here like that all by yourself, love," said the woman, who was heavily made up, had a kindly looking face and appeared to be in her mid-sixties.

"Oh, I don't know," said Clara.

"I'm Marie and this is my husband Rory, by the way."

"Clara Tomkinson. Pleased to meet you."

"Do you have relatives here in Rhu, love?" asked Marie warmly.

"Uh no, not exactly."

Marie and Rory sat back in their chairs and sipped their drinks.

"I'm helping a friend. Genealogy, family trees, that kind of thing."

"Oh? How intriguing," said Marie, leaning forward. "My husband's mam does a little of that, doesn't she, Rory?" she said, looking to her husband.

"Aye," said Rory.

"Oh really?" said Clara, smiling at Rory, who appeared reluctant to interrupt his wife.

"Yes, she's convinced that she's descended from The Bruce," said Marie, laughing amidst snorts from the neighbouring tables.

Although the chatter in the public bar had resumed, Clara was acutely aware that her every word felt louder than everyone else's.

"Yes, the family name is Crawford, do you know them?" asked Clara.

The laughter and chatting quickly faded away and Rory looked over at the green velvet chair next to the fireplace with a faraway look in his eyes.

"Oh," said Marie, turning her head back towards Allan the joker, who was now leaning forward from the other table. Clara felt uneasy as the atmosphere had taken on a conspiratorial edge, yet she breathed out slowly, hoping that she'd touched a nerve.

"Charles and Anna Crawford? I believe they live here," said Clara, glancing from Allan to Rory and then to Marie in the now silent barroom. She then looked at the empty chair and the letters *Mr C*.

"Mr Crawford?" she asked, with a gesture of her hand. Marie nodded and Allan brought his pint over, sitting down at the table next to Rory.

"Aye, Mr C was a real gentleman," said Allan looking over at the green velvet monogram. "A tragedy."

"Tragedy?" asked Clara.

"Lachlan?" said Allan as he turned to look over his shoulder.

An elderly gentleman with a pronounced stoop, thinning grey hair and broken spectacles held together with sticky tape, made his way over and joined Clara's group. The rest of the regulars resumed their banter, albeit somewhat muted.

"They say Mr C was of the Crawford clan, but we never liked to ask," said Lachlan, sitting down.

"Charles Crawford. We're talking about Charles Crawford and his wife Anna?" asked Clara. She needed to be sure.

"Aye. A tragedy what happened to his wife. He was devoted to her. You could just see it in his eyes."

"What happened?" asked Clara.

"She died in childbirth, so they say," Lachlan said, staring at Mr C's chair.

"How awful. When was that?"

"Oh, way back," said Lachlan, shrugging.

"And the baby? What about the baby?" Clara asked, almost gulping as she did so.

"They say Mr C had the wee lad adopted," said Allan, turning to Clara.

"A little boy then?" Said Clara hopefully.

"Aye."

"Who adopted him? Where is he now?"

"Mr C would never talk about it and nobody asked. Well, you wouldn't would you? He wasn't a well man, actually," said Lachlan.

"You were here then?"

"Lived here all my life love. I remember when they arrived. They'd just got married and settled into High Brae Farm, up yonder," he said, nodding in the direction of Clara's hotel.

"He wasn't a well man *then* either. They call it depression nowadays, I think, but he was a different man when he was with Anna," continued Lachlan.

"Go on," said Clara

"In those days, the navy men used to come here a lot. You know, from the submarine base, as it is now, and Mr C and Anna were always in here drinking with them. Naval officers, that's right. They were officers," said Lachlan, pointing and remembering some long forgotten detail. "That's when the rumours started."

"What rumours?"

"There was one navy man who was always in here with them. I can't remember his name just now. Anyway, they never spoke to us of course. You know... officers," he said, pushing his nose upwards with his forefinger. "But they were always together, the three of them and people began to talk."

"Talk? What did they say?" asked Clara, finishing her beer.

"I think it was very unkind myself. People reckoned that there was something going on, some kind of arrangement, something odd anyway," he said, dismissively.

"Come on, Lachlan," said Allan. "Spit it out. Anna was having an affair with that officer and Mr C knew all about it. At least that's what I heard," he said, sitting back in his seat.

"Some say it was more than that Allan," said Marie, piping in.

At that moment, Clara felt she needed to just let them talk amongst themselves, so she got up, went to the bar and asked for another pint. As she was waiting, she turned and looked out of the window and saw that the rain was still sheeting down, the wind was lashing it against the glass and lights twinkled dimly across the loch on the opposite bank. Craig handed her pint over the bar.

"You've stirred them up now, young lady."

"I don't mean to cause any trouble, really I don't."

Craig shrugged his shoulders and made his way to the other end of the bar where all the action was, as Clara made her way back to her seat. They were still talking about Anna and the rumours and Clara felt she needed to draw them out a little more.

"This officer, what was he like? What did he look like?"

They looked at Lachlan, who continued. "Fair looking man, tall, distinguished. Dashing, the ladies used to say."

"Och, get away with you man!" said Marie. "My mam told me. He was more than just dashing, he was a catch. That fair hair, those icy blue eyes. Even she fancied him. They all did!"

"And Anna?" asked Clara.

"Very quiet from what I remember," said Lachlan. "Tall, fine looking lass. Poor thing."

"No point asking them, love," said Marie. "She was the sultry type, dark haired according to my mam. It was quite the scandal at the time. Tell her, Lachlan."

Lachlan took a long drink from his pint and sighed in resignation.

"People said that Mr C didn't have it in him, all pale and lanky as he was and when she got pregnant, we all said it must have been Jack. Yes, Jack that's right. I remember now," he said, pointing at Clara.

"Aye, Jack. Yes, that's right. I'd completely forgotten," said Allan.

"Ay, la mierda!" said Clara, not quite under her breath.

They all glanced at her looking puzzled.

"Oh sorry," said Clara. "And the baby?"

"The wee bairn was adopted, that's what we heard," said Marie. "Mr C had a breakdown apparently. Some say he found out the wee one wasn't his and put him up for adoption. He couldn't cope."

Marie then took a tissue from her handbag and began dabbing her eyes. The group fell silent and each stared at the nearby log fire or into their beer glasses, some of which were now empty.

Clara, eager to break the mood, stood up and asked if she could buy them all a drink.

"Ach, nonsense, lass. Sit yourself down now," said Allan standing up. "Same again, love?"

Clara felt a little guilty, yet she was warmed by her new friends' generosity and how they had been so open with her. She accepted the offer of a drink and then went on to tell them about her life in Buenos Aires, confessed to being a journalist which elicited very little surprise and simply said of her enquiries, that she was looking into something for a friend. She was sure her questions would eventually connect the name with that of the president, so she quickly steered away from any further talk of Argentina.

During her third pint of bitter, which she was enjoying far more than she had expected, Allan, Lachlan and Marie told her what they could remember of the Crawfords and the mysterious Jack.

The local talk was that, following Anna's untimely death, Mr C had locked himself away in High Brae Farm and become a recluse, answering the door to no one, until the worried villagers finally gave up. However hard Clara pressed the issue, no one could remember what had happened to Jack. He never returned to The Rhu Inn, so most people thought he'd been posted overseas or had left on a long naval patrol. Then, in the mid-eighties, a woman buying groceries was seen in the post office general store, and she turned out to be a distant cousin from Anna's side of the family. Soon, Mr C began to be seen in the village a couple of times a week, until he eventually became a permanent fixture in the pub, where he would be seen as a sad, lonely figure sitting next to the fireplace, smoking his pipe and drinking a pint which he would make last for hours on end.

"About eighteen months ago he just stopped coming in," said Allan. "I went up to the farm with Craig, didn't I, Craig?" he said looking over at the bar. "It was all closed up and deserted like he'd never even existed. Very sad."

"I heard that the farm had been a bed and breakfast for a while. What happened there?" asked Clara.

"Didn't last long. His heart wasn't in it. Besides, he was down here most of the time," said Lachlan, looking at Mr C's chair. Clara also looked at the green velvet chair and asked them about it.

"We all chipped in a few years ago and had it made for him. He was a real gent. Didn't say much, but when he did, everyone listened," said Allan.

"What did he talk about?" asked Clara.

"The Crawford Clan, generals, his ancestors, battles they'd fought in. That kind of thing. He was a mine of information, you know," said Lachlan.

Clara's eyes widened on hearing Lachlan's reply and wanted to press him further, but felt that she had heard enough for the night. She could always return the next day, she pondered. Finishing her drink, she looked at her watch, said she was tired and needed to get back to the hotel. She said she hoped to see them all again the next day and made for the door.

She hadn't noticed Rory get up from his seat earlier and, as she was opening the car door in the pouring rain, a voice said, "Jack Forsyth."

"Hello?" she said, looking around the car park. "Rory, is that you?"

But he had disappeared into the gloom as quickly as she had heard the words.

CHAPTER 36

"My fellow Argentines," the president started, keeping a close eye on the teleprompter. "We live in interesting and challenging times, none more so than today. As many of you will know, my vice president was recently taken ill and he will be undergoing surgery later today for a suspected hernia so please pray with me for his speedy recovery."

The president paused briefly, looking solemnly into the camera. That was all he felt the people needed to know about the vice president at that point and for the first time in the country's history he was delivering the presidential address in English with Spanish subtitles on the all-channel broadcast. For that reason he spoke more slowly than usual.

"The security of the nation is paramount and protecting our borders from foreign threats is a matter that I personally, as your president, take very seriously indeed."

He paused again for effect.

"Later this month the brave men and women of our armed forces will be conducting a series of military training exercises with the armed services of Great Britain, which as you know are held in the highest regard as the most professional in the world. My minister of defence will be giving further briefings and press conferences in the coming weeks, and I urge you all to welcome our guests in our usual warm, Argentine way," he said, pausing again.

"So please, when you see the ships of His Majesty's Royal Navy at anchor in the Rio de la Plata and other locations around our great shoreline, please show your happiness in every way you possibly can. They are our friends after all."

Seated at his glass and steel desk, with a view behind him of the tranquil river and palm trees blowing gently in the breeze, he paused again and then continued, smiling broadly.

"Our new currency, the pound sterling, will continue to improve the lives of families with its spending power. We have opened the doors of trade with Great Britain and other major trading partners with our most favoured nation status, and I'm delighted to inform you that our old enemy inflation is now recorded at an all-time low. So rejoice, fellow citizens, and join me in this bright new future for Argentina. Viva la patria!"

Roxy Pla who had been watching the speech from behind the camera, broke out into applause, jumping up and down excitedly.

Robert grinned and adjusted his tie as they arrived at the communications centre to a tumultuous welcome from the staff as they rose from their computer screens in a huge round of applause.

Luis de la Mano had just passed through immigration at Buenos Aires Ezeiza airport and was making his way to the exit when he stopped to watch the president deliver the last thirty seconds of his speech on a TV screen near the exit. His knowledge of English was practically zero and he stared at the smiling face of the president in open mouthed astonishment.

"Hijo de puta!" he said through clenched jaws. "Who the fuck does he think he is?"

Such was his fury that his face and neck turned crimson, prompting him to drop his suitcase and ball his hands into fists, which he opened and closed at his side, as the sweat trickled down his back. When the president asked the people to join him in his bright new future, he grabbed his case angrily and headed to the exit doors, swearing profusely to himself as his driver opened the rear door of the awaiting Mercedes.

Clara caught a TVN recording of the president's speech on an obscure satellite channel late in the morning at the Rosslea Hotel and she too was left practically speechless. It wasn't so much the Pound Sterling or the vice president's illness; she loathed Pérez anyway. Not even the military exercises had surprised her. President Crawford had had the brazen temerity to deliver his speech, not in Spanish but in the language of the very country he was hell bent on emulating. She liked Robert, she really did, yet as she thought of his many charms, his good looks and disarming smile, she couldn't shake the growing worry that his presidency may not be the work of just one man.

Having slept for almost twelve hours and missing breakfast, she asked for coffee to be sent to her room. As she poured herself another cup whilst sitting cross-legged on the bed, she began to wonder if it mattered whether she found the president's real parents. What difference would it make to anything? And then she remembered what Rory had said when she left the pub. Who the hell was Jack Forsyth anyway? Did it matter if he really was Robert's natural father?

After a shower, she opened the curtains to find that the rain had become a fine drizzle, so she dressed in the same warm clothes as the night before, thinking about Jack Forsyth as she did so. If he was still in the navy, which she doubted, he would probably have made admiral, she thought absentmindedly, although she had no idea of the inner workings of the Royal Navy or any other navy for that matter. But the Internet did know, so she plugged her laptop into the hotel room telephone socket, and a search for Jack Forsyth revealed, to Clara's astonishment that he was First Sea Lord of the Admiralty and effectively head of the entire Royal Navy. She also discovered that he was two years away from retirement in 2003, and considered by the British press to be an influential advisor to the prime minister, although Clara found that information on him was scant, other than official entries in government websites. The only photograph she could find was the same old black and white official shot which appeared to have been taken some years ago, head and shoulders only, showing an array of medal ribbons and the dolphin badge on his upper left breast. She looked closely at the off centre angled photograph, his clear eyes, the neatly brushed fair hair and his confident, commanding expression. She then brought up a recent picture of Robert and put them side by side on the screen. There was certainly a resemblance; the cut of the jaw and general profile were similar. But were they father and son? And if they were, who else knew?

At that point, she felt there was little reason to stay in Scotland any longer and even less in returning to The Rhu Inn. Mr C had vanished and as far as she was concerned, it was highly likely that Admiral Forsyth was the key to events in Argentina anyway and she intended to discover the truth herself. But how to get close to him? He appeared to be a shadowy figure at best and there were no known interviews published as far as she could see, apart from a recent reference to Admiral Forsyth in a BBC article about the upcoming joint military exercises with Argentina. But that was all she could find online. Clara knew that there had to be channels and established journalists would know of those channels.

As she was packing the last of her belongings into her backpack, she paused as she thought of Jenny Lane at The Crusader and how they had worked together on her articles on the last military dictatorship. They hadn't been in touch since the dark days of President Cristal, but she felt sure she could talk to her. In fact, she would probably want a story, so she called the newspaper.

Clara gave her name, simply saying it was a personal matter and on being told that Jenny couldn't be located, she thanked the receptionist and hung up. But she and Jenny had communicated through a number of email addresses in the past, so she fired off a message to three addresses Jenny had once used, simply saying, 'Will be in London later tonight. Need to talk about a matter of mutual interest. Here's my cell phone number. Love Clara.'

Jenny had had good reason to use throwaway email addresses; her articles on the Argentine military dictatorship had ruffled more than just a few feathers and Clara hoped that she still checked at least one of them from time to time.

By midday she had reached Glasgow and the sky had cleared leaving a warm sunny day, with puffy clouds skitting across the powder blue sky from the west. Stopping for coffee and a sandwich at a roadside café, she checked her voice mail and found nothing from Jenny, so she decided to hire the motorbike she had dreamed of for so long. After all, she wanted to ride to London, not fly.

The car hire company, phoned ahead for her and as the taxi dropped her off at on Glasgow's Great Western Road, she could see the black and chrome Triumph cruiser waiting on the forecourt practically inviting her to twist the throttle and let rip on the tarmac. The company had prepared everything for her, from the black leather protective suit and gloves to matching black helmet and when she opened up the bike on the M74 through the soft, rolling hills to the English border, she felt utterly free and for a while all thoughts of the strange discoveries she had made seem to evaporate. She had to smile when she passed the village of Crawford, which jolted her into thoughts of how she was going to handle the next stage, but for the next eight hours she simply enjoyed the ride.

Stopping at a service station on the A1, she grabbed a sandwich, found an Internet café, hoping for an email from Jenny, but there was nothing. She resent the email with her cell phone number again, then phoned ahead, booking a room at a hotel in London's Docklands. Arriving at the hotel, tired but exhilarated after her trip, she showered, changed and walked in search of a pub, finally finding a small family local about five minutes from the hotel.

Just as she had paid for her pint and was sitting down in the corner of a red velour bench seat, Jenny called saying she would be there within the hour.

Jenny Lane, a smart, no-nonsense journalist in her early fifties and dressed in blue jeans, a white blouse and a long, dark blue raincoat, was cut from the old school of journalism and a veteran of numerous war zones around the world. Getting her hands dirty, wearing flak jackets and a helmet were what she enjoyed most and Clara looked up to her with great respect, especially since the unadulterated truth was the beacon they both held so dear.

"So, do tell, what's all this about?" asked Jenny beaming enthusiastically as she kissed Clara on the cheek and sat down opposite her.

Clara told her what she had discovered in Scotland and ended by saying that the only way to be sure was to meet Jack Forsyth face to face, but confessed that she had no idea how to get to him.

"That's quite a story, Clara," said Jenny, her eyes wide. "But also a tall order. Serving military personnel are notoriously reticent about giving interviews to the press and with good reason; they're usually told not to, full stop. You're going to need something pretty persuasive to even get past his inner circle."

"He's head of the navy, so his immediate boss would be who? The chief of the defence staff if I'm not mistaken and his boss is the prime minister. True?"

"Go on."

"Surely this military training exercise should be seen as a major publicity coup for the UK. A show of power if you like and frankly I'm very surprised that the British government isn't making more capital out of this. Especially since relations have improved dramatically since Cristal was impeached and Crawford came to power. Not to mention the cooling of the UK's relationship with the U.S."

"You still have access to the president don't you?" asked Jenny.

"I have to believe I do, especially after the Charley Cristal affair. You mean…?"

"That's exactly what I mean. The only way you're going to get to Admiral Forsyth is with a nod from President Crawford. Couch it as if you're going to write a piece on the military exercises and you could even suggest a joint interview. You and me, even."

"But Jenny, if Admiral Forsyth truly is the go between for Robert Crawford, will they really want to be seen giving interviews?"

"Clara, wake up and stop being so naïve. You've heard the expression 'hiding in plain sight' haven't you?"

"Yes, of course I have," replied Clara, feeling a little prickly at Jenny's typically forthright manner.

"It's an open secret that what happened in the UK that night was nothing less than a coup d'état. Terrorist threat, my ass! I've written about it extensively and so have others, but as you would expect, total silence from the government. What I'm trying to say is that the reins of power are now so strong and so firmly established that they probably feel untouchable. And if what you suspect about President Crawford is true, a thought which hadn't occurred to me for a second to be honest, it would make sense."

"It's only a theory, Jenny, and that's all it is for the moment. But from what we know about Sancti Spiritu, Robert's real parents, what's supposed to have happened in Scotland all those years ago and now what's been happening at home since he came to power, I just can't see it as anything else."

"As anything else? As what exactly, Clara?" Jenny asked, looking intently at her friend as she sipped her gin and tonic.

Clara shifted nervously in her seat, played with the chain holding her spectacles around her neck and took a long breath before continuing.

"I think Robert was placed in my country for the sole purpose of…" she paused, not quite able to find words suitable for what was as clear as a picture in her mind.

"Yes, Clara, go on," Jenny said, leaning forward.

"For acquiring the country," said Clara, finally. "You've seen what's going on. The fact that he probably wasn't even born in Argentina is pretty damned significant wouldn't you say?"

"Not that significant, no, Clara. It's only significant if the constitution stipulates that only a natural born citizen can be elected president."

"For fuck's sake, Jenny, are you with me on this or not?"

"Doing your homework is ninety percent of the battle, darling. You know that," said Jenny, smiling benignly.

"I've done my homework already and I know the constitution inside out thanks very much. It clearly states that only a natural born citizen of Argentina can become president. Now, are you going to help me on this or not?" said Clara standing up and throwing her coat over her shoulders.

"Oh sit down, Clara! I'm with you, you know that. Come on, let's get another drink."

Jenny bought them both a drink at the bar and when she returned, Clara said, "I think this whole thing is a re-run of The Maitland Plan."

"The Maitland Plan, you said?"

"Yes, why?"

"Because I heard talk of a group and I'm pretty sure it sounded like Maitland or something," Jenny said, frowning.

"Go on," said Clara sitting up in her seat.

"There's a private club over in The West End called The Compass. Anyway, a friend of mine who's ex-army, is a member and he mentioned the name Maitland to me once. He'd been hoping to arrange an important luncheon in the private dining room but it had already been booked by another group."

"And how does Maitland fit into that?"

"Don't you see? That other group was called Maitland. The Maitland Group, I think he said it was."

Clara looked across at her friend and, deep in thought, tried to make sense of the possibilities. Could it be that the original Maitland Plan was now the blueprint? Or was this simply a coincidence and the group was in fact some industrial concern or an old school tie reunion?

She then told Jenny everything she had gleaned from historical portals about the original Maitland Plan and then asked her what she knew about the club.

"Very much an old school tie, old boys' network kind of place. I went there once and it was like stepping back in time about a hundred years. You know, men in cravats and double breasted suits, that kind of thing," she said, rolling her eyes and laughing. "I was amazed that they actually let women in!"

"Stepping back in time..." said Clara absentmindedly. Jenny studied her for a few moments before she spoke.

"Backroom deals, Clara. It's places like that where most of Britain's future history has been made. Deals done over brandy and cigars, countries divided up, governments toppled. And not just British governments either."

"Are you thinking what I'm thinking? If we could somehow arrange an informal meeting with Admiral Forsyth, you know, to discuss a potential interview and somehow steer him in the direction of that club?"

"Perhaps he wouldn't even need to be steered there," said Jenny.

"He may already be a member you mean? Could you ask your friend? Maybe show him a picture of Admiral Forsyth when you see him next?"

"I can do better than that. Hang on, I'll ask him," said Jenny, taking her phone from her handbag and tapping the keys a few times. "Done! Now let's see what he says."

Clara took a sip of her beer and flicked a stray lock of hair from her eyes.

"Is he your boyfriend or something?" she asked, looking at Jenny.

"Oh don't be silly, he's just a friend. We help each other out sometimes."

"I wasn't being silly, Jenny. I'm curious. You've never mentioned anybody."

"Because there isn't anybody. Well, there is someone but…"

"Want to talk about it?"

"No, not really. It's a bit…how do you say in Spanish?"

"Delicado?"

"Yes, something like that," said Jenny, her eyes glistening.

"Oh, how rude of me. I didn't mean to pry, really I didn't."

Jenny held Clara's hand.

"No, you could never be rude, Clara."

They were silent for a few moments and as they sipped their drinks Jenny watched Clara's eyelashes as she blinked and the way she ran her tongue over her upper lip.

"Listen, you know as well as I do that he'll never give the interview don't you?" asked Clara. "But he may well talk to us informally?"

"You do realise who we're talking about here don't you?" said Jenny.

"The head of the navy."

"He's much more than that, much more. After the coup, which nobody and I mean absolutely nobody wants to talk about, except people like us, most believed that it was Jack Forsyth pressing all the buttons. All that terrorist crap the PM was banging on about was a lie, a smokescreen. Do you follow what I'm saying?"

"I think so," Clara said weakly.

"Clara darling, not long after the coup or should I say, the so called terrorist alert," said Jenny, rolling her eyes again. "The second European referendum was cancelled, the defence spending cuts were reversed retroactively and by about ten years I might add. Britain's doors were slammed firmly shut and the Faslane submarine base was relocated lock, stock and barrel to Portsmouth. What does that tell you?"

"I know what you're saying, Jenny, and yes, it stinks. But I've been so wrapped up in this Crawford business lately…well, you know what I mean."

"Your man becomes president of Argentina a few months later, then overnight it's Cool Britannia south of the border. You couldn't make this shit up. It's fucking brilliant!" said Jenny almost choking on her drink. "So, welcome to the big boys club, Clara."

"I know, I know," said Clara, sighing. "So anyway, fancy your friend hearing about Maitland. Sounds too good to be true."

"Listen, we need to be absolutely sure about this Maitland group or whatever it is, first. If my man confirms…"

At that moment Jenny's phone vibrated in her handbag and she quickly checked the tiny screen for a message.

"He says he doesn't recognise him. Not seen him there. Damn…oh hold on," she said, studying the phone intently. "He says he knows the head waiter so he's going along for a drink."

"What, right now? I hope he doesn't make it too obvious."

"Yep, that's what he says and by the way, he's the senior defence correspondent at The London Times. He knows what he's doing, Clara."

CHAPTER 37

Luis de la Mano sat at the head of a table of eight men in a ramshackle plywood hut in the centre of Villa 36, recently earmarked for demolition by President Crawford. The red and white chequered plastic tablecloth flapped in the breeze from the open door and sunlight pierced through holes in the corrugated tin roof, creating sunbeams through the smoky room. Half a dozen bottles of cheap red wine, Coca Cola, mineral water and numerous baguettes were scattered around the table as the diners were finishing off chunks of beef and pork, cooked on the blackened brick and bedspring grill that smoked and hissed on the floor in the corner. His dining partners, all leaders of national union blocks and fervent supporters of the law of the street, looked over towards him as he rose from his seat wiping his greasy hands on his black trousers.

"This madness will soon end my friends, have no fear," he started, taking a long gulp from a glass of red wine.

"The US puppet Crawford will be gone by the end of the month," he said, turning to spit on the dirt floor. "And I don't need to remind you all of the need for total secrecy in this matter."

There were concerned, serious nods of agreement around the table.

"But we will not be alone in our struggle. We have friends ready and waiting. I only have to give the order and they will arrive..."

"Excuse me, Luis, and please don't take this the wrong way," interrupted one of the union leaders. "Are we right in thinking that you've hired an outside force to join our struggle?"

"I have indeed and I returned from a most satisfactory meeting with our friends only yesterday."

The hard faced union leaders looked at each other and then back to De la Mano.

"And who is paying for this? Why were we not informed?" asked another.

"My friends, it's all been taken care of. All I need to do is give the word, the money will be transferred and…"

"What money?" asked another, standing up.

"I had to think quickly, since I'm a signatory to the emergency funds."

Lucio Melia, who had remained largely silent at the other end of the table, jumped to his feet and strode over to the sweating De la Mano. Grabbing him viciously by the front of his shirt, he pushed De la Mano against the plywood wall.

"And I am the other signatory, together with our friend Ramón. Isn't that right Luis?" said Melia tightening his grip.

At that moment a very loud pop was heard from the darkened end of the hut, the assembled diners winced as they ducked their heads and Lucio Melia fell to the ground clutching at his bleeding throat. Out of the shadows strode a tall man wearing a white shirt and black trousers with black swept back hair, carrying in his hand a large revolver which he placed at the end of the table, then stood back again in the shadows and folded his arms.

A moment of shocked silence descended upon the group. After a moment, De la Mano calmly knelt down and felt for a pulse at the bleeding neck of Melia, who at that moment let forth a gurgle in an effort to breath.

"Victor?" said De la Mano, nodding his head towards the table. The man in the shadows slowly approached the table, picked up the gun and calmly handed it to De la Mano who took it, stood up and fired the weapon point blank into Melia's forehead. As he handed the gun back to Victor he grabbed some paper towels from the table, nonchalantly wiped the blood spatter from his face and arms and then leant forward resting his palms on the blood stained plastic tablecloth.

"Gentlemen. Do you want your country back or not?"

The remaining seven men, shocked at what they had seen, either were still seated or had pushed their chairs away and were trembling, ashen faced in the shadows.

"Sit down all of you please and Victor, remove Melia," said De la Mano.

Slowly, the remaining union leaders took their seats, some reaching for the wine with trembling hands.

"This is how it's going to be. Melia was removed as a signatory to the emergency funds as soon as you idiots reinstated him after the fiasco with Virginia. He couldn't be trusted and Ramon, Victor and I now control the joint assets. Do any of you have a problem with that?"

A few shook their heads, but most of them simply looked at De la Mano in horror and disbelief. As Victor was dragging Melia's body across the dirt floor, De la Mano continued.

"We could never take the country back alone, you all know that, which is why I have enlisted outside help. None of you will ever know the identity of the group assisting us, but you will be made aware of the plan, when we intend to strike and where you and your members will need to be. The less you know the better as far as I am concerned, especially since all of you have failed miserably in your duties to support the cause, but I expect you to, now. I hope I'm making myself clear. Ramón?"

Ramón, a diminutive, bearded man in his mid-fifties stood up at the other end of the table, thanked De la Mano for his initiatives and outlined the basics of the plan to remove President Crawford from power.

"Gentlemen, as Luis has already said, we expect full cooperation from you and your members, and I have to assume that that is all but assured today. Am I right?" he said looking around the table, where he received some glum nods of acceptance.

"We plan to strike at the heart of the gringo Crawford's government during these so called military exercises at the end of the month, when their attention will be focused elsewhere. It's also imperative that his whore, the Campos woman, be taken alive, which is where Victor will play a vital role, but more on that from Luis. Crawford is who we want and he will be hunted down for the traitor that he is. I'd even shoot him myself given the chance and deliver his body to our comrades in the plaza to do with as they wish, but we need him alive. At least initially."

He paused for a moment and sat down. "Luis?"

Luis de la Mano stood up again and began to walk around the small, dingy and smoke filled lean-to hut.

"Do any of you have any questions," he asked as he stopped next to Ramón.

After a pause, a union man who had showed very little emotion during the previous moments, stood up.

"And once you've removed Crawford and murdered him, what then? Who will be president? You, Luis?"

"No, Damien, that is not how it's going to work. This is not a revolution you know, and this not a military coup d'état or some other personal crusade to put myself in the Casa Rosada. We are giving Argentina back to the people, to the workers…"

"Call it what you like, but the country will need a president Luis. Have you thought of that?"

"Yes I have, Damien, and we will respect the constitution as we have always done. Now, moving on…"

"No Luis, you haven't answered the question. We all know," continued Damien boldly, "that you have always wanted to become president. You failed once, the people spoke and they rejected you. I say this is your personal bid to take the presidency for yourself," he said, looking at the other union men for support which was not forthcoming since they all, to a man, hung their heads and stared at the table in front of them.

Luis de la Mano walked slowly over to the doorway, shut the plywood door, leant against it with his arms folded and jerked his head upwards towards Victor Valiente, who calmly walked over to Damien, stood behind him and grabbed his right arm which he forced flat onto the table.

"Show him please, Victor."

Victor removed a photograph from his pocket, placed it on the table in front of Damien, placed his victim's hand over it and in a lightning fast action, thrust a hunting knife through both, pinning Damien's hand to the table amidst the blood curdling screams. At that, De la Mano walked casually around the table and threw a photograph of their families in front of each of the terrified men, whilst Damien moaned in agony until he finally passed out.

"Do I need to repeat myself, gentlemen? This is the way it's going to be. It's very simple. We know where your families are and from this moment on I expect your full cooperation. I hope that's clear enough," he said calmly, before returning to his own seat and pouring himself a full glass of wine.

He knew he had terrorised the men; he had anticipated as much and as he looked at each of them in turn, some now shedding tears of anguish, he also knew he had them where it hurt the most.

"Victor here is my most trusted and loyal friend, aren't you, Victor?" he said, with an upward nod in his direction. "And he will be taking care of the president's bitch. Of that you can be absolutely certain. We know her movements, where she works, where she lives and if it comes to that, we'll even take her on the island if we have to, won't we, Victor?"

Victor remained motionless standing in the shadows and simply sniffed with a slight shrug of his enormous shoulders.

Luis de la Mano continued. "We will meet here again in two weeks and I expect you all to maintain absolute secrecy. If not, you know what is at stake and I'm not just talking about the future of our country. You will be watched at all times, but when the moment arrives, you will rally your men and women throughout the nation and they will be at every plaza in the land!" he finished, smashing his clenched fists on the table.

"Ramón will contact you about our final meeting and the strategy we intend to put in place. Now get out of here!"

The six union men, including the pale and bleeding Damien left the shack slowly without a word among them. Afterwards Victor shut the makeshift door and took up his position standing guard in front of it.

"Ramón, get me a coffee and some brandy. Victor, dispose of Melia's body. You know what to do."

As Victor left the hut with the body of Melia over his shoulder, Ramón rummaged about in a corner fixing up some coffee, then placed on the table a bottle of cheap brandy and a couple of small glasses.

"Ramón, we need to get Victor into the presidential detail, pronto. Can you fix that?"

"Shouldn't be too difficult. He's already seconded to the ANI and we already have one of ours in place. Marco Bueno, remember him?"

"Yes I do. When did you place him?"

Ramón brought the coffee, sat down and poured them each a coffee and a brandy.

"Only a couple of weeks ago. It was tough getting him past Chief Forza, but at least he's in."

"I like Forza, the misguided fool. Anyway, I want Victor in there as soon as you can manage it. His ANI credentials should vouch for him and I've kept him low profile for just this opportunity. Two men need to do this job, so we need him in there with Marco as soon as you can fix it."

"Got it, Luis. Anyway, are you going to fill me in on the operation or what?"

"Listen Ramón, the less you know the better for your own sake. But what I can tell you is that eighteen hours after I give the green light, the specialists will arrive at strategic points around Buenos Aires. They are tasked to eliminate resistance, establish control over key government ministries and installations which, when this is completed, they will hold until Crawford has been captured. That is our task, as I simply couldn't stomach the idea of that traitor to the motherland being taken by some foreigner. That's our job, the people's job and that's what we're going to do. His woman? We'll hold her and deal with her as we see fit. Crawford will be desperate without her of course and the bitch will be our prize. I told you about that fucking barbeque didn't I?"

"Yes, you did, Luis. About sixteen times actually and at least three times last week," said Ramón laughing and pouring them both another brandy.

"I was tempted to shove a glass in her pretty little face there and then, I can tell you."

"She's not stupid, Luis, no matter how much you might hate her. If she gets wind of anything, it could get tricky…"

"Which is why I want Victor in there. He won't hesitate. Marco Bueno? I'm not so sure about him."

"Tell me, Luis, why do we want her anyway?"

"To humiliate him just like he humiliated us. That fucking cage, the townships, all that English crap, destroying the peso. All that shit. He's going to pay for it and I want to see him beg, just like he made our people beg to keep their homes. Believe me, he'll be on his fucking knees when he sees her on video, which is the closest he'll ever get to her ever again."

"As you wish Luis, but do you still think he's part of a Yankee plot? It doesn't look like that to me. It's got British stamped all over it."

"CIA, black ops, English pirates? Doesn't really matter anymore does it? They can play their war games, but one way or another, Crawford is finished."

CHAPTER 38

Clara and Jenny enjoyed another drink, chatted about the work they had done together on the military dictatorship and then decided that if Clara had any hope of getting close to Jack Forsyth, she would need a shoe-in from the president or the exercise would be entirely futile.

"Clara, this will be plain old journalism. You need to sell the idea to the president that Britain's military power is as potent as ever and Argentina is seen as a strategic partner that the UK can do business with. But more importantly, that President Crawford has emerged as the new strongman and Britain's most important ally in the region. There must be no mention of Maitland and you must see it as an ego stroking exercise. Oh and if you do get the interview with Admiral Forsyth, don't expect him to see you in The Compass. I would imagine he sees that place as sacred; hallowed ground if you like. But then, pigs have flown before, as you well know."

When Clara woke up the following morning, Jenny's words came rushing back to her, bouncing about in her mind. Drinking her coffee at the window bar of the hotel reception, she watched through the rain as a dredger moved slowly in its monotonous work through the murky waters of the river Thames. She'd spoken to Robert since he became president how many times? Four, five? Was it not she who had pretty much singlehandedly paved the way for his presidency by giving him that video? And hadn't he been the one who had phoned her with the news of Cristal's impeachment?

She took out her phone, scrolled down to Robert's number and remained staring at it for a few moments. His security team had probably issued him with a new number, she thought. All his calls would be screened anyway, not to mention the invisible wall that would have been placed around him, but she dialled the number anyway. After six or seven rings, she gave up and then remembered when she'd last seen Margarita. She would know how to get hold of him, and hadn't she given her own number to her on that awful day when her husband Stefan had been knifed to death?

Margarita answered on the third ring.

"Clara, how lovely to hear from you again," said Margarita, telling her that she'd just stepped out of the shower, which reminded Clara that it was only seven thirty in the morning in Buenos Aires. After a few pleasantries, Clara explained that she couldn't reach Robert.

"I'll call him myself if you like, and I know he'll talk to you. He often mentions you, especially about…well, you know. Anyway, it's a bit early yet, so give me an hour or so to get myself organised."

Back in the hotel room, Clara unfolded her laptop on the bed, took a sip of coffee and delved into the Net to see what more she could discover about the shadowy Jack Forsyth, knowing that she was treading on ground that she had already covered numerous times.

Apart from the banal and entirely predictable official resumes of Admiral Forsyth's illustrious career in the Royal Navy, she could finding nothing else of interest. No scandals, nothing in the tabloids and absolutely no salacious gossip she could sink her teeth into. He appeared to be hermetically sealed, she thought, as she lay back on the bed, wondering how on earth she was going to handle such a delicate situation. Then her phone vibrated.

"It's Jenny. Any news?"

"I'm waiting, or at least hoping that Robert will phone me," said Clara lying back on the bed as she told Jenny about her chat with Margarita. "And your man from The London Times?"

"Nothing yet, but…"

Clara interrupted her and said breathlessly, "Jenny, I'll have to call you back. I've another call coming through and it could be him!"

"Go for it, girl!" said Jenny as she disconnected.

"Hello?" said Clara nervously and sitting up straight.

"Clara, it's Robert. How are you?"

"Oh, I'm fine, Mr President…" she said, instantly regretting it.

"Clara, come on now. It's Robert, if you don't mind. Partners in crime, if you remember," he interrupted.

"I'm sorry, but so much has happened since last year and now you're, well, you know," she said.

Clara wasn't often lost for words, but she felt that what she now knew about her old friend made her feel she was talking to a completely different person and she dug her fingernails into her arm simply to remind herself that now she really was in the big league.

"So, to what do I owe the honour and where are you by the way?" he asked. "I haven't heard from you in ages."

"In London, actually."

"An exciting story, I hope?"

"I think so, or at least it would be if I could speak to the man concerned."

"Well Clara, if there's anything I can ever do to help. You know that, don't you?"

Pausing for a moment, she took a deep breath and continued.

"Yes, those military exercises you've got planned later this month? Operation Blenheim?"

There was a pause from Robert's end. Not long, but long enough.

"Yes Clara, and what about it?"

"A big moment for Argentina, don't you think? In fact an historic event; unprecedented in fact, and all because of you."

"Where's this going, Clara?"

"Do you think you're making enough capital out of this joint operation? I mean, some are calling you the new strongman of South

America, a breath of fresh air and other such compliments. Wouldn't you like me to shout it from the rooftops for you?"

"You want a story, you mean? But of course. I mean, who else?"

"I knew you'd understand. Thank you, Robert."

"When you get back, come to the island for lunch and we'll fix something up. I'll give you the full rundown. How does that sound?"

"Sounds lovely. Oh, just one more thing. How do I get to talk to Admiral Forsyth?"

This time there was a longer pause and Clara imagined the president snatching the phone from his ear and looking at it as if it had just bitten him.

"I believe he is the most senior military officer in the British government is he not?" continued Clara.

He fleetingly considered denying any recognition of the name, Jack Forsyth.

"My, my. You have been doing your homework, Clara," he said with nervous humour.

"Needs must. The thing is, I have no idea how to get in touch with Admiral Forsyth so that I can set up an interview. Would it be possible for you to…?"

"He's a very busy man you know, and I'm not even sure if he gives interviews."

"But if you were to ask him?"

"Well, let's see. How long will you be in London, anyway?"

"A few more days. I fly back on Friday."

"That's a bit tight you know. The admiral is a very busy man indeed. I'm not sure if I…"

"Who found the video for you? Who brought you Lucio Melia?"

This time Robert lowered the phone to his waist, sat down on the sofa in his study and rubbed his forehead. He had never expected her to call this one in. Not Clara, sweet Clara. Maybe he had underestimated her, he thought as he clenched his jaw tightly. He knew he would have to give her something, so he lifted the phone back up.

"Oh, one good turn deserves another. Look, I'll see what I can do but I can't promise anything."

"And I'd like my colleague, Jenny Lane to join me. You'll call me tomorrow then?"

"I'll try my best. Look, I need to go now."

"Thank you, Mr President," she said, barely containing her glee as she dropped the phone on the bed, bouncing up and down and pumping her fists into the air.

"Jack, we may have a problem," said Robert as he marched up and down the study and recounted his conversation with Clara.

"I'm surprised you hadn't thought of this yourself, Robert. She is, after all, a very competent woman is she not?"

"I'm concerned that she may have made a connection and..."

"Oh nonsense. How could she possibly have done that?"

Robert could think of no tangible evidence that Clara had an inkling of the truth from what she had said, but what worried him was her determination to get the interview with Jack and her unexpected, nay, sinister, reference to the video.

"She's fishing, Jack. I know her. She doesn't let go."

"She can fish all she likes, but she won't catch anything. Besides, have you not considered the benefits that a positive profile of your presidency could do for you? Not to mention the South Atlantic Alliance we are embarking upon. There are infinitely more positives than negatives here, Robert, and you should embrace this opportunity with open arms, as I intend to."

"But this goes entirely against my better judgement. Her reference to the Melia video was way out of character. Not the Clara I know at all."

"Wake up, dear boy! You never considered that she would call that one in one day? I'm sure I would have done. Anyway, this line you're taking can serve no further purpose, so please advise Miss Tomkinson that I will meet her and her colleague at The Compass on Thursday at twelve thirty, sharp. And if she's late, there's no second chance."

"The Compass, Jack? Of all the places…"

"It's practically the only place in London where discretion is assured, my dear fellow. I can't have reporters queuing up at the ministry. It's just not done. Not cricket, old chap."

"And what precisely do we intend to make public about Operation Blenheim?" asked Robert.

"As much as any civilian would need to know and nothing more. His Majesty's Armed Forces, in cooperation with the armed forces of the Republic of Argentina will be conducting joint training exercises in the South Atlantic, as part of the renewed friendship between the two countries, etcetera, etcetera. Need I say more?"

Robert replaced the satellite phone in his desk, locked it, walked out onto the balcony and gripped the tubular steel handrail as he leant forward and gazed out at the horizon. He had wanted to inform Jack of Pimpi's impending resignation, but that would have to wait. It was Clara who now occupied his thoughts. There was something terribly prickly about how easily Clara had connected him to Jack. On the other hand, who would he, as president, be in direct contact with in the British government on the matter of military exercises? It wouldn't have been terribly difficult for her to guess. He already knew that the British broadsheets hadn't fallen for the terrorist exercise cover story and he was pretty sure that Clara hadn't either, if she was as bright as he thought she was.

He lit a cigarette and remembered how he'd once read in some dull corporate sales manual that had crossed his desk one day at the law firm where he once worked, that the key to success was to go right to the top. Forget the organ grinder's monkey, the lackey, the second in command, and go for the jugular. Wasn't that exactly what Clara had done? He'd probably have done the same if he were a journalist, he thought with a smile. But then, he also knew that journalists always wanted a good story and military exercises in the southern hemisphere were far too run of the mill for a journalist of Clara's calibre. She had something; of that he was damned sure. Jack was simply playing the devil's advocate. And dangerously so.

Once she had calmed down a little, Clara called Jenny with the news.

"Nice work. I'm not sure I could have done better myself, but listen to this. My man at The London Times has been very busy and not only has the head waiter pinged the admiral, but there's something else. Something really big."

"Go on," said Clara, clutching her phone even tighter.

"No wait. Where are you?"

"Hotel room. It's pissing down outside."

"Give me half an hour."

As Clara felt cabin fever beginning to set in, she was longing to climb aboard the Triumph, if only for a couple hours. Peering through the window again she saw the rain falling as hard as ever, so she sent a message to Jenny and asked to meet in the pub from the night before. She needed a change of scene.

Because it was a weekday lunchtime she was practically the only customer. As she carried her glass of Coke and toasted sandwiches for two to the table, her phone buzzed once again.

"Clara, it's Robert. Twelve thirty on Thursday lunchtime at The Compass and don't be late."

"Thank you. That makes us quits."

"Step lightly, Clara. You've no idea who you're dealing with," he said as he disconnected.

And he has no idea who *he's* dealing with either, she thought. But when, and indeed if, to use her trump card. That was the question needling her as Jenny swept into view, shaking the rain off her blue raincoat.

"Thursday midday at The Compass," said Clara casually as Jenny kissed her on the cheek.

"Well I'll be…" said Jenny as she sat down.

"I know."

"I have a bit more for you," said Jenny, lowering her voice.

"Go on."

"The Compass is closed on Mondays, but my *Times* friend knows the head waiter pretty well and guess what? He likes to talk."

"About?"

"A lot. My friend managed to lead him astray in a private session last night. Apparently he has a room above the club, a perk of the job if you will, and it turns out that his discretion is a tad fallible."

"He bribed him?" whispered Clara leaning across the table.

"No, of course he didn't. He got him a little tipsy and discovered that our admiral isn't exactly on his Christmas card list, due to some long standing feud in some submarine or other. But anyway, it's more than that. He says he found some books. Diaries or something."

Clara had been about to take a bite from her toasted sandwich, but let it drop to the plate and quickly looked across at Jenny.

"Did he say what they were?"

"No. Apparently he's not terribly bright and has only been in the job a couple of years, but he does know every inch of that place, which is how he found them."

"You've no idea what's in them then?"

"Nope, *nada*."

"Here's my theory then," said Clara. "This group, whatever it may be called, Maitland or whatever, meet at the club a few times a year, they bang the drum for The Maitland Plan, harp on about what might have been and somewhere down the line they come up with a plan for Buenos Aires. A plan to return, something like that."

"Which is why you need to get your hands on those diaries, Clara. They could be the key to all of this."

"Did he say where he found them?"

"As I said, hiding in plain sight. They were behind a drawer in a cabinet in the private dining room, which makes you wonder how important they are. Or not, as the case might be."

"I'm getting another Coke. Want one?"

"Christ no, I'm not drinking that shit. Get me another G & T please."

As Clara went over to the bar, Jenny took a small compact from her handbag, looked into the tiny mirror, rearranged her greying blond hair, quickly dabbed a little gloss on her lips, which she then smacked together, hoping that Clara wouldn't notice.

"Oh, you got your wish by the way. You'll be there too," said Clara as she returned with the drinks.

"And when you finally wrap this up, what are you going to do then?"

This was the prickliest of questions and one that she had been agonising over since the night in The Rhu Inn. Going public on what she knew would bring down not one, but probably two governments. The impact would be unthinkable.

"I don't know, Jenny, I really don't. On the one hand, I have a duty as a journalist to deliver the truth, but at what cost? I've already been instrumental in putting one president in prison, for legitimate reasons, I might add, and now this. Christ..." she said as she put her hand to her mouth with tears welling up in her eyes.

"Oh, Clara," said Jenny, holding her hands across the table. "You know, events have a strange way of levelling things out sometimes. You really shouldn't have all this on your shoulders you know. It's just too much for anyone to bear."

Clara wiped the tears from her eyes with a paper towel and managed a weak smile as Jenny held on to her hands.

"It reminds me of when Pascal and me went to Sancti Spiritu," she said with a trembling voice. "I knew from the moment Mrs Menéndez described Rose's husband that we had found his father. And Pascal? I underestimated him, Jenny, and he rose to the occasion when I least expected him to. What I'm trying to say," continued Clara, still sniffling, "is that we found the truth at that moment, but in the end we couldn't or wouldn't do anything with it. Does that make any sense?"

"Entirely, darling. You're dealing with people's lives, real feelings and this is what held you back. With Pascal, that could only ever be his decision and not yours. It's the same with Robert, surely?"

"No it isn't," said Clara forcefully. "That decision lies with Forsyth and him alone. As far as Robert is concerned, Rose and Horacio are his parents. He neither suspects nor knows anything else. I'd put money on it."

"What are you driving at?" said Jenny, releasing her hands and leaning back in her seat.

"I don't know how he did it but I will find out, believe me. Forsyth is the architect of the fraud of the century. Can't you see it? Christ I see it now as plain as daylight," said Clara, standing up and holding her forehead with her right hand.

"Go on, Clara, you're amazing," said Jenny, smiling.

"Scotland, late fifties, dashing naval officer seduces beautiful sex starved Crawford wife and that's when the plan is hatched. Don't you see it? Somehow Forsyth managed to smuggle the young Robert into Argentina and by the way, all the locals in Rhu thought he was adopted which suited Jack Forsyth's aims to a tee. Robert is brought up by Rose and Horacio, who truly believe he is their son, he's conditioned for the presidency and the rest is history."

"Except he's not truly a Crawford is he?"

"Precisely, but then as far as Forsyth was concerned, the end had to justify the means and I'll bet you that his original idea was to put a true Crawford at the president's desk at any cost. But poor Mr C, whose life was ruined, by the way…"

Clara trailed off again and sat back down, unable to continue as the tears fell again, making little pools next to her glass on the shiny wooden table.

"Oh Clara. Come on, let's get you back to the hotel."

"Yes, all right," said Clara quietly.

Through the driving rain, they ran back to the hotel, Jenny with one arm around Clara's waist and the other holding the umbrella as they giggled and shrieked whilst dodging the puddles. Once back in her room, Clara collapsed onto the bed and stared at the ceiling.

"I'll make us a nice cup of tea. That'll cheer you up," said Jenny as she filled the electric kettle.

"It's always a nice cup of tea with you English, isn't it? The magic cure for everything," said Clara.

"Wars have been won on the back of a good brew, so don't knock it," said Jenny as she lay on the bed next to Clara, with her arms behind her head. For a few moments they both became lost in their own thoughts, as the splashing sound of cars passing on the sodden road filtered in through the half open window.

"I'm wondering about those diaries," said Clara to the ceiling.

"What are you're going to do with them?" asked Jenny as she turned over to face Clara with her head propped up on an elbow.

"That depends on what's in them. Either way, Forsyth is going to admit to his actions, if not to Robert, then at least to me."

"To use that awful cliché, you do seem to be playing God, Clara darling."

Clara turned quickly to look at Jenny. "Do you call everyone darling?"

"Never really thought about it. Why?"

"Sounds a bit odd, that's all," said Clara, returning to the ceiling. "Tea ready yet?"

"Coming up," said Jenny as she stroked Clara's hair back from her forehead, then headed for the electric kettle.

"You know, of one thing we can be certain. The Compass has a fire alarm," said Clara, sitting up on the bed.

CHAPTER 39

R oxy, what's the latest on the vice president?" asked Robert, as he stopped by his cabinet chief's office the morning after his conversation with Jack.

"I um...let me check sir."

Robert walked into Roxy's office and leant over the front of her desk.

"Miss Pla, every morning at eight, without fail, I want a report on my desk on the health of Vice President Pérez. Is that clear?"

"Yes, sir."

"Now, get me the British ambassador and patch him through to my office."

"Yes sir."

As she watched the president stride purposefully towards his office, closely shadowed by Guy, Roxy tried to remember when she had last seen him look so angry. His usual charm and suave good manners were what she most liked about him, and she began to wonder if he was hiding a serious problem. She was his cabinet chief after all, and their briefings were usually candid and open. Was he hiding something from her? Well, apart from the times he would lock himself in his office and talk for hours on the phone. But what phone? The phone records always showed nothing more unusual than calls to Mrs Campos, cabinet members and other normal day to day activity. As she was wondering, she dialled the rehab clinic and was told that the vice president was much improved and would be ready to go home in about another seven days.

If she was honest with herself, she was rather enjoying her job without Pérez around. Not only was he a constant interference, but his lecherous glances at her when he thought she wasn't looking had forced her to dress in the dullest and least alluring clothes she could get her hands on, which only had the effect of his harassing the other female members of staff instead. As she was getting up to walk over to the president's office, her phone rang.

"Where's the ambassador?"

"I'm sorry sir, I was…"

"Just get him on the god damned phone will you!"

"I'm not your secretary," she said, biting her lip.

"In my office, now!"

She threw the phone down, slammed her office door shut and pushed Guy aside as she strode into the president's office.

"What the hell's the matter with you? Why are you treating me like this?" she asked, standing in front of the president's desk with her hands on her hips.

Robert stood up, walked over, closed the door and asked her to sit down.

"Look, we're about to begin Operation Blenheim, which is probably the most ambitious military exercise this country has ever undertaken. The vice president is otherwise disposed, requiring me to do his job as well, and you can't even get the British ambassador on the phone for me…?"

"You have your secretary, Lara, for that."

"Yes, I know I do. But there are certain matters that I prefer you to handle."

"Listen, Robert. I'm not your secretary, I'm your chief of staff, your cabinet chief. Or at least I try to be when Pérez isn't constantly leering at me or looking over my shoulder. If he comes back, I'm going," she said, getting up from her seat.

"Roxy, sit down please."

"I mean it. I just can't work with him."

"I know, which is why he's not coming back, amongst other reasons."

"Oh?" said Roxy, sitting down again and adjusting her glasses with her forefinger.

"You're one of only a few people who know of Pimpi's problem, which is the way I intend it to remain."

"Yes, of course."

"I will be asking for Mr Perez's resignation as soon as I'm able to speak to him. Personally, I mean."

"Oh, I see," she said, shifting in her seat.

"Did the rehab clinic give any indication of when he'd be going home?"

"Yes, about a week."

"Listen Roxy, I'm sorry I was a little prickly earlier. It wasn't my intention and in fact I expect you to be taking on a bigger role in future."

"Oh really?"

"Yes. I'm asking Martín Katz to step in as vice president, but his remit will be nowhere near that which Pimpi was given, and that's where you come in. I'd like you to take on greater responsibilities. Be my campaign manager for the midterms and act as my spokeswoman. You know, put a friendly face forward. Pimpi was never much good at doing that."

"That's putting it mildly."

"Well?"

"Thank you, sir. Now, when would you like to see Mr Pérez?"

"Tonight if you please and I'd like you to come with me, once you've prepared his letter of resignation and any other documents that we may require. I think it's best that Pimpi resign as soon as possible, but only whilst he's under supervision, so you'll have to call the clinic and make the arrangements. I also want the entire proceedings to be recorded, so could you also make that happen please?"

"And the British ambassador?" she asked mischievously.

"I'll take care of that," he said with a genuine smile. "And Roxy. Lara may be my secretary, but that's as far as it goes. She and any of the other staff here are to be told only what they need to know, which isn't very much. We understand each other don't we?"

"Perfectly, sir."

At seven that evening, one hundred kilometres west of Buenos Aires, President Crawford's helicopter landed on the vast lawns of the ultra-modern rehabilitation clinic. The complex was chosen primarily for its isolation and privacy, as it was surrounded by tall cedar and eucalyptus trees and had one single access road from the nearest town of Mercedes, about thirty kilometres away.

The president and Roxy were met by the institute director and escorted to the first floor boardroom of the industrial looking concrete main building, where cold drinks, coffee and other non-alcoholic refreshments were made available. A notary sat at the head of the boardroom table, trying his best to keep a low profile by rummaging around in the briefcase he'd placed on the table in front of him.

"Mr President, we are very pleased with Mr Pérez's progress, but I must warn you that any stressful situation he may encounter could set him back quite severely. Alcohol and drugs are not his only problems, as you may be aware," said the director.

"I am fully aware of your worries, Mr Director but, unpleasant as it may be, I have matters of national importance to discuss with the vice president. He will, of course, remain under your supervision until it is deemed appropriate for him to return to his duties and his home. Now, if you could arrange for Mr Pérez to be brought to me, I would be most grateful."

"Yes, Mr President. I shall see to it at once," said the director with a brisk nod of the head as he took his leave.

"He makes a fair point, Mr President. How do you suppose Mr Pérez will react?" asked Roxy.

"Fait accompli, Roxy. I can't imagine for a moment that he wouldn't have foreseen this."

A few moments later, Pimpi Pérez arrived escorted by two serious looking men in security uniforms. He towered over his two escorts and was dressed in a black, long sleeved shirt, which was tucked into a pair of black cargo trousers and on his feet he wore a huge pair of black combat boots. His hair was crew cut and his beard was gone but he didn't appear to have lost much weight. His six foot five inch frame still looked menacing, and Robert wondered if the entire look had been intentional.

Robert walked over and shook his old friend warmly by the hand, at which point, Pimpi put the back of his hand to his mouth and bowed his head. Robert pulled his friend towards him, put his arms around his huge shoulders and held him tight for a few moments.

"Gentlemen, you may leave us now," said Robert as he gently released Pimpi.

Guy hovered in the background as usual, and took a position next to the door as Roxy set up the video camera on a tripod. Robert gently ushered his old friend over to a sofa and chairs below a picture window, where they sat down opposite each other and remained silent for a few seconds.

Pimpi appeared a defeated man, hanging his head, as if awaiting the executioner's axe. His normally cheerful features were replaced by a pale, blank expression.

"You know why I'm here, don't you, Pimpi?" asked the president.

Pimpi leaned forward with his arms on his legs, playing nervously with his fingers and staring down at the sand coloured floor tiles.

"I often wondered why you took me on in the first place, actually," said Pimpi without looking up.

"I never wondered about that and probably never will. It's not been a problem for us, until now," said Robert, raising his arm without looking around. "Roxy?"

Roxy handed the president a large white envelope which he opened on the low table. He placed a copy of a multi-page document in front of each of them and then summoned the notary to witness their signatures.

"Sign here, here and here, please. The notary will witness both our signatures and then we can be on our way."

Pimpi picked up the pen which Robert had placed on the table and as he was about to sign, he looked up. "You know, everything changed when you met that woman. You changed. It was never really the same again between us."

"Yes, Pimpi, you're probably right," said Robert, looking down at the table with an air of disinterest.

"You're my oldest friend, but what you're doing to my country right now is dangerous. It isn't going to work. I only went along with it for your sake..."

"I hear you. Now let's move on shall we?"

Pimpi's hand hovered over the documents and he looked up at Robert again.

"That's your trouble, you see, you just won't listen, will you? This isn't the English Home Counties and it never will be. You can't just turn the clock back two hundred years and create some Utopia that never existed. You think I don't know what you're doing, don't you? You pushed me around like a dog and you thought I wouldn't notice. Well I did." Pimpi's tone was flat and entirely lacking in emotion.

"But of course you did. That was the whole point. We could never have come this far without you, and the nation owes you a debt of gratitude..."

"Gratitude my ass!"

The notary coughed nervously and adjusted his tie as the two men glared at each other over the table.

"You'd have gone ahead with this model with or without me, so please don't give me that crap. But I'm warning you. There are serious rumblings and I've heard them," he said, pausing. "There are some dangerous people out there and believe me, they're not going to stand for all of this."

"You wouldn't be threatening me, would you, Pimpi?" asked Robert as he leant back on the armchair.

"No, I'm warning you."

"As you warned the girl in the Fiat that night? Is that what you mean?" said Robert icily, as he leaned forward looking directly at Pimpi.

The rest of the group exchanged nervous glances as the president picked up the pen that had fallen off the table.

"Yours, I believe," he said as he handed the pen to Pimpi.

Pimpi Pérez took the pen, unable to look his friend in the eye, and signed the documents in complete silence, with Robert adding his own signature afterwards. He then got up from the sofa and asked Guy to fetch the two uniformed men, as Pimpi rose slowly to his feet with a lost, dejected expression on his face. The two guards approached and stood behind the sofa as if awaiting further instructions.

"Pimpi, thank you for everything you've done," said Robert, extending his hand which Pimpi shook half-heartedly. "Gentlemen?" he said, turning to the two guards, who moved slowly to either side of their charge. As Pimpi was escorted towards the door, the group watched him walk slowly away without looking back.

The helicopter flight back to the capital was a largely silent affair. Roxy scribbled down some notes, Guy spoke intermittently to Chief Forza through his headset and Robert sat staring blankly out of the window as the black empty plains of the interior swept past below them. Occasionally Roxy looked over to Robert, who sat deep in thought on the seat opposite her, his legs crossed, his hands neatly clasped on his lap and his head angled slightly in an effort to look through the small window.

Roxy felt mixed emotions. On the one hand she was relieved to see the back of Pérez; the letching, the bullying, not to mention his bad tempered hangovers. But she also felt for her boss, who seemed to have dealt with the problem the only way he knew how. Heck, how would she have handled it, she wondered. The media had already destroyed what little credibility Pérez had left; the compromising photos of him falling out of bars in the seedier parts of town, not to mention the speculation of his rehab treatment. All this, in spite of the cloak of secrecy they had all tried so hard to create. It was a private moment for the president, yet she felt an odd duty to lighten him up a little.

"Coffee anyone?" she asked, producing a flask from her oversize handbag.

The president looked at her smiling. "You think of everything, Roxy."

"A brew? Excellent!" said Guy.

"It´s white-without and we´ll have to share the cup, I´m afraid."

"As long as it´s wet and warm," said Guy.

As they passed the plastic cup around, Roxy leaned over to Robert. "Mr Pérez looked well, I thought."

"Yes he did. Better than I expected actually," he replied, moving his gaze to the window once again.

Roxy was itching to ask about the girl and the Fiat, more out of curiosity than a sense of mischief, but how sensitive would the president be?

"What will he do now? I mean, he'll need something to do, won't he?" she asked.

"Yes, he will, Roxy. You're quite right of course," said Robert perking up noticeably. "He needs to keep busy. That's the bottom line really and he'll need as much encouragement as possible."

Roxy knew of the long friendship between the president and Pérez, which made watching his discomfort all the more poignant.

"So, have you thought of anything?"

"PR. He's an ideas man, always has been," he replied.

He went on to tell Roxy a little about their time in university, their rise through the political ranks and Pimpi's imaginative campaign tactics through the years.

"Yes, you're right. I can't really see him doing much else, actually and he could do a lot worse than opening his own PR agency. I mean, who's going to employ him now?"

"That's what I've always liked about you, Miss Pla: your brutal frankness. But you're right and if I'm also being frank, I'm finding it hard to imagine Pimpi's not being involved in at least some part of my life."

"As long as he's not part of mine, Mr President, I don't really care what he does."

"Point taken," said Robert, looking at his watch.

"Another half an hour, sir, and we should be landing," said Guy, almost shouting.

"Tell the pilot that I'd like to go straight to the island, please. I've had it for today."

"Will do, sir," said Guy as he leant forward to speak to the pilots.

CHAPTER 40

K illing thirty six hours in London wasn't difficult for Clara, especially with Jenny as her guide. They spent the rest of Tuesday afternoon in her East London office at *The Crusader*, meeting her colleagues and preparing for the big interview. The following day, she fired up the Triumph and persuaded Jenny to ride pillion, as they enjoyed riding around the Essex countryside, taking lunch in a village pub and barely saying a single word about Crawfords or Forsyths.

When Thursday finally arrived, Clara picked Jenny up from her office an hour before the meeting with Admiral Forsyth and, weaving through the traffic to the West End, parked the bike and found a coffee house on Wardour Street to decide their final strategy.

"Someone once said to me that the surest way of being late is to have too much time on your hands," said Clara absentmindedly as she looked at her watch.

"Yes, and when I started in this business someone once said to me that I should remember the four P's. Phone, park and pee!" said Jenny, laughing.

"I'm wetting myself now, actually. I've never been so nervous before. Where's the best place to start, anyway?"

"He's probably just a big old softie. Look, follow my lead to start with, okay? He's not going to give us much and you can be damned sure he won't want to be recorded."

"And what exactly do we want him to give us?"

"Well, apart from what you've got up your sleeve, everything we can squeeze out of him. Anyway, I didn't dress up like this for nothing, and neither did you by the look of it," said Jenny with a wink.

"Are you sure your *London Times* friend understood what we wanted? Otherwise this could all be a huge waste of time."

"You'd be surprised what we'd come up with for a good story and yes, he's on the case as they say. Now listen, you need to home in like an Exocet on his relationship with Crawford. That's the only way you're going to pick up anything. Watch his body language above everything else. Notepad?"

"Notepad, check," said Clara, looking at her watch again. "Come on, let's pay the bill and make a move."

"You've already paid the damn bill. This isn't Buenos Aires, you know," said Jenny, touching Clara's hand across the table.

"Sorry, I forgot," Clara said as she put on her black leather coat and made for the door.

"You look fabulous in that top, by the way."

"It's not too revealing, is it? It's Pascal's favourite," replied Clara as they walked past The Ship.

"We'll soon see if it's revealing enough won't we," said Jenny as she put her arm through Clara's and squeezed her tight.

They walked the seven blocks to The Compass, chatting cheerfully, with Jenny trying her best to calm her friend down and within a minute or two she had relaxed at least enough to crack a smile.

"It's halfway down the next block," said Jenny. "What time is it?"

"Twenty past."

"He didn't say anything about being early, did he?" said Jenny, leading the way.

When they arrived at the correct street number, all they could see was a tall, narrow, brick built building and a blue painted Georgian style door with brass fittings. An intercom was fitted to the sandstone wall at the side of the door, and on closer inspection, Clara saw a tiny gold plaque at the very top of the door that read

The Compass
Private Club

"Is this it? It's tiny," said Clara.

"Press the buzzer, darling. It's already twenty five past."

Clara pressed the intercom button, and within a few moments a stern sounding male voice could be heard.

"Compass."

"Hello? I'm Clara Tomkinson, and I have an appointment with Admiral Forsyth."

"One moment please," said the deep, stern sounding voice.

"Sounds like a sergeant major to me," said Clara, smirking.

Before Jenny had a chance to reply, the blue door opened slowly and a short, powerfully built man dressed in an immaculately pressed black suit stepped back, held the door open and beckoned them in with a nod of his head. Once they had walked past him and waited in the narrow, gloomy corridor, he shut the door, locked it and walked briskly over to them. Standing to attention, he clicked his heels together and then nodded sharply, which reminded Clara of a black and white film she had once seen, and she tried hard to hide a giggle.

"This way please, Madam, Madam," he said in a very precise manner, nodding at each of them in turn.

"I told you he was a sergeant," said Clara as they followed arm in arm a few steps behind the well-dressed military man and trying their best not to giggle too loudly.

As they proceeded down a very narrow, low ceilinged, carpeted hallway, the lighting improved slightly and they noticed that almost every scrap of wall space was taken up with faded paintings and photographs, military portraits, battle scenes and other military paraphernalia, including a few swords and old pistols. Shortly they could hear a low hubbub of conversation in the distance and the distinct aroma of beef roasting, combined with the faint smell of tobacco and the sweet smells of beer and liquors.

The military man stopped at the end of the creaky corridor, stood to attention again and simply raised his arm in the direction in which he wished them to proceed.

Walking past him, they smiled in thanks, turned the corner and entered a warmly lit and welcoming oak panelled dining room with a mahogany laid bar running down half of its right hand side, where they stopped and looked at each other, not sure what to say next or even where to go. Around the bar were three or four wooden bar stools, occupied by suited, middle aged gentlemen drinking pints of beer, or gins and scotches. Other groups of stiff looking men wearing dark suits and of a military bearing stood chatting, many of them with one hand clasping a drink and the other placed behind their backs or in their front jacket pocket.

Flames licked the back of the fireplace beside the spot where one group stood, above which were dozens of colourful shields depicting coats of arms. The centre of the entire display was given over to two crossed swords, which gleamed in the light from the two crystal chandeliers. Numerous circular tables laid with silver cutlery and immaculate, embossed white table cloths were spread around the room, and two waiters dressed in red MC uniforms hovered silently around serving drinks or attending to some finishing touches at the unoccupied tables.

"Welcome to the lion's den," whispered Jenny.

"What now?" asked Clara in a raspy voice.

At that moment, a tall, distinguished man nodded to the small group with whom he had been chatting next to the fireplace and made his way over.

"That's him," mouthed Jenny.

Clara fiddled with her spectacle chain as she watched the tall figure move briskly towards them. Dressed in a dark blue, double breasted suit, a light blue shirt and a perfectly knotted red, white and blue striped tie, he instantly reminded her of Robert. The resemblance was uncanny, as was the cut of his jaw and the dazzling, pale blue eyes.

"Jack Forsyth," he said with a beaming film star smile, while extending his hand to Jenny. "Miss Tomkinson?"

"Um no, I'm Clara Tomkinson," said Clara, shaking his hand. "And this is Jenny Lane."

"I'm dreadfully sorry to have kept you both waiting. Please, come and join us," said Admiral Forsyth as he extended his arm towards the fireplace in welcome.

"I trust your journey was agreeable. It can get quite beastly out there at times, I'm afraid."

"Oh no, everything was just fine, thank you, Admiral. We came by bike," said Clara.

"Bicycle?" he asked abruptly.

"No sir, a motorbike," said Clara smiling, trying her best not to overdo the nervous laughter she felt bursting to get out.

"Oh, a motorcycle. How terribly adventurous of you. I always hankered after one of those, you know. Anyway, let me introduce you to some old friends while we take your order for drinks."

As Admiral Forsyth began his introductions, a white-gloved waiter took their coats and another, with an embossed white towel over his arm, hovered near them, waiting to take their drinks order.

"Allow me to introduce Mick Gordon, Dick Jennings and Spike Davies. Gentlemen, Clara Tomkinson from Buenos Aires and Jenny Lane from *The Crusader*."

With the introductions over, the waiter took their drinks order and they were soon making small talk with the four most powerful military men in the entire country. Within less than a minute, the waiter returned with their drinks and they were met with a joint *chin chin* from their new friends and they soon began to relax a little.

"I see you've taken a taste to our British bitter, Miss Tomkinson," said Mick Gordon.

"Yes, sir, I have. It's rather hard to avoid, actually," she replied, raising her pint glass and giving rise to some hearty laughter.

"I imagine it's a bit a thin on the ground in Buenos Aires isn't it?" said General Davies with a warm smile.

"We make do with what you call *lager,* sir, especially in the heat," she replied.

"Quite so, quite so."

"You, of course, are a Londoner though, aren't you Miss Lane?" asked Admiral Forsyth.

"Yes, Admiral. You may have come across some of my work at *The Crusader.*"

"Indeed we have, Miss Lane, haven't we gentlemen?" he replied, looking at each of his colleagues.

Jenny couldn't help noticing the hint of a sneer in his reply, which surprised her not one bit, as she remembered the ferocious articles she had written condemning the so called terrorist threats, not that many months since.

As the aroma of roast beef and other temptations wafted over from the direction of the kitchen, Clara's taste buds came alive and she almost forgot that she was there to get some serious work done. She was rescued by the voice of Jack Forsyth.

"Ladies, I've taken the liberty of reserving a table for us," he said, tilting his head in their direction. "I trust that will be satisfactory,"

Clara glanced at Jenny with a look of relief, in the certain knowledge that they would be going upstairs to the private dining room.

"Yes, we have a table laid for six, just here in the dining room. I do hope you don't mind the imposition of my colleagues joining us for lunch."

"Certainly not," said Jenny quickly. "We are your guests after all."

A brief silence ensued, followed by some murmuring between the other three military men.

"Admiral, could we trouble you for the ladies room, please?" asked Clara.

"Certainly, Miss Tomkinson. I'll have Bennet show you."

They both followed Bennet out of the dining room, up a creaky flight of blue carpeted stairs and down a short corridor, where he stopped and indicated where they needed to go.

"You're Bennet, the head waiter, aren't you?" asked Jenny quietly as the man was about to take his leave.

"I am, madam."

"You know who we are, don't you? You received the text?"

"Yes indeed, madam."

"The fire exit?"

"Ground floor, far end of the dining room madam," he replied politely and without a hint of recognition. "Will that be all?"

"For the moment, yes. Thank you, Bennet."

Once in the ladies room, Jenny took Clara by the hand and guided her to a wash hand basin, put an index finger to her lips and turned on all the taps.

"That roast beef smells good, doesn't it?" said Clara as she waved her mobile phone at Jenny, who nodded.

"Bennet seems like a good man, don't you think?" said Jenny as she applied some lipstick and played with her hair.

"Yes, and Admiral Forsyth is exactly how I imagined him to be."

"Anyway, I thought you were driving," said Jenny as she continued to examine herself in the mirror.

"Dutch courage. We'll take the Tube."

"You got the text then?" whispered Jenny.

Clara nodded.

"Rather cramped our style with those other three joining in. Still, can't be helped."

"Come on, let's get this over with."

"Could get interesting," replied Jenny giving her lips a final smack together in the mirror and turning off the taps.

"So, Miss Tomkinson, how may I help you?" asked Admiral Forsyth as he took a sip of Châteauneuf du Pape from a cut crystal glass.

"As you know, Admiral, I'm writing a series over the coming weeks on the close relations that have developed between Argentina and Great Britain. How do you see the role of the military in this new South Atlantic Alliance?"

"In any new political alliance, a fundamental aspect will be military cooperation. We are certainly looking forward to sharing our expertise with the armed forces of the Republic of Argentina in the coming weeks."

"Operation Blenheim, as it's being called?"

"Precisely, Miss Tomkinson," he replied.

For the next fifteen minutes, Admiral Forsyth outlined the general scope of the operation, the timeline, the manpower, the considerable amount of hardware being deployed and the envisaged cooperation of the local armed forces. The two generals and the air vice marshall added their perspectives and Clara jotted down her notes as she listened, simultaneously trying to eat. As far as she was concerned, the admiral's dissertation was entirely predictable, economical with the truth and as dull as ditch water. It would be an absolute yawn to write about.

Admiral Forsyth concluded by saying, "as we speak, the fleet is already on the high seas, moving through Biscay and expected to regroup at Ascension Island. This is the largest peacetime force to put to sea in a generation, Miss Tomkinson, and I'm extremely proud to have taken my very small part in its preparation."

"Sounds more like an invasion force to me, gentlemen," said Jenny, taking a bite of roast beef from her fork. The assembled chiefs glanced at each other and laughed nervously.

Admiral Forsyth poked his silver fork in Jenny's direction. "You see, this is what makes this country so great, Miss Lane. The freedom to utter such banalities, yet not be strung up for high treason," he said without a hint of sarcasm. "More wine?"

"Yes please," Jenny replied, maintaining eye contact with the admiral.

There followed a brief pause where all that could be heard were the clink of silverware on china and the low murmur of the other diners. This made Clara uncomfortable and, wishing to regain the initiative, she placed her knife and fork down carefully on the plate and took up her notepad and pen.

"I'm interested in your relationship with President Crawford, Admiral. How long have you known each other?" asked Clara, taking a sip of wine and looking directly at Admiral Forsyth.

Caught momentarily off balance by the question, he paused with the glass halfway to his lips, a detail which was not lost on Jenny.

"We met a little while after he became president, if I recall correctly. He is, as you know, a very good friend of the United Kingdom," he said scratching his temple with his forefinger.

"Oh? You know, I've always had the impression that Great Britain took a pretty dim view of my country, particularly following the Falklands War and that we were all a bunch of *sudacas*," retorted Clara.

"Sudacas, Miss Tomkinson?"

"Spanish slang for South Americans, Admiral. You know, inhabitants of banana republics? Su-da-cas," she spelt out.

"Never heard of that before, young lady, and it's far removed from the image we have of your beautiful country," replied Admiral Forsyth, looking at his colleagues.

"You mean since Crawford was handed the presidency, Admiral?"

"I think you mean, *won* the presidency Miss Tomkinson, surely?" replied Admiral Forsyth with a thin smile.

"Indeed sir, indeed. But returning to your relationship with President Crawford if I may. Isn't it true that you have both enjoyed a close friendship for much longer than the eighteen months since he became president?"

"It's certainly possible that our paths may have crossed here in London, yes. Perhaps as part of some visiting delegation, maybe?"

The two generals moved uncomfortably in their seats, with the air vice marshall putting a hand up to his mouth and coughing nervously.

"You appear to be fishing in a dry river bed here, Miss Tomkinson, but please, don't let me stop you."

"Is it not true that Robert Crawford is a regular visitor to this very club, The Compass?" asked Clara, with a sweep of her hand towards the bar and dining area.

General Davies stood up, dabbed at his mouth with a napkin and lightly touched Admiral Forsyth's shoulder.

"We'll be at the bar, Jack. Ladies? If you'll excuse us," said the general as the other two stood up and followed him away from the table.

"I have indeed entertained the president here in the club Miss Tomkinson. It's no state secret and neither is it a crime to enjoy good company in convivial surroundings, such as this delightful place. But please, don't let me stop you continuing with this fanciful charade. I'm all ears actually," he said, smiling and nodding to the waiter, who made his way over with a tray of selected cheeses and a decanter of fine port.

"Could I indulge you?" he asked, looking at them both in turn.

"If you would excuse me for one moment please, Admiral. Nature calls," said Clara, rising from her seat as a waiter assisted at the back of her chair.

"Of course," he said, standing briefly and dabbing his mouth with a napkin.

Clara put the large computer bag over her shoulder, adjusted her glasses and, with a lightning quick glance at Jenny, made her way back up the stairs in the direction of the ladies' room, with a flutter of nerves in her stomach.

"Miss Lane? Could you be tempted? A little Port, perhaps?"

"No thank you, Admiral," said Jenny, lighting a cigarette, inhaling and leaning back in her seat.

"Oh, you don't mind do you?" she said. "I mean, it's a private club and the normal rules don't really apply here, do they Admiral?" she asked, leaning forward again. "Actually, I've changed my mind. I will take that Port, if you don't mind."

"Certainly, Miss Lane, here we are," he said, pouring her a glass and passing it over.

"Thank you," she said, taking a sip.

"You know, there's something about you people that has always amazed me," she began, blowing the smoke straight at the admiral.

"Do go on, Miss Lane," said Admiral Forsyth, raising his eyebrows.

"Your complete and utter disdain for civilians. You know, like Clara and me," she said, hoping that Admiral Forsyth would show the tiniest of cracks in his armour plating.

"We live in entirely different universes, Miss Lane, and reconciling those two worlds is utterly futile. Surely I don't need to spell that out to a journalist of your calibre?"

Just hold him on this tack, she said to herself, as she clung to what she had agreed with Clara. It would be counterproductive to get him too angry at this stage, even if she could, so she continued with a little ping pong and, glancing at the watch on Admiral Forsyth's wrist, she knew she had less than three minutes to do just that.

At the top of the stairs, Clara stopped and looked around. She could still hear muffled chatter rising from the dining room and so far, nobody had followed her up. Closing the door to the ladies' room, she entered a cubicle, locked the door and sat on the toilet seat. She took her mobile phone from her back pocket and quickly sent a text message to the number that Jenny had given her earlier. Then she waited as her mind darted to and fro.

When she began her career in journalism, she never imagined that she would be sitting in a toilet cubicle sending text messages to waiters in private clubs in the West End of London, but she was grateful it wasn't in some grimy public railway station in Buenos Aires. Come on, come on! She said to herself as she stared at the tiny grey screen.

"And you still continue with that fanciful cover story of the terrorist alert that you put forward nearly two years ago, Admiral?" Jenny asked, barely able to contain the glee at having the target of her many years of work finally sitting in front of her.

"Miss Lane. I've read all your stories and let's face it, that's all they are, stories. Interesting stories, I'll give you that. You certainly know how to spin a yarn, but that's all they are, Miss Lane. Yarns, concocted by that empire builder proprietor of yours. What's his name again?" said Admiral Forsyth, lighting a cigarette of his own.

"Christ, you're so full of…" she started to say and was cut off by the sound of an ear splitting klaxon that began to wail up and down, over and over. Admiral Forsyth calmly stood up, brushed some imaginary crumbs from his jacket, buttoned it up and offered Jenny his hand across the table.

"Sounds like the fire alarm, Miss Lane," he said.

But Jenny, having put her hands over her ears could only see his mouth moving. He beckoned her over and she followed him to the end of the dining room, then to the fire exit, clearly marked in large green letters under an emergency light. Waiters were running hither and thither, the lights had dimmed and Jenny watched as Admiral Forsyth lifted his leg and kicked on the safety bar of the emergency door, forcing it open.

"Mick, get everyone down here, please," said Admiral Forsyth calmly. "And Spike, clear the kitchens and ask Bennet to clear the rooms upstairs. Miss Lane, would you mind stepping outside please?"

Jenny did as she was told, with Admiral Forsyth taking her by the arm and leading her down the steps to the small courtyard at the back of the building, which was clearly marked with green assembly point notices.

"It's probably a false alarm, Miss Lane, so please don't worry yourself," he said, sipping from his glass of port.

The waiters, other diners and kitchen staff were hurrying out of the building as the siren continued to wail, and she saw Admiral Forsyth asking her a question.

"I'm sorry Admiral, what did you say?" she shouted, moving closer to him.

"I said, where's Miss Tomkinson?"

On hearing the alarm, Clara rushed from the cubicle, out through the door and around a corner where she saw Bennet waiting for her.

"In there, on the right. It's unlocked. Hurry, you've got about five minutes until the fire brigade arrive," he said, before rushing down the stairs.

Clara moved quickly into the private dining room, closed the door behind her and leant against it, trying to gather her thoughts. *What the hell am I going to do with these things once I've got them?*

Walking quietly past the long mahogany table, she saw to the right of it and against a wall, a tall oak dresser, open at the top, displaying silverware and cut crystal glasses. The bottom section had four ornate doors on either side, above which were two sets of drawers. *Which to open?* Jenny had said that the books were behind some drawers, she remembered. She pulled each drawer out one by one, but found nothing. Then she opened one door, then the next and found nothing but glasses and napkins.

"What the hell?" she muttered. "Behind the fucking drawers, but where?"

Feeling panic setting in, she looked at her watch. Three minutes left. She frantically searched the entire dresser, all the drawers and cupboards one more time and found nothing that looked even vaguely like a book. She banged her head against the dresser and mumbled, *think, think!*

Behind the drawers? Behind the dresser!

She then went down on her hands and knees, peered behind the dresser itself where it butted up against the wall, but couldn't see anything at all. It was too dark. Torch, torch! Scrabbling in her bag, she found a small penlight on her keyring and shone it behind the dresser, seeing nothing but cobwebs and dead flies. Other side! Scurrying to the other end of the dresser, she lay on the floor and poked the light into the gap. The skirting board, about three quarters of an inch thick, created a gap of around three inches and she prayed that it was enough to create a secret hiding place. Then the penlight began to flicker, so she banged it against the dresser and it brightened up a little. Shining it into the gap one more time, she could just make out a blue object and let out a sigh.

"Miss Lane, I'm a little concerned about your friend. Where do you suppose she is?"

"Will someone turn that fucking noise off please!" Jenny shouted. "What did you say?"

Admiral Forsyth took Jenny by the shoulders, pulled her towards him and spoke loudly at the side of her head. "I said, where is your friend? Miss Tomkinson?"

Jenny cupped both hands around her mouth and shouted, "In the toilet!"

Admiral Forsyth beckoned General Davies over and asked him to go and look for Clara, at which Jenny interrupted him. "I'll go first. She might be stuck in the ladies'."

"Spike, go with her just in case she breaks her neck or something," said Admiral Forsyth, rolling his eyes upwards. "Lord above!"

Clara lunged with her arm behind the dresser but couldn't reach whatever it was she had seen. "Why the hell didn't they just put them under the fucking floorboards for Christ sake?" she hissed.

Her face and hair were now damp with perspiration and she mentally counted down what few minutes remained. Anchoring her feet against the wall, she gripped the back edge of the dresser and pulled with all her strength. After a couple of grimacing pulls, the dresser began to move forward across the wooden floor rattling the crystal glasses, so she gave it one more massive effort until she heard a loud clunk. With the faint and dying glow from her penlight she could just make out two bluish objects lying vertically between the skirting board and the dresser. Reaching in, she grabbed one, brought it out and lay there hugging it to her chest, panting like a thirsty dog.

Noticing that the alarm had gone silent, she listened as the stairs creaked to footsteps climbing up. She quickly thrust her arm into the gap once more, grabbed the second book, stuffed them both into her computer bag and zipped it up.

"Miss Tomkinson? Miss Tomkinson?" she could hear faintly, the voice coming closer from behind the door.

A man's voice, but it wasn't Bennet and certainly not the admiral. Shit, what to do? She couldn't get to the toilet, they'd see her. The emergency light had switched off, but she could see by a faint light coming from beneath the door and, try as she might, she couldn't move the dresser all the way back to the wall. Fuck it, Bennet will have to move it back, she thought.

As she stood frozen beside the door, with her hand on the old brass handle, she listened.

"General, I'll just check the ladies' room again. Could you check the gents' downstairs just in case? She might have got lost," came the muffled sound of Jenny's voice.

"All right, madam, I'll have another look."

Hearing the general's footsteps going down the creaky stairs, Clara slowly opened the door, peeked around and closed it quietly after her. She then headed for the ladies' room and bumped into Jenny coming out. Screaming hysterically, she then ran down the stairs and towards the bar. Jenny quickly followed, grabbed her by the shoulders and steered her outside into the small courtyard.

"It's all right, darling, it's alright. Everything's fine now," said Jenny, trying her best to sound serious.

"Is everything all right, Miss Lane?" asked Admiral Forsyth with genuine concern.

"She got lost in all those bloody corridors of yours. Look at her for God's sake, she's hysterical!" said Jenny, holding onto Clara's arm.

"I'm so sorry, Miss Lane. Look, the fire brigade said it was a false alarm so we can all go back in now. Come on and we'll get Miss Tomkinson something to revive her."

With concerned expressions on their faces, the four military chiefs followed as Jenny helped Clara up the steps and back into the bar area, where she guided her to a sofa next to the fireplace. Bennet and another waiter fussed around them and Bennet asked, "may we bring you some refreshment, madam?"

"Something cold, please. A Coke if you have one," said Clara, rubbing a hand over her forehead.

"Well, no harm done," said Admiral Forsyth. "We'll be over there if you need us," he said, indicating the bar.

When their dining companions had moved away, well out of earshot, Jenny moved a little closer to Clara and tilted her head.

"Did you get it?" she asked quietly.

"Them. I got *them*," Clara replied shakily as the waiter returned with the drinks.

"Erm, thank you. This is thirsty work," said Clara smiling and taking a long gulp of her drink.

"I don't suppose you managed a peek did you, darling?"

Clara laughed. "You've got to be kidding me. Anyway, how did you leave it with Forsyth?"

"I was a little direct, shall we say."

"Look, Jenny, I don't want to leave here under a cloud so could you ask the admiral to come over for a minute, you know, so we can tie everything up and he doesn't end up with a nasty taste in his mouth. I know what you're like."

Jenny went over to the bar and returned with Admiral Forsyth who sat down opposite them with a coffee and brandy.

"I trust you are feeling a little better now, Miss Tomkinson?"

"Yes I am, thank you, Admiral. I don't know what came over me. When it all went dark, I just panicked."

"Happens to the best of us, my dear," said the Admiral, patting her knee. "I'll get Bennet to call the electrician, as I can't for the life of me think what happened for it all to go so dark. We don't want a repeat performance now, do we?"

"Oh, and I'm sorry I was a little overbearing, Admiral. Must have been the heat of the moment I suppose," said Jenny, as contritely as she could possibly manage.

"I would expect nothing less, Miss Lane, especially from you," replied Admiral Forsyth, smiling, his white teeth gleaming.

They concluded briefly with an outline of what they hoped to print, with Admiral Forsyth insisting on reading any drafts prior to publication and Clara breathed an inward sigh of relief. She then stood up, saying that they really ought to be going.

"And please thank the other gentlemen for their company, Admiral."

"My pleasure ladies. It's been a most entertaining afternoon,"

CHAPTER 41

Holding onto the overhead handrail on the Tube back to the hotel in Docklands, Clara quickly sent a text to Bennet which simply read *'check the dresser'*. She cuddled the computer bag close to her chest, as if at any second she expected it to be snatched away by persons unknown.

"I'm itching to see what's inside those, you know," said Jenny yawning and with her head on Clara's shoulder.

"Me too, but what's going to happen when they find out that they're gone?" asked Clara, lowering her voice.

"You're assuming they have something to do with you know what."

"Yeah or someone's unknown sales ledger," said Clara with a roll of her eyes.

Back at the hotel, Jenny flopped onto the bed yawning, while Clara took the two pale blue books from her bag and laid them side by side on the vanity unit in front of the bed. Neither book had any markings on the outside, they both measured twelve by six inches, and the covers were a finely, gold embossed blue leather. Carefully opening one, she went to the first page and found written, in elaborate handwriting, the words, *Maitland Group,* and below that *1815 to...*followed by a blank.

"This is it, Jenny! Quick, take a look," said Clara without taking her eyes from the page. Not hearing a response, she turned and saw that Jenny had fallen asleep cuddling a pillow to her chest.

"Peace and quiet at last, darling," she muttered.

Leafing carefully through the journal, she found short entries for every year up to 1935, with names of group members in attendance carefully annotated and a very brief synopsis of each meeting. Only when a meeting of importance took place was the entry expanded to give more details, which was the case for the very first in 1815, where it was noted *"retake Buenos Aires and establish British garrison"*. Most of the other entries in the first journal showed little information of interest, except for the members in attendance and ended with the words *"no quorum"*. It was almost as if interest in retaking the country had not been particularly high on the group's agenda for one hundred and twenty years, she thought.

Flipping back to the first page, she turned it over and found on its reverse face the words *Maitland Group* and underneath *Principal Aims*, followed by a flowery paragraph setting out the key objectives.

"Defeat unitary forces in city of Buenos Aires. Expel Spanish.

Fortify city around central garrison. Recruit local forces.

Establish positions on all frontiers. Appoint governor general."

"So I was right," murmured Clara, her neck tingling as she opened the second book, which contained an extended entry for 1944, ending with the word *aborted*. She then leafed further through the pages until she found what she had really been looking for in the years 1957 to 1979. Jack Forsyth's name appeared numerous times, along with Charles and Anna Crawford, Horacio and Rose Crawford and a new name, Carmen Pack. Reading further into the 1958 entry, she found written *"Horacio and Rose Crawford to raise child in Sancti Spiritu. Lt. Forsyth to brief next meeting on return from Scotland. Michael Gordon and Richard Jennings to assist. CP."*

As Clara turned the pages she found that the notes went on to refer to Robert's progress through the years in very short, two or three word entries. It was practically a diary on the president since the day he was born, so she quickly turned to the last entry dated April 17th 2003, which she had to assume was the date of the last meeting. She then concluded that she had just over four months until the theft of the books would be discovered. But she also knew there was always the risk that someone from the Maitland Group or even the admiral himself might check, the very notion of which gave Clara a sharp stab in the pit of her stomach.

She normally hated sleeping in the afternoon so, stepping into the shower, she turned on the water and let it blast over her face and hair for a minute or two as she mulled over what she had found and what possible use she could make of the journals. What could be gained by going public with what she now knew? Who would it benefit? Should Robert know?

Wrapping a towel around herself and combing back her wet hair, she went back to the bedroom and found Jenny leaning against the wall by the half open window. She was smoking a cigarette and sipping something from a white plastic cup.

"Hey, what about me?" asked Clara.

"Oops, sorry, you were in the shower and the minibar looked rather tempting. Vodka?"

"Oh, no thanks. Isn't there anything else?"

"I'll have a look. It's packed with goodies."

Jenny took a miniature Scotch from the minibar and dangled it for Clara's approval, then tossed it over to her.

"So? Are you going to tell me then?" asked Jenny, returning to the window.

"You mean you haven't taken a peek yet?"

"They're your babies, and I do still have some ethics left, you know," she said, blowing smoke through the window crack.

"I know you do and yes, it's all there," said Clara, looking over towards the vanity unit, which prompted Jenny to quickly flick her cigarette out of the window and rush over to Clara.

"I knew it! So tell me, what's in them?" she said, holding Clara by the arm.

"Here, I'll show you."

Turning the final pages of the second journal, Clara pointed out what she had found.

"It's all pretty much as we suspected. They place Robert in Argentina, condition him, mould him, monitor his progress and well...there he is now. Look, it's all here," she said, looking up at Jenny.

"But Clara, why so glum?"

"Oh I don't know..." she replied, falling backwards on the bed.

"Clara listen to me," said Jenny, standing over her, folding her arms. "We have to make copies and then get them back to the club. I'll get Bennet to meet me somewhere with the journals and tell him to put them back where you found them."

"No," Clara said, taking a sip from the miniature. "I'm not doing that."

"Why not?"

"They're my insurance policy, and I want Forsyth to know that I have them. I may not use them against him, I don't know yet; but he'll get them back when, and only when he's confronted Robert and told him who he really is," she said, sitting up again and holding the damp towel in place with her forearm.

"Oh Clara," said Jenny, kneeling in front of the bed. "Jack Forsyth is not the kind of man I would want to cross, not like this anyway. Think, think. Surely it would be enough for him just to be aware that you know?"

"I just..." said Clara quietly as tears filled her eyes.

Jenny sat on the bed and held Clara's hands.

"Listen. Just let me help you with this, will you?"

"Perhaps you're right," said Clara sniffling.

"I'll do anything to help, you know that," said Jenny softly, as she wiped the tears away from Clara's cheeks.

Clara felt a little lighter, as if a burden had been lifted. She felt an urge to hold Jenny and her heart beat a little quicker in her chest. Jenny put her arms around her waist, drawing her a little closer and her touch made

Clara shiver a little, barely noticing the damp towel falling slowly to her waist.

"Better?" she whispered.

"Yes," said Clara, sniffling as she pressed her face into Jenny's neck, the wetness of her tears stinging her skin. As Jenny ran her fingers through Clara's wet hair, she too felt a tremble in her hands with the closeness of her body. Slowly moving her hand down to Clara's waist, her arm lightly brushed her breast, which made Clara gasp from a sensation she didn't fully recognise. She pulled her face back a little until she was looking into Jenny's eyes.

"I don't..."

"I know," said Jenny touching Clara's cheek with her fingertips.

"I like you, I do. But not in that way," said Clara, looking down.

"In what way?"

"You know" she said, as her breathing quickened a little. "I just..."

"Don't say any more," said Jenny, wanting so badly to kiss her lips.

Clara then fell back onto the bed again, took another sip of Scotch and pulled the towel back up over her chest.

"Could you get me another one? This one's empty," she giggled, dangling the tiny bottle in front of her.

Jenny raided the minibar again, returning with a handful of plastic miniatures and a tiny can of Coke which she placed on the bedside table.

"Drink it with the Coke. It's falling over juice," she said, giggling.

"Let's listen to some music," said Clara, pouring herself a Scotch with a dash of coke.

"Celebrating?"

"Might be."

Jenny found a soft music channel on the TV and turned the volume down low as Acker Bilk's *Aria* was just beginning.

"Oh my God," whispered Clara, biting her little finger.

"Now, close your eyes and don't look," said Jenny.

Clara knelt on the bed and playfully pulled the damp towel over her eyes as Jenny slowly unbuttoned her light blue blouse, dropped it to the floor, unbuttoned her jeans, wriggled out of them, and knelt on the bed facing Clara.

"You can look now."

Clara pulled the towel down from her eyes and gazed at Jenny's taught body in her blue lacy underwear.

"You look…"

"Fifty two?" sighed Jenny as she flopped down on the bed.

"I was going to say you look lovely."

Jenny looked up at Clara and struggled to hold in what she knew she shouldn't say.

"You know, I wanted to be with you ever since the other night in the pub. Oh God, I shouldn't have said that…" she said, turning her head away.

Clara had no idea what to say next and Jenny moved closer, kissed Clara very softly on the lips, then slowly pulled away.

"I've been wanting to do that all day," she said, biting her lip.

"But we're…" Clara said, looking down.

Jenny put her hand on Clara's cheek and kissed her again for a little longer. Clara hesitated, not knowing where to put her hands, her heart beating a little quicker and then gently pulled away, confused. She had enjoyed it.

"I lay awake last night thinking of you, wondering what would happen, what it would be like if I kissed you," Jenny said quietly, lying back on the bed.

Clara leaned over Jenny to fetch her drink from the bedside table, trembling a little more.

"When I woke up, I remembered what I'd thought about and panicked."

"Oh?" said Clara sipping her drink.

"I never really thought you would want to."

Clara couldn't reply. She simply couldn't think of the words.

Jenny then got to her knees and popped the clasp at the front of her lace bra, allowing it to fall gently from her arms. She lay back down slowly, with her arms around Clara's waist pulling her with her. Clara hovered above her as their breasts softly touched.

"Clara, are you sure?"

"No, I..."

Jenny slowly pulled the towel away from Clara's waist and gazed at her, her eyes barely open.

"I think I love you Clara. Is that wrong?"

"No. But for me it's..."

"I know..."

"No, but..."

Jenny ran her fingers through Clara's wet and slippery hair as she kissed her harder, their bodies slowly entwining. Clara wasn't sure how many times the ripples came and went from her fingertips to her toes and afterwards, as they lay side by side gazing at each other, the perspiration trickling down their backs and between their breasts, they didn't speak.

As the rain lashed against the windows, they held on to each other in the faint glow of the street lights, letting their eyes and the tips of their fingers wander over each other.

Clara felt something she had never imagined, and as she looked at Jenny's tiny imperfections, her high cheek bones, her full lips and dark eyelashes, she felt contented and at one, not only with herself, but with another human being. Not in her craziest, wildest dreams had she thought she could feel such purity with another woman, someone so much like her, yet so different. Someone whom she understood with no words being spoken. She felt not the slightest shred of guilt, not even as she thought of Pascal. It was theirs, they had found their moment, if only for today.

Clara's flight landed in Buenos Aires at seven thirty five on a hot and very humid Saturday morning, not forty eight hours after her night at the hotel.

She had slept fitfully during the thirteen hour flight, attempted to read and had even tried to watch a film on the tiny screen on the seat in front of her. But it had been no good, she simply couldn't get that night out of her mind. Every thought returned to it and as the hours to Buenos Aires counted down, her happiness turned to guilt as she pictured Pascal waiting for her anxiously at arrivals.

As her thoughts turned again to Jenny, she tried to put her mind in neutral, to put her feelings for her in a place where she thought they belonged; a bright, special place that she would always cherish. Then she thought again of Pascal and how he would be waiting nervously for her, checking the arrivals screen every ten seconds and the way he would adjust his clunky old sunglasses and his long ginger ponytail. Tears of joy had filled her eyes as she thought of him waiting, and as she ran through the arrivals gate and felt his big, strong arms around her, she knew she had come home.

CHAPTER 42

The fleet's arrival in the Rio de la Plata was greeted with muted enthusiasm by the crowds gathered on the shoreline, from Olivos to Costanera Sud. The president had instructed Roca to distribute Friendship Flags around the city, but as he watched the live TV report he was disappointed to see that only a few small children were waving the flags whilst jumping up and down excitedly next to their parents. He saw some parents snatch flags from their children and discard them on the pavement and then walk away, pulling the protesting little children back to their cars.

He had worked enthusiastically with Pimpi on the Friendship Flag, an amalgam of the Argentine and union flag of Great Britain, hoping that citizens would embrace the message of unity. He couldn't blame Pimpi; it had been a brilliant idea which he had warmly embraced, especially since it marked a new beginning for his friend who had recovered remarkably quickly since setting up his new PR firm.

"Not the welcome I was expecting, Jack," said Robert as he paced up and down, glancing at the TV.

"The least of your worries. In fact, Sir Michael tells me that the operation is ahead of schedule and that your forces will be opening their bases to our people by the end of the week, as we discussed."

"Yes, Jack, but I was told that the fleet commander needed several days to prepare the logistics, landing craft and so on."

Following a short pause, Jack continued.

"Robert, you should know that we need to bring the main operation forward."

"But your plan had always been to mark the anniversary of General Craufurd's original advance on the city on the first of July, Revolution Day."

"Indeed, but we have reason to believe that Revolution Day may be marked in other ways. This information has only just come to my attention."

"Go on."

"De la Mano?"

"What about him?"

"We have reliable information that he has hired a mercenary force to depose you on the first of July," said Jack solemnly.

Robert took the satellite phone from his ear and stared at it in disbelief. His intelligence agencies had been watching De la Mano for months, but clearly not close enough and now he felt the first tingling of fear stab at his stomach.

"We've been watching him, Jack, and there's been no indication that he was planning a stunt like this. None whatsoever."

"Not close enough, quite clearly."

"Our resources are limited, you know that, in spite of the loans and grants you extended to us."

"I am aware of that, however you should also know that he has planned simultaneous marches by the worker's party and all the other hardline union sympathisers, on every capital city throughout the country. This is why we have to move quickly and position our forces within the next forty eight hours at the very least."

"Jack, I receive daily reports from the director of the ANI, whom I appointed personally, I might add and the indications I was given, were a series of street protests on Revolution Day and nothing more. That's pretty much par for the course down here, you know that."

"And who does the director get his information from? Which field operatives?"

"More to the point, where are *you* getting your information from?"

"My security agencies have had a presence in Argentina for many years, Robert."

"I have no doubt, Jack. But under the circumstances, do you not think that I am owed the common courtesy of...?"

"A mere oversight on my part. Now, I repeat, where is the director getting his information from?"

Robert swore under his breath. He felt he was losing control of the situation, but decided not to push Jack on the matter, for the moment, anyway.

"Victor Valiente, Marco Bueno to name just two and Chief Forza is seconded to the agency by special decree and reports directly to me. Why?"

"There you have your answer."

"Not Marco surely? We go back years, Jack, and certainly not the chief."

"We're not entirely sure about Bueno. Forza has been strung a line, but Valiente, yes. He's the one. He has to be."

It now made sense to Robert. Chief Forza had presented him with a recommendation for Victor Valiente to join the presidential security team, with Marco forcefully backing him up.

"I had no idea, Jack."

"Then deal with him, but first you need to tighten up. Have a quiet word with them all or at the very least give this to Forza. That is, if you can still trust him."

"Jack, I trust Chief Forza with my life, as does Guy. I'll have a quiet word."

"And what do you propose to do with De la Mano? If you can find him, that is. We seem to have lost him."

"I had considered smoking him out of Villa 39 by flattening it, but that would give him even more reason to proceed. I'll let you know."

"Listen, you don't have much time. Our armed forces need to be in place quickly. In fact, less than forty eight hours would be ideal, if we possibly can. I'll speak again with C in C Fleet, directing him to issue new orders to the fleet commander."

"May I suggest, therefore, that the troops disembark at night, under the cover of darkness?" asked Robert. "Meanwhile, I'll arrange some friendly publicity stunts in and around the points of entry. You know, our troops and commanders arm in arm with British troops, that kind of thing."

"Precisely my thinking. We should talk later. Must dash," said Jack, knowing that he had already issued the new orders.

Luis de la Mano sat at his usual seat at the end of the table in the crumbling hut deep inside Villa 39. His street gangs patrolled the perimeter and inner circle while he held court over his group of union men, who now swore undivided loyalty to him, or so he fervently believed.

"Friday morning at dawn it is then, my friends. Revolution Day will be written about as the day we took our country back. The traitor Crawford will be removed and once more the people will unite behind our beloved country."

The men assembled around the table sat in silence as they listened, afraid of making the slightest gesture that could be interpreted as dissention.

"Tomorrow, Victor will be at the heart of the Crawford circle and he will steal the prize held so dear to the puppet president. The whore will be taken from him and he will do our bidding."

He took a large slug of brandy and wiped the sweat from his forehead with a grimy rag that he kept in his pocket.

"I've already given the go ahead to our friends in the north, and they will commence operations in the motherland at the break of day on Friday. Inform your men and women that they will be recognisable by a unique marking on their fatigues and helmets. A diagonal white strip with a vertical red line running through it. Make this information available as soon as possible to avoid friendly fire. You've all received the weapons we distributed?"

There were grim nods around the table as Damien stared at his still bandaged hand, wondering what madness he had just heard.

"There won't be any questions today, gentlemen. You all know what to do, we've done it before, but this is the big one. The big punch. Now, return to your people and prepare to take your country back," he shouted, pumping a fist into the air.

"Chief, Marco, take a seat please," said the president, ushering his two close friends into his office at his island residence. He then pressed some buttons on his speakerphone, a dial tone was heard and a gruff voice answered.

"Boss?"

"Guy? A minute please."

He stood behind his desk and looked out of the window with his hands clasped behind his back. Moments later, a soft knock was heard at the door and the imposing figure of Guy Farlowe-Pennington appeared, taking up the entire door frame. He closed the door, stood in front of it and scanned the office, folding his arms.

"Gentlemen, it seems we may have a problem," said the president slowly.

Marco Bueno and Chief Forza sat staring at the president's back. The chief turned to Marco, shrugged and held his hands out as if posing a question.

"Luis de la Mano."

Marco Bueno shifted nervously in his seat as Robert turned around, leaned forward and laid his palms on the desk, his blue eyes looking at each in turn.

"It seems the intelligence I'm receiving is incomplete, to say the very least. What the hell is going on?" he demanded, banging the desk with the palm of his hand.

Marco Bueno raised his forefinger as if he imagined himself back in the classroom.

"Yes," said the president, straightening himself up.

"I was approached."

"And you didn't think to tell me?"

"No."

"Why not?"

"Because I wanted Ramón to think..."

"And does he?"

"I believe so, Mr President."

"You believe so and yet you still didn't come to me or go to your superior, Chief Forza here?"

"No, sir," said Marco, looking down at his shoes.

"What have you told them?"

"Nothing they didn't already know. Your published movements, that kind of thing. I wouldn't really say they were terribly bright," he offered.

"No, just dangerous fucking lunatics. Chief?"

Chief Forza held his palms face up in defence.

"I'm sorry, sir, I should have seen this coming. *Mea culpa.* What can I say?"

"You can tell me that my security hasn't been compromised, Chief. That would be a good start."

"I'll do what is necessary, yes, sir. But I just approved a request from a Victor Valiente to join the team, so it looks like I'll have to put that on hold now..."

"No. You let that proceed as planned. Put him with Marco, lose any of the other team members you have doubts over and we'll replace them with British personnel. No, come to think of it, ditch all of them. Guy here will bring in his own men and he can show them how things are done. And

Marco, I want you to find out what Victor's real agenda is and report back directly to me."

The president sat down behind the desk, picked up a couple of envelopes and tossed them over to Marco and the chief.

"That's De la Mano and his crew," the president said, wagging his finger. "They intend to strike on Friday morning and I don't mean downing tools and walking out. They plan to depose me."

He then outlined what he had learned during the course of the day and how he hoped to tackle the situation.

"So you see what we're now faced with, gentlemen, which is why I've decided to bring forward Operation Blenheim. The security of this country cannot be guaranteed, especially given the dire state of our armed forces. We simply haven't had the time or the resources to give our military the tools they need to fight off an armed uprising, let alone a mercenary incursion."

The two men looked up at the president, their eyes wide and their mouths partially open, whilst Guy leaned against the door, arms folded, his face as stern as a rock.

"I'm not sure I fully understand you, sir," started Chief Forza. "Are you suggesting that the British forces taking part in those military exercises will be taking an active role in hostile action? Here on Argentine sovereign territory?"

"That is precisely what I'm suggesting, Chief. Can't you see? We're going to be attacked on two fronts. Barbarians and mercenaries," said Robert. "So you see I'm faced with little choice."

"But inviting the British to fight our private war? They would never agree to that, surely?"

"That isn't a matter which need concern you for the moment, Chief. In the meantime, I want you to ensure that the integrity of the presidency and cabinet are safeguarded. I've just signed an emergency order giving you full authority over the Federal and Provincial Police forces of Buenos Aires, including our anti-terrorist and border control teams."

"Do you know anything about this so called mercenary team, Mr President? I mean, who are they? How are they going to strike?" asked the chief.

"The reports that I have suggest they have been hired by De la Mano which is all you need to know for now. Your job is to protect the presidency and secure all the key government agencies and hold them. Marco, I want you to stick to Valiente like a blanket and report directly back to me. That's all gentlemen," said the president, standing up.

"Guy, what do you think?" asked Robert, as looked out of the window.

"If the British forces don't assist, you're finished and it's not the mercenaries you should worry about, it's the mob. You could be looking at over a million angry people taking to the streets and they need only one or two strong leaders to whip them up into a frenzy. You've seen it before."

"I know, and I was afraid you were going to say that. What size do you expect the mercenary force to be?"

"Small, I would say. One-fifty to two hundred, tops. They simply wouldn't have the resources for anything bigger. The costs are enormous and anything larger would be available only to a government run show. The US for example."

"Jesus Christ," muttered Robert as he stood looking through the window again considering his options. He turned around quickly to face Guy.

"Surely this mercenary group must know of the British military presence by now. I mean, it must have been hard to miss. It's been all over the world news, BBC, CNN, everywhere in fact," said Robert.

"Go on, boss."

"Guy, you've been in this business a long time. You know your way around. Is there any way you could find out who this group is and send them a message?"

"Yes, I could do that," said Guy. "But think about it. They would need authentication for the kind of message you're thinking about, otherwise it could be from any old Tom, Dick or Harry."

Robert took off his jacket and hung it on the back of the chair as he paused for thought, looking out through the window.

"Who sent you over here, Guy? I mean, who approached you after I'd requested your help?"

"Come on boss, you know I can't tell you that."

"Very well. Army, navy or air force?"

"Well it wasn't the last two."

"And I would hazard a guess that your man, whoever it was who sent you, would know who these people are."

"I'll tap into the old boys' network, then."

"We don't have long, Guy."

"I know we don't, boss, but anyway…"

Guy moved over to Robert's desk and leant on it with his knuckles.

"Listen, if they get their hands on you. Or even Mrs Campos…"

Robert quickly turned around with a look of anger and fear.

"Mags?"

"She needs to be here. On the island. It's probably the safest place there is at the moment," he said, pausing. "They could take her, you know."

"They wouldn't, would they?"

Guy simply nodded as he remained leaning over the desk and Robert slumped into his chair, angrily pushing a hand through his hair.

"I can fetch her, boss. And I mean, right now."

"Fine, I'll call her. But Guy, make sure you've got back up."

As Guy was heading for the door, Robert stood up and intercepted him at the doorway.

"I need those mercenaries called off quicker than yesterday, Guy."

CHAPTER 43

Try as she might, Clara found it difficult to settle back into a normal life since her return from London. Pascal had been nothing but tender and loving, but even he couldn't help with the heavy burden he knew her to be carrying. She had thought of Jenny constantly ever since their night together, but as the weeks passed, she was able to put it all away in a locked up box, thinking that one day, she might open it again.

On the Sunday evening of the week leading up to Revolution Day, she was at home working on a dull corruption piece concerning one of the president's ministers and her enthusiasm for the story was rapidly waning. She perked up when she heard Pascal's keys jangling outside and as he came through the door, she ran over, stood up on tiptoes and hugged him.

"Whoa! I missed you too, my lovely," he said, kissing her on the forehead.

"I know," she said smiling as they walked into the kitchen diner.

"I'll fix us something tasty for later," he said, taking a bottle of beer from the fridge, as Clara sat on a stool and began uncorking a bottle of red wine.

"I still don't know what to do with those copies we made, you know."

Pascal sighed as he prized the top off the beer bottle.

"Clara, we've been over this already, I don't know how many times."

"Yes I know, but..."

They sat opposite each other at the breakfast bar of their small flat, and Pascal delicately poured the beer into his glass as if it were an art form.

"You said Jenny had given the journals back to that waiter. What's his name again?"

At the sound of Jenny's name, Clara looked away and reached for the bottle of wine.

"Bennet."

"Right. He put them back, you kept the copies and brought them over here with you, so what's the problem?"

"The problem is, I still don't know if I should tell him the truth."

"Who? The president or that man Forsyth?"

"That's the problem," she said.

"Clara listen to me. You couldn't tell Horacio and Rose about me and I would never have let you, you know that. You also have no right to tell the president who his parents are or aren't, for that matter. You just don't have that right."

"I may not have that, no, but as a journalist I have a duty to expose Forsyth for what he is. A fraud of the worst possible kind..."

At that moment Clara's phone vibrated in her back pocket.

"Hello?"

She paused, frowning.

"Yes, speaking."

Clara slowly got up from the stool listening to the caller. Pascal could vaguely hear a man's voice as she stood completely still a few feet from him. She then put a hand up to her mouth and breathed in very suddenly, her face, pale.

"No, no..."

"Clara, what's the matter? What is it?" said Pascal rushing over to her side.

"No! When?" she asked the voice. "Oh my God!"

She burst into tears. Pascal thought she was about to pass out so he held her by the shoulders.

"I can't...Pascal take this, will you, I just can't...talk to him..."

He took the phone as Clara slumped down on the floor against the fridge sobbing, with her hands over her face.

"It's Pascal here. What happened?"

He listened for a few moments, nodding his head and looking down at Clara from time to time.

"Is she...?" followed by a pause.

"I see,"

"Yes...yes, all right, I'll tell her. Yes...fine. Look, here's my number...right, okay. Thanks, Tim."

Pascal knelt down in front of Clara as she sobbed into her hands and he pulled her towards him.

"She's in the hospital and they're looking after her," said Pascal.

He felt powerless and knew Jenny was probably in a worse condition than Tim had wanted to say.

"...oh God," she said flinging her arms around him.

"Come on, over here," he said, helping her up.

Clara sat back on the stool wiping her eyes, and he passed her a tissue.

"What did he say? Is she badly hurt?" she asked blowing her nose.

Pascal looked down at the floor.

"Well? What happened? How is she, for Christ sake?"

"He was calling from the hospital. It's not good, Clara," he said, then paused. "She's in intensive care."

"Oh my God, no. Not Jenny, not Jenny," she said, the tears streaming down her face.

Pascal lit a cigarette. The last thing Tim had said was that Bennet had lied. He hadn't put the journals back, but how could he tell Clara now? She would blame herself for everything, but she had to know.

"That's not all," he said.

She looked up at him as he took her hand.

"Bennet never put the journals back," he said in a low voice.

"Oh Jesus!"

Clara jumped from the stool and put her hands on her head, pulling at her hair

"Tim thinks Forsyth found out and well…"

"What happened, Pascal? Tell me, will you?" she shouted.

He told her that Tim had found her lying at the bottom of the steps leading down to her basement flat. He had been trying to call her most of the evening.

"Forsyth. It was him, I know it. …" she said, bursting into tears again.

"Clara, listen to me will you?" said Pascal, standing up quickly. "This is dangerous now. You're in way over your head and you need to drop it. Now!"

Clara turned around and slapped Pascal furiously across his face.

"Don't you ever speak to me like that! Jenny's lying in hospital and could have been killed. She didn't deserve this!"

He put his hand to his face, examined it and then looked at her, his eyes wide in astonishment.

"And you've been behaving like a primadonna since you got back from London. Jenny this, Jenny that. What the hell's going on?"

"If it hadn't been for her I would never have got this far. So if you can't handle that, well too bad," she said waving her arms at him.

"Why can't you just be a *normal* journalist then?"

She had never seen this side of Pascal and, as she leant against the breakfast bar, she wondered if maybe he was right. Straightening up, she poured herself another glass of wine, took a cigarette from Pascal's pack, lit it and threw the lighter across the worktop.

"But Clara, you don't…"

"I do now," she said with a defiant edge to her voice. "I'm going to bury Forsyth. I'll sell the story to the highest bidder. Journal and all."

"Christ," he muttered. "Has it not even occurred to you that *we* might be in serious danger now?"

"What? Forsyth is going to send a few of his heavies over and sort me out? Don't make me laugh," she said, whilst crying and laughing.

"You know, sometimes you can be incredibly stupid. He probably already has people here anyway, for all we know."

"So, what are you saying? We've got spooks?"

"Clara listen! I think we should go somewhere for a while. Away from here."

Clara thought for a moment before replying.

"Where?"

"Rufino, my parent's."

"You barely talk to them, Pascal and after, well you know…"

"That's the least of our worries."

"I'm not doing anything until I know that Jenny's all right. Can't we call the hospital?"

CHAPTER 44

Tim Hetherington paced up and down outside the intensive care unit in St George's Hospital, and outside, a single police officer stood guard. He had just disconnected his call to Clara and feared the worst.

"Mr Hetherington?"

He turned to see a doctor closing the door to intensive care and walking over to him.

"Yes, doctor. How is she?"

"She has sustained some very serious injuries, probably from a knife or some other sharp object. We have her stabilised but…"

"Yes?"

"We may have to operate if her condition deteriorates. I'm sorry but we are doing everything we can."

"May I see her?"

"I'll let you know as soon as I can. Does she have any family?"

"I'm sorry but I really don't know. I mean, I'll see if…"

"Just a moment, sir," the doctor interrupted, looking over Tim's shoulder towards the nurse's station. "The police are here, you should…"

"Yes of course. I'll be…well, you know where to find me, doctor."

Tim walked slowly over to where the policemen were waiting and he knew that because of him, Jenny was fighting for her life. He had kept the journals, not because he wanted them, but because he knew he couldn't trust

Bennet. And now? In the pit of his stomach he knew he had failed her. He felt wretched and helpless.

The two police officers took him to a spare doctor's office. He told them what he knew; that he had found her in a pool of blood and barely alive. He had immediately called an ambulance and followed it to the hospital. Had he seen anything? Anyone running away? No he hadn't. Would he please come down to the station and make a statement? Now? Yes, now.

Returning to the hospital ninety minutes later, he sat in the waiting area drinking coffee from a white plastic cup. He went over in his mind what he had said to the police in his statement. How long had he known Jenny? She was a close friend and no, they weren't in a relationship. What stories had she been working on, as far as he knew? He told them that he could remember only the coup d'état conspiracy stories she'd been involved in. They didn't need to know about the journals, so he hadn't told them.

He knew that was a mistake and, one way or another, they would probably find out. But he had prepared for that. The two journals were now sitting in a safe deposit box at a branch of his bank in Wimbledon. Trusting Bennet had been his big mistake, and from the moment he had persuaded the ex-navy chef to be part of the ruse to steal the Maitland journals, he had regretted it. Bennet's loathing of Forsyth was matched only by the size of the chip on his fawning and simpering shoulders, and he knew for certain that he would have used the journals for his own nefarious purposes. Blackmail probably. No definitely, he thought.

"Mr. Hetherington?" said a voice.

"Hmm, yes?" he said looking up, surprised.

Standing up quickly, he saw the intensive care doctor standing in front of him.

"I'm sorry, doctor, I was…how is she?"

"No change since we spoke earlier. Her family, have you…?"

"Her colleagues at *The Crusader* are trying to contact them, doctor. Can I see her now?"

"Under the circumstances, I can allow you to see her for a couple of minutes but no longer. Come, I'll take you myself."

He followed the doctor down the corridor. Upon on seeing the police officer outside the door to intensive care, the doctor nodded and swiped his card over the door lock. They entered when the door clicked open, and he led Tim to the far end of the ward. He heard soft beeping noises, clicks and the muffled sounds of voices as nurses went about their business, quietly caring for the patients. Then he saw Jenny lying on a bed in a corner of the ward. She was propped up at an angle, an array of tubes and coloured wires were attached to her, multi-coloured monitoring equipment blinked and small screens showed wavy lines and bars that he didn't understand, although they seemed familiar.

"Don't sit on the bed," said the doctor quietly. "Sit on this chair," he said pointing. "I'll be just over there."

Tim sat down slowly on the chair, found Jenny's hand and held it lightly, looking over to the doctor, who nodded.

"Jenny?"

She was breathing steadily but slowly and he saw her eyes flicker a little as he stroked her hand lightly, not wanting to disturb her.

"Jenny. It's me."

Slowly she opened her eyes a little and turned her head towards him.

"Clara?" she said, looking past him into the distance.

Tim held her hand, felt the salty tears fall to his lips and knew he couldn't find the words he wanted to say.

"Clara?" she said again as she drifted in and out of consciousness.

After holding her hand for a few minutes and gently stroking her hair, Tim stood up and kissed her on the forehead. Holding her right hand for a few moments, he gently released himself and then turned to leave.

As he was about to open the door, a loud and piercing beeping shattered the calm. He turned and saw the doctor and two nurses rush to Jenny's bed, where the doctor immediately held her eyes open and shone a light across them.

"Defib!" said the doctor calmly.

Tim backed away and leant against the wall with a hand over his mouth.

"Clear!"

He watched as the doctor applied the whining defibrillator paddles to her chest and Jenny's body arched upwards. The doctor looked intently at the monitor. A nurse injected something into Jenny's chest and the doctor issued the same instruction again.

"Clear!"

The doctor looked up at the screen once more and pursed his lips.

"Clear!"

He repeated the same actions once more, looking intently at Jenny's lifeless face for twenty more seconds, then turned to one of the nurses and shook his head. The other nurse put a hand up to her mouth and turned away. The doctor pulled the curtains around the bed and turned to Tim who had made several steps towards Jenny's bed.

"I'm sorry," were the only words he heard.

CHAPTER 45

Margarita had time to pack a couple of suitcases about ten minutes after Robert had hung up the phone. Half an hour later, the intercom in her flat buzzed and within minutes she was sitting in the back of the presidential Range Rover, flanked by two burly ex-Parachute Regiment soldiers. Guy was sitting in the front passenger seat and once they had entered the tunnel she leaned forward and tapped him on the shoulder.

"What's going on, Guy?"

"Oh just a precaution, Mrs. Campos. Those crowds can get a bit rowdy and you know what they're like when they all get together with those damned pots and pans," said Guy, trying to make light of the situation.

"Do you think I'm fucking stupid or something?" she said, sitting back in her seat and folding her arms.

The ex-paras coughed nervously and turned to watch the lights of the tunnel flash by like a huge kaleidoscope.

"No madam, I don't, as it happens," said Guy as he turned back to face the road ahead.

"So, are you going to tell me?"

Guy didn't reply, so she glared at the tunnel ahead, hoping she would never have to endure the torture ever again.

"Robert, why have you brought me here like this? What's going on?"

"This is just precautionary, Mags. It will all blow over in a few days, you'll see."

She was standing, arms folded with her back to the window in his private living room in the cupola. Wearing black jeans and an oversize white long sleeved shirt, she had just kicked her shoes off under his desk.

"Crap, that's just crap. I can tell when something's wrong and now you're just lying to me."

Robert rose from his desk and took her hands in his.

"Look, I'm sorry Mags, I..." he said, then paused. "Here, let me show you something."

He took her by the arm, opened the sliding doors to the balcony and led her to the patio at the far end with its view over the huge river delta.

"You see those ships down there?"

"Yes Robert, they've been all over the damn news," she said dismissively with a wave of her hand.

"Months of hard work went into this operation and there are certain elements who want to ruin everything, bring this country's name down and drag it through the mud. Remember De la Mano?"

"Nasty little shit. How could I forget?" she said, turning away from the view.

"On Friday, he and his supporters will be marching in protest throughout the entire country and we have reason to believe that his intentions are not peaceful. Mags, it's going to get nasty and people will die."

Margarita put her hand to her mouth.

"You see why I wanted you here now?"

"But," she said, looking up at him. "I would have been perfectly safe in my flat, surely? Twenty floors up?"

"Mags, you're the president's partner, the first lady, and you know what they call you don't you? I'm sure you don't need reminding."

"Yes, I've heard, thanks."

Robert put his arms around her and kissed her.

"I'll be here when you need me, you know that. And when I'm away, the staff will look after you, so don't worry."

"I suppose so."

"Anyway, Marco's here and you know most of the others."

"It's going to feel like we're prisoners in this damned place."

"Come here."

He held her close as she snuggled her face into his neck.

"I won't let anything happen to you, Mags, I promise," he said softly.

"Pascal, I can't get anything from the hospital. They won't talk to me," said Clara sitting at the breakfast bar.

"Probably because you're not a relative?"

"And Tim's not answering his phone," she said, pushing her hair back. "There's something wrong, I know there is."

"Look, why don't I try *The Crusader*?" he said as he walked into the living room pressing some keys on the phone and sitting down on the sofa.

Clara began looking intently at the black letters on the screen of her phone, pressed a few keys and her eyes widened.

"Hang on, there's a voice message here. I never noticed it before. Here, listen, I'll play it," she said. But Pascal wasn't listening. He was talking quietly on the phone and staring at the floor, with one hand on the back of his head.

She pressed a key once more and a crackly, broken up voice could be heard through the tiny speaker. A woman's voice.

Clara.   Be   careful...Forsyth...Operation   Blenheim is...invasion...call back. Love you.

Clara felt a strange tingle in her tummy at the sound of Jenny's voice, then a stab in her gut as she put a hand up to her mouth.

"You know what she's trying to say don't you? I have to get back to the president. I have to stop this," she said, turning around. "Pascal?"

"Pascal, I said…"

He stood up and looked over at her, his face expressionless.

"Clara, Jenny's dead."

CHAPTER 46

A t zero seven hundred, the captains of the Royal Navy warships, together with senior officers of all the other units in Operation Blenheim, were driven to each of the dozen military bases in and around the city of Buenos Aires, where they met with their Argentine counterparts. Following a slick and meticulously planned agenda, each of the British commanders brought with him selected specialists in the fields of munitions, engineering, bomb disposal, airborne and amphibious assault, including special forces trained in deep penetration behind enemy lines. During the next forty eight hours, junior members of these teams conducted classroom training sessions with the local forces, followed by a few hours of more tactical training in and around the military bases, before returning to the classroom barracks. Meanwhile, the more senior British commanders had persuaded their Argentine counterparts to allow them full access to their command and control structure from the top down, including army, navy and air force, always in the guise of training purposes.

The local commanders, overwhelmed by the professionalism of their British counterparts, opened their doors and systems in a spirit of cooperation not seen since the US military's influx into Britain in 1942. They conducted exercises simulating assaults by land, sea and air, following which, the commanders were billeted with their own quarters in each base, backed up with vehicles of all descriptions, including battle tanks, troop carriers, countless Land Rovers, Rapier missile systems and tactical support vehicles. The amount of hardware on the ground was just enough to facilitate the training exercises, yet not enough to represent a perceived threat. This was much admired by the poorly equipped local forces. They relished the chance to crawl all over the equipment and were encouraged to do so by all the British commanders in each base.

General Roger Sandiford, DSO, Officer Commanding, had been appointed in overall command of Operation Blenheim. Following his evening review of operations in each of the bases, he was to be found drinking a refreshing gin and tonic at a cocktail party in the officers' mess, hosted by the Teniente General Suarez 1st regiment of fusiliers' headquarters, twelve kilometres north of the capital.

"Not a bad day's work, gentlemen," he said quietly whilst scanning the officer's mess.

Near him were standing four other British officers of similar rank from the navy, army and air force, all cheerfully sipping their drinks as waiters passed between the groups, with trays laden with refreshments.

"The local forces seem pretty enthusiastic, don't they," said one.

"Hardly surprising when you see the state of their kit," said another, jovially.

"Indeed, they probably couldn't fight off a pygmy invasion with that lot. Might as well have their men issued with spears," said another, snorting with laughter.

"Gentlemen, I'd hate to spoil the party, but you should know that the main operation is being brought forward by forty eight hours. Trouble brewing locally apparently," said General Sandiford, lowering his voice. "Problems?"

"No, certainly not, Roger. No problems on our end. Quite the contrary; the lads are keen to get stuck in," said one, an opinion shared enthusiastically by each of his colleagues.

"The operation will now commence at 0100 on Wednesday morning and you should receive those orders within the hour," said General Sandiford quietly. "You should all know the drill by now. This should be seen as a training exercise with your forces taking up the agreed positions and waiting, until the final order to execute is given."

The officers all nodded in unison.

"And when that moment comes, we expect resistance to be minimal," the general continued.

"Futile," said one and echoed by the others.

"Well, *chin-chin* gentlemen. We really ought to mingle you know. Don't want to upset the natives, what?" said general Sandiford as he bowed his head a fraction of an inch and clicked his heels imperceptively.

The British officers enjoyed drinks and snacks with the Argentine officers of all ranks late into the night, assisted by numerous official translators and by midnight were returning to their barracks in staff cars or being ferried back to their ships in launches and rigid inflatable craft.

On the bridge of the flagship, HMS Lionheart, Admiral Milton 'Sparky' Hudson sipped his hot chocolate as he leaned against the starboard wing and watched the launches cut through the calm waters off the capital. A junior officer walked slowly up and down inside the wheelhouse and, as he lit a cigarette, the admiral wondered what on earth he was doing, sitting in an aircraft carrier not six months out of mothballs, playing war games off the coast of a troubled state like Argentina. He'd been a career naval officer since being packed off to Dartmouth Royal Naval College at the age of eighteen and here he was, in his last major posting before retirement, commanding the largest fleet he had ever seen, all for what? To train some third world banana republic how to defend itself?

But then everything in his life changed in an instant when he heard the words...

"Sir, signal for you."

The junior officer had walked across and handed him a small, sealed brown envelope marked *secret*, which he opened and then read and deciphered with a small credit card sized decipher device he carried with him at all times.

It read…

Mission objective updated
Secure Buenos Aires
Establish Crown Colony

His heart had been lifted by the signal, as he knew that in twenty four hours, he wouldn't simply be watching two or three launches skimming across the water, but fleets of amphibious landing craft, RIBS, Chinook and Apache helicopters roaring along the coast in all directions. He wasn't entirely sure whose bright idea it had been, but since military history was a pet subject of his, the failed River Plate invasions of the nineteenth century he well remembered from his naval warfare courses, were examples of how not to win a battle. He knew that tomorrow would change everything and reverse the course of history, probably earn him the knighthood he so richly deserved, and indelibly mark the name, Milton 'Sparky' Hudson in the history books, in perpetuity.

He questioned neither the morality, nor the ethics, nor cared for the politics. It was a military operation and a point of enormous pride, since the Royal Navy, the senior service, was taking the leading role. As he watched the city lights and the cars moving to and fro along the distant coast roads, he knew that tonight he would sleep a contented man.

"Clara, this is a very busy time for me. Surely you got everything you needed last week? I mean, can't it wait?" asked the president.

After numerous attempts, Clara had finally managed to get through to President Crawford, and at that precise moment she felt numbed to his excuses. If Jenny's death meant anything, she knew she had to be the one to stop the madness.

"Clara, I don't have much time, so can we please move along?"

She paused and switched the phone to her other ear.

"The Maitland Plan, Mr President," she said in a calm, monotone voice.

She waited as the line went silent for a long moment.

"I'm sure I don't know to what you're referring," he said with a faint defensive chuckle.

"Ten thirty tomorrow morning," she said.

"If there's some detail about Operation Blenheim you're not sure about, I can get Roxy to call you."

"Miss Pla, Mr Pérez and even Margarita are aware of the Maitland Plan, then, are they?"

He felt a rush of adrenaline in the pit of his stomach.

"Very well. You've got ten minutes," he said, disconnecting the call and slowly placing the handset down on his desk.

Robert walked to the balcony window, pulled at the handle angrily and slid it open, taking a long breath of fresh air. Yes, he had seen the news about Jenny Lane. Yes, *The Crusader* had, not surprisingly, made it their lead story. And yes, they had described her death as an assassination, going on to outline her work on the numerous conspiracy theories she had written about, not least her views on Operation Blenheim which they knew was under the control of Admiral Forsyth. They had stopped short of actually implicating him in Jenny's death, the very idea of which was absurd, thought Robert.

But where was their proof of an assassination? He could deny the existence of anything that sounded remotely like Maitland. After all, neither he nor Jack had ever been stupid enough to actually write anything down, had they?

Anyway, he knew that the stories had all been discarded as fanciful speculation by most of the other media, thanks to Jack. Heck, even the prime minister had publicly debunked Jenny's articles, so who would everyone believe?

But Clara hadn't mentioned Jenny, had she? Why not? Perhaps she was just fishing, he reassured himself.

"Probably," he said, with a shrug.

As most of the twenty five million inhabitants of Buenos Aires slept, a low hum could be heard from the river as landing craft splashed across the small waves, heaved up on the narrow beaches at numerous coastal locations, from Vicente Lopez to San Isidro, pouring out their human cargo. The surrounding roads had been closed to all traffic and pedestrians by the local police, who saw it simply as part of the Friendship Flag exercise, paying little attention to the sudden activity. Chinook helicopters whooshed in, carrying Land Rovers and other cargo on long lines and cargo nets suspended from their bellies, with Apache attack helicopters following them inland. On the bridge of his flagship, Admiral Hudson watched through binoculars and listened with enormous pride to the cacophony of orders and the living sounds of the ship in action as, one by one, the jets roared with their take off preps, screamed along the ship's runway and flew gracefully up the ramp, and into the sky.

It was a sight he had long dreamed of, and when at zero five thirty his captain reported that the operation had been completed thirty minutes ahead of schedule, he looked once again at the twinkling street lights, felt the silence of the dawn, shivered a little from the chill and made his way to his quarters, a proud man.

After Robert hung up, Clara slid the phone into her back pocket and returned to her laptop on the breakfast bar. She then called Pascal and told him about her conversation with the president.

She knew he still wanted them to go away somewhere safe, but she had been adamant about seeing it through to the end, whatever the cost. When he had told her of Jenny's death, it had shaken her badly and she had spent the rest of that night prone on the sofa, not wanting to talk. Pascal, sitting alone in the dark of the kitchen, smoking and drinking, had resolved to support her and he woke the following day with the same conviction.

"Clara, all this will do is stop the military...um, whatever it is they're really doing. But what about me?"

She had to admit it to herself. She had been so caught up in events that she hadn't given Pascal the time he needed. Here was a man who had discovered a truth that neither had fully confronted. Hadn't he put his feelings aside for her, she asked herself.

"I know and I'm sorry."

"I thought it would be enough just to know they are my parents, but now it's not Clara. It's not and it won't be for him either. He has to know the truth and there's only one person who can tell him."

"Forsyth?"

"No. He never will. He just wouldn't. Ever."

"But who then?"

"Mrs Campos. Margarita."

She knew he was right. He had calmly worked it through and come up with the only answer to the question she had struggled with for so many weeks. She was the rock that Robert leaned on.

"What do I tell her?" asked Clara.

"Everything. It's what I would want to know, and one day perhaps I will."

She had already told Pascal what she knew about Robert from the journals. What more was there to tell, she wondered.

"It will break him, Pascal."

"Maybe, maybe not. But look at me. At least now I *know*. But you know what? It's not enough and it doesn't feel right."

"What do you mean?"

"Because I know how he's going to feel and probably much worse."

Pascal paused and she knew there was something else. Something he really needed to say.

"This may sound odd, but it feels like he's my brother."

CHAPTER 47

C lara, this way please," said the president as he led her up the sweeping stairs of the island residence. "I'm a little pushed for time today, so you'd better make it quick."

This wasn't the usual Robert Crawford, but then, what did she expect, she wondered as she followed him.

"Oh, this shouldn't take long, Robert."

"It's Mr President actually, young lady."

She ignored the comment and sat on the cream leather sofa as he sat behind his desk.

Turning to her, he looked at his watch and raised his eyebrows as Clara swallowed nervously and crossed her legs. Placing her old dog-eared notepad on her lap and holding her pen at the ready, she knew she wouldn't need either.

"Tell me. Have I not always been truthful with you?" she asked.

He frowned, wondering what was coming next.

"Without question," he replied.

"But you haven't always been truthful with me, have you?"

"To the best of my knowledge, I believe I have, yes," he said, clicking a pen nervously.

"This so called Operation Blenheim," she said, struggling to hold back her distaste. "It's the largest peacetime military operation ever conceived by Great Britain, but what I neglected to ask you when we last spoke was, what exactly are the main objectives?"

He vaguely remembered her having asked him the same question already, so he reeled off the lines he had given to so many other journalists and TV channels, ending with a characteristic smile, his hands clasped together in front of him.

"So you see Clara, Argentina, with the kind assistance of His Majesty's government will be safer and more prepared than it's ever been. Essential training and partnership you see. Our citizens will sleep soundly in their beds, safe in the knowledge that our borders, our shorelines and our airspace are secure against any possible threat."

"And all planned nearly two hundred years ago over Claret and expensive cigars in the private dining room of a small gentleman's club in the West End of London," she said calmly, raising an eyebrow.

Robert felt a familiar sensation just below his rib cage, reminding him of a time long ago when the headmaster would call him into his study for a punishment he knew was inevitable.

"You know, Clara, that's what I've always liked about you," he said standing up, pointing at her and moving to the front of the desk. "Your boundless ability and imagination."

Remaining seated, she sat up a little straighter and continued.

"And you didn't think for a moment that anyone would notice because the people of my country would, as you just put it, 'be sleeping soundly in their beds' while you quietly invaded *my* country."

Robert propped himself against the front of the desk with his hands as he faced Clara, a trickle of sweat forming on his left temple. As he looked passively towards her and then beyond at the grey ships sitting peacefully at anchor, his mind worked furiously to bend to the lies he had always lived with. But all he could picture was the headmaster standing over him with that belt in his hand.

He squeezed the top of the desk with his fingers and knew that whatever words he uttered now could only be his own, so he opened his mouth to speak.

Clara, sensing his discomfort, was not inclined to allow him any leeway and she quickly cut him off.

"I know everything, Robert, and it's time all the lies ended," she said, her eyes focused on his. "I've read everything there is to know about The Maitland Plan, how Jack Forsyth made you and moulded you in his own image. You are his. You always have been. You are his British President."

He walked slowly past Clara to the windows, slid them open and stood on the balcony, his hands gripping the stainless steel handrail.

"How?"

"Jenny Lane," she said without turning around.

"Jesus."

Clara remained seated. She didn't turn around, but checked the mini recorder in the top pocket of her black leather coat. Yes, it was still recording, she noted.

They remained silent for a long while. Robert took a box of king size filters from his shirt pocket, lit one and inhaled, blowing the smoke out slowly as he looked down at the brown waves lapping against the triangular cement blocks below.

"What do you want?" he mumbled.

Clara rose slowly from the sofa, put her notebook and pen carefully in her pocket and zipped up her coat as she felt a chill from the breeze coming through the window. She put her hands in her pockets, shrugged her shoulders a little and moved a little closer to Robert, who was still silently leaning against the rail.

"That this charade ends now. Right here, today."

"Or?"

"You know what I do."

He turned around to face her as he fought the anger raging inside.

"If you go public with this, I'm as good as dead."

"I won't need to. You're going to call Forsyth."

"I see," he said, lighting another cigarette from the one he already had in his mouth.

"Are you aware of what is going to happen on Friday?" he asked.

"Día de la Revolución?"

"It's a little more than that this year," he said with a short explanation of what he knew was about to take place.

"This changes nothing whatsoever."

"I will lose my country, Clara. Can't you see that?"

"It isn't your country and you are not my president."

Clara was desperately fighting the temptation to tell him everything she knew. Scotland, specifically Rhu, Mr C and Pascal were pushing at the front of her mind. She knew she had to give him something more, a doubt, however small.

"I won the presidency fairly and squarely," he said, with his hands raised. "You know that and assisted me in that. It may be the nature of the beast, but I am still your rightful president, in spite of everything."

"No you are not."

Rubbing his forehead and flicking the cigarette over the balcony, he began to feel lightheaded as he walked back to his desk.

"Listen, Clara," he started, trying his best to summon up a smile. "I concede that I may have overstepped the mark with Operation Blenheim, which by the way I carried out in the very best interests of this country, but I am and will remain its legitimate president."

She swallowed hard for what she knew was the only possible way for him to doubt himself.

"You are not who you think you are, Robert."

With those words he stood up angrily and smashed his fists on the desk.

"For pity's sake what do you want, woman?" he pleaded, his face contorting with frustration.

"That you order the withdrawal of all British forces from my country, right now, here in this office…"

"And?"

"And get Jack Forsyth on the phone. You need to speak to him."

"This is absurd, Clara," he replied with forced, nervous laughter.

She stood up, walked over to his desk and picked up the phone, at which he grabbed her wrist and forced her to drop the handset.

"That won't be necessary," he said with a tone that frightened Clara.

"I'm warning you. I have enough material to sink both you and what remains of the British government, not to mention that monster Jack Forsyth," she said, standing over him and rubbing her wrist.

"I could of course have you removed with just one press of a button and that would be the end of all this."

Clara looked at her watch and pointed at it.

"No, Robert, I don't think so. You see, if Pascal and others don't hear from me by noon, the entire Maitland Plan will be uploaded to the Internet."

He stood up and faced her, his arms folded.

"You don't honestly think anyone is going to believe some fanciful plan your friend Jenny Lane came up with do you?"

Clara had reached the closest point in her entire life to actually striking someone. She bit down on her lip, turned and fetched her computer bag, which she unzipped and withdrew a single sheet of paper.

"This, read it," she said, placing the sheet on the desk.

He rested his hands on the desk and read for about fifteen seconds, then slumped down in his chair. Having now read a summary of the journal entries for the five years leading up to his election as president, the Cristal impeachment plan, Jack Forsyth's approval to proceed with Maitland and its ultimate objectives, he had seen enough and pushed the sheet of paper away from him.

"Every single page of these journals will be published in the fastest manner known to man. Call off the invasion of my country. Now!" she said loudly.

He remained impassive in his seat, clasping his hands together, joining and unjoining his fingers. He just doesn't get it, does he, she thought.

"Listen to me, Robert. Has it never occurred to you that your life has been a series of well-orchestrated rehearsals?"

"No Clara, no!" he shouted, banging his fists on the desk once again.

But deep in his memory, the times he would sneak around at night and listen to their grown up conversations came back to him. Those mentors, Jack, and the feelings of self-doubt that he had always felt, rushed back to him in vivid technicolour flashes.

Clara moved a few steps from the desk and put her hands in her coat pockets.

"If you make me leave now, you'll regret it for the rest of your life, Robert."

He sat back in his seat, angrily pulled at his tie, which he then ripped off and tossed across the room.

Clara, her lower lip trembling, then leant across the desk, placed her hands palms down and slowly enunciated the words so that there was no mistake in what she wanted.

"Pick up the phone and call Forsyth."

As he looked into her eyes, he slowly picked up the phone, dialled a number and waited.

"Speakerphone," she said, loudly.

He obeyed by pressing a button and the long dialling tone echoed through the office. After a few moments, they heard a woman's voice.

"Admiral Forsyth's office. Jill speaking."

Robert paused. He had no idea what to say, so Clara made an upward inflection with her head and the seconds passed.

"Hello? This is Admiral Forsyth's office. May I…"

"Jack Forsyth, please," said Robert in a monotone voice.

"I'm afraid he's not here at the moment, sir. May I ask who's calling?"

"Find him, damn it!"

There was a pause on the line and the sound of a nervous cough.

"One moment please…"

They looked at each other, Robert standing, with his hands spread flat on the desk and Clara now rooted before him, her arms folded and one hand playing with a tissue.

"Putting you through…" said Jill.

"Forsyth."

"Jack, it's me…"

"My dear fellow, this isn't our usual channel…"

"Not now, Jack. There's someone here who wishes to speak to you. You're on speaker," he said, pushing his chair back from the desk.

There was a moment of silence.

"This is Clara Tomkinson," said Clara calmly.

"Miss Tomkinson, this can serve no useful purpose you know…"

Clara cut him off and leant over the desk.

"Listen to me Admiral. I have the journals here in Buenos Aires and they're somewhere safe, where not even you can find them. You see, Jenny never had them in her possession, but you had her killed anyway, didn't you?"

Silence descended on the room, the only sound being a sigh from the speakerphone.

"Abort the invasion of my country, Admiral."

"You have absolutely no idea, do you Miss Tomkinson? Just like that Lane woman. She should never have…"

"I'll let Robert be the judge of that."

"Miss Tomkinson, I'm warning you…"

Robert stood up, put on his jacket and adjusted the sleeves.

"Jack, the entire operation is aborted," he said and then stabbed a button, ending the call.

"I'll make my own way out," said Clara, picking up her computer bag. "Oh and you can keep that," she said, pointing at the photocopy on the desk. "I have plenty more should you decide not to respect the will of the people."

She closed the door gently behind her, walked slowly down the stairs and as she was approaching the doors, bumped into a smiling and radiant Margarita.

"Clara, what's the matter? You look a bit flustered," said Margarita, tilting her head to one side.

"Could you call me?" said Clara as a man in uniform opened the front door.

"It's important," she said, looking back at Margarita, as she stepped into the car.

As she drove her Jeep out of the tunnel and into the sunlight, Clara tried to compose herself. She adjusted her hair, crumpled what remained of the tissue in her hand and gazed ahead out of the window. She watched as people went about their normal lives. Mothers pushing babies in prams, beggars with their hands out asking for money on street corners and bus drivers with their hands on their chins, looking frustrated at intersections. She opened the window a crack and smelled peanuts roasting, churros cooking in hot fat, the aroma of dark tobacco and the unmistakeable fragrance of Buenos Aires drains. She smiled and cried as the tears fell down her cheeks and bit her lip as she saw Jenny's smiling face.

Margarita rushed up the stairs, ran down the corridor to Robert's office and burst through the door. She turned and saw him speaking at his desk, rushed over to him and stopped as he turned to look at her, his face full of anguish.

"Robert? Are you there?" said a man's tinny voice, then a click as Robert quickly leaned across the desk, pressed a button and silenced the call.

"Oh, Mags, it's you," he said, his voice weak and trembling.

"What is it? What's happened?" she said, standing completely still.

"It's everything Mags. I'm losing everything."

"Is it Clara? That bloody woman…"

"No, it's me," he said, pointing at his chest. "It's me, I've, I've…"

"But, darling, what's happened?" she asked, moving closer.

He buried his face in his hands and put his forehead on the desk. Margarita rushed over, took him by the arm and led him to the sofa where she sat them both down.

"I don't know what it is, but you haven't lost me," she said stroking his hair.

He blinked his eyes and looked up at her.

"Will you please tell me what's going on?" she asked as he raised his head, wiping his eyes.

"You have to tell me," she said quietly and running her hand over his cheek. "Please?"

"It was Jack Forsyth I was talking to when you came in."

"Who? I'm not sure if I…"

"He…"

"Yes?" she said, holding his hands.

"I think he had Jenny Lane murdered in London. You know, Clara's friend."

Margarita put her hand to her mouth and breathed in sharply.

"Oh lord. Oh no," she said.

He then lay his head on the back of the sofa and told her everything he could remember, from the ranch in Sancti Spiritu, his trips to London, right up to Clara coming to see him.

For a long time they sat in silence and Margarita listened to seagulls screeching, the waves crashing outside and the wind whistling through the small window gaps. Robert remained with his head on the back of the sofa and stared at the sun reflecting in ripples on the ceiling, his eyes moving slowly from detail to detail.

Finally he spoke. "You'll probably want to go now won't you?"

"Why?"

He sat up slowly and then stood up.

"Because well…I'm not the man you thought I was. Christ, I'm not the man I thought I was," he said, looking out over the river.

She stood up and took his hands in hers.

"You are the man I always thought you were, my love. I can't think of you in any other way. Why should I go? Why?"

"I've, I've…"

"I'm not going anywhere and I never will."

"There was always something, Mags. It was always there but I couldn't figure out what it was. Just something, you know?"

"I think so. No, no, I don't really."

"When I was a boy at the ranch, just something I felt. I can't really explain it. Jack has been using me my whole life. Clara was right. I just couldn't see it."

She pulled away slowly and looked up at him.

"But Robert, you're the president. The people voted for you and you won fair and square."

"No, Mags, it was all planned, fixed. I was meant to be president. I was always meant to be president."

"I'm sorry, but I just don't understand all this," she said, backing away.

"Neither do I Mags, but I intend to find out."

"What are you going to do?"

"What time is it?" he asked, turning around quickly.

"There on your wrist. Look!" she said, pointing.

"Eleven forty five. Right!" he said, marching over to his desk, where he pressed a button on the speakerphone.

"Ambassador Brabant please!"

Margarita whispered to him, asking if he would like a drink. He nodded and she disappeared into the kitchen, where the clinking of glasses could be heard.

"Brabant!"

"Sir Michael, it's Robert Crawford."

"Yes, Mr President. How are you?"

"Sir Michael, I'm formally advising you that the republic of Argentina has withdrawn its support for Operation Blenheim with immediate effect. All British forces have twenty four hours to leave our sovereign territory, including our airspace and national waters. Any British military remaining after that deadline will be seen as hostile and dealt with accordingly."

Robert could hear the clink of ice going into glasses from the kitchen as he waited for a response.

"And one more thing, Sir Michael."

"Yes, Mr President?"

"All hardware, including vehicles, tracked and untracked, landing craft, aircraft, missile systems, armaments and ammunition currently in place on Argentine soil, including all and any installations on the island of Martín García, are hereby embargoed and deemed property of the Argentine state. My security forces are, as we speak, in transit to make a full inventory of such hardware, and I expect your full cooperation," he said, pausing for a moment. "I trust that is clear."

"Understood, Mr President, but just one question if I may. How do you expect our men to return to their ships?"

"Commercial and military vessels will be made available to HM Forces, Sir Michael, and they will assist in the orderly transport of the men to their warships. Other than that, improvise. After all, you Brits are pretty good at that kind of thing, aren't you?"

"Will that be all?"

"A written order will be issued by my home affairs minister and couriered directly to your embassy within the hour, Sir Michael. And I don't need to remind you that this matter should be handled in the strictest of confidence. Oh and if there is any doubt in your mind as to the seriousness of my intentions, I would suggest that you speak to Admiral Forsyth directly," he said, finishing.

"That is all thank you, unless you have anything you wish to add?"

"No, sir."

Robert looked at his watch. It was eleven fifty five so he called Clara. It mattered little that he wasn't using a secure line. He was simply delivering a message, he thought.

"Hello? Yes?"

"Operation Blenheim has been terminated with immediate effect," he said, then disconnected the call.

He then called Roxy Pla at the Casa Rosada, and instructed her to contact the home affairs office; he also told her to call the minister of internal security to arrange the inventory. He then dialled three more buttons and asked Guy to see him immediately.

A few moments later, Margarita returned with his whisky, which he took over to the balcony, leaned on the guardrail, breathed out heavily and lowered his head.

"Guy's here," said Margarita, quietly behind him.

Guy saw the president on the balcony and walked over, stopping just before the French windows.

"Guy, I need that information now more than ever," he said, without turning around.

"Boss, I've identified three possible groups. One Russian and the other two are US outfits."

"And?"

"We're discounting the Russians because it's beyond their scope. The Americans? I have someone making contact and I should have an answer later today."

"That's not soon enough, man!" said Robert turning around. "Operation Blenheim has been aborted due to technical issues, so *now* do you see the problem?"

"This is going to be…"

"I know. Now please, Guy, that message must get through before it's too late. Get moving, we haven't got much time."

"Yes boss," said Guy, turning quickly to leave.

Since his arrival in Buenos Aires, Guy had always thought things were not quite as they seemed, yet he knew that discretion was his primary asset. His years of training had seen to that, with his friend Robert and the lovely Mrs Campos being his primary charges. He liked them, enjoyed being close to them and knew that his only function was to protect them.

He remembered when he had first met Robert, before the dark days of the military dictatorship. They had clicked as friends, enjoyed wild parties and lived dangerously. He had seen leadership qualities in him, even then, but somehow he felt that Robert was losing whatever tenuous grip he may have had on the country and it worried him. His bizarre measures to bring Britain to the streets, towns and cities of Argentina had always struck him as outlandish, nay, romantic colonial idealism, and now it had backfired badly.

But he wasn't there to question President Crawford's politics, he was there to protect him and Mrs Campos, as best he could. He of all people knew that Friday would be a day of reckoning, and he had been surprised at Robert's clever idea to alert the mercenaries to the British presence. In fact, Guy had to admit to himself that Robert had beaten him to it, but he was sure it had been a fluke. Robert was many things, but he wasn't a strategist.

As he pressed *dial* on his phone, he tapped his fingers on the door of the presidential security chalet, hoping that his old friend Shorty Winehouse had found what they needed.

"Guy?"

"Yep."

"It's SOF 19, I'm certain of it."

"Do you have anyone in there?" asked Guy.

"I have at least one in most of the groups, mate."

Shorty, ex 22 SAS, ran a small 'logistics' consultancy firm from a converted chapel in Brecon, South Wales, specialising in training special forces soldiers looking for employment following their discharge from the British Army. He ran a tight ship and only ever dealt with people he knew and trusted.

"Look," said Guy. "This is the message they should receive: '*Large contingent British force active in your zone. At least two divisions and a substantial naval task force. Your call.*' Then make sure they see these aerial shots of their current status which I'm emailing to you now. Christ, they only need to look at the news, anyway!"

"Got that."

"How confident are you, Shorty, mate?"

"Ten minutes?"

"Okay," said Guy, hanging up.

CHAPTER 48

Luis de la Mano switched on his filthy and coffee stained PC, checked the balance of the Amalgamated General Workers Union's bank account and smiled as he saw a transfer notification to the account number in Malta he had been given. Two and a half million US was a staggering amount by anyone's reckoning, yet he truly believed that his presidency was worth that and probably much more. But that was a mere detail, he thought, as he typed in the instructions for the final payment, once the Crawford puppet had been unseated and dealt with.

He knew the down payment was non-refundable, but he also felt that those no-nonsense tough guys he had sat talking to in Albuquerque, not forgetting that delicious redhead of course, were the kind of people he could do business with. They understood him and although he hadn't been given the chance to explain why he needed their services – they had each put a hand up to stop him, with one actually slicing a finger across his throat, which he found highly amusing – he felt they understood and could probably feel the passion burning within him from where they were seated. He smiled and stuck his chin out at the thought.

"Ramón? Get in here," he shouted from his small office in the union headquarters, two blocks from Dock Sud.

Ramón poked his head around the office door.

"Luis?"

"Shut the door and sit down."

Ramón sat on a wobbly blue plastic schoolroom chair hoping it would take his weight.

"All set. They have the fifty percent down payment, so you need to confirm by entering your password just here, authorising the final payment for when they've completed the job."

Ramón dutifully did what he was told and then asked if Victor had done the same.

"I wouldn't trust that streak of piss to tie his shoelaces up. It's just you and me now, so, not a word," he said, tapping the side of his nose.

Ramón nodded. He loathed De la Mano in direct proportion to how much he feared him.

"There won't be another meeting, since I'm bringing everything forward by thirty six hours."

"But Luis?" said Ramón, looking at his watch. "That's less than two days away."

"You'd better get moving then, hadn't you? Get on the phone and call them. What are you waiting for?"

"Yes Luis, I'll get straight onto it…" he said, quickly standing up.

As De la Mano was completing his online transaction, the phone rang on his desk, which he quickly answered and listened intently for several seconds.

"Yes, yes. No problem. He'll contact you directly."

Smiling and nodding as he listened, De la Mano stood up, balling his fist triumphantly.

"That will be dealt with immediately. You've been a great help to the cause, Mr Pérez."

CHAPTER 49

By early evening on Tuesday, Robert felt the entire weight of the previous days bear down on him. They had enjoyed lunch together, he had succumbed to a few too many glasses of Rioja and Margarita had led him into the bedroom, closed the curtains and kissed him whilst propping his head up on a pillow. He had closed his eyes almost immediately and she had shut the door quietly, then made her way downstairs to the gym, cell phone in hand.

Sitting on an exercise bench, she sent a text to Clara asking her to call. She well remembered the pained expression in her eyes when Clara had asked her to call. It was unusual, she thought. Clara had always been so jolly and carefree, but she felt there was something she needed to tell her. She had seen it in her eyes, just as she had seen the effect on Robert after Clara had left his office.

As she was lost in her thoughts, gazing at the distant shoreline through the windows, her phone trilled into life.

"Clara, it's you. I was just about to call," she said, cheerfully.

"How's Robert?" Clara asked.

"I don't know really. I've never seen him like this."

"I can't really tell you what I said to him I'm afraid. You'll have to ask him, if he'll tell you. Sorry, that could have sounded better..." said Clara.

"Listen, I don't get involved in his work, I never have. But I know something's wrong. I overheard him talking about the operation. You know, Operation Blenheim, anyway…"

"No, Margarita, it's not that."

"Then why did you ask me to call you?" Margarita asked.

She waited as Clara paused.

"Come on, I know there's something. I've always known," said Margarita.

One of the reasons Clara had always admired Margarita, was her strength. She well knew what was being written about her, how people whispered so many ugly things about her, but she had always known that she loved Robert above anything in her life.

"Which is why I can only tell you. No, I *have* to tell you."

"Well, what is it?"

Clara took another deep breath before continuing.

"None of what you're seeing is Robert's fault. I want you to understand that. He's been manipulated in the worst possible way. I still find it unimaginable, but I'm afraid it's true. Since the day he was born. No, even before that in fact."

"What are you trying to say? You're really not making much sense, you know."

Clara went on to explain what she knew of Robert's birth in Scotland, his upbringing in Sancti Spiritu, the secret meetings of the Maitland Group and the manipulations of Jack Forsyth.

"Jesus," said Margarita, putting a hand to her mouth.

"I am absolutely certain of all this, and have evidence to prove it…"

"You're not going to…?"

"Publish? No, I'm not. But there's one more thing of which I am absolutely certain," she said, pausing. "Jack Forsyth is Robert's father."

Margarita wondered why she wasn't surprised at what she'd just heard and then she remembered the times he had taken her to *Las Siete*

Palmas ranch and the stiffness she had felt between him and his parents. His parents, yes they were still that after all, she thought.

Clara visualised Margarita standing before her. She saw the strong woman she had always known and felt that maybe she had underestimated her. Maybe everyone had, she wondered.

"He's a lucky man, you know."

Margarita didn't reply at first, but as she looked over at the windows again, she felt a little less confused, as if part of a riddle had been solved.

"Clara, I know why you told me this and I would have done the same. But do you honestly think for one moment that I'm going to tell him?"

"You're not?"

"No, because as far as he's concerned, Horacio and Rose are his parents. They've always been, so why does he need to know?"

There was brief silence as Clara breathed in.

"Because they are Pascal's parents."

Margarita hung her head down to her chest.

"Oh God. And Pascal knows?" she asked quietly.

"Yes. We found out together. Not all that long ago, actually."

"How?"

Clara told her about their trip to Rufino and ended by telling her about their encounter with Mrs Menendez.

"They were swapped?"

"Yes."

"Oh God, Clara. What am I going to do?"

"You have to tell him."

"Clara, I really do not want to do it…wait, have you spoken to Pascal about this yet?"

She had and she hadn't, she said to herself. She hadn't actually sat down with him and asked him what he really wanted, since they had returned from Sancti Spiritu. He had barely mentioned it, apart from the other day. It was almost as if he was content in just knowing that they were there. That they existed.

"No, no I haven't. Not really. Well, sort of."

"Then perhaps you should, Clara. After everything you told Robert today, this would crush the life out of him."

"Maybe, maybe not, but either way he has to know that Jack Forsyth is his father and you're the only person who can tell him that. Not me, not Pascal, only you."

"I don't know, Clara, I really don't," she said, raising her eyes to the ceiling.

"Margarita, what he does when you tell him, is up to him," said Clara. "Listen, I know this must sound strange, but I think you should know what Pascal said to me."

"Yes?"

"He said that he felt like Robert was a brother to him now."

"Yes, I think I see now. He should know what Pascal knows and maybe they could both talk to each other. You're right, it's not up to us anymore."

As the sun rose over the smart Buenos Aires port area of Puerto Madero, Pascal shuffled to the kitchen in his boxers and faded *Tangerine Dream* tee shirt, filled the electric kettle and looked over at the suitcase and backpacks by the front door. He would let Clara sleep a little longer, as they had talked long into the night. He then poured the remains of a bottle of wine down the sink, his head pounded, and he wondered if he could really look at Horacio and Rose in the same way ever again. Taking a mug of coffee into the bedroom, he kissed Clara's sleeping face and stroked her hair as he put the mug down on the bedside table.

Drinking his coffee, he opened the usual news sites on his PC, all of which headlined stories on the planned marches and protests for Friday. TVN carried a story describing the protests as many times larger than those seen during Virginia Cristal's impeachment and estimating that the turnout would be more than three million. It reminded him of why he loathed the mainstream press so much and how they so loved to turn a crisis into a drama.

He then checked the newsgroups and forums that had been forming, such as 1J which he quickly realised was 1 July, the date of the marches. They had each attracted nearly a million members, eclipsing his own online efforts by an embarrassing figure he didn't want to even think about.

He felt relieved that Clara had finally agreed with their escape to the tranquillity of Rufino and the dingy hostel. He had come to see it as their secret refuge from the madness of Buenos Aires, and felt a surge of excitement at the thought.

He thought of Maria and Sebastian, whom he would be confronting with the truth, so he lit a cigarette, as Clara came into the kitchen sipping her coffee, and ruffling his hair lovingly on her way past.

"All set?" she asked, pulling up a stool and sitting down.

"I think so, but I wonder what we'll come back to," he said.

Margarita always enjoyed her mornings on the island, but this time she felt trapped.

She let Robert sleep on, and as she was making a coffee she noticed his phone vibrating on the kitchen work surface next to the toaster. Picking it up, the display was showing 'unknown caller', so she decided to leave it vibrating. She knew he hated mobile phones, never allowed them in the bedroom and usually muted his at night, then never remembered where he had left it. As she sipped her coffee watching the TV news, the phone vibrated again but she ignored it and turned up the volume on the TV. She watched as the news presenters pointed to maps of Friday's marches, the planned routes and the chaos they were predicting.

"Christ, how depressing," she said, switching off the TV. When Robert's phone vibrated yet again, she rolled her eyes, grabbed it and pressed the green button, put it to her ear and waited. She didn't hear anyone speak, so as a reflex she said 'hello?'

"I hope you're enjoying your last days of freedom, bitch, because he will never see you again, whore of the puppet…"

She dropped the phone on the table and stood shaking with a hand over her mouth.

"Robert, Robert!" she shouted, running into the bedroom.

She shook him awake and he looked at her with fear in his eyes.

"What? What is it?" he asked, leaping out of bed.

She told him what she had just heard and he sprinted to his desk, pressed a few buttons on the phone and summoned Guy as she stood anxiously behind him.

"Up here now, Guy!" he said.

Holding her by the shoulders, he asked if she knew who it was.

"De la Mano, I'm sure of it," she said, her eyes wide.

They heard a knock, Robert unlocked the door and Guy appeared, his gun at the ready in both hands, pointing downwards.

"Problem, boss?" he asked, closing the door with his back.

Robert explained the phone call to Guy, and then asked Margarita to make them some more coffee as he led the way into his study.

"The tactics of fear, boss, nothing more."

"How did he know she was here, for Christ sake? And how did he get her number?"

"I think I would have managed the same, wouldn't you?"

"Probably. That Victor fellow?"

"No. I thought the chief had reassigned him to the Casa Rosada. Didn't he tell you?"

"No he didn't. And the other matter? Have you heard yet?"

"I was about to make the call when you…"

"Now, Guy, if you please. They have to be called off, damn it!"

At that moment they both heard a shrill but muffled ringing coming from Robert's desk.

"Now Guy, please. I need to know!"

Robert looked at him as the ringing continued.

"Guy, just go, will you please!"

"I'm on my way," said Guy, glancing at the desk.

Robert then walked slowly to the desk, unlocked the drawer and answered the satellite phone.

"You're making a big mistake, my boy…"

"First, I'm not your boy, second, you are the mistake and third, never contact me again," he said, pressing a red button and throwing the device back into the drawer.

"Shorty, mate, I'm getting some flak this end. Any news?"

"The message was delivered. I also had confirmation it was authenticated and that's as much as I can do, mate."

"What's the normal procedure then?"

"There is no normal procedure."

"So how do we know they'll act on it or not?"

"You don't."

By ten thirty that morning, Clara and Pascal were nearly half way to Rufino. They had stopped for a late breakfast at a roadside filling station, their Jeep parked in the shade of a line of Eucalyptus trees at the side of the cafeteria. Dogs slept near the shady entrance and others sniffed around the petrol pumps hoping for scraps of food from passing motorists.

Inside the cafeteria, a cheerful and buxom, middle aged woman served them coffee and croissants, then returned to her position on a tall stool behind the cash till, remote in hand as the TV news loudly speculated over Friday's coming events. An old man lay asleep in a wheelchair opposite the wall mounted television.

"It's almost as if the entire country is about to explode," said Pascal as he stirred his coffee.

"You remember the big marches in the nineties, don't you?" she asked.

He nodded.

"Even the most conservative estimates put those numbers at only half a million people. This is going to be at least five times as many and frankly, I don't know how Robert is going to survive. Politically, I mean."

They looked across at the TV which was showing stills of the president giving public speeches and waving at the people from the balcony of Casa Rosada. The old man in the wheelchair suddenly woke up, pointed a finger at the screen and began shouting and swearing.

"Traitor! English pirate son of a bitch. Fuck off back to where you came from!" he shouted, spitting on the floor, his eyes wild and his untidy grey hair falling over his eyes.

"Now, now, Pa, take it easy," said the lady from behind the cash till. "Oh, I'm sorry about him," she said smiling, turning to Pascal and Clara. "He gets a bit carried away. Just ignore him."

They smiled benignly at her, neither knowing how to reply.

"It's not his political survival I meant Clara…"

"I know, I know and you were right," she said, holding his hand across the table. "We had to get out."

"Guy, I need to talk to the people and I need to be seen. Make arrangements for extra security and for the cars to be ready at seven am. I want this going out on the midday news tomorrow."

"Boss, are you sure this is wise?"

"I should be back on the island for lunch at one, so make the arrangements please."

"I'm really not comfortable with this, sir. They may bring the protests forward. We'd be trapped."

"Nonsense."

"As you wish, but you should know that as your personal guard, I'm strongly advising against this."

"Your advice is noted, Guy, but what the country needs now is leadership. I must be seen to be in charge and not to be terrorised by a small group of trouble makers."

"Hardly a small group, sir…"

"I've made my decision."

"Very well."

Robert spent the rest of the day coordinating the departure of the British forces, reading reports on the hardware inventory and watching through his binoculars as numerous vessels plied to and fro between the warships and Buenos Aires port. Two hours before the deadline expired, he received a call from his home office minister confirming that all the British forces had returned safely to their ships, there were no casualties, accidental or otherwise and that the entire impounded inventory was accounted for. It was also reported that the British fleet were making preparations to steam and that, barring any last minute hitches, they would be weighing anchor within the hour.

He asked Margarita to join him on the balcony, where they watched the fleet prepare, as black smoke belched from the funnels and men could be seen, as small as ants, scurrying around the decks. He smiled as he noticed that each of the three aircraft carriers was deserted of aircraft, and he tried to imagine the two container carriers bereft of any military cargo, requiring them to take in extra ballast for the trip home. He looked at his new acquisitions as a goodbye present from Jack. It was after all, the very least he could have given him in return for his silence.

"You've done the right thing, Robert," she said, holding on to his arm. "I'm very proud of you. I hope you know that."

"How about that cup of coffee you mentioned," he said, kissing her forehead. She squeezed his arm and then headed back inside.

Returning to his office, he called Chief Forza, asking him to liaise with the minister of internal security and to prepare the positioning and distribution of the weapons they had recently acquired from the British. Robert also insisted that the locations should not be overt until they were advised otherwise. He then asked the chief about Victor Valiente.

"Marco has him under his wing, sir."

"Go on."

"He's been overheard reassuring De la Mano that he is where he is expected to be. Marco is sticking to him like glue and as you know, only you and the major have keys to the residence."

Margarita returned and placed a hot mug of coffee by the steel railing.

"Very good chief. One more thing. I'll be arriving at Casa Rosada with Major Pennington Farlowe at zero eight hundred tomorrow…"

Margarita then pulled at his arm and looked at him, frowning.

"Make the necessary preparations please, Chief. We'll speak later," he said, hanging up.

"But Robert, what are you talking about?" she asked him.

"Mags, I'm not having a discussion about this. I have to address the people from government house, live and in person before everything goes to hell. And not from this island fortress. That is the end of that." he said, putting the phone to his ear again.

"Pimpi?"

"Yes sir," answered Pimpi, standing up quickly behind his desk.

"I need you to put a speech together for a public address I'll be making tomorrow morning from the Casa Rosada please. Can you prepare something which will help pull the people together?"

"Yes of course, Mr President, it will be an honour."

"Very well. I'd also like you to make your way over there first thing. Can you do that?"

"Yes of course sir, thank you, sir. Uh, will Mrs Campos be with you for the speech?"

"No, she won't, but Roxy will be expecting you, and I've asked the chief to meet you in the underground car park. He'll brief you on the current crisis that we're facing, so don't be late!"

Pimpi smiled as he put the phone down, rubbed his voluminous chin and set to work on what he believed the president should say to his people. He then sat back, rested his legs on the desk, clicked the pocket tape recorder and began to speak.

Robert watched as the Royal Navy warships weighed anchor one by one, sounding their horns, sending a tingle down his spine. It was a bitter sweet moment, since he had nothing but the deepest of respect for His Majesty's Forces, but the spectre of Jack Forsyth and how he had so ruthlessly used him, made him grimace and look away. He noticed that Margarita had gone back inside, where she was sitting on the sofa staring at the floor.

"What is it Mags?" he asked, sitting down next to her and noticing that she had been crying.

"Are you out of your mind?" she asked, dabbing her eyes with a tissue.

"Mags, I have to do this. I have to try to save something from this mess, and hiding away here is sending all the wrong signals."

"Can't you take me with you?" she asked, sniffling.

"No, Mags, I can't. In fact, I won't."

"I'm worried that's all. What if..."

He held her hands in his and looked into her eyes.

"I promise you, nothing is going to happen tomorrow," he said, smiling. "Stay here and watch me on TV. I'll be back for lunch. You'd like that wouldn't you?" he said as gently as he could.

"Just be careful, damn you," she said, putting her arms around him.

"Look, I've got a few more calls to make," he said, looking at his watch. "So why don't you fix us a drink and afterwards I'll cook us that dinner we had the first time you came. Remember that?"

"All right," she said, smiling and dabbing the corner of her eyes again with a tissue.

Later that evening, as darkness was falling, fleets of buses could be seen approaching the capital from all directions of the country. The major motorways from south, west and north, saw a huge increase in traffic. Ancient flatbed trucks, packed with people waving banners and banging huge drums, streamed towards Buenos Aires, followed by bright orange and white school buses with their windows open, the occupants hanging national flags and makeshift signs from their arms. The TV news, whose helicopters were following the night-time procession, reported the phenomenon as the largest movement of vehicles the country had ever seen.

As the hours passed and buses and trucks began to line up and park beneath motorway bridges, in huge football stadium car parks, in plazas and on recently demolished shanty town land, many people began to set up camp. Makeshift tented villages sprouted up throughout the city, chorizo and hamburger stalls were set up, loud music played from huge speakers and a carnival atmosphere pervaded the area. All the major TV stations sent their roving reporters to wander through the many thousands of camps, where they interviewed the occupants, asking them of their aspirations for the coming days. A prominent reporter, Edgardo Dacosta, who had so enthusiastically reported from what was now known as *The Cage of Shame*, ended his report on an upbeat note as he swung his arm towards a circle of tents on a small lawn in the centre of the floodlit Plaza de Mayo.

"It's heart-warming to know that there is still an element in this beautiful country of ours that practices peace as their core value," he said, dabbing an eye and hoping he could conjure up a few tears.

"The peace camps you see here and many more being set up around the capital and beyond, are a true reminder that Argentines simply wish to protest peacefully, as is our democratic right," he continued, his lower lip trembling almost too perfectly. "Now back to the studio."

"Chief, are you seeing this?" asked Guy, sitting in his chalet, watching the TV.

"Yes, but I can't say that I like what I see."

"And the president is still going to address the nation tomorrow, up on that damn balcony. You know I advised him against it, don't you?"

"As did I, but I can't see him changing his mind. He's determined to stick his neck out, Major."

"Listen, Chief, I'm really not comfortable about all this. We should cover all the options."

"Go on."

"The boats in the island harbour: have they been prepared in case we need to use them?"

"Well no, apart from the usual maintenance. You're not suggesting that the president is going to try to escape, are you? I'm sure it won't come to that," said the chief.

"Covering our options, Chief, that's all. Will you please authorise me to oversee their state of readiness for sailing then? I can be down there in a few minutes and to make sure we've got enough weapons as well."

"I think you're getting a little carried away, Major, with all due respect."

"It's your country, Chief, not mine. But from what I can see, the shit is going to hit the fan sooner than you think. Do we understand each other?"

"As you wish, but I think you're wasting your time."

"I'll be in the boatshed if you need me."

"You don't want the TV on then?" asked Margarita as she cleared the plates from the dinner table.

"Wall to wall peace camps every minute of the day, not to mention those moronic reporters are enough to put me off my dinner, so no. Why do you ask?"

"You're not the slightest bit concerned about all those people camping out tonight then?"

"We've been over this already, Mags, so can't you just drop it please?" asked Robert, pushing himself away from the table. "I'm off to bed now. It's going to be a long day tomorrow."

She threw the rest of the plates in the dishwasher, slammed it shut, kicked her shoes off, then poured herself a large whisky. He just never listens, she reminded herself.

CHAPTER 50

S tanding behind bullet-proof glass panels, on the balcony of the Casa Rosada, just one storey above the Plaza de Mayo, President Crawford gripped the sides of the wooden lectern and began to speak.

"In the last one hundred years, Argentina has faced many challenges..."

As he spoke, he gestured with his hands, nervously adjusted the two microphones and directed his address to the many thousands he imagined had turned out especially to see him speak. As Pimpi had suggested, he kept his focus on a spot near the middle of the plaza, where he could easily see the Pyramid Monument through a sea of people. TV cameras rolled from high scaffolding around the plaza, yet it wasn't until sixty seconds from the moment he began speaking that he noticed more organised movement at the edges of the crowd, near the Cabildo at the far end of the plaza. Groups of men carrying what he thought looked like rolled up banners pushed their way through the crowd and began moving to the front, just below where he was standing.

"...as we defeat the forces of chaos... we are building a country for you, your children and their children..."

As other groups from neighbouring streets joined the already swelling crowds in the square, he sensed a very real change in atmosphere. What had begun as rhythmic chants, banner waving and smiling faces, now became a low murmuring and he sensed a growing air of menace within the crowd. Hundreds of armed federal police officers stood guard behind tall crowd control barriers just below him, at the entrance to the Casa Rosada.

"As your president, I promise you a…"

As he continued, he found it increasingly difficult to maintain his focus on the speech in front of him. He saw more groups of men with rolled up banners moving to the front and as he perspired in the late morning sunshine, his hands gripped the wooden lectern more tightly. He sensed fear creeping into every word he spoke, his palms were clammy and he felt a sudden urge to flee.

"…as we move forward…"

When he saw the glint of black steel, he took a step back and felt the words leave his mouth as if in slow motion.

"…we are united…as brothers, arm in arm…"

The first bullets whistled past a stone column to his left and by the time Guy had brought him crashing face down behind the glass panels, pieces of lead were ricocheting in all directions from the surrounding steel supports. Face down with Guy spread-eagled on top of him, Robert lay with his head turned to the cracked, milky glass panel now barely protecting him. Through it, he could just make out vague shapes of men holding long weapons. With Guy's hand spread firmly upon his head, he became aware of a voice speaking to him amidst the cracks of gunfire that continued from below.

"Don't move. Stay exactly where you are. Do you hear me?" said Guy.

"Yes."

"I'm going to slide backwards on my stomach and you're going to keep your eyes on me. Clear?"

"Yes."

With his face lying in a sticky mess of blood and sweat, he slowly turned his head back towards Guy as splinters of glass and pink stone flew around the balcony. He saw Guy lying face down, inching his way backwards, using his feet to guide him, and his hands to push himself away.

With the fingers of one hand, Guy pointed at his own eyes, urging the president to focus on him. Turning to face him, Robert began to crawl, cringing at every shot pinging the glass panels and every crash of lead smashing into the columns around him, as the shooting increased in its ferocity.

"Hurry, man! That glass won't hold much longer," said Guy, extending his arm without taking his eyes off him.

With his hands bleeding from glass cuts and metal impacts, he made himself as small and as flat as he could and with one final and desperate scurry across the shiny tiled floor, he felt Guy's hand yank him to safety and around the corner. He lay on his back panting like a dog on the wooden parquet floor, blinking quickly and not daring to move. A few seconds later he heard a grinding noise, then a high pitched squeal, as steel and glass went crashing to the ground below.

"Boss, you need to come with me," he heard Guy shout through the sounds of gunshots and screams from the plaza.

Trembling with shock and with blood trickling down his forehead, he got to his knees, then quickly followed Guy down the stairs and into a nearby bathroom, outside which, the other bodyguards stood, their weapons at the ready.

"I hate to say it boss, but…" said Guy, brushing broken glass from his shoulders.

"Just don't, okay?" said Robert, ripping off his jacket and looking in the mirror.

"I'll fetch someone to look at those cuts. Stay here," said Guy as he rushed out of the bathroom.

Looking at himself in the mirror and dabbing at the cuts on his face with a paper towel, he knew he had made the most catastrophic mistake. His thoughts drifted back to a night so many years ago when he had watched another president standing in the very same spot, his white shirt also stained with his own blood.

"This was meant to happen," he mumbled to himself, blood still dripping from his face as he leaned over the wash hand basin.

The door opened and Guy rushed in, followed by a matronly, middle aged woman dressed in a blue uniform, who looked quickly at the president's injuries and ordered him to follow her. She led them downstairs to a small room equipped with an ambulance trolley, oxygen cylinders and other medical equipment, where he collapsed on a chair, put his head back and slowly breathed out.

"Lie down over here please, Mr President," said the blue uniformed nurse, pointing and propping up one end of the trolley.

"I'll be in the security centre, boss. Nurse Carmen will take care of you," said Guy, dabbing his face with a bloody towel as he left the room.

Peering from a tiny window in a top floor bathroom of the Casa Rosada, with a view down to the plaza, Guy watched as the multitude of protesters below seemed to grow by the minute. He could see that many were now armed and as he looked upwards, he noticed shadowy figures taking up positions in the windows of office blocks overlooking the plaza. He calculated that they had a clear aim, should the president be foolish enough to show himself near the smallest gap in a window. The shooting below the balcony had trailed off to an occasional pop and he had ordered the huge doors behind the balcony to be closed and locked shut.

Down below, the crowd was being spurred on by a large vociferous group of heavily armed men in army fatigues, standing on the roofs of flatbed trucks and four wheel drive vehicles, just meters from the entrance to the Casa Rosada. Their faces wore the angry expressions of tribal chiefs and as they faced the seat of government, brandishing weapons above their heads, their leader spoke through a handheld megaphone demanding that the president be handed over to the people or they would take him by force. The federal police had not been moved to action and stood impassively by, as events unfolded.

Luis de la Mano, his face filled with hatred, thumped his chest as his voice carried around the plaza, whipping the entire crowd into a frenzy of shouting and clattering of metal.

As he watched from the small window, Guy saw that the demonstrators no longer banged humble pots and pans as they had always done. Those without firearms brandished makeshift aluminium shields which they struck rhythmically with sharpened steel spikes, fashioned to razor sharp tips. The entire plaza shook to the sound of steel upon shield and stamping feet which gradually quickened pace, rose to a crescendo of furious clattering and was repeated time and again as De la Mano goaded them noisily through his megaphone.

Walking quickly back down to the security centre, he realised that De la Mano had out manoeuvred the president in a coordinated pre-emptive move and the question that most bothered him was, *will SOF 19 show their faces?*

After Nurse Carmen had treated his wounds, assuring him they were mostly small cuts and grazes, Robert made his way up the stairs to the security centre on the second floor, where he found Guy, Chief Forza and two high ranking federal police officers pointing at an array of TV screens hanging from the walls. When they heard him enter, they turned around and welcomed him, their expressions quickly turning to relief, with the chief being the first to shake his hand. Robert was grateful for their concern, but it held little meaning for him.

"Have we lost control, Chief?" he asked.

Chief Forza glanced at the two other police officers who remained silent.

"Well?" he insisted.

"There is a small element of the police taking sides with the crowd, sir," said the chief.

"Right, which is why the shooting continued," said Robert. "Now, answer the question. Have you got your forces under control?"

"A small element?" interrupted Guy. "From what I could see, the police turned a blind eye. All of them!"

One of the other police officers interrupted and quietly introduced himself as a Captain Fernandez.

"If I may sir?" he said, pointing at a screen showing a full aerial picture of the plaza. "There, there and there, I have teams ready to snatch the ringleaders and in those areas," he said pointing again, "we will prevent further ingress to the square."

"Thank you, Captain, but how do you expect to bring your police officers into line?" asked Robert.

"I'll do what I can, Mr President," said Fernandez, grabbing a radio.

"The ringleader you really need is De la Mano," said Guy.

"We're trying our best to get close to him, Major," said Fernandez.

"Try harder then," said Robert, loudly. "Guy, come with me."

As he turned to leave, Robert noticed Pimpi Perez sitting motionless at one of the central desks and staring at a large computer screen. His face was pale, his eyes were wide and he was trembling. Robert gripped his shoulder. "Just stay here and you'll be fine," he said as Pimpi held on tightly to the briefcase sitting on his lap.

Guy followed Robert down the ornate marble stairs and into the central garden patio on the ground floor, where heavily armed federal police officers were standing guard every four metres around the perimeter walls. Sitting on a granite bench opposite the central fountain, he lit a cigarette and beckoned Guy over to join him.

"Just don't say it, okay?" he said, blowing the smoke up towards the gap in the building.

Guy placed his hand firmly on his boss's shoulder, hoping to reassure him. Although Robert was trying his best to appear calm, in his gut he knew he was facing the fight of his life.

"Boss, we need to make a move," said Guy quietly.

Robert looked up at the vast opening in the building and watched as birds called to each other and fluffy white clouds glided slowly across the powder blue sky, interrupted only by the incessant din of the baying crowd outside, which reminded him of a series of express trains rushing past.

"I know, but the question is, how?" he asked, standing up and stubbing out his cigarette. "Look, here comes Forza."

The chief approached slowly, his gun held low and pointing down at his right side. In his other hand he held a two-way radio that hissed sporadically as he made his way towards them. Robert signalled him over with a nod of his head as the noise of the crowd filtered down from outside.

"Forza, what do you think? What would you advise?" asked Robert, his hands on his hips.

"Sir, the vehicle tunnel has been compromised, at least from what we've seen on TVN and from what my men near the tunnel are telling me. There are hundreds of armed men surrounding the entrance and they've dragged concrete blocks across the tunnel access road. The police who are still loyal to us, are standing by and managing to prevent any further incursions towards the entrance, but I don't know how long they'll be able to hold out for," said the chief.

"And the entrance gates to the tunnel? Can we open them?" asked Robert.

"No sir, at least not from this side. The mob have pushed so many obstacles against them that the mechanism keeps jamming," said the chief.

"For Christ sake, Chief, what about the other side. The island side I mean."

Chief Forza began walking slowly back and forth between the palm trees, talking into his radio.

"Margarita is on the island you know, Guy, and I'm pretty sure the drivers left the gates open that end. I've warned them about it and so have you. Those gates have to be shut damn it! It's not only me they'll rip to pieces," he said, his jaw stiffening.

"Boss, listen. There must be another way. There has to be."

"Hang on, Guy…"

As the chief spoke into the radio, a crackly male voice could be heard and Forza looked over at Robert, nodding, his expression serious but purposeful. Finally he clicked the radio one more time. "And make sure they stay closed!"

Chief Forza limped slowly back towards them, holding his radio up.

"Sir, the gates are now closed. About fifty protesters managed to get through the police line and must have forced the gates this end. They could hear them running into the tunnel, but they managed to force them back…"

"Well, thank God for that. Now listen, instruct the police to clear that mob away from the entrance on this side and further down. Flush them out, then remove all the obstacles and see if there's a way to get through."

"This could get messy, sir," said the chief.

"Listen chief, you are to use all necessary force, but I want minimum injuries. Is that clear? Make sure Captain Fernandez is aware. Now get going."

As the chief returned to the communications centre, Robert turned to look at Guy and shook his head.

"This feels familiar," he said.

Guy leant forward and cracked his knuckles, nodding his head.

"I wasn't expecting to end up on this side of the fence though, boss."

They both looked at each other, smiling weakly. Stubbing another cigarette out on the ground, Robert slapped his good friend on the shoulders.

"So, how the hell are we going to get out of this mess then?" asked Robert, standing up.

"Helicopter's out, obviously, but…"

"But what?"

"Maybe we can find some plans. You know, architectural plans?"

Robert beckoned Guy to follow him as he strode quickly up the stairs towards the security centre again.

"Chief, can we get plans of this place? You know, blueprints?"

"I would think so, but why do you ask, sir?"

"Well, remember when Cristal was president? The rumours that went around when no one saw her leave this place during the riots three or four years ago? And she magically reappeared on the island?"

"Yes, I heard about that," he said pointing. "She was never seen leaving in a car or even the official helicopter and some said she had gone through a secret tunnel. But how?" asked the chief, rubbing his chin.

"Precisely, Chief. Can you get someone on that please?"

Guy turned to Robert.

"Are you thinking what I'm thinking, boss?"

"I'm absolutely sure that when she built the island residence, she had a service tunnel installed. How else would she have mysteriously arrived back at the island? We all wondered at the time, but she never gave interviews and every time it was mentioned, her cabinet chief said we were all paranoid. Damn, why did I never ask about it?"

Within a few moments, a smiling chief Forza returned.

"I knew immediately what you were thinking, sir. Here, look, these are the plans," he said, unrolling them on the granite bench.

They gathered around and examined the rolls of paper, moving their fingers around the blue and white architect's drawings. Robert turned and looked at Forza with a puzzled expression.

"But there's nothing here, Chief. Yes, there's the main vehicle access tunnel to the island," he said, stabbing his finger at the plans. "Well, part of it anyway. But I can't see any service tunnel at all. Can you?"

"There wouldn't be anything on the plans, would there, sir? These are pretty much public knowledge and Cristal would have insisted on only the doctored plans being made public. Anyway, there's something else."

"Well come on Forza, spit it out man!"

"I reckoned that if anyone knew, it would be the head of maintenance, Gonzalez. He's been here for more than thirty years. Remember, he's the one who put that cage together for Mr Pérez."

"Well, get him down here. Now!"

"I can do better than that, sir. Would you like to follow me?"

Chief Forza took them down a narrow staircase which ended abruptly at a grey steel door with a green and white sign that read *maintenance*. He tapped a digital security pad, the door mechanism buzzed and he pushed the door open, revealing a large, low ceilinged area, with hanging strip lights, work benches, lathes and other machinery placed around the edges of the large room.

"Gonzalez?" shouted the chief.

Out of the gloom at the end of the workshop, a small man with wiry, untidy grey hair appeared. He was wearing a light brown overall neatly buttoned up at the front and spectacles held together by bits of wire. He was wiping his hands on an oily rag, which he then stuffed quickly into his pocket.

"Gonzalez, the president would like a word with you," said the chief.

The old man shuffled over to greet the president, clearly humbled by the experience and he bowed reverentially as they shook hands.

"Listen, Gonzalez, we don't have much time," said Robert. "Could you show us, please?"

"Of course, Mr President," he said pointing to the end of the workshop. "Over here."

They followed Gonzalez past more machinery and workbenches, down a further set of narrow concrete stairs, where he stopped and flipped a wall switch. They continued along a narrow corridor lit by wall lights, at the end of which they saw a large black door fitted with four locks.

Robert looked at Forza and then back to Gonzalez.

"Where are the keys?" he asked.

"I've got them here, Mr President," said Gonzalez, casually producing a key chain from his belt. "I keep them with me at all times."

"Let's get it open, then!"

The old man turned each lock carefully, tried in vain to pull the huge door open and beckoned for help. They all grabbed an edge of the handle and slowly the door moved backwards with a blast of wind rushing through their hair, revealing the huge door to be six inches of reinforced concrete and steel. The old man stood back as the three others squinted into the blackness and heard nothing but the distant dripping of water and the faint echoes of the protesting mob. Robert walked forward into the darkness, peered further in and fumbled around on either wall, looking for a light switch, then turned to Gonzalez.

"When was the last time you came down here?"

The old man shrugged his shoulders, produced a small torch from his coat pocket, stepped through the doorway and turned to his right where he unlocked a junction box and flicked up a series of twelve breaker switches. One by one, long fluorescent ceiling lights hummed and flickered into life, cascading into the distance as far as a right hand bend about one hundred and fifty meters into the tunnel.

"I come down here about twice a year, Mr President. I'm supposed to just to test the lights and check for leaks," he said, looking at the ceiling. "Every one hundred meters there's a service door see, down there on the left," he said pointing. "And I check that they open correctly. They're supposed to be emergency evacuation doors in case of a fire in the main tunnel. But the thing is, Miss Cristal insisted they be fitted with locks that can only be opened from this side," he finished, pursing his lips together.

Robert shook his head and turned to the others. "Look, it's a little over two kilometres to the island, which will take us how long? About half an hour or a little less if we run?"

"Sir, not necessarily," said Gonzalez. "May I?" he said, gesturing down the tunnel.

They followed Gonzalez about twenty meters along the bare concrete tunnel until he stopped at an alcove recessed into the right hand wall. Neatly parked in the recess was a six person golf cart, plugged into a wall socket with a thick, black and yellow cable.

"She seems to have thought of everything," said Guy looking over the unexpected gift. Robert then turned to Chief Forza.

"Chief, can you wait here with Gonzalez? I need to go back to my office to collect a few things. Keep the door to maintenance locked until we get back. Oh, and have you got another one of those radios? Our phones won't work down here and there's a chance those lunatics will get to the phone masts if it turns really ugly out there."

"It's already turned ugly out there, boss," mumbled Guy as he followed Robert back up to the palm tree patio.

After collecting a couple of two way radios at the security centre, they arrived at the president's office on the second floor, where two heavily armed policemen stood guard. They both stood to attention and stepped aside with a cursory nod to let them pass. Robert slowly approached the windows at the back of his office by inching himself along the wall, where he stood to the side and peered around. The plaza at the rear of the Casa Rosada was filled with a sea of protestors, all with their faces turned in his direction. In the distance he could just see the island and his thoughts turned to Margarita, waiting for him.

They quickly gathered as many of Robert's possessions and sensitive documents as they could, including his satellite phone, threw them in a mail trolley, wheeled the lot into an elevator and returned to the security centre on the second floor.

"Fernandez, once you've secured the tunnel entrance, send in a team and flush out any remaining protesters. That tunnel must be cleared and I don't care how you do it...tear gas, those flash bangs you people use...whatever it takes, but nothing lethal. Just get them the hell out of there," said Robert, turning to leave. "I don't want any dead protesters on my hands..."

"And if they're shooting at us, sir? I mean..."

"Shoot back, but this is not shoot to kill. Disable them. Is that clear?"

"Boss?" interrupted Guy. "Take out De la Mano and you cut off the head of the snake."

"Assassinate a union leader you mean?"

"A union leader who has sworn to kill you, vowed to bring down this government, but has also threatened Mrs Campos directly, sir."

Hearing her name, Robert felt a painful twinge in his stomach. He knew Guy was right is his assessment, but assassination was not a solution he had ever considered.

"How?"

Guy looked across at the two police captains who shrugged their shoulders.

"Find me the right weapon, preferably a Remington 700…"

"Sorry, Major, you won't find anything like that here. The best we can offer you is an M14."

"Any scopes?"

"You'd have to talk to the tactical boys on the ground floor."

"Boss?" asked Guy.

"I'm not comfortable with this, Guy. How do you plan to…?"

"The roof, and I'll need a couple of men to cover me. There's good cover up there and I'll have a clear view of the plaza," said Guy, omitting to say that he'd already scoped out the roof as a routine aspect of his duties.

Robert rubbed the back of his neck as he was thinking.

"Okay, we'll wait for you on the island. But Guy…I can't promise anything. We may have to leave very quickly. You understand that, don't you?"

"Clear as day, boss," said Guy, smiling at the thought of eliminating De la Mano.

"Very well. Fernandez, give the major everything he needs and send your whole tactical team with him."

Guy began to speak but Robert put his hand on his shoulder.

"No buts. You do it my way or not at all," he said, turning to leave. "I'll see you on the other side."

A second later, when Guy had run down the stairs to find the tactical team, Robert returned to the security centre, looking for Pimpi.

"We think he went to the bathroom, sir," said Captain Fernandez. "He doesn't seem to be taking this very well."

Sitting on a toilet seat in a cubicle, Pimpi swigged from a bottle of Old Smuggler and wished he was in a bar. Any bar, far away from the shooting, the anger and all the screaming.

"Pimpi, come out," he heard as the bathroom door opened.

He took another long slug of whisky, screwed the cap down and stuffed the bottle back into his briefcase, where it clinked next to a bottle of vodka. If I'm going to die, I don't want to feel it, he mumbled.

"I'm leaving right now, Pimpi, so if you want to stay here, that's just fine. But remember this. When they take you, it's the end."

Pimpi quickly opened the latch, cuddled his briefcase under his arm and pushed past the president to the wash basins, where he splashed water over his face. Robert looked at him, smelled the alcohol on his breath, shrugged his shoulders and took him by the arm.

"Come on man, there's a golf cart waiting for us."

Margarita stood in the living room of the suite, watching the news on the TV and, looking on in horror, she nervously fingered the mobile phone in her back pocket as Robert's speech was cut short by the gunfire. The image of him being thrown to the floor by Guy was being repeated time and again by every channel she switched to. She had dialled his number several times since the incident, but why hadn't he answered or called her? The TV presenters were re-running the segment in slow motion asking if it was a bullet hitting his head or a splinter of glass. She couldn't be sure, and reassured herself that Guy had got to him just in time. On the other hand, he may have been hit, or she was simply convincing herself that none of it had happened at all.

As she sobbed, she poured her seventh coffee of the morning and dialled every official number she had in her phone, all of which were engaged. Then she heard a soft musical tone, the one she reserved for Robert and tapped *answer*.

"Darling! I was so worried, why didn't you call me? I've been going out of my mind up here."

"I'm sorry, Mags, it's been…"

"Oh, thank God you're all right. But what are you going to do? I'm stuck here and all I can see is what they're showing on television. It looks terrifying."

"Listen, we've found a way to get there."

"Please be careful, Robert. I can see smoke coming from the city now and the TV is showing looting and fighting with police. I'm really scared."

"Listen, stay where you are. The chief and me should be with you in about an hour. Don't let anyone up in the lift unless it's one of Forza's men. It's the only way to the suite, you know that."

The line went quiet for a few seconds and Robert thought he could hear faint sniffling.

"Mags, Mags? Are you all right?"

"No, not really."

"It's not as bad as it looks, believe me. Just stay focused on seeing me come through that door, okay? I *will* be there."

Between a line of humming air conditioning units, Guy inched himself along the roof, looking to both sides as he crouched. As he reached the end of the flat section, he saw that his view was obscured by the two foot parapet he already knew to be there, so he lifted the M14 onto the edge and set up the tripod. As he was securing the feet, his peripheral vision caught movement from a window in a building to his left overlooking the plaza. He was sure he saw a man's head move ever so slightly, so with the scope an inch from his eye, he breathed in, taking aim at the man's shape, then breathed out and squeezed the trigger. His silencer took the noise of the shot and as he kept his eye looking through the scope, he saw the man being pushed backwards by the force of the bullet and disappearing from sight.

"One down," he mumbled.

To his right he was protected by more air conditioning ducts, so he moved his weapon over the parapet, leaned his right shoulder against the aluminium casing and scanned the scope downwards to where he could hear De la Mano shouting through the megaphone. He saw him standing on a red Toyota pickup, so he zoomed in, the man's angry, hate filled mouth coming fully into his view. He checked the weapon, pulled it into his shoulder and brought the crosshairs to settle just above the union leader's right ear.

In a tenth floor office window, Guy couldn't see the man dressed in fatigues who had Guy's trigger hand in his sights and as Guy breathed in and slowly released his breath to squeeze the trigger, he leapt backwards when a bullet pinged past his rifle, hitting the concrete parapet in a cloud of pink dust, just as he pulled the trigger.

"Shit!"

He quickly pulled back, leaned against the aluminium again and pulled out the radio.

"What the fuck is going on? Take out those shooters, now!" he shouted to the tactical team.

He quickly repositioned himself, heard two distant pops, saw a window collapse in the building to the right and brought the scope to his eye once again.

De la Mano, now with his back to Guy, continued to bellow through his megaphone. Guy had never shot anyone from behind; it simply wasn't in the playbook he had always followed. No women, kids or old people, unless they were aiming directly at him. De la Mano wasn't either, but he was sure he would slot Guy if he had the chance. Clamping his jaws together and breathing slowly through his nose, he brought the crosshair to the base of the man's skull, breathed out normally and squeezed the trigger.

In the fraction of a second that his brain issued the instruction to his finger, Guy saw De la Mano, turning his head up towards where he was positioned, the bullet striking the inside wall of the concave plastic megaphone, shattering it into fragments which then embedded themselves into the union leader's face. He fell backwards into the loading area of the truck, his right hand having left his arm and his face a bloody pulp of shattered bone and hanging flesh.

Through his scope, Guy watched, as De la Mano's body fell, heard the screams and zoomed in on what remained of the man's face. He was pleased to notice that the bullet had performed more than satisfactorily, having not only blown the megaphone to pieces, but travelled on through the eye socket.

"That's for Margarita," he whispered.

He folded the tripod, leaned against the metal casing again and spoke into the radio, amidst the screaming and chaos that he had just unleashed below.

"Pull back. Pull back."

Only four of the team responded, so he ran back towards the stairwell, stopping at each air conditioning vent for a few seconds for cover. At the last one, he stopped and caught his breath as he watched the other four team members quickly move to the stairs near the helipad, noticing that two were each carrying a body over their shoulders.

"Go, go, go!" he shouted as he crouch-ran forward to the covered stairwell. Four metres from safety, he felt his legs collapse beneath him, an enormous weight pull in his chest and he fell on his back clutching at his neck, struggling to breath. For a few moments he lay there choking, heard several pops of gunfire and then felt himself being pulled. Someone was pulling the collar of his combat suit and ten seconds later he felt his body bumping down the stairs and then into darkness.

"Sir, this is Captain Fernandez. The tunnel is clear. The tunnel is clear," Robert heard on the radio as he led Pimpi down to the service tunnel.

"And, De la Mano?"

"We cannot confirm yet, sir. I advise you to make all haste."

"Fernandez, get on to the minister of internal security right now please. He has instructions to position the hardware we requisitioned from the British. Do it now and control the situation," he said, pausing. "And the staff need to be evacuated right now. I'm holding you personally responsible for their safety. Is that clear?"

"But how, sir?"

"Do I have to spell it out to you, Captain? You are authorised to use non-lethal force to clear the area at the rear of the building and evacuate the staff. Find transport, buses, trucks, any fucking thing with wheels."

"We could airlift them out, sir."

"Too risky. Do whatever you have to do, Captain and I will contact you again once I've reached a place of safety."

"Sir, if you use the main tunnel, I cannot guarantee your safety…"

"Captain, just do as I say. That's an order!"

As they walked quickly towards maintenance, the federal police guards were rushing to all entrances and exits on the ground floor. The noise of clattering shields coming down the shaft of daylight in the centre of the palm tree patio sounded like a hornet's nest had just been opened. Robert could hear women screaming hysterically, thousands of shouting voices and the constant banging of shields reverberating through the building. Stopping outside the maintenance door, he quickly realised that he could no longer hear De la Mano shouting, so he called Guy on the radio.

"Guy, Guy?"

The static continued…

"Guy?"

More static, then… "the major has been hit."

"Shit! Can you bring him down?"

More static…

"Five minutes…"

"Just get him down here, now!" shouted Robert into the radio. "Pimpi, wait here and don't move. Not Guy, please. Jesus Christ!"

Robert ran back up the stairs to the first aid centre, grabbed a frightened Nurse Carmen by the arm and pressed the top floor button for the lift.

"I'm coming up," he shouted into the radio.

"No, we're coming down, sir. We're in the lift," said a voice over the radio.

"Nurse, we're going to need everything you've got," he said as they waited on the ground floor. Clearly upset by the situation, Nurse Carmen took the medipack from her shoulder, laid it on the floor and examined the contents.

"I think we have everything we need, sir," she said, looking up.

As she said that, a soft tone was heard, the lift doors opened and four tactical team members carried Guy out of the lift and lay him on the floor. His eyes were wide open, his breathing was irregular and dark blood was oozing from the top of his flak jacket.

Robert held his hand and spoke to him calmly. "We're taking care of you, Guy, but we can't stay here. We have to keep moving."

Guy nodded and one of the team moved forward, speaking quietly. "We gave him a shot of morphine, sir. It's all we had."

"Look, you did just fine. The other two?"

They shook their heads.

As they were talking, Nurse Carmen knelt over Guy and checked his vital signs.

"Sir, he's been wounded badly in the shoulder, just under the collar bone," said Nurse Carmen, pointing. "Look there, it must have entered just above the straps. I'm leaving the vest on to help with the pressure, but he's losing a lot of blood and he's in shock."

"Nurse, get what you need now from the clinic and I mean everything, then meet us down in maintenance. Two of you go with the nurse and find a trolley. He's going to need it."

Robert called Chief Forza on the radio asking him to meet him and once Guy was strapped into on the trolley, they wheeled him carefully down the stairs arriving at the service tunnel, where the golf cart was waiting. The nurse put a line into Guy's arm and hung a bag of saline from a pole on the trolley.

No one noticed Pimpi sitting in a dark spot of the tunnel, swigging occasionally from his Old Smuggler. He barely noticed them either.

"Nurse, you're coming with us. You two are also," said Robert looking at two of the tactical team. "You other two go back to security and take Gonzalez with you. Move it!"

Collapsing the legs of the trolley, they carefully rolled it lengthways onto the golf cart and strapped Guy's arms and legs down. As he tried to lift his head, the nurse stopped him. "Sir, I think he wants to say something," she said.

Robert moved closer and leaned over his friend.

"He won't be playing the harmonica again for a while," he croaked, almost smiling.

"Fuck's sake Guy," he said, strangely pleased by what he had just heard.

Robert began pacing up and down next to the trolley. He felt sure he was missing something.

"Gonzalez, where does this tunnel exit on the other side?"

"The car park sir. The underground car park."

"Keys?"

The old man, now very frightened, handed the keys to Robert and stepped back. Robert then remembered his cabinet chief, Roxy Pla.

"Chief, you go on ahead with the cart, I'll take one of these men with me and Gonzalez. I need to get Roxy down here. We'll catch up," he said, handing him a key.

"What about me?" asked Pimpi, staggering to his feet.

"Christ, Pimpi. Chief, keep an eye on him and stay in radio contact."

The golf cart hummed into life and the three of them watched as it slowly moved away into the distance with nurse Carmen sitting next to Guy and holding his hand.

CHAPTER 51

On the island, Margarita waited. The last five hours felt like the longest of her life and as she looked at her wristwatch again, she only felt more trapped. She knew she was safe in the presidential suite, yet she now thought of it as a huge birdcage, loathing every single minute that passed.

Looking again at her phone, which showed seven minutes past four, she poured a whisky to calm her nerves. Sipping the whisky she heard the familiar tone of the intercom. She knew the only access to the suite, was by using a unique key or if she authorised use of the lift by intercom. Maybe it was Marco, she wondered.

"Yes? Hello?" she said, pressing the button on the wall.

"Mrs Campos, it's Marco. I'd like to double check the security upstairs if I may," said the crackly voice.

He was probably just checking up on her, she concluded, so she pressed a green button authorising the lift doors to open. Walking into the kitchen, she checked the fridge. Yes, plenty of Coke. He might be thirsty.

In a few moments the soft tone of the lift sounded and she heard the doors open.

"Over here, Marco, I'm in the kitchen," she said cheerfully.

She heard footsteps approaching very slowly and imagined he was probably tired.

"Can I get you something?" she asked casually, without looking around. "A coke?"

"No thank you, Mrs Campos," said the tall figure wearing a black suit and white shirt.

"Who the hell are you?" she demanded, turning around quickly, not recognising his voice.

Without answering, the man took a 9mm pistol from his belt.

"Where's Marco?" she asked, stepping back.

"Downstairs, somewhere."

She fumbled for her phone, dropped it and ran to the living room.

"There's nowhere to run, you know" he said pointing his weapon and following her slowly.

Margarita stopped with her back against the windows in the living room, her arms folded as if trying to protect herself. He smiled as he advanced towards her, then stopped when he was standing at arm's length. She could smell his perspiration and cheap cologne, so she felt sick and put a hand to her mouth.

"Don't touch me!" she shouted.

Lunging at her, he grabbed the back of her head, dragged her across the room and forced her face down on the sofa.

"This is a special present from Pérez and when I've finished with you, whore, no one will want you," he said, turning her over to look at him.

She spat in his face and kicked him as hard she could, at which point, he grabbed at her blouse and lifted her towards him, laughing.

"The Crawford whore. Now look at you, *puta*!"

Her eyes filled with tears of rage and fear as she smelled his foul, tobacco and wino breath, her face not two inches from his.

He began to laugh again and, ripping her blouse open, his eyes widened as she clawed at his face with her fingernails, digging them in with all her strength, then ran screaming onto the balcony, sliding the door shut. Running the entire circumference of the balcony screaming for help, she reached the patio, where she stopped, looked back and saw him coming towards her from the living room. In desperation, she took off her shoes and threw them at him as he began to run towards her. Spotting the bedroom door, she opened it quickly, ran in and slammed it shut.

She didn't hear the lift arriving and as she lay on the floor behind the bed, a dark figure silently slipped between the one metre partition wall and a wardrobe at the entrance to the bedroom.

Her attacker was laughing now, muttering obscenities and breathing rapidly. From just behind the pillows, she moved her head up a little and, peaking past the wardrobe, saw him slowly taking off his belt and unbuttoning his shirt.

"You're mine now, bitch," he said in a low guttural voice as he approached the doorway. Cowering behind the bed and holding a hand to her mouth, she felt the tears run down her cheeks. Waiting for him to find her, she could hear nothing but his laboured breathing. She daren't look over the bed again, so curled herself into the smallest person she could imagine and trembling, put her hands over her ears.

He had thrown off his shirt and was breathing rapidly as he approached the doorway to the bedroom. He knew where she was hiding, he could hear the sobbing which he would silence and finally make her his. Two metres from the doorway and now breathing even faster he quickly took the gun from his belt, put it in his pocket, pulled the belt away and threw it to the ground.

When he felt the crack on his head, he stopped, his vision blurred and he put a hand to his head. The second blow brought him to his knees and he looked up to see the barrel of a handgun held by two hands pointing at his face. The third blow brought numbness to his whole body and he crashed forwards into blackness.

Marco Bueno kept his eyes firmly fixed on the man now lying prone on the floor, then nodded to his colleague, who removed the gun from the intruder's pocket and secured his hands and legs with duct tape. Marco, still pointing his gun at the man, then put his palm up and moved quickly into the bedroom and around the bed, where he found a shaking Margarita curled up, and holding her hands around her head. He then signalled to his colleague to remove the man from the room.

At the sound of a voice, she winced.

"Mrs Campos...it's over. He's gone," said Marco, softly as he looked down at her.

Turning a little and looking upwards, she pushed the damp hair from her eyes.

"Who? What?" she asked.

Marco knelt down on one knee and spoke gently to her. "It's over. He's gone."

"Oh God!" she said, the tears falling down her cheeks and her whole body trembling.

"Mrs Campos, you're safe now," said Marco. "Come, take my hand."

Sniffling and wiping the tears from her face, she took his hand and slowly stood up, trying with the other hand to pull the ripped blouse together over her chest, as Marco looked away.

"Who the hell was that, Marco?" she asked, trying to rearrange her blouse.

"I'm sorry, but I've got no idea," answered Marcos.

"Pérez sent him!" she shouted.

"I don't think so, Mrs Campos..."

"But I know it was, Marcos..." she pleaded.

"Look, I'll be right outside the door if you need anything," he said, gesturing to her, leaving the bedroom and shutting the door quietly behind him.

Still holding the torn blouse to her chest, she ran to the bathroom, slammed the door, leaned back against it and looked in the mirror. Christ, what a mess, she thought as she removed the remains of her blouse and dropped it on the floor. She moved a little closer to the mirror and ran a finger over the bleeding scratch marks on her neck and chest.

"Fucking Pérez," she murmured, taking off her bra and wincing at the pain. After she had spent fifteen minutes showering, she rubbed a little antiseptic lotion on the scratches, dressed herself in a black polo neck sweater and faded blue jeans and gathered up all the clothes she had been wearing during the attack, which she then stuffed into a black refuse bag. She then washed her hands again and made her way to the kitchen and out onto the balcony, where she found Marco and another member of the security team looking through their binoculars.

"How the hell did he get in?" she asked, angrily.

Marco let the binoculars drop around his neck and turned to her.

"I'm terribly sorry, Mrs Campos. It seems that he sprung one of our colleagues, Javier and assumed his identity."

"And Javier? Where is he now?" asked Margarita.

"I'm sorry, Mrs Campos…"

CHAPTER 52

R oxy, there you are," said Robert, finding her in a group of government employees huddling in the boardroom.

"Please don't be alarmed. We have arranged transport for everyone until this all clears up," he said, rubbing his hands together.

Many were still crying from the shock of seeing the president shot at on live TV and the shooting of De la Mano had been too much for many to accept. Seeing him flanked by two heavily armed men dressed in black caused them to huddle together even tighter.

"But when, sir?" asked one.

"No more than half an hour, madam. Please wait here, everything is under control. Miss Pla, this way please," he said gesturing to the hallway.

Once outside the door, he held her by the shoulders. "You have to come with me, Roxy. You're my chief of staff and there's a big chance they'll be looking for you."

"No, Mr President, I'm not going anywhere," she replied, surprised he had even asked her. "My responsibility is with those people," she said pointing.

"I don't want to spell this out, Roxy, but it's likely that the government will fall and we're running out of time. You are a figurehead and even with protection, I cannot guarantee your safety."

"I'm sorry, sir, I can't leave these people. You do what you have to do," she said, turning to walk back to the boardroom, at which, Robert nodded to the two guards, who intercepted her at the door and blocked her path. She turned around with her hands on her hips.

"Bring her with us," he said pressing the lift button. "Gonzalez, go on. Go with them in the boardroom. You've done your job."

Watched over by the two guards, Roxy quickly collected her belongings from her office and they made their back to the service tunnel, where Robert locked the door to maintenance and finally the huge service tunnel door.

"Chief? Do you read me?" said Robert into the radio. There was no reply, only the sound of hissing static, so he tried again. More static.

"We had better start walking then, hadn't we?"

In the boardroom of a low, two storey building on the outskirts of Albuquerque, four impeccably dressed men and a red haired woman sat at a long mahogany table and looked at a TV on the wall at the end of the room. They watched as thousands of people ran from a handful of riot police who were firing rubber bullets and lobbing tear gas canisters.

"A close call," said one, playing with a ball point pen.

"Oh I don't know," said another, smiling. "Would have been right up our alley."

"If it's a private war we have a chance of winning, yes," said another.

"Too many imponderables, gentlemen," said the red haired woman. "We didn't sign up for this, just to take on the British Empire."

"What British Empire?" said the first one.

"An empire that's still alive and kicking, by the looks of it," said the red haired woman.

"Still, not a bad day's work. I don't expect we'll be hearing from our friend again," she said, standing up and straightening her skirt.

As Margarita watched Marco and his colleague scanning the river, she overheard them talking.

"About one kilometre out?" asked Marco.

"Looks like, what? Twelve vessels, maybe fifteen," said the other.

"Weapons?" asked Marco.

"Probably, but I can't see any yet."

Jesus, she thought, it's really happening. She walked over to them, they heard her footsteps and lowered their binoculars.

"What's going on out there, Marco?" she asked.

"Oh, Mrs Campos. Are you feeling a little better now?"

"I think so, but could you tell me what's going on?"

"You need to come with us, Mrs Campos."

"But what about Robert?"

"The president is on his way."

"Can't you talk to him?"

"Madam, the last we heard was that he was arranging a way to access the tunnel. Anyway, their radios won't work properly underground."

"Can't we wait for him?"

"No madam, we can't wait. Look, take these binoculars."

Margarita looked through the huge binoculars, saw dozens of vessels approaching and gulped visibly.

"Do you see now, Mrs Campos? We have to make a move right now. The president will meet us later. I'm afraid we don't have any other choice."

"But where will we meet him?" she asked.

"There's a small harbour on the Martín García Island."

"But isn't it dangerous there?"

"Not any more. It was completely neutralised by the British."

Marcos's colleague who had been scanning the river, now walked over and interrupted them.

"Boss, we need to make a move. They're less than half a click away now."

"Mrs Campos, please pack a bag of clothes. We've run out of time."

Margarita, realised the impending danger and ran to the bedroom to pack what few belongings she had and went back out to the patio with the bag slung over her shoulder.

"As long as you're sure, Marco. If anything happens to Robert…"

"Follow me please," he said, ignoring her comment.

Chief Forza opened the door at the end of the service tunnel on the island and peered into the underground car park. He saw several vehicles, recognising a Jeep and the spare presidential Range Rover. He immediately keyed his radio.

"Marco? Are you receiving?"

He heard the usual static, but nothing else. Still too far down, he thought, so he walked up the stairs to the exit and dialled Marco on his cell phone.

"Marco?"

"Chief, where are you?"

He explained how they'd arrived and also that they had the injured Guy on the golf cart.

"I need help down here, Marco. Nurse Carmen says he needs surgery."

"Where's the president?" asked Marco.

"He went to fetch Miss Pla and said he would follow. It's all a bit tight"

"Look, I'll send a couple of my men down, but we have to get moving, Chief. They're coming by boat, hundreds of them, and it's not looking good."

"I hear you, Marco. Is Mrs Campos with you?"

"Yes she is and we're boarding the presidential yacht now, so you'll have to hurry."

"No, Marco, take one of the coast guard cutters and have one of your men prepare the other one. They'll outrun anything."

"Will do."

The chief ended the conversation and went back into the tunnel, where he helped carry Guy's trolley off the cart and into the car park. Within a few minutes, two heavily armed men arrived dressed in black and escorted Guy and Nurse Carmen down to the harbour.

"Mr Pérez, I'll be waiting here for the president. You can either go directly to the boat or wait with me. I really don't care as long as you stay out of my way," said the chief.

"I'm in no rush, I'll wait," replied Pimpi, his drunken reply hiding the disappointment of hearing Margarita's name.

"Men, the cart has had it, the batteries are shot, so we'll just have to wait it out."

The chief tried reaching the president again on his radio, but all he heard was more hissing static.

Gripping the handrail at the stern of the cutter, Margarita watched as a trolley was being wheeled along the jetty. Seeing a man lying on it and a nurse walking quickly beside it, she immediately thought it was Robert and ran down the gangway, thinking the worst.

As she got closer she immediately saw that it was Guy lying on the stretcher and rushed over.

"What happened to you, Guy?"

"Please Mrs Campos, he really shouldn't talk. Do you mind?" said Nurse Carmen.

"Is there anything I can do to help?"

Marco and two police officers lifted Guy off the trolley onto a stretcher and carried him aboard the cutter, laying him on a bunk in the forward cabin.

"You can help me collect whatever medical supplies there are in the residence, okay?" said Nurse Carmen.

"Come on then, let's go. I know where to find them," said Margarita.

"How much farther?" asked Roxy.

"No more than about fifteen minutes; after all, two kilometres isn't all that far," Replied Robert.

"Sir?" said one of the agents. "It's three, not two."

Robert stopped and turned to look at him. "What?"

"As the crow flies it's two and a half clicks from the coast to the island, but the tunnel is much farther due to the first bend and the distance of the Casa Rosada from the coast. I would say about another forty minutes, sir. Unless we run."

Robert tried to raise the chief on the radio and received nothing more than the hissing of static again.

"Come on then, let's go," he said, taking Roxy's arm. "We really don't want to be down here any longer than we have to."

As they briskly walked, they heard the constant dripping of water, the walls were damp and slimy and the air smelled stale and musty. After another ten minutes, they all felt a rush of air pass over them.

"That's probably someone opening a door, over there, at the end," said one of the agents, pointing.

They all peered ahead, but could see no other light, due to the tunnel now rising up and bending slightly to the left.

"Who designed this damned tunnel? Why doesn't it just go straight, for fuck's sake?" asked Robert.

No one answered and the four of them continued walking as fast as they could, one agent in front, the other at the rear.

CHAPTER 53

The chief stood on the pontoon as the cutter moved slowly away, its bow thrusters pushing it sideways. He threw the stern line over to Marco and one of his men released the bow line as the cutter pushed forward towards the breakwaters and increased to full speed ahead once clear. Margarita stood at the flagpole on the stern, the tears falling down her cheeks as she gripped the railing, wondering when she would ever see Robert again.

Standing back from the pontoon and up on the raised wall of the breakwater, were the remaining six federal agents, their weapons at the ready.

The chief looked up and shouted. "Where are they now?"

The squad leader looked out over the bay and shouted back. "Five minutes, sir."

Walking as quickly as his legs would allow, the chief reached the other cutter, climbed aboard, made the usual checks and fired up the twin turbo diesel engines. The calm water at the stern boiled up and churned into a foamy mass and black smoke spewed from the twin exhausts, soon turning to water and steam as the cooling of the water took effect.

"Full tanks, range five hundred nautical miles, check," the chief mumbled. "Two of you get back to the tunnel and find the president, one of you join me on the cutter and you two guard the entrance. Hurry, please," he said into his handheld radio.

The two federal agents ran back down to the tunnel, through the door and jogged into the dim light, hailing the president as they jogged.

"Sshhh!" said Robert as he put his hand. "I hear them."

They all stopped as a faint echo of running feet and muffled shouting could be heard behind them.

"Come on, run!" he said taking the lead.

"They must not be allowed to enter the marina," shouted the chief to the two soldiers standing on the breakwater above him. "We have to keep them out at any cost!"

Positioning themselves near the end of the breakwater and using the concrete tower of the southern beacon as cover, they watched as small boats approached rapidly, heading for the mouth of the harbour.

"If you can, disable the helmsmen. The president has ordered minimal casualties," shouted the chief above the roar of the cutters engines.

"Easier said than done," said one, as he took aim through his scope at a small fishing boat two hundred metres from the entrance. His first bullet hit the wheel house, piercing the shatter proof glass, the second hit the helmsman in the shoulder, throwing him backwards and the small vessel veered away. His colleague aimed for the engine housing amidships of the second boat and fired six or seven rounds. After a few seconds, black smoke could be seen rising from the housing and the boat stopped dead in the water.

More boats were approaching; bigger boats, offshore cruisers, some with armed men standing on the bows.

"Chief, we need more men. I don't think we can hold them all," shouted one.

"Mr Pérez, get yourself a weapon and help those men." shouted the chief. "Quick, come with me," he said to the other federal agent on the cutter.

Robert put his hand up and the four of them stopped briefly as the sound of running came closer. But this time the running was from behind them, so he looked around with the others and they heard what sounded like a rush, a muted rumble, a clattering from where they had come.

"Oh shit!" he said. "Come on, keep moving!"

"What?" asked Roxy, pulling his shirt as she began to jog alongside the president.

"Just keep going Roxy, we're nearly there," he shouted.

"Hijo de puta," she mumbled, making the sign of the Cross on her chest.

The four of them ran, breathing hard and sweating in the damp atmosphere, the lights passing over them, creating a strange glow in the tunnel. Two minutes later, they saw two black figures rushing towards them, shouting.

"Mr President!"

They stopped as they joined together, all leaning over, their hands on their hips and catching breath. As they did so, the noise from behind them grew louder and more distinct. Roxy knelt on the ground leaning forward, her face pale and her breathing rapid, her face wet from the sweat.

"I can't go on. My legs…they're like jelly," she said, looking up at Robert.

"Come on now, Roxy. I'm not leaving you here!" he said.

"Sir, we have to keep moving," one of the newly arrived agents shouted. "Now!"

One of the original two agents bent over, grabbed Roxy by the waist and threw her over onto his back, putting her legs around his waist. "Sit tight and hold on!"

As they resumed running forward, the lead agent turned to Robert. "It's about another two hundred metres, sir. We're almost there."

Looking over his shoulder, Robert thought he could see lights flickering and he could definitely hear the clattering of running. He looked at the agent in the rear, the whites of his eyes showing determination. Or was it fear, he wondered as he turned to look ahead.

As the lights tapered out at the end of the tunnel and their running slowed a little, they could see nothing but a closed door in the dim light. Finally reaching it, one of the agents grabbed the handle and pushed at the door.

"Why the hell did you close it?" asked Robert.

"I didn't, sir. I left it open," he said, pushing against it furiously with his shoulder.

The rumble behind them grew louder with every passing second and Robert watched as the agent rammed the door with his shoulder.

"It must have slammed shut by the air sucking inwards, when they opened the service door on the other side!" said Robert.

Robert leaned against the door with his palms. What had Gonzalez said? *The evacuation doors can only be opened this side because President Cristal...*

He tried the door with his key and it refused to budge. "It's completely jammed."

"Listen, we need to backtrack to the nearest door back there on the right," he said, pointing.

"But, sir, what do you mean?" asked one of the agents.

"Did anyone notice any doors on our left as we were coming? Come on, will you!"

"But..." said another.

"There are evacuation doors from the main vehicle tunnel. We have to find one," he said, running back into the tunnel.

"Shit," said another, rolling his eyes.

An exhausted Roxy jumped on the back of the nearest policeman and they all ran as fast as they could back down the tunnel.

"Shit, the door is jammed!" said an agent, pulling at the service tunnel door in the underground car park.

"Quick, back around to the other side," he said, pointing. "Look, over there, by the main gates."

The car park was separated into two areas by concrete columns, with the service tunnel exiting into an area reserved for maintenance machinery, the spare Range Rover and one or two staff vehicles. The main tunnel gate led into a larger area for official vehicles and the private lift to the presidential suite.

The two agents ran to the main gate, an ornate design of curved metalwork and vertical iron bars, no more than six centimetres apart. The design was intended to allow air to pass unhindered from one end of the tunnel to the other, but was clearly no defence against firearms.

One of the agents pressed the green button at the side and the gate began to slide open, whirring and screeching as metal past over metal.

"Stop!" said the agent standing behind. "Sshh, listen!"

As they listened, standing with their hands gripped around the bars of the gate, they heard shouting in the distance and a faint rumble.

"They've broken through." said one.

"You stay here. I'll move forward and see if there are any doors down there on the left."

"What are you talking about? What doors?" asked the other.

"How the hell do I know? I've never been here before, but there must be some kind of evacuation system. Fire doors or something. Ask the chief."

The other bodyguard reached Chief Forza on his mobile phone.

"Chief, we need to know if there are fire doors in the tunnel," he asked, putting his free hand to the other ear. As he listened to the broken reply of the chief, he thought he could hear gunfire.

"Yes, every...hundred metres...why?"

"I'll explain later," he said, disconnecting the call. He told his partner over the radio and gave him the information. "I'm coming with you!" he said running into the tunnel.

The coast guard cutter, fitted with a single railgun mounted forward of the wheelhouse, could be operated from where the chief stood at the helm. He gave orders to cast off and manoeuvred the vessel to the narrow entrance between the two breakwaters, pushing the bow so that the nose of the vessel jutted out nearly five metres, giving him a clear view of the approaching vessels.

He pulled down a microphone from the overhead console and switched to public address.

"Any vessels found within fifty metres of the harbour will be deemed a threat and will be fired upon. There will be no warning shots. Turn your vessels around and proceed back to port immediately."

He repeated the warning twice and as he looked through the one inch thick glass of the wheelhouse, he saw the boats continue their approach.

"Well, fuck that," he mumbled. "Disable them? That's a joke," he said as he grabbed the joystick, swivelling the gun, turning it to the port side and pressing the fire button.

After five minutes of running back into the tunnel, Robert stopped, leaned over with his hands on his knees and pointed to the right. "There, there!" he croaked. "It's a fire door."

He felt his lungs burning and a sudden need to vomit as his breathing gradually slowed and the sweat ran down his face. The noise from deep down in the tunnel grew louder and he straightened up, took the keys from his pocket and ran to the door.

"Quick, all of you," he shouted, pushing the key into the lock. Turning it, he pulled the handle down and pushed. "Oh no, it's stuck!"

"Sir, they're coming!" said one.

Roxy took cover behind one of the agents who had knelt down, taking aim with his M14. He put his arm back and held Roxy in place to keep his body working as a protective mass and then gripped the gun again.

While Robert kept downward force on the handle, two of the other agents rammed the door with their shoulders, while the third knelt next to his partner, signalling Roxy to keep low.

The clattering of feet grew louder and the agent with Roxy behind him calculated that they were now less than two hundred metres away. He could hear distinct voices and swear words he recognised.

"Shit, this is not good, there could be hundreds," he mumbled.

Robert's radio crackled into life.

"Hey, *gordo*, you copy, over?"

Robert pressed the talk button on his hand-held. "It's the president, here. Where are you? Over."

"A door. I think it's a fire door. Over."

"Which one, over?"

"First from the main gate, over."

"We're at the second one, over."

"Can you open it, sir? Over."

"It's jammed. Can you help, over?"

"Two seconds. Out."

Agent one turned to his partner. "Find something. A crowbar, anything! They're at the second door down."

Agent two turned and ran at full speed to the garage, skidded on the shiny surface and turned right into the maintenance area. He opened all the doors to the equipment storage, turned over crates, looked up at the racks of assorted tools hanging above a workbench and spotted a red and grey one metre crowbar hanging from a hook. He grabbed it, slid it into his ammo belt, then noticed a long steel bar with flat ends, and two large hammers, which he grabbed and turned back to the main gate.

"Hurry… they're coming!" he heard, broken up on his radio.

"I think it's moving, sir!" shouted agent three as he continued pounding the door with his boot.

As he heard the crowd getting closer, Robert turned and saw the two agents taking aim. "Disable them, god damnit!" he shouted.

Neither soldier answered, but kept their aim on the downward slope of the service tunnel, scanning for the first movement as the clattering sound of running feet approached more loudly.

"Here, use this," said an out of breath agent three as he knelt down next to his partner. He then wedged the crowbar into the narrow gap at the top of the door while the other shoved the flat edge of the metal pole in another gap at the bottom.

"One, two…pull!"

The door gave a fraction and agent one pressed the handset on his collar.

"Push hard your end. Push!"

Back at Robert's end, the two agents began firing single shots from their automatic weapons, trying their best to aim for the legs of the crowd that had just appeared over the slight incline of the tunnel.

"We're working it from this end, sir. Protect yourselves. Over," a voice sounded on Robert's radio.

"Roger, will do," he replied as he pointed to the two agents pushing and kicking at the door.

"Roxy, come over here. Crawl! You two, hold them off."

Terrified, Roxy crawled over to the recessed door and Robert pulled her up into the one metre deep recess, standing her up and holding her shaking body close to him.

"Nearly there, nearly there," he said, stroking her hair and comforting her.

The four agents were now firing at will, single rounds leaving their guns and disappearing into the legs of the incoming crowd. The entire scene became chaotic, men screamed as they were hit in the legs and arms, and their advance appeared to slow a little. One or two bullets ricocheted off the walls as two or three armed protesters returned fire and Robert held Roxy as far back into the recess as he possibly could.

Spurred on by the gunfire of the armed protesters, the crowd surged forward again.

"Sir, we won't hold them!" shouted one of the agents, seconds before he lunged backwards and fell on his back, blood gushing from his right arm. At that moment, they all heard a clatter of metal upon concrete and the fire door swung open with a rush of air, and two men grabbed the president and Roxy as they fell backwards into the now open doorway.

"Fall back! Fall back!" shouted one of the agents through the door to his four colleagues. Now firing indiscriminately as they kept low and moving back on their heels, one grabbed the fallen agent by the top of his flak jacket and lunged back quickly to the others waiting at the open door. They immediately grabbed him, and the group moved quickly towards the main gate.

With Robert's group now safely out of the tunnel, two agents stayed back and slammed the door shut. Being unable to lock it, they jammed the steel bar against the blind, protruding non-functional lock, hoping it would hold.

Now running up to the main gate, they heard gunshots from behind the door they had just left.

"Sir, you need to get to the harbour. Two of us are going to use those vehicles to block the door and the main gate. Hurry!"

Holding Roxy's hand, Robert rushed through the gate, felt her weight as he pulled, then stopped. She had fallen to her knees, blood oozing from the left side of her chest.

"Oh no! Oh Christ no."

He picked her up in his arms, felt his knees give way and as he almost dropped her, one of the agents grabbed her.

"Come on, sir. I've got her!"

As the president's group made their way across the car park and out through the exit to the stairs, two agents smashed open the key locker, started the engines of the armoured Range Rover and a Ford Mondeo estate car and drove them into the tunnel. The Mondeo, they parked with the front end wedged tight against the service tunnel fire door, and the Range Rover, end to end against the rear of the Mondeo. As they were returning for one more vehicle, they heard shots in the main tunnel, with bullets piercing the Mondeo's passenger doors. Taking cover behind the safety of the Range Rover, one of them opened fire and signalled to the other, who ran and fired up a Renault van, which he then squeezed into the remaining gap between the Range Rover and the wall. The two agents moved back quickly and hammered on the big red button. The metal gate slowly closed. They moved two more vehicles in front of both the ornate main gate and the service tunnel door, as an extra precaution.

"Let them try and get past that lot," said one as, panting he sat down against the wall next to the gate.

The other took a swig from a plastic bottle of water and threw it over to his partner as the shots became louder and more frequent from the tunnel.

"I got the crowbar," said the other, brandishing it and laughing. "You just never know when you're going to need one."

"Fuck, you're mental!" the other said, throwing the bottle back.

"And shitting myself. Come on, let's go. They'll be over those cars in no time."

"Wait. There is one thing that will stop them…"

"No, not that."

"It will buy us time, buy the president time."

"I'm not doing that," he said standing up and keying his radio. "Chief, we're on our way."

"You carry on and I'll catch up with you."

"*I'm* mental?" he said, leaving quickly for the door at the end of the car park. "You should be locked up."

"Fucking animals. Let 'em burn," he mumbled as he took aim at the Renault's fuel tank through a gap in the gate.

The bullet hit the vehicle with a ping, just about audible through the shouts of the crowd who had started to climb over the vehicles, shooting blindly through the gate with handguns.

The agent moved to the maintenance area, took cover behind a steel tool cabinet and aimed at the Mondeo, just above the rear wheel, with the bullet thudding into the metalwork.

"Shit!"

He glanced around the workshop looking for a petrol canister. Surely they must have something, he thought. Then his radio hissed and he pressed a button on his flak jacket.

"This is the chief. What the hell are you doing down there, man? You've got five minutes."

"Just one minute more, Chief," he said, looking around the area as his eyes fixed on a large olive green canister sitting at the side of the work bench.

He quickly scrabbled over, keeping low and behind the workbench, grabbed the half empty canister, shook it and as he threw it against the gate, he felt a thud against his shoulder and fell backwards, blood pouring from the wound.

"Fuck 'em!" he said loudly as he rolled over and took aim at the canister, now not caring if he was in full view. As the bullet hit the canister and exploded into flames, another bullet hit him, pushing his head back as he smashed backwards on the floor, blood rushing from his mouth.

"Fuck!" he gurgled.

The crowd had climbed back over the vehicles at the heat of the flames which now began to spread downhill towards them.

The agent eased himself up and, grimacing from the pain, took aim at the Mondeo once more. He fired in full automatic, catching the fuel tank and the car exploded in a ball of fire. He lay down, blood pouring from his mouth, his eyes wide open and he stopped breathing.

Standing on the pontoon, Robert called the chief on his handheld radio.

"Chief! Where's Margarita? Is she with you?"

"She went with Marco and I'm glad she did, sir. He made the right call," Forza answered, hitting *fire* on the console.

"That's another one down," he mumbled as he watched a small twenty foot fishing boat take a hit just below the stern.

"Sir, take the yacht. Quick!" said the chief into the handset.

"But I don't know how to drive a boat, Chief," replied Robert.

"Yes you do. It's just like a car, only bigger. We need to get the hell out of here, right now!"

Robert beckoned the men he could see to join him on the yacht and ran over to help them carry Roxy, who was now very pale and practically unconscious.

"Where's Ramirez?" he asked as two carried Roxy up the gangway. They shook their heads and carried on down into the main saloon.

The third agent, who called himself Maxi, joined the president in the wheelhouse and asked him if he knew how to operate the controls.

"Not really," replied Robert, looking through the glass at the breakwater.

"Mind if I take a look, sir?"

"No, be my guest...fucking hell! What's Pimpi doing up there, for Christ sake?"

The gunfire from the breakwater was now incessant, with Pimpi cackling like a madman and swigging from his bottle of *Old Smuggler* as he took pot-shots at the hulls of the boats now prevented from entering the harbour. He never imagined that he would find himself with a fully automatic machine gun in his hands and lots of targets to shoot at. The *Old Smuggler* spurred him on, and as he stood next to the tactical team members whose shooting had now slowed considerably, he felt indestructible and emptied his magazine into the hull of a ten metre sailing yacht, which quickly began a list to starboard, the crew jumping overboard.

"Beats writing fucking speeches all day!" he shouted.

"Pimpi, get the fuck down here now, will you!" shouted Robert from the door of the wheelhouse.

"Chief, how's it looking?" asked Robert into his radio.

"Sunk three or four, six out of action. They're backing off. Get your engines rolling, Mr President, we're not finished yet."

Maxi ran through various checks on the ship's console and after a quick visual of the forward and aft lines, fired up the engines.

"Sir, Miss Pla is in pretty bad shape," said one of the team members emerging from the saloon. "She's going to need blood."

"Are any of you paramedic trained?" asked Robert.

"Yes sir, but the one with most experience is the Doc, he's up on the breakwater."

"To the yacht, now!" Robert said through the PA system.

With the tactical team members now safely aboard with the other agents, and Pimpi sitting at the stern cuddling his new friend, the M14, next to his briefcase, Robert gave the order to cast off. Two agents singled up on the bow and stern lines, heaved up the walkway and two then took up positions at each end of the vessel.

"Which one's the Doc?" asked Robert.

"Me sir!" came a voice from the stern.

"Get down below and take care of Miss Pla. Maxi? All ready?"

"Yes sir."

Robert then took a final glance back at the island.

"Jesus! Let go forward, let go aft!"

He rushed out to the stern, held on to the guardrail and watched as thousands of protesters swarmed from the car park door and rushed angrily towards the marina. He then walked amidships, looked forward and then aft.

"Are we clear? Are we clear?" he said loudly.

"All clear."

"All clear."

The two remaining agents cast off and took up defensive positions aft and forward with their mates, reloading their weapons as they did so.

Robert signalled to Maxi, pushing his clenched fist in a downward motion and the vessel leapt forward, clearing the port breakwater by no more than a metre. Robert then ran back into the wheel house and spoke to Maxi.

"Full speed now, lad. Use the chief as your guide."

"Aye aye, sir!"

"Shit, that was close," he mumbled to no one in particular as he looked aft.

Thousands of protesters had now overwhelmed the entire marina, the breakwaters and surrounding area. He saw smoke billowing out of the car park doors and flames spreading farther along towards the mansion. The odd gunshot could be heard and a faint sound of screaming and shouting over the roar of the engines, fading away to nothing as they sliced through the water at more than twenty five knots.

"Thanks, Jack," he muttered, looking down at the angry brown foam boiling at the stern. "There's one thing you can be certain of, old boy. Maybe not tomorrow or the next day…"

He walked past Pimpi who was sitting cross legged near the stern, grinning and taking slugs from his collection of bottles. Robert shook his head, returned to the wheelhouse and called the chief.

"That was close, Chief. Where are we heading? Over."

"Yes it was. Call me on my mobile. Out."

"The last message I received from Marco was that he had sailed past Martín García Island, but it was a no go."

"When was that?"

"A couple of hours ago?"

"Where they hell are they now?"

"In all the confusion, sir…"

Stabbing at the keys, he dialled Margarita's number on his phone and listened to the ringtone over and over again, willing her to pick up, but there was nothing.

At around two kilometres from the coast, he still had a mobile signal but he knew that wouldn't last, so he called Chief Forza again and asked if he'd been able to raise Marco on the ship's radio.

"I'm sorry sir, but they could be nearly a hundred nautical miles away by now, and our radios will never reach them. He's not even answering his phone, and we lost him on radar quite some time ago. Sorry, but I'll keep trying."

Robert felt his guts somersaulting and the blood drain from his head, so he steadied himself against the bulkhead of the wheelhouse, imagining the very worst of possibilities.

A minute or so later, the chief called again and he desperately hoped it would be Margarita's voice.

"Sir? I don't know what's happened here, but you need to make a decision."

His heart told him to follow Margarita but he had no idea where to and he felt tears in his eyes.

"Paraguay?" he said in a quiet voice.

"We can't go south and we can't go east. It's our only option now sir."

"Have we lost the city?"

"If you lose the city sir, you've lost the country."

CHAPTER 54

Sitting on a single bed in the small bedroom of their hostel in Rufino, Clara sipped red wine from a white plastic cup and leaned against Pascal's shoulder, as he took a bite from a slice of pizza.

The wall mounted TV was showing the city of Buenos Aires in turmoil, shops being looted, many buildings in flames and thousands of armed protesters pouring into the Casa Rosada.

In a sombre tone, the young reporter told the viewers that law and order had completely broken down, the police were looking on helplessly and the whereabouts of the president was unknown. Closing her report from the relative safety of a twelfth floor studio overlooking the now devastated Plaza de Mayo, she asked the viewers to pray for the broken nation.

"And to think," said Clara, holding back the tears. "No one even knows who Robert really is. Just imagine."

"And that, Clara, is the way it should stay," said Pascal.

CHAPTER 55

Well, that was quite a storm. It went on and on, all night, just like Mr Crawford did, but at least he stopped occasionally.

It's dawn outside now and bright yellow light is burning through those green shutters like razor thin shards, but it's really dim in here and I feel jet lagged.

How peaceful it is, except for that constant dripping noise coming from the tin roof. It's like a leaking tap and it's beginning to irritate me, to be honest.

And then I remember what he told me. It's like stitching old black and white film clips together. Everything is jumbled up, like a perfect jigsaw puzzle, tipped off the table and onto the floor.

Robert Crawford is sitting in a big, red leather armchair, his arms stretched out along its sides. It's like a scene from *The Godfather* and, although his eyes are open, he seems to be in a trance. He's just staring at nothing.

Now I can hear clattering from the kitchen. This jolts him visibly, so he gets up from the chair, opens all the windows inwards and then pushes those green shutters away. The light is blindingly bright and I put my hands over my eyes, then realise that I don't recognise this room at all, even though I've been sitting in it for half a day.

When I look past Robert Crawford, who is now framed as a dark, looming shape in the window frame, I can see a scene of perfect tranquillity. Long, pink, oblong clouds sit motionless over the far horizon and I can see one solitary tree on the line between the land and the sky. It really is quite beautiful, and as I stand behind him, the scene is almost poetic in its serenity.

I'm drawn to the now open front door and when I walk out onto the veranda, I can't find a single word to say. My mouth simply refuses to operate and behind me I hear china clinking and what sounds like teaspoons tinkling.

"Come, let's take our coffee outside," he says, as I breathe in fresh morning aromas of wet concrete, earth and grass. As I sit down opposite him at a table on the veranda, I can see steam rising from the tin shed roof and the red seat of my bike, just poking into view.

As I roll a cigarette, I imagine that he is swimming in agonies that are all now quite clear to me. I ask myself if it's possible to lose everything and still be the same person you were before. But can you really lose something that never belonged to you in the first place?

As he stirs his coffee, I see that he's still wearing his blazer, and the cravat from last night hasn't even moved. It's incredible. How can a man remain so untouched by such a night? Me? I'm exhausted, but I offer him a cigarette anyway, which he accepts without looking at me at all and proceeds to tap it on the table, because it's all misshapen. Then he lights it, inhales and sits back and crosses his legs, as he blows the smoke out while gazing at something far, far away.

I can't remember if I have ever sat with someone and said nothing for such a long time. It's an odd, but calming experience and I want it to continue, even though I know that I will have to shatter it, right now.

"You never resigned as president, yet you were tried and found guilty of treason in absentia. Should I still refer to you as Mr President?"

It's odd, but I still think of him as the president of Argentina.

"The grounds upon which Congress voted, were entirely spurious. I am still the president, but how you wish to address me is entirely up to you. I'm not *your* president after all," he replies, without a hint of emotion or bitterness.

"No, you are not my president, sir. But Virginia Cristal would certainly take issue with your assertion. After all, she has practically wiped your name from the history books since she was re-elected."

He finally turns to face me, just as I'm wondering when we would make eye contact.

"You remember everything I told you last night, I dare say?"

I remember practically every detail and I tell him so. Besides, I also have a full recording.

"Then you should know, in spite of everything that's happened, my greatest disappointment, is to once again see that woman in the Casa Rosada."

"And now, stronger than ever, thanks to you."

"The pendulum of politics is a cruel mistress, young man."

I'm beginning to believe that he just doesn't get it, even after everything that's happened. I feel like banging his head against a wall.

"No, sir. It's national populism and you singularly refused to accept its power, did you not?"

He turns away and resumes his staring into the unknown. I would have to change tack and ask him those burning questions that I left hanging from last night.

"I know this is difficult for you, but..."

"No, it's not difficult in the slightest. Whatever gave you that idea?"

Well, at least he's woken up from his trance. That's something.

"What became of Mrs Campos?"

"Nothing became of her. What an odd turn of phrase. Anyway, Mrs Crawford stayed the night with friends in Asunción," he says, looking at his watch. "She'll be here later, if you'd like to wait."

"So, you married?"

"Yes, indeed. Not long after finding each other again, actually. Here, in Paraguay," he says, smiling at last. "But she didn't want to hear me going on and on last night. She doesn't like to be reminded of it, at all."

I know I have to face the journey back to Buenos Aires, but I also know that I have to meet Margarita. She is the woman I saw in the photograph and the most important person in his life.

"But, sir. I thought she hated Mr Pérez…"

"Good Lord. Pérez doesn't live here," he says, throwing his head back and laughing. "I call when I need him."

I'm about to ask about Guy, Roxy and the Chief, when the tall figure of Pimpi Pérez looms up in the doorway.

"Will that be all, sir?" he asks, his hang-dog expression having been replaced by a nervous smile, as his eyes dart from side to side. I'm not a betting man, but I would lay odds that Pérez is anxious to get away before Mrs Crawford arrives.

"Yes, thank you, Pérez," he says, as Pérez nods, quickly turns away and heads for a small Fiat parked by the side of the house.

"Mrs Crawford will be arriving a little later, at lunchtime, so I suggest you get some rest, young man."

As I head for the bedroom, he takes my arm.

"Pérez wasn't here. You understand that don't you?"

"Old habits die hard, I see," I reply, turning away.

"Lunch is ready."

I'm awoken by Mr Crawford gently shaking me by the shoulder. After a long hot shower, I slowly put my biking kit back on, grimace at the twinge in my back and return to the veranda, where I find a table laid for three and a strikingly beautiful woman stand up and move towards me.

"You must be Margarita," I say, already enchanted by her as we shake hands.

"I'm sorry I missed you last night, but I was with friends in Asunción," she replies, looking at her husband, who is seated at the table and pouring wine into a glass.

She's exactly as I imagined, and how Mr Crawford described her last night. Her dark hair is pinned up and falling untidily around her shoulders, she's wearing tight black jeans, a blue and white striped blouse and those striking green eyes fascinate me.

"Please, take a seat. Wine?" she asks.

"I've got a long ride ahead of me, so a Coke will do fine, thanks."

We talk about last night's storm, they give me advice on which are the safest routes for my ride back to Buenos Aires and I notice that neither of them are keen to re-visit the events recounted to me last night. But I need to know why, and can't stop myself from asking.

"So, Mr Crawford. When will you be returning to BA?"

He looks at me with a severe frown and before he has a chance to answer, Margarita holds his hand firmly and turns to me with a hint of smile from the corner of her mouth.

"That's not going to happen."

I know I had to ask the question and sit back as they look at each other in a private manner that only they can understand.

"The last British president, then," I venture.

Neither of them reply to my half serious comment and as we finish lunch, I watch as they talk, the way they look at each other and how she touches his hand across the table. I see a need they both have for each other and in a curious way, I want to know more.

During lunch I begin to tell them how I would wish to write the book and Mr Crawford points his fork at me, as if to correct me on some point, when the unmistakeable sound of heavy tyres on gravel shatters the peace.

She quickly looks across at him and I see fear in his eyes for the first time.

Within less than a minute we hear several pairs of footsteps approaching on the stony ground and by the time Mr Crawford has stood up, two uniformed police officers and a man in a khaki suit have appeared at the steps of the veranda.

"Señor Crawford?" asks the man in the khaki suit, who is holding some papers in his hand.

"Who is asking?" asks Mr Crawford.

"I am Fiscal Schmidt and I have a warrant for your arrest, so you will please accompany me to Asunción."

"On what charges, Fiscal?"

"An irregularity has been detected on your residency, resulting in your illegal status under Paraguay law," said Fiscal Schmidt, who then looked to either side.

"Officers, please detain Señor Crawford immediately."

As Mr Crawford is being handcuffed and taken away, he looks back at Margarita and me.

"You know who's behind this, Mags. Get hold of Guy and my lawyer right away."

As the sound of the vehicle fades into the dust of the dirt track, I sit down, ran a hand through my hair and breathe out slowly.

"Pérez," is all she says, standing on the edge of the veranda, arms folded, with her back to me.

"You never told him about Pérez, did you?" I ask.

She remains where she is and takes a tissue from her pocket.

"He wouldn't believe me," she says, returning to the table and sitting down opposite me.

"He just won't listen," she says, sniffling and pouring herself a glass of wine.

Now I feel torn. Should I tell her that Pérez was here? I came to ghostwrite his memoirs, but now I could find myself part of their story.

"What are you going to do?" I ask. "He could be extradited to Argentina and you know what that would mean. You really should call his lawyer right now, Mrs Crawford."

I'm finding it hard to fathom as to why she is doing nothing at all and so I decide to tell her.

"Pérez was here," I say, quietly.

"I know. I've always known, but this comes to an end right now!" she says as she quickly gets up and disappears into the house, where after a few seconds I hear her talking, but I don't know how or with whom. I didn't notice any telephone lines or poles when I got up this morning.

I know I should go, but I also know that I have to stay. This isn't finished yet.

As I light a cigarette, she returns with what looks like a huge radio phone in her hand, sits down again and calmly pours herself a glass of wine.

"Would you take me to Asunción?" she asks.

Before I can answer, the device bleeps and she picks it up.

"Yes, thank you, Guy. You know where to find him," is all she says, then presses a button and places it back on the table.

"I'm glad he's still got friends like Guy," I say, unsure what exactly is going on here.

"Well, he's going to have one less friend, now," she says, taking a sip of her wine and smiling from the side of her mouth.

Marc Thomas

41725347R00249

Printed in Poland
by Amazon Fulfillment
Poland Sp. z o.o., Wrocław